Michelle stared at A

"I need an intellige
the same time she liste
A man might let slip to
say otherwise."

"Listen?" she asked icily. "This is all I must do?"

"You must convince anyone we meet you are my beloved mistress."

"I shall not fawn over you and let you touch me like a lover."

"Fawn over me? You?" The edge returned to his laugh. "No, I would not ask such a horrible thing of you. The duties we discussed earlier have not changed. You need to be by my side during meetings and translate for me. To keep from being too conspicuous, I thought I would lament about a war injury that left me hard of hearing. Then you can whisper the translation into my ear."

Michelle was not sure if he was being honest or jesting. "If you wish to be inconspicuous, I don't think that is a very good plan."

"Do you have another?"

"Have you considered the truth? That you do not speak French well and that I am traveling with you to assist you. Very simple and the truth."

His finger moved along her cheek in an aimless caress. When she inched back, his hand on her waist halted her. Resting his cheek against hers, he murmured, "But no one would believe that."

"Why not? It is the truth." She quivered as he chuckled, the warmth of his breath swirling into her ear and through her like a summer storm. His fingers slipped along her back and drew her closer. The brush of his rugged face urged her to soften against him, to touch his muscular arms, to delight in the texture of his skin.

His voice was rough as he whispered, "The truth will not work because nobody would believe that Alexei Vatutin would have a lovely woman like you by his side and let her sleep alone."

Dear Romance Reader,

In July, we launched the Ballad line with four new series, and each month we'll present both new and continuing stories set everywhere from medieval England to the American West—the kind of passionate, romantic stories you love best, written by the most gifted authors. At the back of each book, we'll tell you when you can find subsequent books in the series that have captured your heart.

This month beloved author Jo Ann Ferguson completes her riveting *Shadow of the Bastille* series with **A Sister's Quest**, as a French schoolteacher embarks on a perilous—and passionate—adventure with a Russian count. Next, talented newcomer Elizabeth Keys offers the second book in her *Irish Blessings* series, **Reilly's Gold.** What happens when a man determined to find his fortune in America meets a spirited woman instead?

Beginning this month is a series from rising star Kathryn Fox. In 1874, three men—loyal, brave, and true—ride into the Canadian wilderness to fight for justice as *The Mounties*. In the first installment, a recruit trained as a physician will capture a bootlegger—yet *she* will claim his heart for **The First Time.** Finally, new favorite Shelley Bradley presents the second book in her breathtaking *Brothers in Arms* series, as a Scottish knight bent on revenge finds the power of true love with **His Stolen Bride.** Enjoy!

Kate Duffy
Editorial Director

Shadow of the Bastille

A SISTER'S QUEST

Jo Ann Ferguson

ZEBRA BOOKS
KENSINGTON PUBLISHING CORP.

http://www.zebrabooks.com

For Charis,
Your love of romance is an endless inspiration.

Chapter One

Zurich, 1814

"Frère Jacques, Frère Jacques, dormez-vous?"

Michelle D'Orage counted the tempo with her hand, but her thoughts were not on her students. As she stood in the plain room and watched the little girls in their black gowns, she sighed. Tomorrow would be the sixth anniversary of her mother's death and almost her fifth year of teaching at St. Bernard's School for Girls. She had spent most of her life at this school, first as a student, now as the language teacher.

Startled when she realized the song had ended, she instructed, "Again, but together this time."

Compliantly, the little girls obeyed.

Michelle wandered around the long tables. Usually she was amused by how the ones closest to her sang with extra enthusiasm, but today she barely took note. As she paused by the windows overlooking *Zurichsee*, she stared at the mountains rising from the lake's far shore. To the west was France, the place where she had been born. A place she had not visited since her mother had brought her to Zurich before her first birthday.

"Fraulein?"

She turned to discover that the girls had finished again. Laughing, she said, "Forgive me. My mind is not on Brother John today. Why don't you wash up for dinner?" As they scrambled to their feet, she admonished, "Remember. Frau Herbart expects polite young ladies."

At the headmistress's name, the girls slowed. Their treble voices lingered in the room as Michelle collected the books. Most days the students picked them up, but she was as anxious as they for classes to be over for the term.

"Michelle?"

"Come in, Elfie." She smiled at the rail-thin woman in the doorway. In the black gowns all the instructors wore, Elfie's pale skin looked lifeless, but her blue eyes sparkled.

"Is there something in the air?" Elfie asked in her surprisingly deep voice. "My students had no interest in embroidery today."

Michelle chuckled. "I gave up all attempts to practice French verbs, because they can think only of the holidays next week. We sang." She did not add that she was as unsettled as her students.

"They will come back from holidays forgetting all we have taught them. We have to retrain them how to stand in line and to take turns at the washbasin."

"Listen to yourself. You have been here too long!"

"Not as long as you, Michelle." She gathered up a stack of workbooks. "And you never take a holiday."

If only she had a place to go. . .With her mother's death, she had lost her only family. Mayhap other D'Orages lived in France, but she had no idea where. Her mother had never spoken of the days before the French Revolution had left her a widow with an infant daughter.

"Now that the war is over and Napoleon banished," Michelle said, "I can travel."

"First to Paris?"

"Why would I go there first?"

"Weren't you born in Paris?"

"I believe *Maman* once mentioned that I was born along the Loire."

Elfie stared. "She never told you where?"

"I am sure she did. I just forgot. After all," Michelle continued with a smile as she blew out the lamp on her desk, "what does it matter? Zurich is my home."

"You cannot bury yourself here at school for the rest of your days."

"I'm not burying myself here." She tied her straw bonnet beneath her chin. Drawing the door closed, she walked with Elfie down the narrow corridor. A single lamp lit its length. The long war had made it difficult to obtain even basic necessities. "Where are you going for the holidays?"

"Home." She smiled. "My brother Edel will be there."

Michelle took her friend's hand. "I am so happy for you."

"Mama is thrilled. She has promised delicacies to stuff both of us."

"She is always trying to fatten you."

"She fears I eat nothing here."

"I could write a list for her of all you eat, but it would take too long!" Michelle laughed. Hugging her friend, she repeated, "I am so happy for you."

"Be happy for Edel. He survived the French conscription." She grinned. "Why don't you come home with me? Edel has asked to meet you."

"Me? Why would he want to meet me?"

Elfie giggled. "Because I told him about your ebony hair and dark brown eyes and how you look beautiful even in these horrible gowns we wear."

"Elfie!"

" 'Tis the truth. These are even more hideous than what we wore as students."

Before Michelle could reply, another voice said, "If you have a complaint, Fraulein, you should come to me."

"Frau Herbart!" squeaked Elfie, sounding as young as a student.

The rawboned headmistress was even taller than Michelle. With her steel gray hair pulled back in a bun, she was an imposing sight. Only those who knew her well dared to approach close enough to see the warm twinkle in her blue eyes.

"Elfie, I would speak with Michelle alone." Her resonant voice had the strength of a storm wind.

Nodding, Elfie left after giving Michelle a sympathetic glance.

Frau Herbart opened the outer door and waited for Michelle to precede her. Michelle looked at the sun, which was setting the western sky ablaze. She took a deep breath of the scent emanating from the pines edging the garden. She wondered if anything could be as wonderful as the familiar sight of the gray walls reflecting back the day's last light. The classroom building, the dormitory, and the teachers' quarters overshadowed Frau Herbart's small house. This was Michelle's familiar world.

"You have not spoken of staying at the school during the holidays," the headmistress said as she came down the steps to the stone walk. "Do you have other plans?"

Michelle hesitated. She loved being at St. Bernard's, but her life had been one quiet day after another, save for the brief times when *Maman* had taken her to live in the apartment on Fraumunsterstrasse in Zurich. *Maman* had never explained where she was going when she returned Michelle to school. *Maman* kissed her farewell and simply left. Michelle wanted to capture some of that spontaneity, to spend time following whims and seeking adventure.

But how could she explain this to Frau Herbart? Michelle doubted if the headmistress had ever had a moment of doubt or a yearning for excitement.

"Mayhap you have plans," Frau Herbart said. "If so—"

"I have no plans."

Although her eyebrow quirked, Frau Herbart's voice

remained even. "Would you be interested in a temporary position during the winter holiday?"

"What type of position?"

"I think it would be best if Count Vatutin explained himself."

A dozen questions sprang into Michelle's head, but asking would gain her nothing. Frau Herbart had said this gentleman would explain, and that was the way it would be.

"Thank you," Michelle murmured when Frau Herbart opened the door to her house.

Warmth surrounded her. The headmistress's home was filled with comfortable furniture instead of the utilitarian cots of the teachers' quarters. A lamp spread a welcoming glow, and the snap of embers on the hearth recalled the winter days Michelle had spent with *Maman*.

Michelle took off her bonnet and placed it on the table near the door. Following the headmistress into the parlor, she saw a tall man next to the settee. His back was to them, so she took a deep breath and squared her shoulders without his seeing. Many times in the past five years, she had met a student's parent in this cozy parlor. She could not recall a student named Vatutin, but the man must have some connection with one of the children. No one came here otherwise.

"Count Vatutin?" prompted Frau Herbart.

He turned, and his emerald gaze appraised Michelle candidly. The lamplight gilded his golden hair and full mustache. His severely sculptured face would draw any woman's eyes. When he smiled, her breath caught, for that smile seemed uncomfortable on his lips. She wondered if he usually wore a frown.

Wearing her own strained smile, Frau Herbart said, "Count Vatutin, I would like to introduce you to our mistress of languages, Fraulein Michelle D'Orage." Turning to Michelle, she added, "Michelle, Count Alexei Vatutin."

Although the imperious tip of his head suggested she

should dip in a curtsy, Michelle held out her hand. He bent over her fingers but did not raise them to his lips. She drew her fingers away, disturbed by his cool touch when her palm was damp with sweat.

" 'Tis a pleasure to meet you," she said into the silence.

"I appreciate your seeing me at this hour, Fraulein D'Orage," he replied.

"You are Russian!" Michelle gasped as she recognized his accent. Heat climbed her face at Frau Herbart's admonishing glare, which was aimed in her direction.

Count Vatutin's smile did not waver. "I can guess what you are thinking, Fraulein, but my nation and what is left of yours are no longer enemies. I hope the future can herald a long friendship."

Her eyes narrowed. Words came facilely to him. With these few, he had made her look want-witted.

"I believe we all hope for peace," Frau Herbart said.

"No sane person wants war."

Surprised at his fervor, Michelle was curious whether he had fought in the war, but she asked only, "May I inquire why you wished to see me?"

He chuckled. "I was told you possessed much common sense. I can see that is true."

"Please sit," Frau Herbart said, motioning to the white settee. "I shall ring for brandy if you wish, Count Vatutin."

"There is no need."

"Will you sit?" She smiled at Michelle. "Fraulein D'Orage has had a long day of teaching, and I suspect she would appreciate sitting while we discuss what has brought you here."

As if he were their host, the count gestured for Michelle to sit. She chose one of the chairs opposite the settee. When he sat facing her, she clasped her hands in her lap while Frau Herbart brought a tray from the sideboard. The headmistress avoided her eyes. Frau Herbart must have known Count Vatutin was calling this evening. Why had she said nothing to Michelle before now?

Frau Herbart set the tea tray on the low table between them. "Would you pour, Michelle?"

"Of course. Count Vatutin, do you take sugar or cream in your tea?"

Instead of answering her, he said, "Frau Herbart, I had hoped you would not go to this trouble."

"St. Bernard's School for Girls is proud of our history of hospitality," the headmistress replied in her clipped, correct voice.

"Then I shall not do anything to tarnish your kind traditions." He smiled at Michelle. "Both cream and sugar, if you please, Fraulein. One enjoys the simple pleasures that have been so long denied."

She wondered if the tea would freeze in the pot as his stare, which was alpine cold, focused on her again. Pouring tea, she held a cup out to him with a smile as frigid as his. A flicker of some emotion she could not decipher raced through his eyes. She tried to imagine this elegant man in his splendid clothes fighting in the war, for she had no doubt what his cryptic words meant, and realized she could very easily. He would be a terrifying, crafty enemy.

Michelle handed Frau Herbart a cup. The headmistress gave her a rare smile. If it was meant to reassure her, it failed.

Frau Herbart said, "Count Vatutin, I would like to know why you are anxious to hire someone with Fraulein D'Orage's qualifications."

"Yes, her qualifications." He turned to Michelle, his smile vanishing.

She fought not to flinch. He slanted toward her, and his eyes slitted. He seemed to be searching for something. Only Frau Herbart and years of lessons at the school halted her from asking if his peculiar stare was a Russian eccentricity.

"The answer is simple, Fraulein D'Orage," Count Vatutin said, again smiling as he relaxed against the settee. "I am on my way to Vienna to take my place at the Congress. I need someone fluent in several languages, especially French, to serve as my interpreter." His green eyes fixed her with another uncompromising stare. "Exactly what are your qualifications for this position?"

Irritation scored her. He need not ask as if daring her to prove her worth. If all Russians were as haughty as Count Vatutin, it was no wonder the Allies disdained them. She raised her chin. "Of course, I speak German. It is our primary language here at St. Bernard's. In addition, I am fluent in French and Italian. Also I can manage English with some difficulty."

"Do you speak Russian?"

"No, my lord."

Looking back at Frau Herbart, he asked, "How long can you spare her?"

"We have a holiday for several weeks."

"Starting when?"

"Next week."

"I cannot wait another week. I leave in the morning." He set his cup on the table. "Frau Herbart, can you spare Fraulein D'Orage earlier?"

The headmistress looked at Michelle. "I do not believe that she has said if she is interested in your position."

"She is interested." Adding another spoon of sugar to his tea, he smiled. "Aren't you intrigued at the idea of seeing history unfolding before your eyes, Fraulein? I assume you have never been to Vienna."

"No, I have not," Michelle answered.

" 'Tis one of the most beautiful cities in this world, mayhap even lovelier than Paris or St. Petersburg. I am sure you would agree."

"I could not say. I have not seen either of them."

"Not even Paris?"

"I was very young when I left France, Count Vatutin." She would not let him rile her into revealing how a small voice in her mind teased her to jump at this opportunity to satisfy her long-suppressed longing for adventure.

Watching what she said would be very important while she was in Count Vatutin's company.

"Frau Herbart," he said, "I know you can see the benefits if Fraulein D'Orage accepts this position. Emissaries from every nation in Europe are gathering in Vienna. Fraulein D'Orage will be exposed to many experiences that she can share with her students."

"That is true." She tapped her chin with a thoughtful expression. "Those experiences could be an asset to the school."

"Exactly."

"But it must be Fraulein D'Orage's decision."

Michelle almost smiled as Count Vatutin frowned. If he had thought he could get the better of Frau Herbart, he had been shown how mistaken he was.

"And what is your decision, Fraulein?" he asked. "Will you come with me to Vienna?"

Her reply died on her lips when his intense gaze caught her eyes again. Common sense told her to thank him and bid him to enjoy the rest of his journey without her. She had other ways of spending the holidays. She could stay at the school. She had an invitation to visit Elfie's family. A shudder of dismay raced along her, for if she turned down Count Vatutin's offer, her days would continue to unfold as they always had. But to accept . . .

Count Vatutin stood. "I take your silence to mean you are not interested, Fraulein. Thank you for allowing me to disrupt your evening and enjoy your hospitality, Frau Herbart." He set his silk hat on his head. "Good evening."

"Wait!" Michelle set herself on her feet. "My lord, I am interested." She waited for the second thoughts to taunt her, but her heart beat with anticipation. *Maman* would have taken this chance to see a new city. She must, too.

"Is that so?" His eyes lost their icy edge. "I rather thought you might. However, there remains the problem that I must leave tomorrow morning."

"The term is nearly over." She could not relinquish this

possibility of adventure now. "Frau Herbart will, I am sure, allow me to leave a few days early."

He smiled at the headmistress again. "Is that so?"

"It is possible," Frau Herbart replied, lowering her tea-cup to her lap.

He held out his hand. "We are in agreement then, Fraulein D'Orage. You will, of course, be offered a fair salary. I assume you can be ready to leave at dawn."

"I shall be waiting then." She put her hand in his.

His fingers closed over hers and, trapped by his strong hand, she could not flee. But did she want to? She was not sure as he stepped closer and lifted her hand to his mouth. Green fire from his eyes seared her, seeming to see far too much when she could discern far too little. She feared she was face-to-face with the devil, who had tricked her into this covenant that would fulfill her dreams and cost her her soul.

"I look forward to your joining me on this journey, Fraulein," he murmured.

His warm breath brushed her hand in the moment before his lips did. When his mustache grazed her skin, ripples of pleasure rushed outward from his touch and spiraled deep within her. He raised his head, and she tried to cloak her reaction, but he must have sensed it through her quivering fingers. Nothing he had done went beyond the boundaries of propriety. Yet his smile dared her to denounce him.

She should tell him she had changed her mind. She should tell him it was inappropriate for her to travel with him to Vienna, even if she were in his employ. She should . . . She saw his amusement. He really might be the devil if he could gauge her thoughts with such ease.

"Until tomorrow, Fraulein D'Orage." He slid his fingers from around hers. The lingering caress was as intimate as a feverish kiss.

"Yes," she whispered like a student reciting her lessons, "until tomorrow."

When Michelle heard the door close, she flinched. It was too late to call after him now. By accepting his offer, she was entering a world populated by her nation's enemies. The men meeting in Vienna were eager to carve out the largest share of Europe for themselves. They would use anything or anyone to achieve their ends. She did not doubt that Count Alexei Vatutin would be their match.

The only difference was that he might be using Michelle D'Orage.

Chapter Two

Frau Herbart put a hand on Michelle's arm. "Please sit. I have something you must see before you leave with Count Vatutin tomorrow."

Michelle perched on a chair and folded her hands in her lap. How could she have been so skimble-skamble as to accept an offer of employment from a stranger? Frau Herbart must have checked into the count's background before she allowed him to speak with Michelle. That would explain why she had been prepared with tea for this visit.

How astonished the other teachers would be to hear of her plans! Mayhap as astonished as she was that she could not wait to begin the journey across the Alps.

Frau Herbart returned with a small package. The headmistress sat where Count Vatutin had and held it out without speaking.

Michelle untied the strings around the brown paper to discover a small box and another package wrapped in linen. She opened the box and stared at a gold ring on a piece of black velvet. An odd design decorated one side. Her fingernail traced the lightning bolt.

"Your mother requested that you be given this when you left St. Bernard's." An uneasy expression crossed the headmistress's face. "I was unsure if she meant when you finished your studies or when you departed, so I have delayed."

"But what is it?"

Frau Herbart murmured, "I believe it was her wedding ring."

"With such an odd design?"

"It may have symbolized something to her and your father. Did she explain in the letter?"

"I don't see a letter."

Frau Herbart leaned forward. "When your mother gave me this package, she also gave me a letter for you. It must be there."

Michelle shook the brown paper. Nothing fell out.

"I shall look for it in the morning," Frau Herbart said. "It will be waiting when you come back from Vienna."

Michelle tried to smile, but could not. She slid the ring on and found a perfect fit on her middle finger. Dear *Maman*. Even after her death, she was reaching out to her daughter.

She ran her finger along the ring, realizing she could not recall her mother wearing it. If it had been her wedding ring, *Maman* must have set it aside after her husband's death.

"Why don't you open the other package?" the headmistress asked. "Mayhap what is in there will explain."

Michelle picked up the box, which was as long as her forearm and about as thick. Pulling off the cloth, she found a latched case. She opened it and stared at the coins inside. "Oh, my!"

Frau Herbart said with a gasp, "There must be hundreds of francs in there."

Michelle counted out several coins. She closed the box and handed it back to Frau Herbart. "I will take enough to pay for my journey from Vienna if the situation becomes . . .'' She sought the proper word. "Intolerable.''

"I think that is wise." She smiled as Michelle stood. "However, I think you and Count Vatutin shall do admirably.''

Bidding the headmistress a good evening, Michelle went into the hall. She put the coins on a table as she tied her bonnet into place. The coins twinkled in the lamplight. How had *Maman* amassed this fortune?

Maman had been like no one else Michelle knew. She had shown no interest in remarrying, although the lot of a widow could not have been an easy one. The cost of boarding Michelle at St. Bernard's had not been insignificant, and every Christmas and birthday had brought gifts, and Michelle's gowns never had been allowed to become threadbare or too short. Somewhere, somehow, *Maman* had garnered enough money to pay for the apartment as well as her daughter's schooling and this generous bequest. But how?

She was asking too late. *Maman* had died when a rock slide hit her carriage near the French border. Tears blurred the sparkle of lamplight. Raising her hand, she stroked her mother's ring. The past was over and dead. It was time to put aside the life *Maman* and others had chosen for her and discover the life she wanted.

Dawn painted the distant mountains with rosy light, but sunrise had not reached the valley. Night clung to the gray stone buildings as Michelle huddled by the drive. In the distance, she could hear the exuberant students as they prepared for the day. It would be more than a month before she heard that familiar noise again.

Taking a deep breath, she tightened her black cloak around her. She sat on her small portmanteau and balanced her scuffed satchel on her lap. A yawn pulled at her

lips. Sleep had not come easily last night as she waited to
be thrust into a new life.

Wheels rattled on the road. She gasped. The approach-
ing carriage was as ornate as the coach of a fairy-tale
princess. Gold trim outlined the doors and accented the
buttons on the driver's coat, which was as scarlet as the
wheels. She should have guessed a Russian count would
possess something this grand.

The coachman jumped down and opened the door with
a flourish. When Count Vatutin stepped out, his clothes
matched the opulence of his coach. From his white leather
gloves to the shine of his well-polished boots, he reeked
of wealth. He brushed wrinkles from the black coat he
wore over nankeen pantaloons.

"Good morning, my lord," Michelle said, her tongue
almost tripping over the few words. She berated herself
for being intimidated. She was not a schoolgirl.

"Are you ready, Fraulein D'Orage?" he asked, his deep
voice rumbling beneath the sound of the children's.

"Yes, my lord."

"Good." His eyes narrowed as he looked at her trunk.
"Is this what you are bringing with you?"

"I can bring less if—"

"Less?" He laughed. "You may bring all you wish. The
boot has plenty of room."

"This is enough." She did not add that everything she
owned was packed in this box. Two dresses and her under-
clothes were folded over her low boots and the few books
she had slipped into the corners of the portmanteau.

"Enough? I have met ladies who could not cross the
street with so little."

"It should be plenty for the length of time I shall be
working for you, my lord."

He motioned to the coachman, who hurried to place
her things in the back of the carriage. Pointing to the open
door, he added, "If you please, Fraulein D'Orage."

His icy gaze followed her toward the carriage. Was he

displeased with the discrepancy in their appearances? Her clothes reflected her station. She recoiled as a hand was thrust in front of her.

"Allow me, Fraulein." Count Vatutin's polite smile did not match the challenge in his emerald eyes.

She must not let him think he could overwhelm her with simple courtesy, even though he had. She put her fingers on his palm as he handed her into the carriage.

"Thank you," she said.

"Indeed, it was my pleasure."

She winced. His answer was too smooth.

"Relax, Fraulein D'Orage," he continued.

Michelle started to reply, but paused when she saw a man sitting on the backward-facing seat. She glanced from him to the other blue velvet seat. Twisting the strings of her reticule, she wondered where she should sit. A lady should be allowed to ride facing forward, but she was serving Count Vatutin, and he might wish that seat for himself.

She looked back at the man. His blue gaze drilled into her from an emotionless face. Wrinkles suggested he was older than Count Vatutin, and his hair was almost gray. Although his clothes were not as well made as Count Vatutin's, they were sturdy and clean.

Michelle said, "Good morning. Do you think I should—"

"Do not waste your breath asking Rusak questions that he cannot answer," came the count's voice from the door.

She looked at Count Vatutin. He took her hand and seated her on the forward-facing seat. Then he sat beside her, taking more than his share of the seat. Although she was tempted to edge away, she resisted. He would not appreciate her showing that she found it uncomfortable to be so close to his tightly restrained strength. Insulting him would not be a good beginning.

"Rusak?" she repeated, unsure if that was a name or a title.

He gestured to the other man. "Feodor Rusak, my assistant."

"He does not speak German? I can—"

"I know what languages *you* speak." Drawing off his gloves, he said, "Rusak does not speak any, Fraulein D'Orage. He met with misfortune during the French army's ignoble retreat from Moscow."

Rusak opened his mouth. His tongue was gone.

She pressed her hands to her chest and recoiled, bumping her head against the hard line of Count Vatutin's arm. In shock, she realized it was resting behind her. She was trapped between these two men she did not know. She should tell the count she had changed her mind. She should . . . She rocked back against Count Vatutin's arm when the coach began down the road away from St. Bernard's School for Girls.

As Michelle tried to repair her tattered composure, she sensed Count Vatutin's gaze on her. She should expect that he would be curious about the woman he had hired. She was curious about him, but his cool eyes had kept her from asking any questions. Slowly she faced him. She hoped the motion appeared natural instead of calculated. Pretending was idiotic, she realized, as her eyes met his. Amusement glistened there, warning he had taken note of every nervous motion.

"How long will it take us to reach Vienna?" she asked.

"We are in no hurry, Fraulein." His pleasing voice resonated through his smile. "The Congress is officially open, but, with Napoleon imprisoned on Elba, the delegates wish to celebrate. I suspect little will be accomplished before the new year."

"The new year?" She gasped. "My lord, I must be back at school in six weeks. When—"

His smile halted her. "When our work is done, you may return."

"But why weren't you honest? I would have told you I

could not come." Horror filled her. Was everything he had told Frau Herbart a lie?

"I need your skills, Fraulein."

"I have no idea how you do things in Russia—"

"Differently than you do in France."

"I know little about France, my lord."

"But you were born there."

She frowned. "You are trying to cloud the issue. I cannot go to Vienna for so long. If you will return me to the school, I am sure—"

"No!" He added as her eyes widened at his abrupt change from jesting to fury, "I have hired you, Fraulein, because you suit my needs. I doubt if there is another who would do as well."

She sat straighter, hitting her black bonnet against his arm. "Stop this vehicle! I shall walk back if you will not take me there."

"No."

"I . . . I . . . I—"

"Stop sputtering like a hen." When she flushed, he crossed one leg over the opposite knee. "The note I left for your headmistress explains the delay in your return."

"You did what?" In desperation, she looked at the silent man on the facing seat, but he was smiling. "You presume much!"

Count Vatutin shrugged. "I need you. Therefore, I told Frau Herbart we had decided you would stay with me as long as necessary. I doubt if it shall be more than a few months."

"You are mad!"

"Fraulein D'Orage, the world is insane." His eyes glinted with frustration. She was not sure if it was aimed at her or someone else. She hoped it was someone else. "A generation of children has grown up thinking war is normal. Do you wish to turn your back on them?"

Michelle tried to pull her fingers out of the strings of

her bag, but they were so twisted, she was caught. "I have an obligation to St. Bernard's."

"Which you can fulfill when we are finished." Smiling, he took her hands and began to unwind the string cutting into her gloved fingers.

She looked from his face to his broad hands. Without his gloves, she could see they were hardened from a life much more strenuous than this one with elegant clothes and a luxurious coach. Count Alexei Vatutin was no more a gentleman diplomat than she was, but she could not guess what he might be.

"Do you often get yourself into such predicaments, Fraulein?" he asked.

Michelle bit back her sharp response, hoping he meant her reticule instead of how he had entangled her life with his. "I make every effort to avoid them."

"I suspected that."

She tried to pull her hands out of his. "I can just slip that off."

As if she had not spoken, he undid the final twist and let her purse drop across his knee. Massaging her fingers, he smiled again. "Would it offend you if I thank you in advance for your help? I know I have approached this in what to you seems an unorthodox manner, but the work we do is important."

"No, you would not offend me." She was not sure what else she could say. Drawing her hands away, she snatched her reticule from his lap.

He chuckled. "I am glad my fingers were not tangled in that! You would have pulled them from my wrist."

Her gaze rose along the sturdy length of his arm to the breadth of his shoulders. The idea that she could do anything to this powerful man was ludicrous.

She gasped as he took her hand and turned it over on his. Running his finger along the lines in her palm, he mused, "We must be a team, Michelle." He paid no attention to her gasp when he used her given name. Slipping his finger along her wrist, he etched an invisible pattern on her arm.

Fearing she could not breathe as his face came closer, she stared at him. Slowly he curled her fingers beneath his, capturing them in a heated prison of flesh. A warm, silky sensation flowed along her as he drew her toward him.

He tilted her wrist beneath his lips. Raising his gaze, he smiled. He held her eyes as he teased her wrist with a swift kiss. It was as if the lightning had escaped from her mother's ring to rivet her with sweet, dangerous fire.

His mustache brushed her wrist as he whispered, "I must know. Are you coming with us?"

She stared into his eyes, which were half-hidden beneath the golden hair dropping over his forehead. "Do I have a choice?"

"Only one correct one. Before you answer, heed what I wrote to Frau Herbart. If, at any time, you decide to depart, I shall immediately arrange for your transportation to Zurich at my expense."

"Why didn't you mention that before?"

A queer sound came from the other side of the carriage. Michelle choked back her despair when she realized it was Count Vatutin's assistant's laugh. She had forgotten he was here witnessing how easily the count had seduced her into giving him his way.

"Rusak," cautioned Count Vatutin in a tone that suggested he was trying not to laugh. "What have you decided, Michelle?"

Fearing she was being foolish, but unwilling to turn her back on adventure before it began, she said, "I will continue to Vienna with you."

"For as long as I need you?"

"For as long as I can."

When he smiled with satisfaction, her unease grew. It was not too late to change her mind. Or was it?

* * *

The carriage rolled to a stop in front of a country house as the sun sank beyond the mountains. Count Vatutin stepped out and held up his hand. "Fraulein D'Orage?"

"Thank you." Michelle was proud her voice sounded serene. Placing her fingertips on his palm, she allowed him to assist her to the ground. She lifted her hand away and took a steadying breath.

All day, Count Vatutin either had not noticed her discomfort or had chosen to ignore it. She must set it aside. She was going to Vienna, the very heart of the Hapsburg Empire. In Vienna, she would walk the same streets and view the same sights as kings and queens and emperors. This was the adventure she craved.

As Count Vatutin gave instructions to the coachman, she looked at the inn. The wooden house rose four stories through a row of trees. The steep roof swept down to shelter the porch as well. Along the front of the house, small windows were separated by boards to protect them from the stormy weather off the *Zurichsee.*

Michelle smiled at the lake. They had followed its shores all day. Drawing her cloak more tightly around her, she walked toward a pier. A rickety rowboat waited, rocking with the gentle waves. She had loved rowing with *Maman* on this lake.

"It's lovely, isn't it?"

She flinched when Count Vatutin's voice shattered her memories. A shiver ran along her back. He must have followed her. She hoped he did not intend to intrude on everything she did.

"I think it must be the most beautiful lake in the world," she answered.

"You were lucky to be here. This was one of the few peaceful places in Europe."

"Not all of Switzerland has been peaceful." She could not keep her bitterness silent. "The French renamed us the Helvetic Republic and tried to remold us into a miniature of themselves. When that failed, they stole our young men to fight a war that we never wanted. Now, at last, it is over."

"Is it?"

She turned. The light wind ruffled his hair. With the waning light on his face, its stern angles were emphasized by shadows. His mustache camouflaged his expressive lips, but the emotions in his eyes refused to be concealed. Rage burned there as brightly as the setting sun.

"It is over," she whispered, "for as long as we are vigilant."

His lips tilted in a smile. "You have an excellent grasp of the dangers awaiting us if we become complaisant. I am impressed, although I should not be surprised."

"As I think that may have been a compliment, thank you."

"It was indeed a compliment, Michelle." When she glanced at him in surprise, he added, "I trust I may continue to call you that. It would not be inappropriate."

"No, it would not," she said, knowing of no way she could explain how even this slight intimacy seemed too much when so many of her thoughts today had been haunted by the fire in his eyes as he kissed her wrist. When the breeze slipped beneath her cloak, she shivered.

Count Vatutin's keen eyes must have noted it. "Let's go inside and see what meal awaits us. I, for one, shall be glad to sit on something stationary."

Michelle delighted in the familiar crunch of pine needles beneath their feet. The forest prepared for night while the wind sang a lullaby through the firs. She listened as Count Vatutin spoke of his journey from Paris, where he had been since the Russians dethroned Napoleon.

"Coming to Zurich has taken you many miles out of your way," she said as he opened the inn's door.

He smiled. "I had my reasons, Michelle. One of which you have fulfilled quite well."

"You could not find someone to translate for you in France? That—"

"Count Vatutin, welcome, welcome," called a round, apple-cheeked woman in a dark dress with a brightly embroidered apron. "I am Frau Offenbach. I am honored you have chosen to be our guests."

Count Vatutin took her hand and bowed over it. Frau Offenbach giggled, her cheeks becoming a deeper shade of rose. He put his hand on Michelle's elbow. She was shocked by the familiar motion and the spark his fingers etched into her.

"Frau Offenbach, this is my companion Fraulein D'Orage."

The plump woman smiled, but curiosity filled her eyes. "Welcome, Fraulein."

"Thank you," she said, not sure what else to say.

She followed the bustling woman into a huge room that was open and airy. The furniture fit its rustic warmth perfectly. Wooden floors glistened with constant care and reflected back the flames on the huge hearth. When hands grazed her shoulders, she gasped.

"A problem, Michelle?" asked Count Vatutin.

Warmth spread up her cheeks as she realized he was lifting off her cloak. She avoided looking at the good humor that must be in his eyes as he gestured for her to follow Frau Offenbach.

Michelle nodded a greeting to Rusak, who was waiting by a long table beside the fireplace. When he ignored her, she wondered what she had done to make him dislike her. That she had been shocked by what had happened to him surely had been the exact reaction the two men had wanted.

"Will you sit, Michelle? Rusak and I are tired, too."

At Count Vatutin's impatience, she flushed. She had been living in a children's world for so long she had forgotten the men would not sit until she did.

"Thank you," she managed to mumble.

When he pushed her chair in, his fingers lingered along her back. She glanced up to ask if something was wrong. The glow in his eyes immobilized her. She wanted to look away. She wanted to shrug off his fingers, which quested in a gentle circle. Each caress suffused her with sweetness flowing outward from his touch.

She did not look at him as he pulled out the chair next to her. When a bowl of steaming stew was set in front of her, she picked up a spoon. It was simpler to eat than make conversation.

Michelle was surprised that the food in this roadside inn was so good, but she simply nodded when Count Vatutin asked her if she liked the stew. By doing that, she did not have to look at his piercing eyes.

Only when he had chased the last of the meat out of his bowl with a chunk of bread did Count Vatutin speak. "Rusak, I have made arrangements for Michelle and myself upstairs. Frau Offenbach assured me she has a comfortable room for you on this floor."

Rusak glared at her. She wanted to remind him that, if he disagreed with Count Vatutin's plans, he should not be angry at her. When he rose, he nodded to Count Vatutin and hurried across the room.

"He shall become accustomed to you, Michelle. 'Tis not easy for Rusak."

"I suppose not."

Putting his elbow on the table, Count Vatutin rested his cheek on his fist. His other arm settled on the back of her chair. When she glanced at it, he smiled, but did not move it away. "I know you are bursting with questions. Go ahead."

"Here?"

"No one is paying any attention." Laughing, he picked up a mug of beer and left foam streaking his mustache. "Go ahead with your questions before they erupt past your pretty lips."

She refused to let him taunt her into reacting to his

bold compliments. Folding her arms in front of her, she said, "Count Vatutin, I believe I would be more effective in helping you if you explained my duties more clearly."

He poured wine into a glass and offered it to her. "I thought I'd made my needs very clear. I need an interpreter. Already I have seen that your German is superior to mine."

"Thank you." She sipped the wine and forced herself to swallow without coughing. She had forgotten the bite of wine that had not been watered for children.

"It was not intended to be a compliment. I trust you will not be dismayed if I ask you to do a few other tasks for me."

"Such as?"

"Nothing onerous, I promise you." A smile teased the corners of his lips. "Taking notes, making arrangements when we entertain, and such things. I trust you can handle that."

"Yes, it shall be no difficulty." Curiosity urged her to ask, "But why did you come to Zurich to hire me?"

"You don't think you have a reputation for competence?"

"Mere competence does not explain why you came to Zurich when you could have found someone in Paris."

He chuckled. "Do you wish me to shower you with compliments, Michelle?"

"Only the truth."

"Which I shall endeavor always to give to you." His eyes dared her to contradict him. "A few queries gained me your name. I decided to see if you were interested in the post. As you are, the situation is perfect."

She intended to ask another question, but a yawn interrupted. "I was up late last night preparing for the trip," she hurried to explain when he laughed.

Swallowing the last of his beer, he stood. As she rose, he drew her hand within his arm. "Then let us get you to bed posthaste. I want you fresh when we reach Vienna, for the pace will be one I am sure you shall find hectic after a girls' school.''

"Thank you for a pleasant evening, my lord."

"Pleasant?" He laughed. "My dear Fraulein D'Orage, I would hate to know what you considered an *uncomfortable* evening. You spit like a furious cat each time I have tried to engage you in conversation."

"I do not! I—" She flushed as he chuckled. Mayhap he was correct; yet, if he would answer a question directly, she might have been more at ease with him.

When she yawned again, he asked, "Do you think you can stay awake until we get upstairs?"

"I am not used to inactivity. It is more tiring than teaching."

He motioned to the staircase beyond the hearth. "Then I think you shall find Vienna invigorating."

"Are you attending the Congress?"

"That is undecided at this point. I shall be given my orders when I arrive." A grim smile drew his lips taut. "This Congress is very nebulous. No one has selected a location for meetings, despite the fact that work should have started more than a month ago."

She lifted her skirts to climb the stairs. The other women in the inn wore their skirts much shorter than hers. Some gowns revealed the tops of their shoes. Although she had paid little attention to fashion while at St. Bernard's School for Girls, she could not ignore the amused smiles aimed at her.

With a start, she realized she might be attending meetings of the Congress. In that case, Count Vatutin must advance her a part of her salary, for she had no money to spend on such frivolities as clothes. *Maman*'s coins must not be used for anything but an emergency.

A hand at the center of her back startled her. She turned to discover Count Vatutin's eyes level with hers, for he stood on a riser below her. Refusing to be daunted by their jade sparkle, she said coolly, "I can climb without assistance, my lord."

"I realize that."

"Then—" She bit back her words. He was her employer and, as such, due her respect. "I would appreciate if you remember that our situation does not require such intimacy."

His laugh rolled along the narrow stairwell. "You are perfect, Michelle."

"I assure you that I am far from perfect."

"But you are. Such refinement was exactly what I had hoped for." He withdrew his hand from her waist and moved to stand next to her, although there was barely enough room for her on the step.

She did not dare to take a breath, for her breasts would brush his coat. It seemed odd to look up at someone, for she was accustomed to being the tallest. Now her eyes were even with the line of his lips. "Count Vatutin—"

Offering his arm, he said, "Allow me to treat you in a refined manner as well."

She thought of protesting, but Count Vatutin's mind was as honed as the faceted sparkle in his eyes. Whatever she said, he countered with ease. Yet . . . She sensed he enjoyed her retorts.

She gathered up her gown and continued up the stairs. His leg brushed her skirt with every step. Glancing at him, she saw a wisp of a smile beneath his mustache. He was enjoying every moment of this, but was it because he liked jesting with her or because he shared the startling sensations that were roiling within her? She did not dare to ask.

Something about Count Vatutin convinced her that everything he did was for a reason. If he wanted to overmaster her, she could foil him by pretending to be oblivious, something that was growing more difficult each time he touched her.

The upper hallway was poorly lit, but wider than the staircase. He kept her hand on his arm as they walked along the carpet, which had been worn to a dull gray. The doors were closed, and she saw no sign to tell her which one was to be her room.

"One other thing," he murmured.

"Yes?"

"I failed to mention that your position requires one very specific task."

"If you will explain it, I shall endeavor to do my best."

He pulled a key from beneath his coat and inserted it in a door. Pushing it open, he put his hand on her arm as she was about to enter. He turned her to face him, and a slow smile lit his eyes. "Actually, 'tis easy to explain. I want you to be my mistress."

"Excuse me?" She gasped, sure she had misunderstood him.

His arm swept around her waist and tugged her against him. When his fingers tilted her chin, she stared up at his hooded eyes. His lips were moist against her cheek as he whispered, "You heard me, *Liebchen.* I want you to be my mistress."

Chapter Three

Alexei Vatutin cursed in every language in which he was fluent and several in which he was not as he caught Michelle before her senseless body could hit the floor. *Verflucht!* He had not thought she would faint. She came from sterner stock, but, he reminded himself, he must not forget she had been raised in the cocoon of that girls' school.

Lifting her into his arms, he walked into the simple bedchamber. He shoved the door closed with his foot and looked about. Their bags were stacked in front of the wide bed. A chair was set next to a window beneath the sloped ceiling. More light came from the fire on the hearth than from the single candle on a low table by the bed.

Perfect. It was just perfect.

Just like . . . He smiled as he examined Michelle's face, which was softened in her faint. The finely drawn curves of her cheek and the gentle line of her nose were so familiar, so sadly familiar. From the moment she had walked into that stuffy room with that even stuffier head-mistress, he had realized one search was at an end. He would have recognized Michelle D'Orage anywhere, even in the quiet girls' school that seemed the least likely place to find her.

No, he argued with himself, as he carefully carried her to the bed and placed her on the pillows that smelled of the fresh pine needles beyond the window. St. Bernard's School for Girls had been the exact place he should have been searching. It was his good fortune—and Michelle's—that he had been the first to realize that.

A soft moan bubbled from her lips, and she shifted on the pillow. He drew the pins out of her bun, smiling as her thick, silky hair washed over his hands. He guessed it would fall to her waist, but now it billowed like an ebony cloud around her. She was lovely, just as he had expected she would be. Tall and willowy, she possessed a grace that drew the eye. As she breathed shallowly, the shapeless form of her dress hinted at the feminine curves that had been pressed to his chest when he drew her into his arms.

He raised her hem only enough to undo her shoes and pull them off. Smoothing her skirt over her ankles, he let his gaze slip along each curve to her lips, which were parted gently. He needed only to bend to put his over them. As sweet as her skin had tasted, he guessed her lips would be luscious.

No one had to tell him he was a fool. He knew that, but some debts had to be paid, no matter what the cost. This was one. Rusak did not understand. His friend had been furious when he discovered what Alexei planned. So furious, Alexei suspected that if Rusak could have spoken, he would have refused to do so.

Alexei had not bothered to try to explain. Rusak knew old debts did not die, not even when death took everything and everyone who mattered. Today had only begun to even the obligation Alexei owed, and he suspected the rest of it would not be settled soon. Too many people would like to see him fail, for as many reasons as his enemies could devise. Even his superiors would be outraged to know of this little errand to collect Fraulein D'Orage. He did not care. This one thing he had to do.

Taking a cloth from a shelf over the table holding the candle, he went to where a bucket of fresh water waited by the door. He pulled off his coat and draped it on the footboard. Quickly he rolled up his shirtsleeves. Dipping the cloth in the water, he wrung it out. He heard another low groan.

Michelle opened her eyes and stared at a strange pattern of water stains on the ceiling. Candlelight fluttered fitfully. They were not the familiar stains of her room at school. After so many years of looking at that ceiling, she would have recognized the brown stains left by a long-ago rain-storm.

If she was not in her room, where was she? Memory refused to stir.

"Awake? I didn't think you were the type to swoon, Michelle."

She flinched at the male voice. She turned her head on a starched pillowcase that rustled beneath her hair. "Count Vatutin!" The sound of her own voice ached through her skull. Vowing never to drink unwatered wine again, she tried to piece together what had happened. Nothing formed in her mind.

"Hush," he murmured.

A cool cloth was placed on her forehead, and she closed her eyes to savor the comfort. She had not thought Count Vatutin would tend to her so gently, but she was grateful. Not wanting to do anything that might upset her precarious hold on her senses, she waited as the world steadied. She forced her eyes open.

Count Vatutin sat by the bed. "How are you feeling?"

"I shall be fine." She hoped it was not a lie.

"Undoubtedly." He relaxed back on the chair and regarded her with disdain. "I trust you do not make a habit of such feminine faints."

"Faints? I don't faint!"

"You just did."

She was ready to retort, but swallowed her harsh words. She could not recall how she had gotten to this lumpy bed where every spring cut into her back. *Bed!* She was talking to Count Vatutin while lying in *bed?* She struggled to sit.

Gently he put his hand on her shoulder. "Rest a moment longer." The twinkle in his jade eyes warned that her face had betrayed her thoughts.

"I don't make a habit of fainting," she said tightly. She sat and sagged against the headboard as the world whirled. Clutching her head, she waited for the room to halt its mad dance. Hands on her shoulders moved her forward slightly, and she feared her stomach would embarrass her. The hands leaned her back again. She closed her eyes as she sagged into the plump pillows behind her.

"Thank you," she whispered.

"As I caused this rare swoon, I should be sure you recover from it."

Michelle was not surprised to see a smile tipping one corner of his mustache. She sat straighter with a gasp as she looked around the sparsely furnished room.

"What is wrong?" he asked.

"I thought ... I did not want ... I ..."

He smiled. "Rusak is no good in the sickroom. Even if he had been here when you dropped so enticingly into my arms, he would have found something else to do with all speed. You don't like Rusak, do you?"

"I don't know him well, Count Vatutin."

"Under the circumstances, you need to learn to be comfortable calling me Alexei."

"Under ... ?" As she stared at him, she remembered what had prompted her faint. Shaking her head, she slid to the far side of the bed. She stood and stared at her stockinged feet. He must have removed her shoes. Just the thought of him touching her was disturbing. Not only was Alexei Vatutin a stranger, but he had tricked her into coming with him by weaving his lies so smoothly. No matter what he wanted, she would not include in her duties sleeping with him.

When she saw her shoes at the foot of the bed, she slipped her feet in them. She bent to button them, but a hand on her arm halted her. Brought upright, she was whirled toward Alexei.

"What is wrong now?" he demanded.

"Take your hands off me, or I will scream."

He laughed. She stared at him in disbelief as he said, "Scream if you think it will do you any good. You are not leaving until you listen to what I have to say."

"I have heard what you have to say. If a harlot is what you want, you should not have looked at St. Bernard's."

"I'm not interested in a whore." When she winced at his crude language, he laughed again. "My dear Fraulein D'Orage, you misunderstand me. I do not intend to ask you actually to be my mistress. I want you to play the role of my mistress in Vienna. I need an intelligent woman who can play the part at the same time she listens to the conversations around her. A man might let slip to a lovely woman what he would not say otherwise."

"Listen?" she asked icily. "This is all I must do?"

"You must convince anyone we meet you are my beloved mistress."

"I shall not fawn over you and let you touch me like a lover."

"Fawn over me? You?" The edge returned to his laugh. "No, I would not ask such a horrible thing of you. The duties we discussed earlier have not changed. You need to be by my side during meetings and translate for me. To keep from being too conspicuous, I thought I would lament about a war injury that left me hard of hearing. Then you can whisper the translation into my ear."

Michelle was not sure if he was being honest or jesting. "If you wish to be inconspicuous, I don't think that is a very good plan."

"Do you have another?"

"Have you considered the truth? That you do not speak French well and that I am traveling with you to assist you. Very simple and the truth."

His finger moved along her cheek in an aimless caress. When she inched back, his hand on her waist halted her. Resting his cheek against hers, he murmured, "But no one would believe that."

"Why not? It is the truth." She quivered as he chuckled, the warmth of his breath swirling into her ear and through her like a summer storm. His fingers slipped along her back and drew her closer. The brush of his rugged face urged her to soften against him, to touch his muscular arms, to delight in the texture of his skin.

His voice was rough as he whispered, "The truth will not work because nobody would believe that Alexei Vatutin would have a lovely woman like you by his side and let her sleep alone."

"I—" Her voice caught as his fingers cupped her chin and brought her mouth beneath his. Slowly, so slowly she wondered if this was some exquisite torture he had devised, he lowered his face toward hers. His hand roved along her back to press her to the unyielding wall of his chest.

Suddenly he cursed and released her. She gripped the footboard of the bed as she watched him stride to pick up the damp cloth and toss it into the bucket. Struggling to regain her breath, she wondered how long she had been holding it.

His hand fisted. When he pounded it against the ceiling that brushed the top of his head, she flinched. A dozen questions filled her mind, but she did not dare let a single one pass her lips.

"Alexei?" she whispered.

He faced her, and she wished he had not, for his eyes gleamed with green fire. Walking back to her, he lifted a strand of her hair from her shoulder. "There shall be times when I must hold you," he said, each word squeezed past his straight lips. "You cannot act as if you have never been in a man's arms before."

"I haven't—I—"

His laughter halted her. "I guessed that, but now you have been."

When he walked away again, Michelle resisted snarling a curse after him. He considered this amusing, but it was not. Quietly she said, "I think it would be best if I returned to St. Bernard's in the morning."

"I think you are wrong."

"This was not what I agreed to do."

Alexei turned to her. As he regarded her without comment, a blush banished the cool ashen color from her face. If she was embarrassed by such a slight hint of intimacy, she had much to learn before they reached Vienna. The lessons needed to begin now. She must learn to accept his arms around her without emotion . . . as he must.

Loosening the cravat at his collar, he watched her eyes widen. She could be spectacular in this role, for one touch had shown him how her composed exterior covered an inner tempest. She must throw aside her virginal ways and pretend to be sophisticated in the ways of diplomacy and of love.

"You agreed to help me," he said.

"But you never said anything of such a licentious situation."

"Licentious?" He closed the distance between them. When she pressed back against the bed, her dress pulled across her breasts. He thought of those soft curves against him when he had carried her to that bed, and an answering need ached all along him. She was beautiful, vibrant, and possessed a sensuality waiting to be tapped.

His fingers combed through her hair as he brought her face to his. Her lips parted, but he did not let her voice her protest. He silenced it beneath his mouth as he succumbed to the temptation to sample the flavors waiting there. Then he silenced his own groan of denial when he raised his mouth away after only the briefest touch.

"That," he said through gritted teeth, "is the most licentious thing you shall have to endure in my company. I vow that to you."

She put her fingers to her lips. Astonishment filled her eyes, but she said nothing. Beneath his fingers, her trembling warned him to cloak his own reaction. He must not yearn to do more with this woman.

"What do you say?" he asked when she remained silent. "Are you going to hide in that girls' school, or will you come with me?"

"I should go back."

"Yes, you should." He smiled coldly when she stared at him. "But will you? Will you be Fraulein D'Orage, mistress of languages, or will you be Michelle D'Orage, presumed mistress of Alexei Vatutin? Will you hide yourself away, or will you be as brave as Sophie D'Orage, who never backed down from a challenge?"

"Sophie D'Orage?" she repeated with a gasp. "You know— You knew *Maman?*"

"Briefly. Sadly, too briefly." He released her and sat on the chair. Folding his hands between his knees, he looked up at her. "She occasionally did work for my government."

"*Maman?*" Michelle frowned, lowering herself to the bed, but keeping the footboard between them. "You must be mistaken."

"Why do you think I came to St. Bernard's and asked for you? I had hoped Sophie had passed on her skill for subterfuge to her daughter." He rested his hand on the other side of the footboard and caught her eyes. She wanted to look away, but froze as he asked, "Did you know nothing about the work your mother did? How do you think she managed to pay for you to attend that expensive boarding school?"

Wanting to tell him he was mistaken, she could not keep from thinking of the box of gold coins. *Maman* had gotten that money somehow. But as a spy? That seemed impossible. There must be another explanation, but what? "Mayhap we aren't thinking of the same woman."

"D'Orage is not a common name, and you look just like her." Pain flashed through his eyes so fast she was not sure if she had seen it. "Even if your appearance had not been enough to persuade me, that would have." He pointed to her finger and the ring her mother had left for her. "That was Sophie's ring."

"You've seen her wear it?"

He nodded. "Often, for it was her wedding ring."

"It was?"

"You didn't know that?"

"No." Rubbing her finger along the raised lightning bolt, she glanced up as the sable softness of a shadow moved along her.

She watched Alexei trace the design as she had. "One evening I was admiring the fine workmanship, and she told me your father had a set of rings made at a jewelry shop in Paris called Mauriac's."

"Why would you remember that?"

He put his hand on the foot of the bed and smiled. "Your mother is impossible to forget."

"I know." She stood and wrapped her arms around herself. "I think of her so often."

"As I do." He touched the ring again. "Sophie told me the rings were designed as a play on their name. *Orage* is French for storm, so I guess Michel used the lightning bolt to signify that."

"Michel was my father's name!"

"So Sophie mentioned often. She loved him very much. He must have been an extraordinary man."

"I wish I had had a chance to know him."

"So do you believe me now? Will you come with me?"

She turned away and twisted the ring on her middle finger. If Alexei was telling the truth—and he knew so much about her family she had to believe him—there had

been a side of her mother's life she had been too blind
to see.

Now it all seemed clear. Those infrequent visits to her
mother's apartment must have been when her mother had
not been working for a foreign government. Tears bubbled
over the edges of her lashes. She hated weepy women, but
she could not halt the sobs that burst from her aching
heart. Why had *Maman* not been honest with her?

"Michelle?"

She whispered, "Today is the anniversary of *Maman*'s
death, but the pain makes it seem as if it were yesterday."

"And you have no one else."

Surprised that he did not make it a question, she nodded. "You know so much about me."

"I know about Sophie."

"You remember after six years?"

"I know." He smiled wryly. "I never forget the most
minuscule details, although I must own Sophie's death was
not minuscule. My memory is why I am considered so
valuable to my government. They know I won't forget anything I hear." He looked directly into her eyes. "I do know
a little about you, Michelle. Enough so I suspected you
would be willing to come with me to Vienna to help combat
those whom your mother fought to keep them from con-
trolling Europe."

"*Maman* was a spy?" She nearly choked on the words,
which were as bitter as bile.

"There are nicer terms for it, but that is what she was."

"And you?"

"You must know that if I worked with your mother, I
have been involved in espionage, too. Now the war is over,
and I can travel as Alexei Vatutin. This assignment is something of a reward for what I have done in the past." He
stroked the tears from her cheek. "Will you come with
me, Michelle? I intend to enjoy Vienna. We could have
such fun."

She put her hand over his. "Yes, I will come with you."

With a laugh, he planted a smacking kiss on her cheek. Then he slapped her on the bottom. When she gasped, stunned by his outlandish behavior, he chuckled again. "I thought you would see sense."

"If you ever do that again, I shall—"

"Do what? This?" He tapped her bottom again. When she started to whirl away, he grasped her arms and pulled her to him. His voice dropped to a roguish whisper. "Or this?"

There was nothing teasing about his mouth over hers. Fire seared her as her hands slipped up his back. He tugged her more tightly against him until every inch of him urged her to soften. A breathless sigh burst from her when his lips tasted the curve of her chin and traced heated joy along her throat.

Rapid flicks of his tongue teased her skin as the sparks deep within her grew into a flame. When her hand curved along his neck, she discovered the warm skin beneath his loose collar.

His mouth found hers again, but demanded entrance to the shadows within as his tongue sought to explore every sleek surface. Urging her to caress him as intimately, he twisted his fingers through her hair. She delighted in the splendid sensation of his mouth. When he drew away, she slowly opened her eyes to see his glistening with passion he made no effort to hide.

Softly he asked, "Which did you mean?"

"Both, I fear."

"I feared that as well." He released her, and she gripped the footboard again to keep her wobbly knees from collapsing beneath her. Brushing her hair back from her face, he said, "We shall do well together, Michelle. We have much to speak of, but for now, go to bed. We have many more days of traveling."

"Do I sleep here?"

"Yes." He went to the chair and got his coat. Shrugging his arms into the sleeves, he said, "I will go downstairs to be sure Rusak can polish off that last mug of beer alone. That should give you all the time you need to ready yourself for bed before I come back."

"You are coming back here?" She gasped.

"Where else?"

"Are you crazy to think that I would sleep with you?"

He rested one elbow on the door frame. "Even I am not that crazy, *Liebchen,* but never forget that, as far as the rest of the world is concerned, you are my mistress. It would be very strange for me not to share a room with you, wouldn't it?"

"But here?"

"There can be no chance of any word reaching Vienna that I did not sleep with you from the moment you left St. Bernard's."

Heat slapped her cheeks, and she knew she was blushing when he chuckled. Too late, she understand Frau Offenbach's puzzlement. The mistress of a grandly dressed man like Alexei Vatutin should wear something more splendid than her simple black gown.

Blowing her a rakish kiss, Alexei went out and closed the door. It opened before she could move.

He peeked around the edge and said, "I shall not be downstairs long. You might want to hurry and change. Good night, Michelle. Sleep well."

"That is unlikely," she said to the closed door. She hurried to her bag and pulled out her simple muslin nightgown. She was glad it covered her from chin to ankle. Unhooking her gown, she shoved it over her hips. She untied her petticoats and let them fall to the floor as she pulled on her nightgown.

She sighed with relief as she scurried to the bed. Taking two of the pillows, she pulled off the coverlet. She placed them on the chair. Let Count Alexei Vatutin sleep on the floor, for he would not sleep with her.

As she pulled back the remaining covers, she glanced at the door. She did not dare let him so close again. With an ease that was frightening, he had orchestrated her into his arms like a conductor leading his musicians to a crescendo. To let him hold her again when they were alone would be madness, for she had been unable to resist his kisses.

With her palm beneath her cheek, she stared at the silhouette of the candle dancing on the wall. She tried to think of something other than his fiery touch. Something . . . anything.

Maman!

Why had *Maman* told her nothing about this other life she had led with Alexei? Had she kept the truth from Michelle because she did not want her daughter to be involved in this world of half-truths? Mayhap that was why Michelle had been sent to a straitlaced girl's school. If that was so, it all had been for naught when Alexei Vatutin invaded her life.

Her thoughts were interrupted as the door opened. Only the clatter of a key locking it kept her from looking up. She shut her eyes and forced her breathing to slow.

Low noises warned her of every motion Alexei made. She heard him curse as he pulled off his boots. Without a bootjack or a valet, the tight boots must be nearly impossible to take off. She hoped the shadows hid her smile at his grumbles. It was a pleasure to discover that the almost too perfect Count Vatutin could be bothered by something as commonplace as boots.

"She makes her opinions quite clear," he mused in a whisper, and she knew he had seen the pillows and coverlet.

Feeling his gaze on her, she froze. She wanted to tense and pull the covers to her chin. With every bit of her strength, she kept from moving as he came to stand by the bed. While he drew the covers over her shoulder, his fingers brushed her cheek lightly, but he walked away as she fought to submerge the fiery river flowing through her.

She dared to breathe again only when she heard him arrange his makeshift bed. Even when the soft rhythm of his breathing filled the room, every inch of her ached for him. She must learn to control this longing for his touch, or she feared that, by the time they reached Vienna, there would be no need to *pretend* to be his mistress.

Chapter Four

The second day of their journey proved even more difficult than the first. Exhausted from not sleeping, Michelle fought the sway of the carriage, which reminded her of a roughly rocking cradle. More than once her head drooped against Alexei's shoulder. He said nothing when she was routed awake.

If her relationship with Alexei had improved even slightly, she could not say the same about Rusak, who tried to ignore her. When it was impossible, he made it obvious with gestures that he found her company disgusting. She did not mention to Alexei how much Rusak's coldness bothered her. She was sure he would tell her to learn to live with Rusak.

The schedule of their journey did not change. They paused only to rest the horses or stop at an inn at night. Slowly Michelle became accustomed to sharing her bedchamber, but she made certain every night that a pillow and a blanket were set aside for Alexei. She did not care if he slept on a chair or on the floor. Just as long as he kept his promise not to sleep with her.

She wanted to believe she was worried about nothing, because, after the first night, Alexei treated her with the kind indifference of a big brother for a vexing younger sister. Yet, when she finally convinced herself of that, she would catch a glance from him that she was not supposed to have seen. The barely quiescent sparks in his eyes cut through her defenses, suggesting ideas that should not be in her head. He was an impossible man, and she hoped he would change when they reached Vienna.

On Sunday morning, Michelle woke as the sun peeked into the window of the *Gasthaus* where they had taken a room high under the eaves. She heard the soft chime of church bells. After the past week's confusion, hearing something so familiar was like unearthing a treasure.

She drew on her dress under the covers and slipped her nightgown over her feet. Hooking her dress, she slid out from beneath the blanket. She wrapped her braids around her head and pinned them in place. It was not neat, but with her bonnet, no one would notice.

Her eyes widened when she saw Alexei sleeping on the floor not far from the door. If he had chosen such an uncomfortable bed each night, she had seen no sign of it. The hard floor of a Swiss *Gasthaus* must seem heavenly in comparison to nights of camping with the Russian army.

Michelle tiptoed across the floor. As light as her footsteps were, she was not overly astounded when Alexei's hand gripped her ankle.

Half-asleep, he grumbled, "Where are you sneaking off to at this godforsaken hour?"

"To church."

"Church?" He muttered something.

"Go back to sleep." She tried to pull away.

Alexei released her ankle and stood. He stretched, revealing his bare chest. Her gaze moved along that firmly muscled expanse. She had never seen so much raw masculinity. Heat as strong as a fever oozed up her cheeks as she realized he was amused with her stare. She thought of

snarling at him for being so vain, but such an admon-
ishment would be a waste of her breath.

"Something wrong?" He laughed. "Your face is the
color of the rising sun."

Again she was tempted to retort. She said nothing as
she reached for the door latch.

He laughed once more and pulled her away from the
door.

"Release me!" She was shocked that he would treat her
so coarsely.

"If you will stay here."

"I am going to be late if you don't—"

"*I* don't like being reprimanded at this early hour. Will
you act reasonably?"

"Me?" She swallowed her rage as her voice broke on
the single word. Taking a slow breath, she said, "Alexei,
I am going to be late."

"Do you think I intend to let you just wander about
alone? You are in a strange village on the border of the
Hapsburg Empire."

Clenching her fingers on her reticule, she snapped, "I
know the dangers, but I doubt I shall be accosted on my
way to church."

"Church?" He laughed. "I thought that was what you
said, but I was still only half-awake."

"Yes, I would like to go to church. If you will excuse
me . . ."

"Sit."

"I am not a child for you to order about."

"Then act like a grown woman and sit while I get dressed.
I don't think you want me to accompany you with my
shirttails hanging down out of my breeches."

She flushed. Before she had met Alexei, she had not
blushed more than a handful of times. As she dropped
onto the chair, she watched as he went to the washtable.

When he poured water into the bowl and splashed it on
his face, she wondered where he had washed since she

began traveling with him. He had arranged for times for her private needs, but never spoke of his own. There were many things that had gone unsaid between them.

Lathering his face, he grimaced at the small mirror. "I assume this churchgoing is a habit."

"Yes."

"I should have guessed. Sophie said often that she wanted you to have a chance at a righteous life."

"Righteous? What do you mean?"

He grinned at her through the soap. "Why are you asking me? You are the one who teaches in that convent."

"St. Bernard's School for Girls is not a convent." She wanted to get up and walk out, but she was fascinated by how confidently he wielded the sharp razor so close to the vulnerable line of his throat. "Zurich is very Protestant. It was at the crossroads of the Reformation."

"Crossroads of the Reformation? Must you sound like a schoolteacher all the time?"

"And can't you ever be serious?"

Alexei yelped as he nicked the edge of his jaw. "You could be less exasperating while I am shaving."

Michelle went to the bowl and dipped the end of a towel into it. Dabbing at the bloody spot, she ordered, "Put this against it. The water will cleanse it."

"I guess I should say thank-you for your quick nursing."

"No need. Just don't talk and shave at the same time."

"I didn't realize you were such an expert on men shaving. Or have you left your school before for an adventure? Mayhap an amorous one?"

She whirled away. "You are disgusting. 'Tis just common sense not to run a sharp blade against a moving object. If you cannot keep your mouth closed, mayhap you should grow a beard."

"I have." He chuckled as he dropped the towel onto the marble washstand. "It looked horrible. All patchy and a dozen shades of blond and brown. I prefer the risk of cutting my throat in front of an exasperating woman."

Michelle considered answering, but the sound of church bells reminded her of the passage of time. "Alexei, if we are going . . ."

"A moment."

She was going to tell him that she did not have time to wait, but more quickly than she would have guessed possible, Alexei shrugged on his best frock coat. He adjusted his stock collar and the cravat closing it. Sitting, he pulled on his boots.

He looked up at her, and the gleam of amusement returned to his eyes. "Damnable boots! Hard to put on and harder to take off."

"You do not have to wear them."

He stood and placed her fingers on his arm. "I am afraid I cannot resist wearing the latest fashion, Michelle. After years of fighting in the mud, the idea of fine clothes is almost as enticing as waking to find your slender legs out from under the covers and so close to my face."

Fire slapped her face. *Um Himmels willen!* He could be a gentleman and not mention such things. When he gave her a bold wink, she lifted her chin. She would not be intimidated by his crass comments. Quietly she said, "Alexei, need I remind you that we are on our way to church?"

"All the more reason to be honest." He unlocked the door, revealing that she could not have left without his knowledge. "And allow me to be honest, Michelle. You are an incredibly lovely woman."

"Which is why you chose me for your supposed mistress?"

He squeezed her fingers and chuckled. "Why shouldn't I have a beautiful mistress instead of a plain one?"

"We shall be late," she reminded him, unsure at the course of the conversation, for his eyes never hid his admiration.

As Alexei led her down the stairs and across the main room of the inn, he chatted as easily as if they took a walk every morning. The bite of the wind silenced him when it swirled through the door. Winter was greeting them here in the mountains.

Bowing her head to its icy caress, Michelle hurried with him down the steps. The brown grass in the center of the small village was lifeless. Only the pine remained green as everything waited for snow.

The church was a simple building. Gray stone edging the door and windows offered the only decoration amid shingles that needed painting.

Michelle adjusted her bonnet as they entered the chapel. Incense billowed out to lure them into the hush. Walking between two rows of stone pews, she admired the intricate altar. She saw the stares of the churchgoers, who must be curious about the strangers who had appeared in their midst.

"It has been a long time," mused Alexei behind her.

"A long time?"

Instead of answering, he pointed to the right. "Over there. There is half a pew empty."

When she heard a rumble from the people closest to them, she tensed. She hurried along the aisle before Alexei could say anything else. His accent identified him as a despised Russian.

Reaching the pew, she sat on the damp stone. He sat next to her and flashed her the smile that continued to disconcert her. When it dimmed and his eyes narrowed as he looked past her, she glanced to her right to discover that the three people who had been in the pew had risen and were leaving.

The Swiss could not forgive the Russians, who first had declared their friendship, then slaughtered the Swiss men conscripted into the French army. Although she empathized with their hatred, Michelle was embarrassed by it.

"You look unsettled." Alexei's fingers covered hers, drawing her hand within his arm. She tried to pull it back, but his fingers tightened on hers as he bent toward her to murmur, "I do not take the insult personally. Neither should you."

"Me?"

"Are they disgusted because they do not want to be contaminated by a Russian or by a Swiss woman in the company of one?"

Michelle was saved from answering by a song from the off-key choir. How had *Maman* handled these complications? Throughout the service, Michelle tried to imagine how she could put her life back together after Alexei and his schemes were behind her.

Had he guessed this would happen? She saw his jaw work as a comment came from behind them, the voice just loud enough so he would not miss the scorn. Mayhap that was what he had been cautioning her about. If he spoke plainly just once instead of acting as if she could not be trusted with even the most basic truths, she would be amazed.

As Michelle came out of the church, she noted every hostile glower. Alexei had been right. They saw her as a traitor who had sold herself to the man who owned the wondrous carriage that was stopping in front of the church.

Alexei stroked her fingers, and she looked at him. His smile was gentle. In spite of herself and knowing she condemned herself further in the villagers' eyes, she smiled back. Odd that this man her countrymen saw as an enemy was her only ally.

As he would be in Vienna.

What had her yearning for adventure gotten her into?

Michelle grimaced when Alexei opened the carriage door, and she saw Rusak inside.

Alexei handed her in and asked, "Is everything ready for the day's journey?"

Rusak nodded.

"You packed all of Michelle's things as well?" he asked as he sat opposite Rusak and slapped the wall.

"My things?" Michelle asked. She yelped as the carriage started. She fell backward onto Alexei's lap.

"This is charming," he said as his arm encircled her waist, "but I do believe there is enough room on the seat for both of us."

"It is not charming," she retorted as frostily as the ice that clung to the grass. "You should have given me a chance to sit before giving the signal to get under way."

"Mayhap, but that does not lessen the pleasure of our current circumstances."

She tried to slip off his knees, but his arms tightened around her. "If you want me to move, you must release me."

"I don't recall saying anything about you needing to move." He glanced at Rusak. "Did I say that?"

Rusak grumbled something in his throat.

"He did not hear me say that, *Liebchen.*"

"Don't call me that!" Fear erupted within her. Alexei had altered from the kind man who shared her disquiet to this haughty fool in a single heartbeat. Brushing away his fingers, which stroked her waist, she gasped when he tipped her face beneath his.

She stared up into his catlike eyes. Green and mysterious, they glittered with potent emotions. Her mouth was caressed by his warm breath as her own caught and burned away all thoughts of anything but him.

"Endearments are used by lovers," he whispered. "You are portraying my mistress. What better way to show my devotion than by calling you *Liebchen?* 'Tis a part of our charade. Unless you prefer . . . ?"

"No!" she cried as his mouth lowered toward hers. Pushing herself out of his arms, she struck the side of the carriage. When she heard Rusak's guttural laugh, she added viciously, "Call me whatever you wish, but do not think you can take liberties because you are my employer. I shall not have you touching me, and I do not want *him* touching my clothes!"

"Don't be ridiculous! Rusak helps me as you do. If you want to waste time on our trip, you must expect he will do what is necessary to get us on our way on time."

She scowled. Their brief camaraderie had vanished as if it had never existed. Drawing her cloak around her, she looked out the window. She must remember that this was a job she had taken in order to see the world beyond Zurich. She must not let her longing for Alexei's kisses make her forget that.

Chapter Five

A knock sounded at the bedchamber door. Hastily Michelle hooked what she hoped was the last button on the back of her gown. She glanced around, but all of her smallclothes were packed away, ready for when they left in the morning. As with each of her baths during this journey, she had not had enough time to soak in the warm water. Sharing a room with Alexei made it impossible. She changed behind a screen, but with only the thin material between them, she was too aware of every movement he made.

Hurrying to answer the door, she winced as a splinter cut into her foot. It was her fault for not putting on her shoes. This *Gasthaus* was not as pleasant as the other inns where they had stayed.

She turned the key and called, "Come in." Then she limped to the room's sole chair. The flimsy piece of furniture squeaked, but she ignored it as well as Alexei's greeting. Tipping her foot up, she frowned at the small, brown sliver.

"What did you do?" Alexei asked.

Looking up, Michelle silenced her retort as his gaze moved along her bare legs beneath her raised skirt. When his eyes met hers, she forgot about her immodest pose. All she could think of was trying to breathe. His green eyes were a maze, daring her to try to solve the puzzles hidden within them. But one thing was clear: the desire she had tasted on his lips that first night glittered in his eyes.

She forced her eyes away. "I have a sliver in my foot."

"Do you need help?"

She started to refuse, knowing the danger of letting him touch her even so chastely; then she nodded. She could not reach the small sliver.

When he squatted, he balanced her foot on the knee of his breeches, which were almost the same color as the splinter. He grinned. "Even your feet are slender and pretty."

"My foot hurts. If you are going to babble, I will remove the splinter."

"No, no, I shall pull it out," he said with a laugh. "There."

Surprised, she asked, "All done?"

He held up the sliver. "See? Here it is." Tossing it aside, he cupped her heel. His thumb rubbed the curve of her instep. "Is the rest of you as soft as this is?"

"Really, Alexei!" She started to stand, but he refused to relinquish her foot and she dropped back into the chair. It wobbled and collapsed.

His arms caught her before she could land on the floor. When she struck his hard body, she wondered if she would have been better off hitting the floor. Her breath exploded out. A rumble sounded beneath her ear. Slowly she realized he was laughing. The infectious sound surrounded her, reaching into her, making it impossible not to laugh, too. As his arm slipped around her, she chuckled and looked at the broken chair.

"I shall have to take the chair's cost out of your wages,

Liebchen." He laughed. "I suspect the innkeeper will charge highly for such an heirloom."

She groaned with mock despair. "It shall take me years to repay it."

"Yes, years." His arm tightened around her, drawing her closer.

When her breasts brushed his firm chest, she laughed to pretend she was oblivious to the powerful emotions in his eyes—emotions she did not dare to explore, for they might entice her into discovering truths she had never guessed existed, such as how perfect his arms were around her.

Her voice barely quavered as she said, "I am surprised either Frau Herbart or I believed your tale that I would be back at St. Bernard's before next term."

He stroked her damp hair before his fingers curved around her nape. "But you came with me, *Liebchen."* He caressed her gently, sending pleasure through her. "This seems as good a time as any to ask you to forgive me for lying."

Softly, she said, "You have me in a difficult position to refuse your apology."

"I don't think this is a difficult position, *Liebchen."* His lips brushed her cheek. When her hands gripped his sleeves, wanting to stay within this embrace of delight, he whispered, "I find this an incredibly fitting position to apologize."

She rose before she gave in to the temptation to steer his mouth over hers. "Alexei, I meant only that I owed you a favor for pulling out the splinter."

"And I wasted that favor on asking for an apology?" He chuckled and stood. "Stupid of me." His finger outlined the shape of her lips. "I should have saved it for something much more delicious."

Michelle picked up a towel. As if it were of the least concern, she asked, "Did you want something?"

"I shall not give you the obvious answer to your blatantly

suggestive question." He chuckled as he sat on the bed, making her too aware of how intimately they lived during this journey. "I thought you might like to join us for a drink before you go to bed. I know you think Rusak and I have ignored you the past few days."

"No, no." That was a lie. The two men had said barely a score of words to her in the past week as the carriage climbed slowly through the mountains.

"You should not have to hide here alone every night."

"I do not want to disturb you two."

"*Liebchen,* I would not call either Rusak's or my reaction to you anything as tepid as disturbing." His smile disappeared as he rose. "Come along. We need to speak of what awaits us in Vienna."

"Why didn't you say so instead of plying me with false compliments?"

His finger traced her cheekbone. " 'Twas not false, *Liebchen.*"

She knew she should step away. She should fire some whetted comment at him that would remind him of his place and hers. When his finger slipped beneath her chin and tilted her mouth to his, she forgot all she should do and thought only of what she wanted to do.

"You look so lovely," he whispered.

"Thank you." Her breathless voice came from the depths of her heart.

"That was honest."

"Yes."

"And are you being as honest when you look at me with a craving to be kissed?"

"I am being nothing but myself." She brought his lips to hers. She could not deny the longing that grew stronger each time he touched her, each time he teased her, each time she found a haven in his arms. Unhurriedly, delighting in every facet of her mouth, he lured her to soften against him.

Her hands slipped up his back to stroke the powerful

sinews covered by his coat. When she touched his skin above his collar, its rough texture teased her fingertips to explore further.

Alexei muttered something and drew back, tugging her hands down to fold them between his. She regarded him with astonishment. She had not thought *he* would be the first to pull away.

"Alexei?"

"Turn around."

"Pardon me?"

He spun her so she faced away from him. When his hands ran along the back of her gown, she gasped and jumped away. If he had stopped kissing her for *this,* he must be shown what a mistaken assumption he had made.

Before she could speak, he stepped in front of her. "Stop being a silly schoolgirl!" His laugh was serrated, cutting into her. "Your buttons are not done up correctly. Let me fix them. You certainly would not want anyone to think we had been surrendering to passion, although they are going to be curious after hearing that crash."

Her cheeks burned with embarrassment, but she did not turn. What, she wondered with a pulse of cold dismay, if he redid her gown wrong simply to serve as "proof" of his tale?

That thought must have been on her face, for he whirled her so she could see the back of her dress in the cracked mirror by the door. "Look. Here." He touched a skipped button among the score running along her back. "And here. And here. You need someone to help you dress, *Liebchen.* We shall have to think about finding you a husband."

"A husband? You think I want you helping me to find a husband?"

"Why not? You are the type of woman who would enjoy marriage."

Keeping her spine straight as his fingers struggled with

the bead-sized buttons, she asked, "What type of woman is that? A *Hausfrau?*"

"That is not what I meant." He bent forward to fix another button. His words oozed warmly past her collar, and she leaned her hands on the footboard in front of her as her bones threatened to melt. "You have incredible passions within you that the right man would be a fool not to release."

She tried to pay his enticing touch no mind, but it was impossible. "Certainly you are not offering marriage."

He chuckled. "Certainly not. I am what the Germans call a *Hagestolz,* a confirmed bachelor. I might like hooking up a pretty lady, but that does not mean I wish it to be the same one night after night."

Michelle did not answer. This personal, very frank conversation unnerved her. He had hinted that they might be in Vienna for several months. Alexei was a virile man. While she portrayed his mistress, he would have fewer opportunities to become involved with another woman. Only fewer, she acknowledged, because she did not doubt that Alexei could do anything he set his mind to.

"I did not mean to embarrass you, *Liebchen.*"

At the unexpected apology, Michelle looked into the mirror and saw his face too close to hers. She could taste his mouth again if she tilted her head so very slightly. Lowering her eyes to stare at the reflection of her clenched hands, she said, "You must remember that I am still Fraulein D'Orage of St. Bernard's School for Girls."

"Only if you want to be." He traced the curve of her lips. "Look at these, and tell me what man could resist them." His finger continued along her jaw to pause just below her ear. He twisted a strand of her hair around it. "This black silk is obscured within your conservative bun." His lips seared fire against her nape. "But to think of it loose and flowing along you when—"

"Alexei, stop!" She had intended to chide him, but the words came out as a desperate plea. With so few words, he was creating captivating fantasies, fantasies in which the man sampling her lips was Alexei Vatutin.

"Why, *Liebchen?*"

She remained silent, knowing she risked speaking the truth if she opened her mouth. Would he laugh if she told him how much she wanted him to kiss her now?

He sighed, stepping away. "When this is finished, I shall find you a list of suitable suitors."

"A list?" Facing him, she asked, "Do you think I wish to go from mistress to courtesan?"

He began to chuckle. When she asked what was so amusing, his answer was nearly lost amid his laughter. "You are so fetching when you endeavor to be a proper lady, Michelle. Why don't you be yourself?"

"This *is* me."

"No," he stated, abruptly serious. "No, the prim Fraulein D'Orage is just what you have learned to be. Inside you is a woman who is as fierce as a dragon, snorting fire at anyone who gets in her way."

Her eyebrows arched. "Is that so? I did not realize that you were such an expert on me, but I should have known that Alexei Vatutin is an expert on everything. At least, in his own mind."

"There." He grinned. "St. Bernard's language mistress would never say such a thing." He held out his arm. "Let's go downstairs. We can argue just as easily there, and I can find something to stanch the wounds left by your glare."

When he started to lead her toward the door, she said, "Wait. I need to put on my shoes and stockings."

He scooped them up and handed them to her with a bow. Sitting on the bed, she put her thick stockings on her lap. "Now 'tis your turn to turn around, Alexei."

"Why?"

"You have already seen too much of my limbs this evening."

Leaning forward, he gave her a roguish leer. He picked up one stocking and dangled it in front of her. Snatching it from him, she reached up to shove him aside. As she touched his chest, she froze, aching to explore its breadth. The mirth vanished from his eyes, disclosing a fierce glow. His mouth lowered toward hers.

With a curse, he turned his back. "Get dressed! I am thirsty."

"Alexei—"

"Get dressed!"

Hurt by his harsh tone, she drew her stockings up beneath her skirt. What had happened? What she had seen on his face could not have been anything but desire—the same desire tormenting her as she thought of his eager kisses.

Michelle sighed. She never would figure out this enigmatic man, and she was not sure if she wanted to. It would be best to forget about his touch and think only of the job she had been hired to do. That was impossible, she knew, as she lowered her skirts and bent to hook the buttons on her shoes.

"Here. Let me help." Alexei knelt again and swiftly closed her half boots. "Why do you wear these clumsy things? Ladies are wearing slippers now."

"Fashion is not important to me."

"That I have noticed." When he offered his arm again, she put her hand on it gingerly.

She was not sure if he would smile or lash out at her. He did neither. While they walked down the narrow steps to the common room, he said nothing.

Her nose wrinkled at the odors left from too many meals. At supper, the meat and bread on her plate had resembled slops given to hogs. Her middle cramped, making her regret that she had eaten at all.

Several men lounged about the room, but she was the only woman. The innkeeper stood behind a table that held a keg and a pyramid of pewter tankards. No candles were lit. The flames from the hearth offered the only light. No one seemed to mind, but she did not want to call attention to herself by tripping over an uneven board.

Or more attention. Every eye was focused on her, including those of their coachman, who was laughing with several men she had never seen. She wanted to flick away their lecherous gazes and was grateful when Alexei motioned for her to sit. Her gratitude vanished when she saw the man across from her.

"Good evening, Rusak," she said softly, trying to be pleasant to this man who considered her an interloper. Whether Rusak was jealous or protective of Alexei, she could not guess. All she knew was that he despised her.

When a mug of beer was placed in front of her, Alexei sat next to her and held up his own mug. "To our good fortune. May our good luck come quickly and frequently." He took a hearty drink and wiped his foamy mustache with his sleeve. "Drink up, Michelle."

"I have never had beer before."

"Then 'tis time that you did."

She recognized the challenge in his voice. She did not look at him as she lifted the heavy tankard. Taking a deep breath, she drank. Beer splashed on the table as she choked on the acrid flavor. Alexei slapped her companionably on the back.

"I am glad I am giving you a good laugh," she said past her scratchy throat.

"Actually, it is good beer."

She pushed her mug toward him. "Then have mine."

"All right." He poured some in his tankard and held the rest up in Rusak's direction. When Rusak nodded, he dumped the rest in his mug.

Some message she could not understand passed between the two men. Alexei comprehended his friend as no one else could. They shared an alien language of glances and motions she doubted she could learn.

When she rose, Alexei glanced up, surprised. "Are you leaving, Michelle?"

"I am tired, and I am interfering with your fun." She frowned. "Of course, you will have to find someone else to hoax once I have left. Good night, Alexei, Rusak."

Rusak nodded with satisfaction, but Alexei downed his beer in a single swallow and placed the mug on the table. He stood. "Get me a refill, Rusak. I shall be back."

"Don't bother," Michelle said. "I can walk up the stairs alone."

He put his arm around her waist and steered her toward the steps. "I am sure you can, *Liebchen,* but I do not like the way the men are watching you."

"Again?" When she started to turn, he pushed her up the stairs ahead of him.

"Still," he corrected. "Pretty ladies like you cause trouble without trying."

She did not answer. When they reached the narrow landing at the top of the stairs, he put his hand on her elbow. She faced him, but remained silent. Tonight she had not said anything right.

"Good night, *Liebchen.* I shall be only a few minutes while I tell Rusak about our route tomorrow."

"Oh! You wanted to speak to me about Vienna."

He put his finger to her lips. "We will have time in the coach on the morrow. Go to bed now. I can lock the door if you wish."

"That might be a good idea," she said, although she could think only of his fingers stroking her arm. The smallest movement might urge him to draw her into his arms again. Thoughts she should not have spiraled through her mind, but she must not do anything to show him how she longed for his kisses.

Softly she repeated, "Good night, Alexei."

"Will fifteen minutes be enough for you to hide under the covers?"

"Yes."

As she turned to the door, he brought her face back toward him. "Are you really tired?"

"Yes." She was tired of the upheavals in her life. Once things had been so simple, so straightforward, so undeniably right or wrong. Nothing was that way any longer. She wanted his mouth on hers and his hands touching her in ways she was only beginning to imagine. He would be glad to oblige before he sought out the next woman who might pass through his life.

She closed the door and heard him lock it. She should be grateful Alexei was being a gentleman. The thought of wrestling with him to keep him out of her bed was not a pleasant one. Yet ... Crossing the room, she pulled her nightgown from her bag. She undid her dress and pulled it over her head. The muslin nightgown dropped over her. Nothing relieved her baffling frustration. She did not know why she was upset when Alexei was doing exactly as she should wish.

She pulled pins from her hair and stared at her hueless face. What she *should* wish. Not what she wished. Brushing her hair with short, ferocious strokes, she sighed.

Everything was wrong, but she could not return to St. Bernard without getting answers to some questions—questions of her past and of *Maman* and of Alexei and of how all three interacted.

Footsteps sounded on the stairs. Blowing out the candle, she hastily climbed into bed and arranged the covers around her. She winced as the thin feather bed shifted to leave her on a wooden slat. When she was about to adjust it, she heard the key rattle.

The door opened with a squeak. A splash of light flowed from the lantern on the landing. Burrowing under the covers, she knew that saying anything would be an invitation to another quarrel. With Alexei or with herself? That was another question she did not want to answer. All she wanted now was to dream of a place where no one hid the truth.

He relocked the door before walking across the room. The floorboards screamed in the darkness. It was a sound she had not noticed earlier when she had been arguing with Alexei.

When the footfalls neared the bed, she scowled. Alexei should have seen his pillow and blanket next to the broken chair. Sitting up, she asked, "Alexei, is there something wrong? If—"

A hand seized her arm as another clamped over her mouth. She was shoved into the mattress. She tried to scramble away, but the hands were too strong.

The shadows congealed into a form. She fought to escape. The bed screeched as the man put a knee on it. Shaking her head, she clawed at the hand over her mouth. It ground into her lips, driving them against her teeth.

She struck the man. He batted her hands away. When the covers were jerked away, she shrieked. She heard a triumphant laugh as the hand over her mouth slipped to her throat. She took a deep breath to scream. Broad fingers cut into her neck, gagging her.

She struggled to squirm away from the fingers moving along her legs. They tugged aside her nightgown. The thought of kicking him flitted through her head, but was lost as she struggled to release the breath imprisoned in her lungs and gasp for another. Blackness surrounded her.

Nothing mattered.

Not the questions that plagued her. Not Alexei and his strange ways. Not this man who reeked of beer and was stroking her legs boldly. None of it mattered. She was nothing. She was—

Fresh air struck Michelle like a blow. She choked, rolling on her side and pressing her hand to her throat. She heard a fist striking someone and a grunt of pain. She sucked in deep breaths. A door slammed somewhere. Voices shouted. She paid no attention. Breathing was enough.

"Michelle? *Liebchen,* are you hurt?"

Hands settled on her shoulders. She screamed. When she was pulled against an unyielding body, she fought for only the second it took her to realize Alexei held her.

"Alexei," she whispered. "Alexei, it was horrible. He . . . He—"

"Hush, *Liebchen*. He will not hurt you again." His hand tilted her face up to his intense gaze. Only now did she realize that someone had relit the candle.

Looking across the room, she saw Rusak by the door. Rage twisted his lips, but, for once, it was not aimed at her. Compassion softened his rigid mouth as he looked at her.

"How did that man get in here?" she asked.

Alexei's smile was honed with fury. "As with everything else tonight, it was my fault. After I left you here, I went outside."

"Outside?"

"For personal reasons." His eyes twinkled for a moment before they darkened with fury. "Your caller got another key somehow. He bragged to his comrade. They thought Rusak was deaf as well as mute. When he overheard their plans for one to keep me busy while you entertained the other, Rusak found me. We have settled our accounts with our innkeeper and his allies."

She rose as far as her knees, but gripped the headboard to keep from falling. "Thank you, Rusak."

Grudgingly he nodded. He seemed grateful when Alexei asked him to bring the carriage from the rickety barn behind the *Gasthaus*. Picking up Michelle's satchel and flinging her dress over his arm, Rusak hurried away.

"Let's go," Alexei commanded. "I have had enough of this place."

"You are hurt!" She touched the scarlet mark along the sharp ridge of his left cheekbone.

His smile became malevolent. Rubbing his reddened knuckles, he laughed. "Not as much as your caller. He shall be sporting at least one black eye on the morrow. If I had not been afraid of killing you, he would have met my pistol instead of my fist."

"Alexei!"

"Do not scold me," he said, framing her face with his hands. His eyes drilled her. "I was not there when Sophie could have used my help, and I will be damned before I let you get hurt, too."

"It was not your fault *Maman* died," she whispered, wanting to comfort him for this raw wound.

"Be careful what assumptions you make, *Liebchen.*"

She inched back. "Are you saying it was your fault?"

"I am saying," he murmured as he held her lips close to his, "that things might have been different if I had been there."

"You might be dead, too."

"Or she might be alive."

"Alexei, you cannot fault yourself for something that is not your fault."

"I am glad you feel that way, *Liebchen,* because it is not my fault that I want to kiss you so much. 'Tis yours." His smile warmed as he tipped her lips beneath his.

She breathed his name in anticipation of rapture, then gasped as he turned her face and kissed her lightly on the cheek. With a laugh, he draped the blanket over her shoulders and scooped her into his arms.

"Wrap the covers around your legs, *Liebchen.* 'Tis cold out."

"I cannot go out in my nightgown!"

"It covers you well enough." All amusement left his face. "Michelle, we will not stay here tonight."

Relenting, because she knew he was being wise—wiser than she was when she could think of nothing but his kiss—she leaned her head on his shoulder. He was correct. If they stayed at the *Gasthaus,* they must guard all night against another attack. As she imagined the long hours ahead of them, she hoped Alexei would hold her close as he did while he carried her toward the stairs. Nothing had ever been so splendid as being in his arms.

She knew the peril she was courting with these thoughts,

but, as she rested against his broad chest, she savored them. There could be no danger in that . . . could there?

Michelle was surprised to see that Rusak was seated in the driver's seat of the carriage. As the snow cut through the blanket, she asked, "Where is your coachee?"

"He is no longer in my employ."

"You gave him his leave? Because . . ."

He pushed aside the carriage door with his foot and lifted her onto the seat. "He was talking more than he should when the beer loosened his tongue." Stepping into the carriage, he lit the small lantern near its roof. "And I suspect he helped your caller."

"Why?"

"Who knows why any man will sell his loyalty in exchange for gold?" He closed the door and slapped the wall. "It does not concern me, for Rusak can drive us the rest of the way to Vienna while you play my devoted mistress, *Liebchen.*"

She drew the blanket more tightly around her. "I wish you would not call me that."

"Now, now," he teased as he wagged a finger at her. "Bad habits take a while to develop. We shall be in Vienna soon, and I must be able to call you that without thinking."

"As long as you do not expect me to call you darling, too."

He laughed as he stretched his arm along the back of the seat and crossed his legs so that his boot brushed the blanket. "No, Michelle, I do not expect you to call me anything but Alexei. For a woman educated at that prim school, I think that in itself is quite a concession."

The carriage lurched into motion, saving her from having to answer. She changed the subject to one she found more comfortable.

Alexei smiled as Michelle prattled on about the mountains around them. Since he had found her at St. Bernard's School for Girls, he had found out how different she was from his expectations. Her mother had been world-weary, tested by years of living two separate lives. Michelle was an innocent, believing that she could change the world simply because she did good for those around her.

Innocent mayhap in many ways, but he could not be unaware of her enticing beauty. Her mother had been an elegant hostess, winning the admiration of men throughout Europe. He should have been prepared to discover that Michelle possessed Sophie's elusive allure, which he had sensed even though Sophie D'Orage had been many years his senior when they worked together. Yet it was Michelle's innocence that made her even more irresistible than her mother.

His hand curled around her shoulder, halting her in midword. When she glanced up at him, her eyes luminous in the dim light, he smiled. A man could lose himself in those eyes, if he was not cautious. It was his good fortune that *he* was always cautious. If he had not been, he would have given in to his yearning to press her back into that bed and teach her how much rapture they could share. She was concerned that he was sleeping on the floor night after night, but she need not be, for he could not sleep, plagued with the intoxicating thoughts of her so near.

"Liebchen." At her grimace, he smiled and repeated, *"Liebchen,* there are some things you need to know about how we must appear when we reach Vienna."

"Such as?"

"Everything said or done in our apartment must never be discussed elsewhere."

Her eyes sparked. "Do not treat me as if I am completely naïve, Alexei."

He flinched at her words. Had she become privy to his thoughts? Warning himself not to be fanciful, he let his hand slip along her arm. He fought his yearning to press her back against the seat and claim her lips. To claim all of her. With her hair flowing along her back and her eyes hooded with fatigue, she had a vulnerability that was beguiling.

He put his hand back up on the top of the seat. His fingers clamped into a fist. Nothing had changed. He had been a fool to kiss her even that first time. And then to have kissed her again ... This torment was of his own making.

His words were squeezed out past his taut jaw. "Treating you as anything but my translator was not my intention." Even though he tried to pull it away, his gaze centered on her soft mouth, which was parted so slightly in an invitation he was sure she had no intention of offering. He shook his head to clear it. He must think only of the reason he was going to Vienna and why she was going with him.

"Then what is your intention? I do not carry tales." She arched her shoulders. "Nor do I have to suffer your pawing when we are alone."

His lips tightened when he realized his hand had cupped her shoulder again. "Pawing? I was only trying to offer you comfort after what you suffered."

"With that man or with you?"

A growl came from deep in his throat as he pressed her back against the seat. As he leaned over her, his hands caught her face between them. "If you don't know the difference between rape and seduction, *Liebchen,* allow me to show you."

He savored her beneath him as he captured her lips with a gentle kiss that startled her, for she stiffened in the moment before she raised her arms to curve around his shoulders. The wind spun her hair about him. His fingers entwined through it as his tongue tantalized her mouth before moving to outline her throat with kisses. Her breath grew frayed, and the answering response raged through him. Drawing aside the blanket, he reached for the ribbon closing her nightgown at her throat.

"Alexei, don't!"

Not sure whether it was Michelle's voice or the echo of Sophie's from his memory, he blinked. Michelle's eyes were wide with dismay. If stealing her innocence had been his goal, he had almost succeeded. It had not been, for he only wanted to show her he was not like that beast at the *Gasthaus,* but he had nearly been overcome with his desire for her. What was wrong with him? He never lost his self-control, but this demure schoolteacher threatened to steal it from him with a single glance in his direction. Slowly he moved away so she could sit.

She turned her back on him. When he started to speak, she said, "I don't want to hear anything you have to say, Count Vatutin, except that you shall honor your vow."

"Vow?"

"That I can go back to St. Bernard's whenever I wish." She looked over her shoulder at him, tears glistening in her eyes. "We must end this right now. I do not want to work for any man who would treat me like this, Count Vatutin."

"You want to leave because I kissed you?"

She shook her head as the tears glistened on her eyelashes. "No, I want to leave because you seem unable to realize I am not my mother."

"What does Sophie have to do with this?" he asked, although he could not forget how that voice had rung out through his head. Sophie's voice telling him to be careful. That had been the first lesson she had taught him, as well as the first one he had forgotten when he drew her daughter into his arms.

"*Maman* has everything to do with this." A sad smile stole across her lips. "*Maman* is the reason you sought me out. You hoped I would be just like her, but unfortunately for you, I am not the woman you love."

"Love? Sophie?" He regarded her with shock. "You are mad! She was my mentor. Nothing more. Not with me or any man, for, as far as I know, she was always faithful to your father's memory."

"So she never had to suffer your idea of a seduction?"

"Michelle, I was just trying to show you—"

"Your fantasies of my mother."

"You are mad!"

Michelle knew she was not. Alexei's eyes glowed each time he spoke of her mother. It was just as well that this was over. She liked Alexei's kisses too much, but no one could compete with a legend, especially when that legend was her mother.

"If you will ask Rusak to stop at the next village," she said, "I can—"

"I will not let you travel back to Zurich by yourself."

"But you said that you would—"

"I am quite aware of what I said. I don't forget conversations. Remember? I remember every damn word you or anyone else says to me. What *you* must remember is that you know too much now for me to risk your returning to Zurich, where someone could convince you to talk."

She crossed her arms over her chest and glowered. The carriage hit a rut in the road, and she was tossed against Alexei. He caught her before she could slip to the floor.

"Let me go!" she cried.

"I told you that you are going to Vienna with me, *Liebchen.* I meant it." She stiffened when he went on in a dark tone, "Don't tell me that you will be silent. If anyone else suspects that you are Sophie D'Orage's daughter, you will find them demanding answers you do not have. They would not accept your tale of ignorance of your mother's life, and the methods they use to ask their questions can be deadly."

"You are trying to scare me."

He nodded, surprising her more. "You are right. You are also right that I did love your mother. How could anyone not love her? She was vibrant and intelligent and, even when I knew her, beautiful. But, *Liebchen,* I loved her as a boy adores a favorite teacher. She taught me everything I must know to survive in this life I have chosen. What I learned from her, I intend to teach you. The first rule is that once you start, you cannot stop. You are the hunter and the hunted. Every day you must stalk without being caught. It never ends."

"But I did not choose this life."

"No, *Liebchen*, you didn't." He sighed. "It was my mistake to choose it for you."

"At least you are apologizing."

"No, I am not, for there is nothing to apologize for."

"You have ruined my life, and you say there is nothing to be sorry about?" She wrapped her arms around herself beneath the blanket.

"Ruined your life? You wanted to put that staid life behind you."

"How do you know that?"

"You would not have come with me if you were not bored with life at St. Bernard's School for Girls."

"If I had had an inkling of what would happen, I would have refused."

He shook his head and sighed again. "You still don't understand. You had no choice. Once I discovered where you were, I knew others would, too. The only way to protect Sophie's daughter was to bring you with me."

"You mean that you would have taken me against my will?"

"If necessary." He caught her face between his hands as she was about to move away. "Your mother saved my life once, *Liebchen*. I never had the opportunity to repay her, so I shall watch over you until I am sure you are safe."

Putting her hands on his wrists, she meant to draw them away. Her fingers froze on his as his cold stare riveted her. He was not jesting with her. He believed what he was saying.

"Safe?" she whispered. "From whom?"

"From the ones who would kill you as they did your mother."

"Maman died in an accident."

"Do you honestly believe that?"

"I—"

"Honestly! *Liebchen*, do you honestly believe that?"

Questions she should have asked years ago taunted her. Questions of why her mother was traveling so far from Zurich in the company of strangers, of why there had been a rock slide on a road where there never had been one, of why no one had come to Sophie D'Orage's funeral but her daughter. And . . .

She shivered and hunched into the blanket, but this cold came from the center of her heart. "You said it was your fault, Alexei."

"I should have been traveling with her. Mayhap I would have seen something she missed, but I had decided to take another route because of an obligation." He looked up toward where Rusak was sitting on the box. "I chose between two friends, and I lost one while barely saving the other."

"You could not have known what would happen."

"I knew. Your mother's enemies are thorough, Michelle. They have been trying to find you, but have been stymied by how Sophie kept her life with you so private. When I learned that they were looking for you, I came to Zurich."

"But how did you find me?"

His smile had no warmth. "I remember all I hear, and your mother spoke of you to me often enough so I could piece the clues together." He cupped her chin. "Until you are safe, *Liebchen*, you shall stay where I can watch over you."

"How long?" she whispered.

"As long as necessary. We might be together far longer than either of us wish." His grim tone made his words a threat as he repeated, "Far longer."

Chapter Six

Opening the door, Alexei motioned for Michelle to precede him into the apartment. It would be home during their stay in Vienna. She hesitated. Crossing the threshold meant another beginning, another collection of unknowns, another farewell to the safety she had known at St. Bernard's School for Girls.

She forced her feet forward. She was exhausted. For the past two days, they had traveled with a stop only for quick meals and for her to change out of her nightgown and into a dress that was appropriate for traveling.

When she paused just within the door, Alexei pushed past. He lit a lamp and bent to start a fire on the cold hearth. Wrapping her arms around herself to keep out the damp chill, she stared around the room.

She had not expected the second floor of the unremarkable, gray building to be like this. The large room had a trio of windows that overlooked the *Platz*. She could see snow flying past, and shook her head to dislodge the flakes that had been driven into her bonnet.

"Why don't you take off your cloak?" asked Alexei without looking up. "I shall light the other hearths while Rusak brings in everything from the carriage."

"Other hearths?" Her teeth chattered.

He smiled at her. Sitting back on his haunches, he held out his hands to the fire. "You didn't think we were going to live in poverty in Vienna, did you, *Liebchen*?" He got to his feet and tossed her cloak over the back of a chair between the hearth and a pair of scarlet settees. Tossing his hat on a marble table near the windows, he laughed. "We have a certain appearance to maintain. As a Russian diplomat, I must live well with my mistress."

She ignored his grin. Rubbing her cold hands together, she glanced at an arch to her left. The darkness beyond suggested it was a corridor leading to other rooms. She hoped one room was a kitchen. They had not eaten since breakfast, for they had wanted to beat the storm into Vienna.

"Will the other diplomats live here?" Michelle asked.

"You mean from the Russian delegation?" He shook his head as he walked toward the arch. "I like being free to do what I need to do."

"Why don't you just be honest? You want to spy on the other delegations and can do it more effectively without your fellow countrymen around."

He shot her a grin. "Now that sounds like a comment Sophie would have made. You are right. Now stop chattering like a chicken and let me get these fires started. You will not want to sleep in the cold."

Michelle walked toward the fireplace. She considered following him to explore the apartment, but she ached from the long hours of riding on the uneven roads. All she wanted to do was sleep.

No, that was not true. She looked at the arch. She wanted to be in Alexei's arms. It was insane. Yet, during the last two days of their trip, he had again treated her with the polite indifference of a brother. She missed his teasing kisses and his bold caresses that dared her to be as brazen.

When the outer door opened, she turned to see Rusak entering. He dropped her bag in the center of the room. Glowering in her direction, he walked back outside. After the attack on her, he had reverted to his scowls. Her hopes that they could become allies, if not friends, had come to naught.

As she untied her bonnet, Alexei strolled back into the room. "What do you think?" he asked, brushing small bits of bark from his coat.

"Of what? This room?"

"You have not stuck your pert nose into the other rooms yet?"

She sighed, for she longed to avoid another argument. She guessed that was as likely as Alexei explaining even one of his strange comments. "I think this room is lovely."

"A grudging compliment." He sat on a settee and placed his feet on the table in front of him. At her gasp, he frowned. "Don't become a nag, Michelle."

She hung her bonnet on a peg behind the door. "This is going to be my home also. I would prefer not to have to have the furniture marked with bootprints."

"This was a stupid idea," he grumbled.

"Bringing me to Vienna was your idea."

Firing a glare, he said with a snarl, "You need not remind me, but that was not what I meant. I meant it was stupid to find you, thinking you would be as reasonable as Sophie was."

"You are forgetting one vital thing."

"What is that?"

Michelle knocked his feet off the table. "My mother would not have been pleased either to be hired under false pretenses. I might be more reasonable if you had been candid with me from the beginning, Alexei." She bent to pick up her bag.

"Let Rusak do that."

"He does not like me. Why would I want to make things

worse by asking him to run errands for me? He is your servant, not mine."

Bounding to his feet, Alexei pulled the bag from her hands. "Are you going to force me to be a gentleman?"

"I did not realize I was forcing you to be anything but your customarily beastly self."

"Beastly?" He stepped toward her, overwhelming her. "If I were to show you—"

The outer door opened behind him. Rusak's expression showed his abhorrence at seeing Alexei standing so close to her. Looking away, he carried her small trunk past the arch.

Michelle watched him, wide-eyed. Rusak's familiarity with the apartment warned that this was not the first time the men had stayed here. She wondered who had shared it with them in the past.

No, she would not even think that. What did she care about Alexei's past? If it had not touched hers, she would not be here now, and her life would not be all ajumble.

Fatigue deepened Alexei's voice as he motioned toward the arch. "Lead the way, so I will not find a knife protruding from my back."

"Alexei, I—"

"Just go. The second door is your room."

"My own room?" The words slipped out. After all the nights of sharing a room on the way here, the thought of being able to have privacy was delightful.

"Is that dismay I hear in your voice?" he asked as they walked down a broad hallway. A lamp had been lit, and it illuminated the paintings hanging along the walls like a gallery. His quick pace gave her no chance to admire the landscapes.

"Hardly, for I cannot wait to be alone. I do hope the door has a lock."

"The one to the hall," he said as he opened the first door.

"I thought you said my door was the second one."

He smiled and, taking her arm, drew her into a room. A gasp of amazement erupted from her. She had never seen such a magnificent bedchamber. A tester bed stretched toward the ceiling, its cloth of gold curtains shadowing its breadth. Chairs and settees as fancy as the ones in the front room flanked the white stone fireplace. To one side a desk was topped by leather.

"This, *Liebchen,* is my room." He reached for another door. "And this is the door that does not have a lock."

When he ushered her into another room, Michelle shivered. A mistress would never deny her lover access to her private room. Another bed, this one smaller but still taking up half the room's floor, was set by a mahogany armoire. The door hung open to reveal that it was lined with a brocade that matched the bedcurtains.

Alexei placed her bag on the chair in front of a dressing table, but Michelle's gaze went to a tub filled with steaming water. Her delight must have been emblazoned on her face, because Alexei began to laugh.

"You should bathe before the water gets cold," he said, coming to stand behind her. His hands settled on her shoulders as he drew her back a half step to lean against him.

"Yes." The idea of a bath was as heady as an opiate; yet she did not move. Being against him like this was even more heavenly, especially when she did not have to look at the devilish twinkle in his eyes. "But how did it get here?"

"Didn't you see me speak to that lad when we stopped to change horses at the edge of the city?"

"He was a lanky lad, nearly as tall as a man."

"I should have guessed you would not miss that." He brushed hair back from her forehead. "Your dark eyes seldom miss anything. I sent the lad ahead with a message for our landlord to prepare a fire on each hearth, to have oil in the lamps, and to get this ready for you, *Liebchen.*"

"Thank you for thinking of the one thing I want right now more than anything else."

His hand on her elbow wrapped her arm around her with his over it. Sifting his other hand up through her hair, he plucked out the pins. He caught the strands that fell over his fingers. "How simple your desires are! To want things within your grasp must be wonderful."

"And what do you want?"

"Other than you?" He lifted her hair and kissed her nape.

She put her other hand over his on her arm as she closed her eyes, delighting in the sweet sensations quivering deep within her while his fingertip roved along the modest neckline of her gown. "Yes."

"I am not sure." There was a tinge of regret in his voice. "Why do you ask me questions no one else has?"

"I don't know." That was a lie. She knew exactly why she asked. She longed to discover an answer to even one of the puzzles that made up this paradoxical man.

"No? I thought you might be spying on me."

"Are you that interesting, Alexei?" Her words ended in a soft gasp as his caress brushed the curves above her gown.

He turned her, enfolding her to him. His legs pressed against hers as she raised her arms around his shoulders. "I could be interesting. For you, I could be, *Liebchen*. I— Dammit!" He stepped away and motioned toward the tub. "You should take your bath, Michelle, before the water gets cold."

Michelle stared after him as he went back into his own room, closing the door behind him. She did not hesitate. Lifting her bag off the chair, she jammed the chair under the knob so the door would not open. Sitting on the bed, she stared at the door. She was more certain than ever that she would never understand Alexei Vatutin, and more uncertain than ever why she wanted to.

* * *

Alexei clamped his pipe between his teeth and scowled at the chair that was meant to keep him out of Michelle's room. Then he chuckled. She was learning, albeit not the lessons he would like to teach her.

Verflucht! He did not need to be thinking about her when he should be considering his next move. There were a few people who must already know he was back in Vienna. They would be making plans, so he must, too. If he could just banish Michelle from his mind . . .

Hearing a sound behind him, he turned. His smile returned when he saw Rusak in the doorway.

"Where is Michelle?" Alexei asked.

Rusak gestured toward his left.

"In the kitchen?"

He nodded.

Alexei chuckled. "Whatever she is cooking smells wonderful. I hope she is making enough for three."

Rusak's lips pursed in a scowl.

"Eat it or not, as you wish." Alexei shrugged. "I had thought, by now, you would see the good sense of having her here. If we had left her in Zurich, everything might be ruined."

He drew his finger across his throat.

"Very funny, unless you are talking about *our* throats, which will be slit in no time if LaTulippe finds out I have double-crossed him."

At the sound of footsteps, Rusak walked in the opposite direction.

Alexei chuckled as he set his pipe on the dressing table. From one problem to the next.

"What are you doing here?" Michelle said, pausing in the open door. She held a bowl from which came enticing aromas of pepper and basil.

He had seen her in her nightgown and wrapper before,

but the sight of her standing in the doorway, wisps of her hair floating around her face as they teased his fingers to touch them, was enchanting. Every inch of him demanded that he pull her into his arms and loosen those buttons on her wrapper as he drew her nightgown up along her legs. Her legs . . . He gulped. That habit she had of sleeping with one leg slipped out from beneath the covers had given him an enticing view of it and added to the maddening need to run his fingers along its slender length. Up over her ankle, along her calf, to her knee, to her thigh, then . . . He cursed silently. How much could he be expected to endure, even for the love of his homeland?

"Alexei, what are you doing here?" Michelle's voice was sharp with impatience, and he wondered how long he had been lost in the thought of wrapping those pretty legs around him in her bed.

"Waiting for you." *Good!* His voice was even. He pointed toward her bag and trunk. "I have been playing your maid while you made supper." He plucked the bowl from her hands. "Is this mine?"

"I think not!" She took it and set it on the table. Her eyes widened when she saw his pipe there.

"You have no gratitude for what a good lady's maid I have been. After I removed your tub, I turned down your bed to take away the chill and put your things in the armoire."

"You unpacked— You dared to—"

"You are welcome, if you are attempting to thank me." He dipped a finger in the soup and, with a yelp, waved it in the air. "*Verflucht!* That is hot!"

"What did you expect?"

Tasting the soup on his scalded finger, he smiled. "And delicious, *Liebchen.* Is there more?"

"In the kitchen." She pointed to the door, then frowned. "I locked the door!"

"Yes, you did." He pulled the chair away from the connecting door. "I had to unlock it because you put this in the way."

"There are two keys?"

"No."

"But you are in here!"

He smiled and tapped her cheek. "*Liebchen,* you should have guessed that I have encountered other locked doors before tonight."

"Ah, the famous spy."

Laughing, he said, "Those two words should never go together. Many of the locked doors I have encountered were locked again without anyone else being the wiser."

Her eyes snapped with dark fire when she folded her arms in front of her. "This, you told me, would be my room. If you want to come in, you must knock like anyone else."

"Anyone else? Who else are you expecting to give you a look-in at your bedroom door?"

"Don't try to confuse the issue." She pointed to the door. "It is unlocked now, and I suggest you make use of that fact."

His arm swept around her. He gave her his most wicked smile, but the fury in her eyes did not dim. "Michelle—"

"If you will not leave . . ." She put her hands on his arms and tried to shove them away. Her words were spat through her clenched teeth. "I will leave, then."

"Not until you listen to me." Putting his mouth near her ear, he whispered, "If you keep squirming so enticingly against me, I shall not be leaving until you do far more than listen."

"You would not dare!"

He was tempted to tell her that she was the one who was daring. If she had guessed the course of his thoughts, she would have turned and fled. His fingers splayed across her back, pressing her in her soft garments even closer.

" 'Tis your good fortune, *Liebchen,* " he said, holding her gaze, "that you are right. At least, tonight." When he released her, she took only a step away before he cupped her elbow again.

She glanced at him. "Count Vatutin, are you going to paw me all night?" A flush climbed her cheeks as he laughed.

He relinquished her arm. "Oh, Michelle, you make it so difficult to remain angry when you act like a child. And, like a child, you must have your lessons repeated to you often before you remember them." He leaned forward. "Do not forget this again, *Liebchen*. I shall go anywhere I please in this apartment. You must accustom yourself to that."

"I do not think I can."

"You will."

She turned away, but he could see her face in the mirror. Her anger was gone. Dismay had replaced it. She closed her eyes, then opened them to meet his gaze. "Do not forget *this* again, my lord: I am your employee, not your mistress. I will pretend to be your mistress in public, but I insist on privacy in this room."

"Brava." He clapped his hands. "What a performance! I cannot wait to unleash you on the unsuspecting delegates. They will never guess that such a cold lady is, in actuality, a schoolteacher."

Michelle pointed to the connecting door. "Will you please leave? I want to eat my soup."

"Can I hope you made enough for Rusak and me?"

"Yes."

In spite of himself, Alexei was amazed. "You did?"

"If you did not spend all your time picking locks and being where you should not be, you might have come to the kitchen to see that." She clasped her hands in front of her. "Will you please leave? I am tired of your trickery and lies."

"Lies? *Liebchen*, do you think I am lying to you?"

"Of course."

With a shrug, he reached for the door latch. "And, of course, you are correct." He opened the connecting door, then paused. "You are correct about everything but one small fact."

"What is that?"

He gave her the grin that always raised her color. *"Liebchen,* I was honest that I would like to stay here and have you in my arms all night long."

With a cry, she whipped her pillow off the bed and flung it at him. He ducked, and it sailed into his room. Picking it up, he turned to hand it back to her. The door slammed so hard that the wood vibrated.

He tossed the pillow into the air. Catching it, he threw it onto his bed. This was, without question, going to be his most interesting visit ever to Vienna.

Chapter Seven

Alexei regarded Michelle over his coffee cup. As he lowered it to the table, he stated, "It is clear that the first thing we have to do is obtain you some decent clothes."

"Decent?" Her hand reached toward the neckline of her gown. It was properly modest.

Laughing, he said, "Let me rephrase that. We must obtain you some clothes that fit with your new life as the mistress of a member of the Russian delegation. No man would be attracted to your funereal feathers."

Her eyes snapped with outrage. It took every ounce of her willpower to hold on to her serenity. "I can understand that you do not want to be seen with a decent woman on your arm. Think what it would do to your reputation! It would be ghastly to—"

He laughed again. "You make it difficult to do anything nice for you." He stood and picked up his cup. Draining it, he set it back on its saucer. "How long will it take you to get ready to go to the modiste's shop?"

"I am ready now," she said primly as she rose. Placing her napkin on the table, she added, "I have no interest in inciting another of your Russian temper tantrums, Count Vatutin."

"You should always call me Alexei here, even when you are having one of your *Swiss* temper tantrums."

She went to the glass over the sideboard. The dining room was situated next to the parlor and overlooked a small courtyard at the back of the house. As she patted her hair into place, she said, "I have told you I shall do my utmost to convince everyone I am your mistress, intent on satisfying your every need. I shall keep my private feelings hidden."

"You, hide something?" He snorted. "Impossible, *Liebchen*. Every thought you have is visible on your face. Such as right now. You are pretending to be angry, but you are excited to be replacing your bleak frocks."

That he could judge her feelings so accurately bothered Michelle, for it left her bare before him. Then she scowled. If he was able to guess what she was thinking, he should be more considerate instead of infuriating her at every opportunity.

He went into the parlor and plucked her cloak off the hook. With a flourish, he settled it over her shoulders. When she reached to hook it, he said, "Allow me, my dearest love." He silenced her retort when he continued, "Don't you understand that it must be different from this point forward?"

"Is it? You will be insufferable, and I shall be your long-suffering mistress."

He finished securing the small buttons on her cape. Instead of stepping away, he slid his hands along her shoulders and down her arms in a languid motion. "It shall be very, very different. You must grant me certain liberties I know you find offensive."

"Yes," she whispered, "offensive." She stared up at him, lost in the emerald seas of his eyes. Brown specks within them fascinated her as his arms slid beneath her cloak to encircle her waist.

"You must be willing to let me hold you."

"I know."

His hand swept up along her back, bringing her to him. "If the occasion arises, you must not appear disgusted by my kiss."

"I won't," she said softly.

His grin returned. "I did not think you would."

"You arrogant, contemptible—"

He laughed as she walked away from him. She could not let him discover how hurt she was that he was playing with her emotions again. Her hand was grasped by his. He placed it gently on his arm and winked.

"I should hate you!" Michelle said, unable to keep from smiling.

"More than you do?"

"I thought you said you could tell what I was feeling!"

He opened the door and led her out, then turned to lock it. Unable to see his face, she was unsure if he was teasing or serious when he said, "I can."

"But I don't really hate you."

He faced her. Although he did not touch her, a warmth oozed from her center as he smiled. "But you would like to hate me, wouldn't you?"

Standing on the landing, she said over the clatter of traffic in the street below, "Alexei, I honestly don't know what to think anymore."

"I do."

"You do?" Her eyes narrowed when she saw that twinkle in his. What mischief was he about to spring on her now?

"I think Rusak will be outraged if he has to wait out in the cold much longer." Holding out his arm, he asked, *"Liebchen?"*

She put her fingers on it. As he led her down the stairs, she wondered what awaited them in Vienna. Whatever it was, if Alexei was involved, it would not be boring.

* * *

A tinny bell rang as Michelle hurried into the small shop. She was glad to be out of the piercing wind that was whipping the snow down Griechengasse. As she shook snow from her cloak, she asked, "Why won't Rusak come inside?"

Alexei chuckled as he took off his beaver hat and brushed snow off it. "Rusak in a *couturière's* shop? He would rather face the French again." In a whisper, he added, "Besides, we must keep up appearances. Don't forget he is our coachman."

"Grüss Gott!" called a rumbling, female voice.

Michelle tried to find a smile for the woman who was as round as the rich sound of her voice.

"Frau Lepper?" asked Alexei.

"Yes," she said, bobbing her head so enthusiastically that her double chins jiggled. "You must be Count Vatutin."

He gave her his most charming smile. "I appreciate you seeing us on such short notice."

"My pleasure, my lord. I am happy to make a wardrobe for your *dear* friend."

Michelle noted Frau Lepper's slight emphasis. This was only the first of the embarrassing situations she would find herself in during their stay in Vienna. From this point forward, she would be an extension of Alexei, for her identity came solely from their relationship.

He drew her forward. "Frau Lepper, my *dear* friend. Fraulein Michelle D'Orage. I think you shall find her more than easy to work with."

As Frau Lepper clucked another greeting, Michelle flashed Alexei a furious glance. It was horrible enough that the modiste used the term *dear friend*. His repetition added to her discomfort.

"Come here, Fraulein," ordered the seamstress. "Turn." She shook her head. "What a shame."

"A shame?" asked Alexei, sitting on a chair by the window.

Frau Lepper glanced at him. "I mean no insult to her, my lord, but such a lovely woman should not be dressed so. Are you in mourning, Fraulein?"

"No," she answered uneasily.

"Then you should never wear black. With your dark hair and pale skin, you should wear soft colors."

Alexei said, "We leave those decisions in your competent hands, Frau Lepper."

"What exactly do you wish to order?"

Although the seamstress had spoken to Michelle, Alexei answered, "Everything from the skin out. She will need dresses for calls and for at-homes and for evening, along with all the accessories to go with them. Do not forget the lacy unmentionables that ladies love to wear." His smile became lascivious. "And men love to have them wear."

"Alexei!" Michelle gasped before she could halt herself.

"Let me spoil you as you spoil me, *Liebchen.*" He clasped her hand and brought it to his lips.

Alexei watched both women. Michelle's flushed face was perfect for her role as his newly acquired mistress. Frau Lepper's smile became more calculating. She must be trying to figure how far his generosity extended. As he released Michelle's hand, the modiste hurried her into a measuring room.

Leaning back in the uncomfortable chair, he peered through the window. It had been almost a decade since his first visit to Vienna. He sighed. That debacle he did not want to remember. Although it hardly seemed possible now, he had been nearly as naïve as Michelle. So simple the answers had seemed. So clear-cut the line between right and wrong. No longer. He nearly had destroyed all that he worked for, but he had been saved by Sophie D'Orage.

He looked at the curtain, which undulated with the movement beyond it. He could not have imagined then that he would return to Vienna with Sophie's daughter.

Resting his hands on his knees, he stared at the floor, which was littered with thread. Finding Michelle and bringing her with him might have been the wrong way to repay Sophie. He wished he could have left Michelle in her cloistered school. He had not had that choice. Those who had lost power sought the daughter of the woman who had worked for their downfall. His fingers tightened on his knee. They could have twisted Michelle into believing their lies too easily.

Or could they have? As sharp-witted as her mother, Michelle resembled what Sophie must have been before her profession hardened her. Michelle was the woman he wished Sophie had been. A woman he could have loved.

"Don't be stupid!" he said in a growl under his breath. He had no need for any woman who did not sleep by his side. He might have seduced pretty Michelle, for she was clearly eager for his caresses, but the debt he owed her mother stood in the way. Sophie had not saved his life so he could ruin her daughter's.

He stood when the curtain was pushed aside.

Frau Lepper bustled out, bubbling with enthusiasm. "I have several patterns that interest your dear friend."

He nodded absently in response to the modiste's questions as Michelle emerged. Her eyes sparkled with anticipation. Satisfaction flowed over him, surprising him. This visit to Frau Lepper's shop had been meant to be nothing more than a part of his scheme to complete his work quickly and efficiently. Yet his gaze was drawn again and again to Michelle's joyous smile.

When she glanced at him, he kept his thoughts hidden. He must not allow her to gauge them as he did hers.

Looking past her to where the seamstress's assistant had found another girl to help her carry the armfuls of samples, he pointed. "That one," he said in an arrogant tone. "The gold one. It would be the perfect foil for your dark hair, *Liebchen.*"

"Alexei, it is so garish," Michelle replied.

He grasped her shoulders and turned her so only she could see his face. "The gold would look lovely on you, my love." He stroked her cheek, but she shook her head vigorously. "Michelle," he warned in a taut voice.

Michelle almost told Alexei the truth. It was not the gown that bothered her. It was her breath-stealing reaction to his touch. How he would roar with laughter if he learned how his simple caress sent a storm of pleasure along her! Her yearning for him nearly ripped every thought from her head.

"Michelle?"

Forcing a smile, she said as if she were his dutiful, adoring mistress, "Of course, Alexei, if you wish, I shall try the gold dress on. It looks large."

"It can be pinned," Frau Lepper chimed in. "This way, Fraulein." Her smile showed she had been listening closely.

Behind the curtain, Michelle shed her dark gown with Frau Lepper's help. The young assistant lifted the gold silk over Michelle's head. It enlightened her skin. While the seamstress hooked up the back and put pins in place to make the dress fit, Michelle stared at her reflection.

Could that elegant woman in the glass be her? Her breasts were accented by the deep neckline. White lace at the high waistline matched the edging on sleeves dripping over her shoulders. When she moved, the gown whispered a song.

Frau Lepper smiled so broadly her bulbous cheeks threatened to split. "A bit long, but otherwise 'tis perfect, Fraulein. Perfect."

Her assistant nodded in awed silence.

Michelle wanted to agree. The dress was perfect, and, in it, she felt perfect, too. Her eyes sparkled back at her as she wondered what Alexei would say when he saw her in it. Suddenly she could not wait to find out.

She pushed aside the curtain. He stood by the window with his back to her. Something was bothering him, for his back was rigid. Wanting to ask what was wrong, she remembered her role as his empty-headed mistress who was interested only in the luxuries he could provide her.

"Alexei? What do you think?" she asked.

What he said under his breath as he faced her she could not hear, but the glow of admiration in his green eyes was unmistakable. "Turn," he commanded.

"It does not look so good in the back where it is pinned," she replied with a laugh.

"Let me judge for myself."

Obeying, she listened to the silk brushing the floor. The shimmering material seemed to possess a life of its own.

When she faced him again, he said, "No, I don't think so. It is not right for you, *Liebchen.*"

Her eyes widened. "Alexei, I—"

"I said no, *Liebchen.*"

She wanted to argue, but recalled how she must act. It galled her to be so meek. "As you wish."

Shocked, Frau Lepper motioned for her assistant to help Michelle take off the wonderful gown. The young woman said nothing as she unhooked the dress. Hanging it carefully, she redid the many buttons along Michelle's black frock.

Michelle bit back her disappointment. For a few seconds she had been a princess. Pushing aside the curtain, she said quietly, "I am ready to leave when you are, Alexei."

"Good." He handed the modiste a card with their

address on it. As he helped Michelle with her cloak, he stated, "Bring the things I ordered to us as soon as possible. You may fit Michelle at our apartment."

"Of course, Count Vatutin. Good day, my lord." A tinge of pity filled her voice as she added, "Good day, Fraulein D'Orage."

"Michelle?"

At Alexei's question that was clearly a command, Michelle put her fingers on his arm. He led her out into the cold slap of the wind. She sighed. She would have been thrilled with what he bought her, if he had not suggested she try on the incredible dress. Even in her dreams she had never imagined herself in such a magnificent gown.

But she would from this point forward.

Alexei handed her into the coach and shouted the address of their next stop to Rusak, who was huddled under a blanket on the box. She did not pay attention, wishing they could go back to the apartment. In her private room, she might convince herself to forget the silly dream of wearing such a dress.

When the carriage started, Alexei's arm settled around her shoulders. He smiled broadly. *"Liebchen,* I knew you would be perfect in this charade. No one would have guessed that you were not truly disappointed to leave that dress behind."

"I was," she blurted. When his smile faded, she mumbled, "I mean, I—"

"You thought I would buy you a gown like *that?*"

"You were so insistent I try it. I have never seen a dress like it before."

"That gown was not for you, Michelle."

"Why not?" She shrugged off his arm. "Because I am just a language mistress in a girls' school?"

His eyes narrowed as he pulled her back to him again. "Because you looked so incredibly enticing that, if you

appeared among the Beau Monde in it, you would create
a sensation that even this blasé city would long remember.
Some charming gentleman would woo you away with an
offer you might find more economically favorable than
the one I have made you.''

"How dare you!"

He caught her hand as it rose. "Now, now, Michelle,"
he warned with a stiff laugh, "that was not meant to be
an insult."

"I shall not be any man's mistress. Not yours. Not anyone
else's."

"So you have no interest in love?"

"Don't twist my words! If I met the right man, I could
love him."

"And marry him?"

"Of course."

With a snort of derision, he nodded. "I should have
guessed. The schoolteacher in her convent—"

"St. Bernard's is not a convent. I have told you that over
and over."

"You are afraid of any emotions that might make you
lose that prim gentility. Fraulein D'Orage is a puppet,
speaking as she has been taught, never with an original
thought in her head." He cursed imaginatively. "If your
mother could see you, she would regret ever sending you
to that school."

"*Maman* had her life. I have mine. If it is too conventional
for you, that is your problem, not mine. I choose to wait
for love, not its tepid cousin lust."

With a laugh, he swept his arm around her and tugged
her into his arms. "Tepid? How did you get the idea that
lust is tepid? It eats like an ulcer within you until you can
think of nothing but soft lips and softer curves. In the
middle of the night, you wake to think of eyes as ebony
as the shadows clinging to the corners of your lonely bed.
Unable to sleep again, you ache for those eyes looking up

from beneath you as sable hair covers your pillow. Are those tepid symptoms, *Liebchen*?"

"You are talking nonsense."

"Am I?"

His mouth pounced on hers, and she put up her hands to push him away. Her fingers spread across his waistcoat when he deepened the kiss. His arms cradled her as his tongue slipped along her lips before delving within. When his mouth glided along her face toward her ear, she trembled with the longing that refused to be silenced. Her uneven breath pulsed through her, a counterpoint to her fiercely beating heart.

"Do you want me to show you more?" he whispered. "To show how I want to touch every inch of you with my fingers and my lips? To warm your skin with mine? To be a part of you at the very moment you learn what ecstasy truly is? To—"

"No," she said in a moan, "don't say anything else."

He nibbled along her neck until she steered his mouth back to hers. She needed to taste his lips, to have them burn into her with their delicious fire.

Slowly he released her. "As you can see, *Liebchen,* there is nothing tepid about the longing that sends a flame along your skin."

"Alexei—" She bit back the rest of her words when he turned away and stared out the window.

Every time she was certain she was learning something about him, she discovered that she knew nothing of him. She was beginning to fear she never would find the single clue to explain why he treated her as he did, bringing her into his arms one minute, then pushing her away the next. Had he been honest about the dress? Did he really believe some man might try to lure her away from him? And had that been jealousy she had seen in his eyes when he talked about another man coming into her life?

She shivered. He had spoken often of the debt he owed her mother, a debt he would repay by protecting Sophie

D'Orage's only child. She looked from the ring on her hand to his back.

One thing was certain. As he had from the beginning, he intended to keep her away from the truth concealed behind his too charming smile.

Chapter Eight

Michelle stretched to reach the buttons in the middle of her back. She had not guessed her new clothes would be a problem. The heavier buttons on her dresses from St. Bernard's had been simple to close, although Elfie and she always helped each other dress. These ethereal gowns might look like a summer cloud, but they were vexing when she did not have help getting dressed.

You need someone to help you dress, Liebchen. *We shall have to think about finding you a husband.*

She scowled, not wanting to hear Alexei's jesting tones in her head. Him find her a husband? She thought not! He probably would approach that as if it were another hoax he could perpetrate on her. For the past week, he had delighted in shifting her hairbrush on her dressing table to let her know whenever he wandered into her room. She had ignored it, hoping he would stop. That had been useless, for he enjoyed jesting about everything.

Her hands fell to her sides as she sighed. No, Alexei could be serious about his work, and she suspected he would be equally grave about finding her a husband. She did not want a husband. *Maman* might have been right. No ties to a spouse, so she could live the life she wanted.

With a hushed whisper from her dress, Michelle sat at the dressing table and put her fingers on the hairbrush. It was impossible, but she could almost believe the heat from Alexei's fingers remained on it.

She had anticipated this new wardrobe almost as eagerly as she had waited for *Maman* to come to visit St. Bernard's. Alexei and Rusak went out night after night to call on other delegates to the Congress. She could not accompany them while dressed in her clothes from St. Bernard's. Finally she could be free of her prison, but how could she leave the apartment with her dress half-hooked?

Frustrated, she pulled off the gown and surged around the dressing screen Alexei had found for her. She hung the dress back in the armoire. There must be another she could manage alone. Peering into the wardrobe, she tried to decide which one would be best.

"Nothing to wear? I find that hard to believe, *Liebchen.*"

Whirling, she kept the door of the wardrobe between her and Alexei. "How dare you come in without knocking?"

"I did knock."

She tried to ignore how handsome he appeared in his new clothes. His stylishly tied cravat was as white as his trousers. The green of his waistcoat deepened the color of his eyes. He pushed back his tousled blond hair to a rakish angle as he stepped closer.

"I did not hear you," she said, tightening her grip on the door, "and I certainly did not grant you permission to enter."

"I thought you might want to show me what Frau Lepper sent over along with her bill." His gaze dropped, and she realized her legs were visible below the door. Her chemise reached only to midcalf, so he was offered a splendid view. He grinned. "I like what I see so far. Why don't you let me see the rest?"

"Get out!"

"Now, now, *Liebchen*. Is that any way to say thank-you?"

"Alexei, I am not properly attired. Please leave."

"I assume you need help hooking up."

Recognizing defeat, she sighed. He was correct. She could not manage these new dresses alone. Pulling the one she had already tried on out of the wardrobe, she dropped it over her head. She drew on the short, puffed sleeves and smoothed it along her. Holding the back closed, she kept the neckline from drooping to reveal the top of her chemise.

"Will you hook me?" She kept her back to him to avoid meeting the amusement in his eyes. She did not want to think of what else would be glowing there, but she sensed his eagerness in the tips of his fingers as he closed the small buttons. "I need a maid to help me dress."

"I know, Michelle." At his abrupt seriousness, she looked at him. "Stand still," he ordered, before continuing. "We need someone to help you and to manage this household. You shall be too busy now to tend to the apartment."

"I do not mind the cleaning."

"But you shall not have the time to tend to it." His chuckle teased her ear as he latched the last few hooks. "The problem is that I need someone I can trust. There are certain things that I would not want a servant privy to."

"Things?" She whirled to face him, not astounded to see the disquiet on his face. "What sort of things?"

"Just things." He sat on the chair and held out her satin slippers. "Things you do not need to know about now."

Her frustration sharpened. "One thing I do know. I do not want you barging in here whenever you want to." She slipped her feet into the elegant shoes. "Don't think I will be insulted if you ignore me. I can assure you that the revulsion is mutual."

Standing, he put his finger under her chin and tipped her head back gently. He smiled. "You do not find me repulsive, *Liebchen*. When I touch you, even accidentally, you soften. You want me to hold you."

"You are flattering yourself." She backed away from him before her hands could slide up his arms, proving her words were a lie. The upright of the bed halted her sharply, and she winced.

His hand settled on her shoulder as she clutched the tester behind her. So easily he proved her wrong. So desperately she wanted him to pull her into his arms and to his lips. As her fingers touched his face, he caught them and pressed them to his lips. She closed her eyes as he ran his tongue along one of her fingers.

"Do not be foolish, *Liebchen*," he murmured. "Stay angry at me. That is much safer for you."

"Alexei—"

"We must go," he said quietly.

"Go?"

"Now." Reaching into her armoire, he pulled out her new coat. The red velvet coat was edged with ermine at the hem and along the short cape over the shoulders. He handed it to her and pulled a hatbox from the top of the armoire. Tossing the top on the bed, he drew out a bonnet of the same red velvet, which was also lined with matching fur.

He put the bonnet on awry. Before she could straighten it, he took her coat and held it up. She slipped her arms into it and hooked the satin frogs at her throat. Tying the bonnet's ribbons beneath her chin, she followed him into the front room. He threw his cape over his shoulders, nearly striking her in the face.

"Watch out!" she cried.

"Don't stand so close then, *Liebchen*. Not only could you get hurt, but you are going to prove that you have not heeded a single word I just said to you."

She reached to untie the satin ribbons of her bonnet. "If you think I am going anywhere with you when you are in such a churlish mood, you are wrong."

"No, *you* are wrong." He captured her hands and drew them away from her bonnet. "I have heard too many questions about you. You must come with me tonight."

"What sort of questions?"

"Either someone saw us going to Frau Lepper's or gossiped with her about you. The curiosity is interfering with my work. People are more interested in discovering the truth about Count Vatutin's mistress than in discussing the news from the Congress." Placing her hand on his arm, he tapped his hat onto his head. " 'Tis time for you to go to work, *Liebchen.*"

"I understand." She could not argue when this was part of what she had agreed to do. Yet she was troubled by making this masquerade public. *Did you have to play these games,* Maman? The only way to get an answer to that was to ask Alexei, and she did not intend to do that.

She should be grateful that they would be among a crowd. When they were alone, it was easy to let snarled comments cover dangerous emotions. And far too easy to drift into his arms.

Michelle could not help staring as Alexei led her into a grand house not far from their apartment. From the moment she had stepped out the door, she was certain she had entered a dream. The short trip here had shown her a part of Vienna she had not seen before. The street lamps had offered pools of light to match the glowing windows of the homes they passed. Unlike in Zurich, the houses of the wealthy were side by side with shops. On nearly every corner there was a church.

And now she was here in this house. Alexei had mentioned as he handed her out of the carriage that it was being leased by a German prince. She should have asked about the prince and his household, but the very idea of being in a prince's house made her as mute as Rusak.

As her coat and bonnet were taken by a footman, she

was certain she had never seen so much gilt in her life. Even the servants' uniforms were trimmed with gold to match what was painted on the intricate wooden molding and the plaster medallions that seemed to be everywhere.

"Excuse me, *Liebchen,*" Alexei said, handing his hat to another footman.

"Alexei?"

"Go on in. I will be with you as soon as I can."

Michelle started to protest, but he had vanished into the crowd of guests flowing toward a wide door. She clenched her hands. How could he be so inconsiderate? She knew no one here. With a sigh, she forced her fingers to relax. He was her employer. He had every right to tell her what to do. If only he could be less maddening and explain a bit more.

Alone, she wandered from the exquisite foyer into the parlor, where even more guests were gathered. They gossiped, their voices overwhelming the music. She saw more painted and gilded medallions on the walls and ceiling. Each one was identical, showing a stag standing in front of a tree.

Michelle accepted a glass of champagne from a servant who rushed over to her. She took a sip and smiled. She had heard about the bubbles in it, but never had had a chance to sample it. The flavor was as fun as she had guessed.

She edged to a spot near a tall window while she waited for Alexei. She listened to the conversations near her and swallowed her gasp when she heard famous names being bandied about with as much ease as she and Elfie would discuss the students. Never had she imagined she would be among such powerful people. This had to be a dream.

When Alexei motioned to her from near a hearth next to a table loaded with food, she hurried to his side. He put his arm around her waist and smiled. Yet, in his eyes, as he bent to brush her cheek with a kiss, she saw his intense expression, which warned her that something intrigued him about the man standing beside him.

The dark-haired man was rotund. Between bulbous cheeks, his nose was an afterthought. When his narrow lips pulled back over protruding teeth, he resembled a terrier.

"Liebchen," Alexei said, "allow me to introduce Monsieur Bontretemps, a delegate from France. Monsieur, this is my dear friend Michelle D'Orage. Because of my ineptness with your language, I ask your forbearance in allowing Mademoiselle D'Orage to translate for us." When she hesitated, Alexei added, "Now, Michelle."

Trying to remember what he had said, she wished he had warned her that he needed her to translate before he had started talking. She smiled tightly as Monsieur Bontretemps bowed over her hand, but concentrated on translating from French to German and back as the two men chatted about people and places she did not know.

When Monsieur Bontretemps laughed suddenly, she tensed. Had she made a mistake? *Impossible!* French and German were the simplest languages for her.

Michelle relaxed when, with a grand motion, he took a glass of wine from a passing tray and offered it to her. "For your excellent service, mademoiselle. Listening to your sweet voice speaking words that were far less lovely is a pleasure."

"You are very kind, sir."

"Not kindness, simply the truth. Where did Count Vatutin find a gem like you?"

Glancing at Alexei, she hesitated. She could not ask him now what he wished her to tell about her past. Why hadn't she thought of asking him on the way here? The safest thing to say would be the truth. "I was teaching languages. When Count Vatutin asked me to accept the position he had to offer, I was delighted to do so."

The diplomat rumbled with laughter, and she flushed. How could she forget that she was rumored to be more than an employee to Count Vatutin? When a hand settled on her arm, she looked at Alexei, who was smiling. He apparently had been honest when he told her that he understood more French than he spoke.

"If you will excuse us, Monsieur Bontretemps," he said in slow French, his accent nearly obscuring his words.

"Certainly." The round man laughed again. "If I had such a flower to savor, I would not waste my time speaking to an old toad."

Michelle smiled uneasily in reply before Alexei led her across the room. He nodded to some of the people they passed, but did not pause. When he reached a window bench, he sat her on it. He glanced about, then lowered himself next to her.

"Don't stop me," he said in a hiss.

"Stop you? From doing what?"

"This." In spite of his hissed warning, she gasped as he pulled her against him. He whispered against her ear, "Put your arms around me, *Liebchen*. Damnit! You are supposed to be in love with me."

"But here?" Every lesson that Frau Herbart had taught about how to act in public rang through her head, keeping her from softening against him.

"Most especially here."

Michelle nodded, trying to ignore the ache within her. She would have gladly gone into his arms if his embrace was genuine. She hated this hypocrisy.

He leaned his forehead against hers in a very intimate pose. "You did well."

"I am sorry I am so slow."

He chuckled. "If you mean your interpreting, I assure you that I think you are doing well. However, your hesitation lends credence to the tale that I keep you with me less for your interpreting skills than for other, more pleasurable skills."

When he ran his fingers lightly up her back, her heart quickened. She fought to ignore the pleasure as she fired back, "You are enjoying the ruin of my reputation far too much."

" 'Tis the only thing you have allowed me to enjoy." Again he gave her no chance to answer as he went on, "However, as difficult as that makes our situation, I suspect it is for the best that the rumors about our love affair are only rumors."

"For the best? Do you believe that?"

"I must." His grim expression returned as his name was called in a strident voice. He glared at a man wearing a bright red cravat. "Stay here, *Liebchen.* I can deal with Stolz alone. Until later . . ." He strode into the crowd.

Folding her hands in her lap, Michelle wished she could be as sure of his opinion as he was. She scolded herself. Why, the single time he was being sensible, did she want to argue with him? Why, when he was doing as he should, was she so tempted to throw aside caution for just one more kiss?

Michelle remained on the window bench and watched moonlight inch across the guests. It leached color from the gentlemen's coats and from feathers piled high on a lady's head.

"Is there a reason why you are hiding here in the shadows, Fraulein?"

She turned to see a man standing to her right. His blue eyes regarded her with obvious interest as he pushed aside his dark hair and smiled. The cut of his clothes was elegant, from his black coat to his white breeches and the dark blue sash cutting across his chest. He wore some sort of medals sewn to his coat, but they dimmed in comparison to the gold fringe on his sash and the gold rings on his fingers.

Wondering who he might be, she said quietly, "I am watching."

He chuckled. "Anyone in particular?"

"No."

"You sound as if you are bored, Fraulein."

She smiled, charmed by his puppylike friendliness. "Not bored. I like to watch people. We are very interesting."

Sitting next to her, he scanned the room. "Yes, we are, aren't we? Can there be many collections as odd as this one? Enemies who are now friends trying to remain allies while we carve Europe as if it were a game bird."

"Yet no one seems in a hurry to do anything."

His laugh surprised her. "You must be recently arrived in Vienna."

"A little over a week ago."

"I thought so. Once you are here awhile longer, Fraulein, you shall learn that the only way this Congress moves is slowly. Have patience. The line of history is woven an inch at a time."

"It just seems that there is more of entertaining than meetings where something might be accomplished."

"You are correct, but then, Fraulein, that is the way of the world." His smile returned. "I trust you shall not find me too bold if I ask you a personal question."

Michelle wanted to ask what, but said, "No, of course not."

"Would you tell me your name?"

She almost laughed. After their conversation, she had expected a query of a different type. "I am Michelle D'Orage."

"A lovely name for a lovely lady. Are you French?"

"I live in Switzerland, sir." She saw no reason to reveal more.

"Switzerland? Then your home is not far from Coxe-Saxony-Colburg."

"Is that where you live, sir?"

He smiled. "Yes, Fraulein D'Orage. My home and the home of many of the guests here tonight." He motioned toward the table, where small frosted cakes were being replenished. "May I suggest we make our selection while there is still a choice?"

"Thank you." She glanced about the room, but Alexei was nowhere in sight. "And will you tell me your name, sir?"

He smiled at her, as if he were amused. "Would you be averse to calling me Bartholomew? I know I am presumptuous to ask you to be so informal on such short acquaintance, but, as I am one of your hosts, indulge me."

Unsure how to react to his charm, she decided to enjoy it. He offered his arm, and she put her hand on his velvet coat. She noted an emblem on his sash, but could not read the tiny print.

When he led her toward the table, she noted four men following. Uneasily she watched them as Bartholomew selected two plates and began to heap them with cakes.

"Bartholomew," she said softly.

He smiled. "Did you want one of the pink ones instead of the one with green frosting?"

"Those men . . . they are watching us."

"Of course," Bartholomew said, selecting another cake. "They are from my country, and they are curious about the beautiful woman who is sharing dinner with me."

"Do not let me keep you from—"

He laughed again. "Michelle—if I may be so bold as to use your given name also—I would prefer to talk with you just now."

"They are with your delegation from . . ." *Oh, no!* She had forgotten which country this man represented. Her thoughtlessness could be construed as an insult. That could make problems for Alexei.

"Coxe-Saxony-Colburg," he replied. "The name is long and resembles other German states. As to the men in question, yes, they are with the delegation. Shall we return to your window seat? I would like a chance to continue our conversation."

Michelle nodded, guessing Alexei would look for her

there. As she sat and nibbled on a delicious cake, she discovered Bartholomew had a delightful sense of humor as he repeated gossip about the guests. The tales of infidelity and flirtations and arranged marriages made the gloriously dressed people far more human to her.

"And why are you here?" Bartholomew asked abruptly.

"I was hired by Count Vatutin to act as an interpreter during his time in Vienna," she said, stiffening as she noted a slight shift in his tone.

"So I had heard."

Michelle's fingers clenched on the plate. She was certain, because he was so conversant with *on-dits,* that he had heard as well that she was Alexei's mistress. Even though she wanted to tell him the truth to salvage her reputation, she knew she could not. A promise must not be broken, even when it was a mistaken one. She should have anticipated what would happen by agreeing to that charade instead of letting Alexei seduce her with promises of adventure and the delight of his kisses.

Not looking at Bartholomew, she added, "I had been teaching foreign languages."

"You were a teacher?" His smile returned as he regaled her with stories of how he had plagued his tutor. He banished her disquiet as she laughed at his tale of putting cheese in the cracks of his tutor's fireplace stones so it would reek throughout the room.

She said, "Your teacher must have had far more patience than I."

"But he was far less delightful to look at, Michelle. But it is better that he was my tutor, for how difficult it would have been to learn anything when I would have wanted only to regard your loveliness."

She lowered her eyes, for the effusive compliment bothered her. When he put his fingers beneath her chin, she pulled away. His touch did not send that mind-draining thrill through her, as Alexei's did, and she must not allow such intimacy with a man she had met only an hour ago.

"I have embarrassed you," he said, his tone rueful. " 'Twas not my intention."

"You are very kind."

"And you are very beautiful." He took her hand between his. "If I may, I—"

"Ah, here you are," intruded Alexei's voice.

Jerking her hand out of Bartholomew's, Michelle leapt to her feet as Alexei walked toward them. She heard a clock chime midnight, and she was astounded. She had not realized she had talked so long with Bartholomew.

"Alexei," she asked, "do you know—"

"We have met." A haughtiness entered Bartholomew's voice. Taking her hand again, he bowed over it. "Michelle, I trust I shall see you again."

She glanced at Alexei and away when she saw his amused smile. "Mayhap we shall meet at another soirée. Thank you for a pleasant evening, Bartholomew."

"My pleasure. Good evening, Vatutin."

Silently Alexei nodded. When Bartholomew joined a conversation not far away, Alexei offered his arm to Michelle. He remained quiet as they collected her coat and bonnet. Each time she started to speak, he shot her a look that warned her to silence.

A slow fury built within her. She had done nothing wrong but enjoy Bartholomew's company after Alexei abandoned her to speak with others. Had he thought she would sit and speak to no one without his permission?

Snow twirled in a lazy pirouette as Alexei led her out into the cobblestone street. White covered everything, save for the tracks left behind the waiting carriage. A hush unlike any she had experienced since they left St. Bernard's had settled on Vienna, which slept beneath its snowy blanket.

Inside, the coach was damp and cold. When Michelle sat, a chill billowed out to encase her legs. She shivered as fatigue assaulted her.

Alexei stretched his legs out on the opposite seat. Too tired to admonish him, she simply stared at his boots.

"And to think," he said with a chuckle, "that I was worried about finding you a husband when this was over." He yawned broadly and stretched his arm along her shoulders. "You are doing quite well by yourself, Michelle."

"Bartholomew was being kind because you left me alone." She drew her shoulders in to avoid his fingers drooping against them. His touch made it difficult for her to think of anything but how much she wanted to be in his arms.

"Bartholomew?" He laughed again. "I thought I heard you call him that, but I was sure I was mistaken. How can you be so naïve?"

"Just because he was kind to me when you vanished, you do not need to insult him. He was being a gentleman."

"You really don't know, do you, *Liebchen?* You did not suspect anything unusual when no one approached you and a quartet of burly men followed everywhere you went?"

"What should I have suspected?"

"That your friend Bartholomew was our host Prince Bartholomew of Coxe-Saxony-Colburg."

"Prince?" she choked out.

"You should be proud of yourself. Not many schoolteachers make a conquest of a German prince."

Michelle pressed her hands to her mouth. She had spoken all evening to a *prince?* She tried to recall what she had said to him.

"Do not be so concerned, *Liebchen,*" Alexei continued. "You did nothing wrong."

In the thick twilight in the coach, she could discern very little of Alexei's expression. Slowly her fingers rose to the rough sculpture of his face. As they moved along his cheek to the thick obstinacy of his eyebrows, she discovered he was not smiling. Her hand slipped up into his hair, wishing she could tell him with her touch what was thudding in her heart. That he was not amused by her *faux pas* offered her some solace.

"He is a prince," she whispered, "and I treated him like . . . like—"

"A person?"

"What can I do, Alexei, if I meet him again?"

"Apologize if you wish. No, no," he ordered as she drew her fingers away. He clasped them and brought them back to stroke his cheek. His arm around her shoulders contracted to turn her to face him. His hand curved along her cheek, and he huskily whispered her name. Then, shaking his head, he released her.

Dismayed, Michelle asked, "Alexei, is something wrong?"

"Nothing, *Liebchen.*"

She grasped his arm when she heard the pain in his voice. "Tell me, Alexei. Tell me, please. If you don't want to kiss me—"

"Don't want to kiss you?" He laughed mirthlessly. "I would like to do a hell of a lot more than kiss you!"

"Then why—"

Again he interrupted her. "Don't whimper like a child, Michelle. Practice your seductive wiles on your Prince Charming. We should recall that you and I have a business relationship. Nothing else."

"Because you care more about your work?"

He looked out the window. "That, *Liebchen,* is not a choice I can make. If you want a reason to remember Vienna, seduce Prince Charming."

"I would never do anything like that!" Fire seared her face.

"Mayhap you should."

"Alexei!"

"There is no reason to keep prattling about it, is there? I worked hard tonight. I did not have a German autocrat playing court on me."

"Mayhap if you are as short-tempered with everyone else as you are with me, no one would want to speak with you."

He gave her the superior smile she despised. "Trust me, *Liebchen*. I had plenty who were willing to speak with me."

Trust Alexei? She would rather trust a hungry bear. Michelle clenched her hands in her lap. Vowing this would be the last time she would let him twist her heart, she stared out at the storm.

Tonight had taught her one thing: she did not need Alexei. Although she would continue to work for him as she had agreed, she would find her own friends. She need not be dependent on a boorish Russian.

That was what she should do. So why was it impossible to imagine doing the sensible thing and putting him out of her life? Mayhap because Alexei could be the kindest, most tender man she had ever met. If only she could find a way to reach that Alexei, she might salvage her heart.

That, she feared, was impossible.

Chapter Nine

Alexei knew he was late. Michelle was going to be vexed at him. That would be no different from any day for the past week. Since she had attended that party at Prince Bartholomew's house, nothing had gone right.

Not that he could blame her, for he had barely said two words to her except to give orders. Reminding her and *himself* that they were here to do a job rather than to engage in a flirtation had been the smartest thing he had ever done. And the most frustrating. When he saw her eyes dim each time he spoke coolly to her, he wanted to tell her why he was insisting on nothing but business between them. He could not, for many reasons—not the least one being that he was not sure why himself.

He sighed. Vienna was one of the most romantic cities in Europe, and he was living with a beautiful, sensual woman who responded with such fervor to his kisses. Yet he was pushing her out of his arms. Calling himself insane in every language he knew, he quickened his pace. It did not help. He could not escape his own thoughts.

Mayhap if this meeting had gone as he had hoped, he

might have a more positive outlook on his other problems. He had wasted the whole afternoon. If LaTulippe was in Vienna, the man had covered his tracks far too well. None of Alexei's allies—and none of LaTulippe's enemies—had offered even a hint to where the man might be.

His steps slowed as he came around the corner by Frau Lepper's shop to see Michelle in animated conversation with an old man who leaned on a cane. His incredible shock of hair sprang in every direction, and a rusty black coat drooped from his reed-thin shoulders.

Who was she talking to now? For the daughter of a woman who had kept her counsel from everyone, Michelle had an irritating habit of talking to everybody. She looked past the old man, and Alexei could see her flinch. What mischief was she getting into now?

At least you don't have to worry about this old man seducing her. Alexei clenched his teeth at the thought he wanted to ignore. Let her flirt with Prince Bartholomew! It would be an easy solution to a problem he did not have time to deal with just now.

The old man must have noticed Michelle's reaction, for he looked over his shoulder as Alexei neared. A wisp of a smile appeared beneath the old man's bushy mustache. "Good day, Fraulein." With a tip of his hat, he strolled down the street like a spry troll.

"Who was that?" Alexei asked.

Michelle spun to face him. "Are you worried that I might leave you for a man who does not make me wait for hours?"

"It has not been hours," he corrected, not wanting her to guess how closely she had assessed his thoughts. As the clock on the corner began to chime, he grinned. "An hour. No more." Reaching past her, he opened the carriage door. "Shall we argue in private, *Liebchen?*"

"Yes!"

The arch of a single eyebrow was his only response. When he put his hand under her elbow to assist her into the carriage, she started to shake it off. His fingers tightened. She scowled at him, but he took care that his cheerful expression did not change as he handed her in.

"Aren't you coming?" Michelle called as Alexei turned to Rusak. She did not understand how he and Rusak communicated, but she wanted to speak to Alexei before Rusak revealed what she had been talking to Herr Professor Waldstein about.

"Don't be a shrew." He swung into the carriage and sat, propping one leg across the opposite knee.

"As you wish, Alexei."

"Why are you being so cooperative?"

She smiled, unable to remain irritated at him when she had this news to share. "Alexei, the most wonderful thing just happened."

"That you agreed not to snarl at me in public? Not quite what I would deem wonderful, but—"

"Hush!" When his eyes widened, she said, "That man I was talking to can help Rusak."

"Help him do what?"

"Help him talk!"

"*Liebchen*, are you feverish?" Putting his hand to her forehead, he laughed as she batted it away. "You must learn not to listen to charlatans on the streets. Did that old man claim that he could sew a new tongue into Rusak's mouth?"

"Be serious! Alexei, Herr Professor Waldstein is not a doctor. He is a teacher at a very special school. I learned about such schools while at St. Bernard's."

The carriage stopped, but she put her hand on his sleeve to keep him from opening the door.

"*Liebchen*, we are already too late for the reception we were to attend this afternoon," he said. "Now we must get ready for this evening's gathering. Can't this wait?"

"No, because I made an appointment with Herr Professor Waldstein for tomorrow afternoon for Rusak to begin to learn this manual language."

"You did what?"

Michelle pulled the teacher's card from her bag and handed it to Alexei. He stared at it, then gave it back to her. He started to speak, but clamped his lips shut when Rusak opened the carriage door, a quizzical look on his face.

Rusak flashed Michelle a frown as they climbed the stairs to their apartment. As they entered, he motioned toward the back and made it clear he was going to his room.

Alexei nodded and waited until he heard Rusak's door close before he said, "A manual language? That sounds like quackery."

"Look at you. You use your hands to express yourself. We all do." She laughed when she used gestures to emphasize her words. "See? Frau Herbart spoke of us learning this way to speak when a deaf child was registered at St. Bernard's. The worsening of the war halted the child's arrival, so we never did learn. But it works, Alexei."

"Are you mad?" he asked as he sat and pulled off his boots. "Rusak is not a schoolboy."

"I agree." She refused to let his gaze daunt her. Sitting next to him, she boldly took his hands. "Alexei, he is your friend! Why would you deny him his best chance for a normal life?"

He rose, crossing the room to look at the hearth, where a fire crackled. "Normal life? How can he have a normal life?"

"What will become of him if something happens to you? Who will hire a man most people would call a freak?"

"Michelle, lower your voice. It will carry into Rusak's room."

"Do you think he does not hear the insults people speak?" She stood. "Please look at me."

Slowly he faced her, but said nothing. She saw his pain and guilt. But why? Alexei was Russian. He had not caused Rusak's injury . . . had he?

"Alexei," she said softly, "give him the chance to try this.

If he fails, you can tell me you were right. If he succeeds, you will have gained a better assistant."

For a long moment, he stared at her. Powerful emotions flared in his eyes. Wishing she could read them, she waited, unsure what else to say to persuade him. Although she had no idea what the manual language consisted of, if a child of six could learn it, Rusak could as well.

"What do you want me to say, Michelle?" Alexei asked. "You have already made up your mind that Rusak should do this. Do you want my blessing on your little project?"

"He will not listen to me."

"That is true." He drew out his pipe and tapped it against the fireplace stones. When ashes fell onto the hearth, he kicked them into the fire. "So you want me to try to convince him?"

She shook her head. "How could you possibly convince him to do something you believe is impossible? Just ask him to give this a chance."

"No, you ask him. I want nothing to do with this idiocy."

"Alexei!"

He strode to the arch and called, "Rusak, come out here!" He smiled. "I never guessed you were aiming for sainthood."

"I am not!" Her chin rose in defiance, but she faltered when Rusak came into the room.

Alexei said, "Michelle has something to tell you."

Rusak shook his head and turned to go back to his room.

"Listen to her!" Alexei ordered, amazing her because she could not mistake the tension in his tone. In spite of his words, he must be intrigued with what might be possible for Rusak.

Michelle met Rusak's vicious glare. "Rusak, that old man who spoke to me is a teacher. A very special kind of teacher. He would like to have you as a student."

He scowled, but she refused to let him intimidate her. Clasping her hands in front of her, she said, "Herr Professor Waldstein teaches deaf students." Rage blistered his face into a deep shade of red, but she continued, "I know you are not deaf, but, like them, you cannot speak." Capturing one of his rough hands, she held it between hers. "You use your hands to speak with already. So do I. So does Alexei. Why not learn to do it better?"

When he pointed at her, she shook her head. "No, I do not know this manual language, but Herr Professor Waldstein is willing to take you as a student. You must be willing to learn. Of course, Alexei and I must learn it also. Are you interested?"

Michelle was shocked when he put his other hand over hers and nodded eagerly. She smiled when he did. Looking past him to Alexei, she said, "Now we are in agreement, so we shall go to Rusak's first lesson tomorrow at two."

"You have it all arranged, don't you?"

"Alexei!" She had thought he would be as pleased as she was with Rusak's interest.

His voice remained sharp. "Rusak, you need to get the carriage ready for us to leave as soon as Michelle changes." When Rusak left with an unusual grin on his face, Alexei sighed. "You want to know why I am against this, don't you?"

"I don't care why you want to deny him this." She folded her arms. "You thought he would refuse, didn't you? I am tired of your selfishness, Alexei Vatutin. If you could think of someone other than yourself and your work just once—"

Grasping her by the shoulders, he pulled her up against him. She struggled to breathe, thrilled to be in his arms. Her delight vanished when he snapped, "You do not understand. The French attack on Rusak's family was just the most recent horror he has suffered. How old do you think he is? Forty? Fifty?"

"Probably closer to forty."

"He is barely thirty, Michelle." When her eyes widened in astonishment, he said in a growl, "Life has aged him too quickly. You are right. He is my friend. My best friend, for we fought side by side. I shall not see him hurt again."

She put her hands up to frame his face. "I promise you, Alexei, I shall do all I can to see that he succeeds. You saw his face. He wants this opportunity. He wants it as desperately as I"—she hesitated before she blurted out her longing for Alexei's kisses—"as desperately as I want him to succeed."

Again he stared at her for a long minute. She tried to guess what he was thinking. When his arm came up to slip around her waist, her heart thundered. She took a half step closer so that her legs were against his. With a groan, he caught her face in his other hand and tilted her mouth toward his.

She gasped as he pushed her back, releasing her. He motioned toward the hallway and said, "You need to hurry, or we shall miss this reception altogether."

"Would it be so horrible if we did not go?" she whispered, reaching out to touch the buttons in the center of his waistcoat.

"You need to go."

"Me?"

He walked back to pick up his boots, so again his face was hidden from her. "Dress in your prettiest gown, *Liebchen*. I understand Prince Charming is going to be at the party we have to attend tonight."

"Prince Bartholomew?" All her delight at Alexei's touch disappeared as anxiety twisted her stomach.

He looked at her, a stiff grin on his face. "You knew you would see him eventually. You might as well see him at this reception and put it behind you." He chuckled, but the sound was as false as his smile. "Mayhap you will find he truly is your Prince Charming."

Michelle lowered her eyes from his. She did not want to talk about Prince Bartholomew when she wanted to tell Alexei how she longed for him to tug her back to him and kiss her until her knees were weak. All she said was, "Thank you, Alexei, for persuading Rusak to listen."

His tight smile eased as he nodded. "You are welcome. *Liebchen?*"

"Yes?" She paused in the doorway. Would he speak now of what was in her heart? *Du lieber Gott,* when had Alexei inveigled his way into her heart? She must be out of her mind.

"I hope you prove me wrong about this teacher and Rusak."

"We shall." She made the words a vow. "We shall."

"Nervous?" asked Alexei as he handed his hat to a servant.

Michelle smiled wryly. "What an absurd question! The last time I called here, I insulted the prince by not recognizing him."

"True." Alexei gave her a lopsided grin.

"I shall be glad when this evening is over. Mayhap I can avoid him."

"Tonight is formal, *Liebchen,* so you shall meet Prince Charming in the reception line."

Her cheeks lost all color. Although she had known she must face this embarrassment, she had not expected it would be so public. She straightened her shoulders and let Alexei draw her hand into his arm. As they walked through the door to the grand parlor, she sensed the eyes of the many guests. They all were aimed at her. Heads bent toward each other as she passed.

Self-consciously, she looked down at her gown, hoping to find something amiss. Then she could blame the stares on that. Her lacy glove smoothed her skirt, which was decorated with a trellis of white flowers. The narrow bodice clinging to her breasts was not too deep, for ruffles edged it. She was dressed perfectly, so she could not blame their stares on anything save her own thoughtless actions last time.

Alexei's hand covered her quivering one. Looking up, she met his surprisingly sympathetic smile. She had thought he would be crowing about her mistake. Had she misread him again? She had been so certain he would kiss her at the apartment, but she had been wrong about that, too.

"Shall we?" he asked with the slightest motion of his head toward where a footman in fancy blue-and-gold livery stood to their right.

She nodded. Fearful of speaking, she hoped this would be over quickly so she could fade into the background once more. How had a friendly conversation escalated into this?

"Count Alexei Vatutin, Fraulein Michelle D'Orage," announced the footman.

Michelle waited for Alexei to step ahead of her, as he should as her employer. She sensed rather than heard the sharp intake of breath as she faced Prince Bartholomew. Hearing Alexei greet him politely, she wished words would form in her head.

"Your Highness," she said as she dropped into the deep curtsy she had learned during etiquette classes at St. Bernard's.

With a jovial laugh, Prince Bartholomew took her hand and drew her to her feet. "Now, Michelle, you were not at all like this last time we met."

"I must apologize, Your Highness. I did not know—"

"I know you did not know to whom you were speaking, and I liked it that way. You were pleasant because you liked Bartholomew, not because you felt obligated to be kind to the heir of Coxe-Saxony-Colburg."

Heir? She looked at Alexei, but he appeared not to notice as he talked with the dowager. She knew he had seen it because he missed little. Why had he failed to mention something as important as the fact that Prince Bartholomew would be the next ruler of his small state? Alexei must have a reason, but she could not guess what it might be.

When she did not answer, Prince Bartholomew asked, "Will you grant me the boon of still calling me Bartholomew while I call you Michelle?"

"If you wish, Your— Bartholomew," she corrected herself when his smile dimmed.

"Not if I wish it alone, for you must find this comfortable as well."

Although she was aware that every word she said was being listened to by Alexei and all the others who were unabashedly eavesdropping, she said, "To be honest, I find everything uncomfortable about this. You are the first prince beyond those in a storybook that I have ever met."

"You are so amusing." He captured her gloved hands and pressed them to his lips. "May we talk later?"

"Of course." When she saw him glance at Alexei, she faltered. She could not forget that she had promised Alexei to portray his mistress. "I believe we can find some time to speak this evening."

"I believe you are right."

Alexei's fingers cupped her elbow. She saw fury flicker through Bartholomew's eyes when he looked at Alexei. She bit her lip to keep from laughing. How much more absurd could this get?

Michelle walked past the people who stared at her openly. She had never felt so much like a leper. When a glass was pressed into her fingers, she raised it to her lips. Instead of wine, brandy cut through her.

"You did fine," Alexei said quietly.

"I wish I was back at St. Bernard's."

"And miss all this fun?" He smiled. "And me?"

"Don't jest with me now, Alexei, please."

He put his fingers over hers on her glass. When she looked at him over it, his face was serious. "*Liebchen,* I wanted only to make you realize that you have done nothing wrong by being kind. Amidst this world where one word can have a dozen meanings, you are a welcome change. No wonder Prince Charming delighted in how you treated him."

"But he is a *prince!*"

"True. He bears the title of prince and is the heir of Coxe-Saxony-Colburg, but he is only a man. Like every other man you know."

"No, not like every other man I know."

"What makes him so different?"

At Alexei's abruptly sharp tone, Michelle drew her hand from beneath his. How could she explain her unthinking words without revealing the truth hidden in her heart? She had not intended her words as a compliment to Bartholomew. Rather, her words spoke of how unlike other men Alexei was, but he would not want to hear how her heart ached for the moment when his arms were around her as his lips found hers.

"I have never met a man who has only one name," she returned with contrived sauciness.

When he regarded her with disgust, she lowered her eyes. He made her feel like a fool. And why not? She was. Any woman who lost her heart to Alexei Vatutin was a fool. He was a man of the wind, going where chance took him.

When Alexei excused himself to speak to an acquaintance, she sighed. She was making a muddle of the whole of this.

"So sad?"

She met Bartholomew's smile. His eyes were innocuous compared to Alexei's. She could not imagine him being involved with the subterfuge Alexei loved. If she had a hint of wit about her, she would forget Alexei, who wanted only to use her to further his ends, and welcome Bartholomew's friendship.

"I am not sad." Her smile became sincere as she added, "Not any longer."

"Or frightened?"

"Frightened? Of what?"

"Of *whom.*"

Michelle's eyes widened when Bartholomew glanced in Alexei's direction and back. Was she frightened of Alexei? Of course not . . . save for his effect on her hapless heart. She could not tell Bartholomew that.

"Only a leather-head would be unafraid among the vagaries of power here in Vienna," she replied.

"You are as intelligent as you are lovely, Michelle." Bartholomew took her hand between his. Again she was aware of the eyes following every motion they made, but she could ignore them all, except for the green fire from Alexei's gaze.

As Bartholomew lured her into conversation, Michelle relaxed. Nothing could make her forget her yearning for Alexei, but Bartholomew's gentleness might help.

Her smile faltered when Bartholomew asked, "Would it be possible to call on you to ask you to join me for a soirée tomorrow evening, Michelle?"

"Call on *me?*"

He smiled. "Don't act awed of me. Please. Last time we met, I was simply your friend Bartholomew. Can't it be the same this time?"

"I am trying."

"So may I call on you?"

"I . . ." She glanced toward where Alexei was talking to several people she did not know. His gaze met hers without emotion. She could not imagine what he would think of Bartholomew's request.

"Ah, your *friend* Count Vatutin," mumbled Bartholomew. "Therein lies the problem."

Her attempt to smile was a dismal failure. "Mayhap under the circumstances—"

"Curse the circumstances!" When she gasped, Bartholomew added in a more tranquil tone, "If your employer does not mind, would you accompany me tomorrow evening? Just a gathering of a few friends. I think they would be as charmed by you as I am."

"Bartholomew, that is impossible. Alexei depends on me to translate for him, and he may have plans for tomorrow evening."

"That is not what I asked. Would you go?"

"The point is moot."

"Is it?" Raising his voice, he called, "Count Vatutin, would you join us, please?"

Michelle wished she could disappear as Bartholomew's question drew everyone's attention once more. How had she gotten mixed up in this bumble-bath? And, more important, how would she extricate herself without insulting Bartholomew?

"Yes, Your Highness?" Alexei asked without looking at her.

"I would that the three of us speak together privately," announced Bartholomew with the pomposity he never used when speaking to her. His command carried throughout the large room.

Michelle stared in disbelief when the servants escorted the other guests out. Bartholomew wielded his power with the ease of one accustomed to it from birth. Within minutes, they were alone.

"Count Vatutin," Bartholomew said as soon as the doors were pulled closed by a silent servant, "I have asked Fraulein D'Orage to accompany me to a small gathering tomorrow evening."

"Do you want to go, *Liebchen*?" Alexei asked.

She saw Bartholomew's lips narrow when Alexei spoke the endearment. Dampening her own lips, she asked, "Do you want me to go?"

His smile was as cold as the snow-laden wind. "You are free, *Liebchen*. A woman held against her will becomes unappealing. If you wish to go with Prince Bartholomew to this *tête-à-tête*, I see no reason why I should gainsay you." He laced his fingers through hers and drew her closer.

She knew she should say something, but all words vanished when she gazed up into his eyes. *Tell him that you want to keep me close.* Could she will him to speak the words that clamored in her heart? *Tell him that you are just jesting, that I mean more to you than just an employee.*

"After all," Alexei said, "Prince Bartholomew wishes only your company among his other guests. What we share needs no one else."

A heated blush fanned across her face as his gaze held her imprisoned in its emerald fire. She hated this farce. In an anguished whisper, she pleaded, "Don't, Alexei."

As if he had not heard her, he said, "As I said, Your Highness, she is free to do as she wishes during the evenings when I do not need her to interpret for me. You understand, of course, that *all* her nights are mine."

"I understand perfectly, Count Vatutin," Bartholomew replied in a tone as taut as his lips. "Now that we understand each other, tell me what you Russians think of this new plan proposed by Talleyrand and the French delegation."

Michelle listened in disbelief. They understood each other? Mayhap, but she did not understand either of them, and she suspected she never would as long as she was a pawn between them. Neither Alexei nor Bartholomew would accept the other as a part of her life for long. She did not want to think about what would happen then.

Chapter Ten

Michelle knocked on Alexei's door—the one from the hallway, for she pretended there was no door connecting their rooms. Even so, she had no privacy in her rooms. She always changed behind a dressing screen and glanced over her shoulder to make sure Alexei had not entered her room.

When she received no answer, she opened the door. She thought Alexei would be here, because he had told her to let him know when she and Rusak left for the appointment with Herr Professor Waldstein.

"Alexei?" she called.

He did not answer, but she saw him bent over his desk, scribbling fiercely. She entered the room, staying close to the door. In spite of herself, she stared at the huge bed. Why had her dreams for the past two nights been of being there with him?

She was crazy! She was certain of that. For the past two evenings, Bartholomew had escorted her about Vienna. They had laughed together, and he had delighted in sharing gossip with her about those they met. Yet, in her dreams, she was always with Alexei, who was making it clear during their waking hours that he been sincere when he told her their relationship should be only business.

He stood and faced her, the brilliant blue stripes of his waistcoat glowing in the sunlight. "What are you doing here?"

She dragged her gaze up from his waistcoat to the open collar of his shirt, which displayed taut skin across his muscular chest and then up to his face. A rage unlike any she had ever seen tightened on his mouth. She took a step backward. "You asked—"

"Why didn't you knock?"

"I did!" She squared her shoulders and gave him a scowl as icy as his own. She was grateful for this anger, which kept her from staring at his honed muscles. "A courtesy you never offer me, because you walk into my room whenever you wish."

He swept the pages he had been writing on into a drawer. "Never come in here while I am working, Michelle. Never!" He put his face close to hers. "Do you understand?"

"I understand. You can disturb me as you wish, but I must not speak to you without your permission."

His hand under her chin tilted her head back to meet his gaze. Sorrow edged his voice. "How can I keep you safe if you sneak in and see things you should not see?"

"Things? What things?"

"Don't ask questions I cannot answer, *Liebchen.*" He caressed her cheek. "You must trust me on this."

"Trust is not something you inspire."

He smiled. "Enjoy your time in Vienna and your flirtation with Prince Charming. Do the work I need you to do, but keep your life separate from mine." With a sigh, he released her and sat again at the desk.

Michelle blinked back tears. Never had she seen anyone so alone. She took a step toward him, wanting to put her arms around him and offer him comfort . . . and more.

His head snapped up, his practiced smile once more in place. "What did you want before I went off in a pelter?"

"To tell you that Rusak and I are leaving for Herr Professor Waldstein's school now."

"Do not forget you must be back to meet Prince Charming later."

"I would not forget something like that."

His eyes dimmed for a single heartbeat. With regret? she wanted to ask, but he gave her no chance, telling her to enjoy her afternoon.

Michelle recognized his dismissal. She walked out, closing the door behind her. As it shut, she saw him open the drawer and pull out the sheets, his frown returning. Whatever he was writing did not please him.

She wondered if anything—or anyone—could.

The school was in a crowded part of the old city. As Michelle watched the lovely buildings pass by, she sighed. She hoped the day would take a turn for the better.

The carriage slowed in front of an unadorned stone building. She must not show her distress. Rusak was already unnerved enough. That a man who had faced his enemies boldly was afraid of going to school did not surprise her. It was a world unlike any he had ever known. By the time Rusak opened the carriage door, she had pasted a fake smile on her lips.

"Ready?" she asked lightly.

He nodded.

She said nothing as he handed her out of the carriage almost as gracefully as Alexei. She was glad for his help as they walked up the icy steps to the house's door.

Rusak hesitated, and Michelle lifted the heavy brass knocker twice. She watched Rusak, who kept looking back at the carriage as if he wanted to flee.

A dour-faced woman opened the door. She nodded when Michelle greeted her.

"Yes," the woman said. "Herr Professor Waldstein is expecting you. This way."

She led them toward the back of the house. As they reached the end of the dark corridor, a door opened to spray the passage with sunshine. A little girl emerged, regarded them with wide eyes, and then scurried toward the front door.

"*Grüss Gott,*" called Herr Professor Waldstein. "Exactly on time. It is a pleasure to see you again, Fraulein D'Orage. Come in and bring your friend with you."

As she drew off her cloak, Michelle stared about her. This room resembled her own classroom with its books and papers as well as tables for the students. Scents of ink teased her. The room was drenched in sunlight from the large window overlooking the street. Until now, she had not realized how much she missed teaching. The laughter of her students, their bright eyes when they understood, their ruffled brows when they did not.

Smiling, she turned to Rusak, who remained by the door. "Herr Professor Waldstein, I would like to introduce Feodor Rusak. Due to an unfortunate incident, he is unable to speak."

"But you can hear?" Herr Professor Waldstein affixed him with an uncompromising stare.

Rusak nodded.

"Then join us." The old man appraised him. "So you once could speak?"

Again he nodded.

"Good. Then you shall be able to learn far more quickly than those who have no idea of language. You, Herr Rusak, possess that knowledge. All we must do is give you the method to convey words again." Without taking a breath, he ordered, "Sit. At this table. You, also, Fraulein D'Orage."

Michelle smiled. Herr Professor Waldstein obviously expected instant obedience.

Sitting across from Rusak, the old man continued, "I shall endeavor to teach you a new way to communicate.

You must endeavor to learn. It is no more difficult than that. Now watch.''

Michelle watched intently as Herr Professor Waldstein made various signs with his hands. He explained too rapidly for her to understand as his fingers flew. Some she could figure out, but others were as confusing as if the professor spoke Russian.

"Slower, please, Herr Professor," she begged. Rusak flashed her a grin, and she knew he was having the same problem. "I cannot remember all of this."

Herr Professor Waldstein smiled and pointed at Rusak. "You will listen and watch very closely. I see intelligence on your face. Prove that to me."

Stretching across the table, Herr Professor Waldstein shaped Rusak's hand into the sign for *hungry* as he said, "This may be the most important sign you can make, for it serves a basic need."

Michelle watched as he curved his hand into the shape of the letter *C* and drew it from his throat toward his stomach. She smiled. That was easily understandable as the path food followed.

Rusak struggled to copy the sign.

"You, too, Fraulein D'Orage," Herr Professor Waldstein ordered.

She tried, but her fingers refused to obey.

"Relax, Fraulein D'Orage," he said with a chuckle. "No one expects you to master this in a single day. It will come slowly. You are babes learning to babble at your mother's knee. You will learn. Your friend will learn."

When Rusak gave the guttural sound that served as his laugh, Michelle smiled. The competition between them to learn would be friendly. It astonished her how much she looked forward to it.

Michelle's life became a blur as she tried to fulfill her obligations to three men. Two afternoons each week, she went with Rusak to class. As Herr Professor Waldstein had predicted, their knowledge expanded rapidly. Her evenings were taken by parties she attended with either Alexei or Bartholomew.

Most often, her evenings were with Bartholomew. She had heard enough whispers to know that he was escorting no other woman around Vienna. The only mention she heard of Alexei was in a laughing aside about the Russian count who was going to lose his mistress to Prince Bartholomew. She wondered if having her at the center of attention so no one would take note of him was what Alexei wanted. She never could be certain with him.

In addition to her busy afternoons and evenings, she spent her mornings dealing with the needs of their odd household. She needed to buy food and cook for the few meals they took in the apartment. As the days flowed into each other, she grew accustomed to being exhausted. She had never guessed she would become tired of adventure.

Today Alexei and Rusak had gone with her to the market. Alexei had spent the whole time talking with a pair of men who were determined not to let her see their faces. She had not asked Alexei about them because she knew she would get no answer.

Returning to the apartment, Michelle reached for the door key in her reticule. She heard Alexei grumbling behind her and laughed. He had insisted on carrying all the packages instead of letting Rusak bring in some after stabling the carriage.

"Hurry!" he ordered. "These are going to slip any minute!"

"I am hurrying!" She pulled out the heavy iron key. She put it in the lock, but the door swung open before she could turn it. "What . . . ?"

"What is it?"

She ignored his question as she pushed the door open farther. Alexei had locked the door when they left, so how had it come ajar? Something crunched under her feet. A shard of glass! She stared about herself in disbelief.

Every piece of furniture was upended. The settee and the chairs had been slashed. All stuffing beneath the cushions had been ripped away. Pictures hung awry on the wall. The few figurines that had been on the mantel lay in ruins on the floor. She saw a book on the hearth, its cover scorched beyond repair. The lamps were broken, leaving the carpet covered with oil-stained papers.

Hearing a curse behind her, she gasped as the packages were shoved into her arms. Alexei rushed past her and through the arch. She slowly lowered the boxes to the floor as she listened to his heavy footsteps resonating along the wooden corridor.

Michelle turned to close the door, but halted when she saw Rusak coming along the hall. He must have come up the back stairs. He looked into the room, and his mouth twisted with frustration. She knew he longed to ask the questions displayed in his blue eyes. The phrases they had learned were for everyday events. They did not have signs for this.

Shutting the door, she leaned back against it. Her hand closed over her mother's ring. *This* was *Maman's* life, a life of secrets and enemies.

Alexei erupted from the shadows near the arch and spat, "Damn fool!"

"Whoever did this—"

"I am not talking about our unexpected guests," he retorted with a vicious smile. "I am talking about me. I should have . . ." He sighed. "Why don't you hang up your coat, Michelle? Then you can help us clean up here."

She nodded. Tonight she was supposed to attend the theater with Bartholomew, but she would have to cancel that. She must devise a message for Rusak to deliver to Bartholomew. It would have to be a lie, for Alexei would want no word of this to filter past their door.

She took a steadying breath as she put her hand on her

room's doorknob. She pushed it open and stared. Nothing had been touched. When she heard a deep chuckle behind her, she looked over her shoulder to see Alexei.

"They did not search my room," she said.

His smile became an intense scowl. "What makes you think they were looking for something?"

"Alexei, I am not stupid! You did not come to Vienna to enjoy seeing Europe's leaders parade before you." Wrapping her arms around her, she wished his arms enveloped her. "You have told me that you and *Maman* were spies. Others must think that you have information here that your enemies would be eager to possess."

"You are right."

"I am?" She had not thought he would admit to any espionage.

"You are not stupid, but neither am I. I would not leave anything valuable lying about." He chuckled. "That was one of the very first lessons Sophie taught me."

"So they got nothing?"

"It would appear that way." He walked past her and opened her armoire. Taking her coat, he put it inside, where nothing had been moved. He patted the fabric on the door as he closed it. "You clearly have convinced everyone that you are nothing more than my mistress, Michelle." His face remained rigid. Despite his jesting words, he was furious.

Softly she asked, "Does that mean we can expect another visit?"

Taking her hand, he led her to the adjoining door. He pushed it aside, and it crashed against upset furniture. She moaned. The room had been devastated. She tried to step over papers and broken ceramic littering the floor, but it was impossible. The rug had vanished beneath the stuffing from the mattress and the chairs.

With another moan, she threw her arms around his shoulders. He pulled her close, burying his face in her hair. Fury coiled within him, but his lips were gentle as they found hers. She leaned into the kiss, wanting to be swept away by this pleasure. He deepened the kiss until she was panting against his mouth. When his hand slid up from her waist to curve along her bodice, she quivered. Sensations, fiery and fragile, flew along her. Her fingers clenched on his coat while his glided along her breast in a sinuous path before a single one slipped beneath the shoulder of her gown and began to lower it along her arm. His arm tightened around her waist as if he feared she would slip away. She wanted to be nowhere but here in his arms.

His mouth followed the lowering sleeve, then moved along her bodice, which was slipping down across her breasts. Boldly, his tongue sought beneath her dress, laving the curve of her breast with a succulent flame. When she whispered his name in a desperate tone, for she could no longer control the need escalating through her, he captured her mouth again and tugged her against him.

Ceramic cracked under Michelle's boot, and Alexei pulled away. She swayed as she held her arms out. Her empty arms. Blinking past the haze of delight, she whispered, "Alexei?"

He walked to his desk and snarled what must be a curse, although she could not understand the word. He looked back at her. "*Liebchen,* when the one who sent them discovers they have failed to find anything, he will send them back to try something different."

Michelle blinked again, then realized he was talking about whomever had ransacked the apartment. "Alexei, forget about that for now." She went to him and ran her fingers up his arm. "Alexei, I—"

"Do not fret," he said as he pushed past her, walking back to the door that connected their rooms. "I am their target, not you. They made that clear by not touching your room."

"Mayhap because they believe I do not use it."

Why was he keeping her so far away when, moments

ago, they had been so close? He was acting as if nothing had happened when she was in his arms.

His laugh was cold. "Now you are beginning to understand, *Liebchen,* why I suggested this charade for our stay in Vienna."

Charade? Was that all this was? No, she could not believe that the passion she had tasted on his lips was feigned. "You suggested it to protect me?"

"As Sophie would have wanted," he said quietly; then he grinned. "I told you that you have been doing an excellent job in pretending to be my almost devoted mistress. Your flirtation with Prince Charming suggests I would not trust you."

"So all of this is part of your plan?"

"I learned to use what comes my way."

"Another lesson from *Maman?*"

His eyes became green slits at her bitter question. "She was a master, *Liebchen.*"

"Then she died."

Crossing the room back to her, he untied her bonnet and lifted it away slowly, but her hair swirled around her face. "Yes," he whispered, "then she died."

"And I can never be her." She clasped her hands to keep from reaching up to the strong angle of his jaw and the lines from laughter at the corners of his eyes. His face was not as classically handsome as Bartholomew's, for life had left its indelible imprint.

He picked up a book and set it on the mantel as he said, "We need to get back and help Rusak in the other room. It will be a huge job."

"Alexei, I am glad you joined me for shopping today." She squeezed his arm, then walked to the door.

"Liebchen?"

She paused as he walked toward her. He looked into her eyes while he gently drew up her sleeve to settle it on her shoulder. When she caught his hand, he pulled it away as gently.

"We need to help Rusak," he said, edging around the broken furniture in the hallway.

Michelle folded her hands on her disheveled bodice. She could not have mistaken the disappointment in his jade eyes. She *had* seen it. But if he regretted not continuing, why had he halted? She wished she could ask him, but he would not answer that question either.

Rusak was stacking the ruined pieces in one corner. Some of it might be salvageable, but very little. When Alexei suggested they all sit, it took a few seconds to find three chairs steady enough to hold them.

"I am going to hire a housekeeper," he said without preamble. He raised his hand as Rusak growled. "I am going to need you to help me with other matters, so you cannot look after the apartment and Michelle."

She flinched. His words contradicted his assertion that she was in no danger. She had not believed him then, for anyone associated with Alexei Vatutin could be the focus of his enemies.

"Nothing important was taken," Alexei went on. He looked at her. "Of course, no one must know about our uninvited callers."

"Really, Alexei," she replied. How could he mistrust her now when she had trusted him to touch her with such yearning? If he had been searching for a way to hurt her, he could not have found a better way. "I think I know better than to babble about this with anyone."

"Even with Prince Charming?"

"You think Bartholomew ordered this?"

With a grin, he put his foot on a wobbly table. "No, I don't think this was Prince Charming's work."

"Then why are you so nasty about him? Just because he is a nice man—"

"Very nice."

Her brow rutted with bafflement. "You make being nice sound like a crime."

"It is when he is being nice to you for only one reason."

He winked bawdily at Rusak and frowned when Rusak did not smile. Dropping his foot back on the floor, he crossed his arms on his knees as he leaned forward to rivet her with his gaze. "Michelle, I don't wish to belittle your obvious charms, but I do not trust your Prince Charming. He wants something, and I suspect it is not as simple as having you as his mistress."

"Thank you for the compliment."

"Don't be petulant. Has he said anything to you about me?"

"I thought you don't suspect him of this."

"I don't, but has he asked you anything about what we are doing here?"

She laughed. "Mayhap you think you should be the topic of every conversation, Alexei, but you are not. Quite to the contrary, he avoids speaking of you. Once someone at a gathering mentioned that I was your mistress, and Bartholomew insisted that we leave."

Startled, he rested back in his chair. He glanced at Rusak, but Rusak grabbed Michelle's arm. He wiggled his fingers rapidly.

"Slow down," Michelle said, "I cannot understand what you are saying."

Alexei mad, he signed. *Alexei jealous.*

"No," she retorted, "you are wrong." She wished she had the signs to tell Rusak how Alexei had kissed her and then pushed her away. She closed her eyes. She could not tell that to anyone.

Rusak patted her arm, and she opened her eyes to see him signing, *Happy Alexei. You happy Alexei.*

Before she could try to figure out a way to ask if he meant he wanted her to try to make Alexei happy or that she did make Alexei happy, Alexei asked, "Will you translate, Michelle? Or do you prefer to leave me out of this conversation?"

Although, as Rusak smiled, she was tempted to say yes, she replied, "Rusak was saying you are very angry and should calm down.'' She refused to add that Rusak believed Alexei was jealous of Bartholomew. ''You would understand if you would attend some of the lessons with us.''

''Am I going to have both of you nagging me?'' He set himself on his feet. ''No matter. Tomorrow I shall hire a housekeeper.''

''I can do that, Alexei.''

''Nonsense. I would not want to interfere with the time you spend with everyone except the man who pays your wages, Michelle. Rusak, let's clean up the mess in my bedchamber while Michelle gets herself all pretty for Prince Charming. She does not want to be late when he calls.''

Sorrow ached through her as she watched the two men go toward the arch. No matter what she did, it was wrong in Alexei's opinion. Even when she did nothing, he found fault with her.

She sighed. Only a few days ago she had fretted about having to decide whether she wanted to spend her evenings with Alexei or with Bartholomew. It appeared that Alexei had made that decision for her.

Whether she liked it or not.

Chapter Eleven

The next day, when Michelle and Rusak returned from Herr Professor Waldstein's class, they were met at the apartment door by a slender woman whose age was wrinkled into her face beneath her white hair. Dressed in a loden green dirndl skirt of the style favored by Austrians, she smiled broadly. *"Grüss Gott.* You must be Fraulein D'Orage and Herr Rusak."

Taken aback to find a stranger in the apartment, Michelle asked, "And you are . . . ?"

"Frau Schlissel. Count Vatutin hired me to take care of your household. I trust I can work to your standards."

"I trust you can," she answered with a soft smile. She wondered what Frau Schlissel thought of the apartment, which still bore scars from the raid by Alexei's enemies. Although some of the furniture had been replaced, several chairs rocked whenever anyone sat on them. She took off her bonnet and hung it next to the door. "Welcome, Frau Schlissel."

"Herr Rusak—"

When he signed, *Just Rusak,* Michelle conveyed the message to the housekeeper, then added, "Rusak can hear you, but he uses these signs to speak."

"I understand, Fraulein. The count explained," Frau Schlissel replied. She looked away as color slapped her cheeks, and Michelle knew Alexei had told the new housekeeper as well that he and Michelle were lovers.

"Shall we go over the household tomorrow, Frau Schlissel? I shall answer any questions you have then. I must hurry if I am to be ready when Prince Bartholomew arrives."

"Prince?" The housekeeper gasped.

"He is a friend and has asked me to attend the theater with him tonight."

"Does Count Vatutin know of this?" the housekeeper blurted.

Michelle's face now was hot. How could she explain without revealing the truth? "Alexei knows of my friendship with Prince Bartholomew. If you will excuse me . . ."

As she hurried from the room, Michelle wondered how she had let herself get caught up in this madness. No wonder Frau Schlissel was baffled that a Russian count's mistress was spending the evening with a German prince. What bothered Michelle most was that she was no longer amazed by it. When had the bizarre become normal?

"Prince Charming is here, Cinderella," drawled Alexei as he pushed aside Michelle's door.

She glanced at his reflection in the glass. "Do you have to be so hateful all the time?"

"I am not hateful *all* the time."

She readjusted her feathered turban. Its pale lavender silk matched the trim on her white gown.

Leaning his shoulder against the door, he laughed. He folded his arms over his chest, but when she rose and tried to walk past him, he caught her hand. He pulled her closer. His fingers touched her cheek before brushing her lips. They parted with a soft breath as his fingertip eased past her chin to the slim column of her throat. Within her rippled a sweet, voracious longing.

"Is this hateful, *Liebchen*?"

"No, but certainly hypocritical." She draped her shawl with its long silk fringe over her shoulders to keep herself from softening against him. He was the most outrageous man she had ever met, taunting her and expecting her to delight at being in his arms at the same time.

"Hypocritical?" he murmured. "Do you think I truly dislike touching you?"

"Mayhap you do, mayhap you don't, but that was not what I meant. 'Tis not your caresses but your sincerity that I question. You ignore me until Bartholomew arrives; then you are eager to pay court on me." She pulled on her gloves. "Alexei, I wish you would halt these childish games. I have not done anything to suggest to Bartholomew that our presumed situation has changed."

"And he has done nothing to convince you to change it?"

"He has been a gentleman." Her smile grew stiff. "Does it bother you that there are some true gentlemen left in this world? Simply because you—"

"Michelle, you are making a prince wait." Again as she stepped past him, he put his fingers on her arm. Drawing her so tightly to him that she was aware of his strength through the thin material of her gown, he whispered, "Don't judge what you do not understand, *Liebchen*. Simply because I have not made love to you does not mean I have not thought of it." His fingers trailed up her arm. "Often."

"But that would interfere with your work, wouldn't it? Let me go, Alexei."

He started to speak, but clamped his lips shut as he slowly released her. The pain in his eyes unsettled her. If her friendship with Bartholomew bothered him, why didn't he say so?

Mayhap for the same reason you do not tell him how much you wish he were your lover.

Michelle flinched at that thought and pushed past Alexei. If he saw that thought on her face . . . *Du lieber Gott!* She was torn between eager anticipation and terror at the very idea.

She wished Alexei would not watch as she went to where an awestruck Frau Schlissel was basking under Bartholomew's charm.

Bartholomew smiled. "Ah, Michelle! How lovely you look tonight." He bowed over her fingers, and his fur-lined evening cape brushed her arm. She waited, but there was no sensation like the explosion when Alexei touched her. Pressing her hand fervently to his lips, he raised his head and looked past her. "Good evening, Vatutin."

"Your Highness."

Bartholomew held out his arm to Michelle, ignoring Alexei's terse answer. "Shall we go, my dear? We want to be there before the curtain rises."

Alexei went to the fireplace. Drawing out a blazing piece of kindling, he lit his pipe. He puffed several times before smiling. "What are you going to see?"

"An intellectual comedy," Bartholomew replied. "Nothing that you would be interested in, Vatutin."

"You might be surprised what interests me." He chuckled and winked at Michelle.

Bartholomew bristled. "I try not to concern myself with such low pursuits."

"Low? Is that your opinion of Michelle?"

Bartholomew's smile dimmed. "Forgive me, Michelle, if you thought I spoke of you."

"I know *you* did not." She gritted her teeth as Alexei's grin broadened. He was utterly impossible!

"Shall we go?" Bartholomew asked.

"Yes." Only by leaving could she put an end to this verbal jousting between the men.

In the carriage, Bartholomew's lighthearted voice suggested that no angry words had been spoken. She did not listen as she sat on the carriage seat and stared at nothing.

Throughout the evening, Michelle said little. There was no need, because Bartholomew seemed determined to fill every moment with bright conversation. It should have been a perfect evening, one filled with wonder at her first visit to the theater. She had not guessed how splendid the actors and the music would be. Even the audience glittered beneath the chandeliers hanging from the theater's painted ceiling. The theater had been followed by a soirée with many delegates from the German states. The chocolate cake that had been served had been delicious, but she had taken no more than a few bites.

Why are you allowing Alexei to ruin everything for you? She knew why, but she did not want to admit even to herself that she preferred his barbed jests to Bartholomew's cloying kindness.

The carriage, as it drove back to her street, was silent. Mayhap Bartholomew had run out of things to say. She knew anything she said would infuriate him, because Alexei's name would be part of it. She wished she could decipher why Alexei was as he was. One moment he was taunting her. The next he was tantalizing her in a totally different way. And then he ended the beguiling moment with an outrageous statement guaranteed to irritate her. None of this made sense. Yet it must. She was not seeing the one clue that tied all of this together.

Some spy you would be! You cannot even see what is right in front of you. Michelle flinched when a hand on her arm ripped her away from her thoughts.

Bartholomew's voice was apologetic. "Excuse me. I did not mean to startle you."

"I was lost in my thoughts."

"You looked so far away. Are you nostalgic for home?"

A smile flirted with her lips. "No, Bartholomew. Mayhap because I am enjoying Vienna so much." That was a lie . . . and it wasn't. She was enjoying the parts with Alexei, even though he was making every effort to persuade her to spend time with Bartholomew. Another question she could not answer was why. She hoped it was not because Alexei wanted her out of his hair.

Lifting her fingers to his lips, Bartholomew gazed down at her. "Could I be so brazen as to suggest that part of the reason you are happy here is my company?"

"How can I say anything but yes to that?" She was amazed how easily these nothing-sayings now fell from her lips.

"That was the idea, my dear."

He released her hands and swept his arm around her in one smooth motion, pulling her to him. She tried to ease away, but he tipped her face up so her mouth met his. Gently, as gently as he had held her hands, he kissed her. Brandy flavored his lips.

Raising his mouth from hers, he smiled. "You are so luscious, my dear. So luscious, yet there is an innocence about you that is incredibly intriguing."

She cursed silently as Bartholomew bent to kiss her again. Turning away, she reached for the carriage door.

He halted her by clasping her hand between his. "You need not go back in there." His smile was a soft shadow in the dimly lit carriage. "You could come home with me, Michelle."

"No."

"Do you love Vatutin?"

"No!" She did not want to guess whether that was the truth or a lie.

He stroked her cheek. "But you continue to live with him."

"Yes." She took refuge in simple answers, because she could not speak of things that she did not know about herself. "Good night, Bartholomew. Thank you for a lovely evening."

"Tomorrow evening?" he asked, refusing to release her hand.

"I don't know. Alexei—"

"Don't speak his name to me! I hold you in my arms

and sample the sweet delights of your lips, but you return to his bed. I should refuse to allow that."

"I am not one of your subjects," she said, putting her hands out to keep him away. "I can do as I wish."

"And you wish to sleep with Vatutin instead of me?"

She shook her head. "It is not that simple!"

"No?" Tilting her chin up, he demanded, "What hold does he have over you? I heard your raised voices tonight. He chides you constantly. Why do you stay with him when I would treat you so much better?"

Pulling away, Michelle flung open the door almost into the face of the footman who was waiting to assist her out. "What is between Alexei and me is none of your business. Good evening."

"I shall call tomorrow afternoon."

"I shall be busy tomorrow afternoon."

"But you will attend the musicale in honor of Prince Metternich with me as you promised?"

Michelle hesitated. She *had* promised to let him escort her there. "Yes, I will attend with you. However, you must understand that it would be better if I accepted no further invitations."

His lips tightened into a rigid smile, but he nodded. When she stood on the walkway, he motioned for the carriage to start. Only when she saw it disappear into a white mist did she realize it was snowing again.

The secrets and lies Michelle carried in her heart weighed on her as she climbed the stairs and turned the doorknob. A single candle burned, nearly gutted, in the parlor. Strange shadows danced on the opposite wall, but nothing was as outlandish as this evening's events. Two men had made it clear that they would be glad to take her to their beds, but neither spoke of love.

Maman, she thought, *how did you live this life? Why didn't you warn me?*

By the hearth, Alexei sat reading. She could not keep from admiring his rugged profile. The fire emphasized every angle along his face as he sat alone. How many friends had Alexei made during his life? Not acquaintances, for he seemed to have an unlimited amount of those. Real friends. Certainly Rusak. Her mother. Mayhap he would count Michelle D'Orage as one.

Or mayhap not, for she could not mistake the glitter of desire in his eyes as he looked up from his book and smiled. "Cinderella, it is long past midnight."

"I do not wish to argue." She bent and pulled off her slippers. "I am too tired."

He patted the cushion beside him. "Sit, and I will get you a cup of tea."

"I don't want tea."

"Churlish tonight, aren't you?" He stood and, taking her cape, tossed it on a chair. He sat her on the settee before bringing the teapot and a cup to where she sat. "Can it be that you and Prince Charming had a lovers' quarrel?"

She drew her feet up under her. "Bartholomew and I had a lovely evening."

"Did you go to Herr Herrschel's after the theater?"

She watched as he poured tea into the cup on the table beside where he had been sitting, then offered her the teapot. "Let mine steep a little longer," Michelle said. When he sat next to her with his feet on a low table, she asked, "How do you know where Bartholomew and I go every evening? Are you spying on me, too?"

He laughed as he stirred the sugar into his tea. "I have too much to do to be a watchdog for you and Prince Charming. It is common knowledge that the delegates from the German states like to spend their evenings together. So whom did you see there?"

Michelle had become accustomed to his interrogations. As she answered his questions, she observed his reaction. She knew when she said something that interested him, because his eyes narrowed.

"The theater was lovely," she said as she sipped her tea.

He stirred his cup again. "I trust you and Prince Charming enjoyed yourselves on the way home."

"How . . . ?" She flushed and lowered her eyes. That he could continue to read her mind with such ease disconcerted her.

Intensity invaded his voice as he murmured, "Just be careful, *Liebchen.*"

"Alexei, I am a grown woman and quite capable of taking care of myself."

A smile hinted beneath his mustache. "And Prince Charming is a man."

"Would you stop calling him that!"

"When you stop evading the truth."

"Which is?"

He set his cup back onto the table. "That you are becoming involved in something you cannot handle."

Coming to her feet, she set her cup beside his. "Good night."

His hand on her arm spun her to face him. Her retort died, choking her, as she stared at Alexei. His face was strained with rage.

"Michelle, you were raised in that convent—"

"St. Bernard's is not a convent!"

"It might as well be," he fired back. "Living with women, you have no idea how to deal with men."

She clamped her arms across her chest. "I assure you, Alexei, that I am quite capable of dealing with men. I have managed with you and Rusak, haven't I?"

"But we are not Prince Charming—"

"Stop calling him that!"

"Who thinks you are my mistress. He is trying to woo you away from me."

"Right now I would go with anyone who promised not to shout at me."

"See? You are acting like a simpleton!" He snorted with derision. "Do you think Prince Charming is going to be happy with just stealing a few kisses from you? He does not know you are the prim and respectable Fraulein D'Orage. He believes you are the mistress of a man he despises. How better to hurt me, in his opinion, than to take you from me?"

"Bartholomew is a gentleman." *And his kisses do not delight me as yours do.* For a moment, she feared she had added the last aloud.

His retort told her she had not. "But even gentlemen are not to be trusted when they are alone with a woman they want."

That his words mirrored her own concerns she would not admit. "I remind you, Alexei, that I am capable of handling my own—"

He laughed. "Your own affairs, *Liebchen?* Undoubtedly you could in Zurich. This is a whole different world."

"Why are you interfering now when you have said nothing before?"

He plucked at her left sleeve, and she saw the dark imprint there. Chocolate from Bartholomew's hand! "If you are curious, *Liebchen,* the mark goes all the way down your back to your waist."

"Oh."

"Just oh?" His fingers glided from her sleeve along her back, following the trail of chocolate. When her breath grew unsteady, he drew her to him. "I do not like that, when I do this, I am following the path left by another man. Nor do I like to imagine him doing this."

As his mouth slanted across hers, she sifted her fingers up through his hair. Her senses ignited with the rapture of his eager touch. She tasted neither the sugar nor the milk from his tea, for the overwhelming flavor on his lips was passion. His hands curved up her back as his tongue delved into her mouth.

She shivered with indescribable delight when her fingers slipped beneath his loose shirt and along his muscular back. Each brush of her skin against his made her want more. Stretching her fingers across his taut skin, she sought to touch as much of him as possible. His kiss deepened until she strained to breathe against it.

As he peppered her bare shoulder with kisses, he abruptly drew back and cursed. Her hands caught within his shirt. He reached and pulled them away from him, but folded them between his.

"Alexei?" she whispered as she had so often. He did not want her to be in Bartholomew's arms; yet he was denying her this pleasure in his.

"This is not right."

Michelle stared at him in disbelief. "It is wonderful."

A smile drifted across his lips, but disappeared into his sad eyes. Gently brushing her hair back from her face, he said, "You are right. It is wonderful and wrong."

"What is wrong about your holding me?" She grasped his arm when he started to turn away from her, as he had too many times before. "Alexei, be honest with me!"

"Honesty?" he said in a growl. "Do you want honesty? Let me start with that you are getting into trouble with Prince Charming."

"Alexei, I have no intention of letting Bartholomew hurt me. That could happen only if I fell in love with him. That cannot happen."

"No?"

"No," she answered with more vehemence than she had intended. Why was he asking her that when she had just melted in his arms? "Bartholomew is my friend. Nothing more."

"Does he feel the same?" When she hesitated, he continued, "Then you are heading for trouble, *Liebchen*. Prince Charming has powerful allies in Vienna. If you jilt him, you may find yourself in more trouble than you can imagine."

She clasped her hands over her ears, wishing he would pull her back into his arms again. She did not want to quarrel. She wanted to kiss him.

He drew her hands away. "What do I need to do to convince you?"

"The truth?"

"All right. I am trying to help you because of the debt I owe Sophie."

"Debt? What do you owe her?"

"My life."

"Your life?" she said in a squeak.

His hands encircled her face as he held her with the fire of his gaze. "She saved my life, Michelle, and I intend to repay her by saving yours."

Alexei watched Michelle's mouth open and close in amazement. It took every ounce of his willpower not to cover those soft lips with a savage kiss that would reveal how much he ached for her. Taking her hand, he sat her on the settee. He did not release her slender fingers as he sat beside her. While he could, he wanted to touch her.

"*Maman* saved your life? How?" she whispered.

He savored the soft huskiness of her voice, but now was not the time to enjoy it. Never would there be a time, he reminded himself. His obligation to Sophie could not be reciprocated by seducing her dazzling daughter.

" 'Twas nothing as dramatic as fighting off a pack of demons to save my soul." His attempt at a jest fell flat.

"I doubt if *Maman* would waste her time on that. If she had won your soul back from the devil, I have no doubts that you would bargain it away again."

"Most likely." He stared at the flames reflected in her eyes, then dragged his gaze away to look at the ones on the hearth. "Sophie watched over me like a mother." He grinned wryly. "Something you would understand better than anyone. When we worked together, she warned me away from potentially dangerous situations. I heeded her every time, but one."

"Who was she, Alexei?"

He shook his head. "Is it that obvious that the problem was a woman?"

"Only because you warned me about Bartholomew and getting too deeply involved."

Standing, he locked his fingers together behind his back. He could not meet Michelle's eyes while he told this shameful story that he had hidden from everyone else.

"Her name was Shanna. I was young. She was beautiful. The second I saw her, I was smitten. I could think of nothing but her, of possessing her, of giving her my heart and my soul." His voice hardened. "How was I to know that that was exactly what she wanted? Sophie told me to avoid her, but, dupe that I was, I could not believe that lovely, angelic Shanna wanted to lure secrets from me and betray me to my enemies. Nor did I imagine she had foes of her own. When Sophie tried to tell me to stay away that night, I refused to listen."

"What happened?" she whispered.

"It was perfect when I arrived. She had sent her servants away, so it was just the two of us. So eager was I to seduce her that I could barely eat." He sighed. "That saved me."

When Michelle slipped her hand into his, he squeezed it gently. He looked at her as she whispered, "There was something wrong with the food?"

"It was tainted with a poison so deadly that I nearly died even from what little I ate. If Sophie had not been concerned about my welfare as well as my idiotic infatuation that could have betrayed everything, I would have died as well. She found us unconscious. It was too late for Shanna, but, after months, I recovered." He released her hand. "It was the year Sophie missed coming to spend Christmas with you."

Her eyes widened. "That was because of you? I was so angry and so sad when *Maman* sent a message. It arrived on Christmas Eve and said only that I must stay at the school through the holidays." She lowered her eyes. "Until *Maman*'s death, it was the worst day of my life."

Kneeling in front of her, he put his hands on hers in her lap. "She was furious that I kept her from spending Christmas with you."

"It would have been our last Christmas together."

He winced at the unhealed pain in her voice. *"Liebchen,* I have thought of that so often." He stood and drew her to her feet. "Now do you understand why I fear for you with Prince Charming? I was as naïve then as you are now."

"But I do not love him as you loved her."

"Love?" He laughed tightly. "I did not love her. I wanted her. Just as Prince Charming wants you." He ran the back of his hand along her cheek. "How could anyone not want you, *Liebchen?"*

It was the wrong thing to ask, he realized when she took a step toward him, raising her hands to his shoulders. How much did she think a man could endure? He had thought she would understand now why he pushed her away when her tempting smile became too enticing for him to resist.

Knowing the reaction his words would get, he gave her the arrogant smile she hated. "Playing hard to get will make Prince Charming even more eager. You could become a princess if you play your cards right."

"Bartholomew asked me to leave you and come with him tonight."

"Did he?" Alexei picked up his cup and sipped. He almost gagged—not on the tea, but on what he must say. "Be careful. Stronger men than I have sold their souls and their countries for lust. Women have found themselves betrayed when the lust for power becomes more compelling than passion."

"You are insufferable!"

"Simply trying to repay your mother by teaching you what she taught me."

"You want me to believe that she taught you to be so coldhearted and cocksure? My mother was kind and loving, no matter what you might say. She may have taught you to be a spy, but she never taught you to care only for yourself and your work, no matter how much pain you brought into other people's lives." She scooped up her cloak and ran out of the room.

He sighed when he heard her door slam. No doubt she

was locking it and jamming the chair up under the knob on the door between their rooms now. Setting his cup down, he murmured, "You are right, *Liebchen*. I had to learn that all by myself."

Chapter Twelve

Herr Professor Waldstein nodded as he watched Rusak answer his question. "Very good," he said. As always, he used signs to match what he spoke, so Rusak would become more familiar with reading signs. "Both of you are doing better than I expected. Rusak, why don't you get your carriage and bring it around front? It is too cold for Frau-lein D'Orage to stand on the stoop and wait."

Good day, Herr Professor.

"Good day to you."

When Michelle rose and stretched her cramped hands, she reached for her coat, which she had folded over the back of the chair. She smiled as the white-haired man took it and held it up for her to slip her arms into.

"Fraulein D'Orage, may I ask you a question?" he asked as she closed the velvet frogs at her throat.

"Of course, Herr Professor."

"Your man Rusak is even quicker at grasping this than I had hoped. He is a man of rare intelligence. Would it be possible for you to afford more lessons for him?" He gave an embarrassed smile. "I would do this without cost,

Introducing Ballad,
A New Line of Historical Romances

*A*s a lover of historical romance, you'll adore Ballad Romances. Written by today's most popular romance authors, every book in the Ballad line is not only an individual story, but part of a two to six book series as well. You can look forward to 4 new titles each month – each taking place at a different time and place in history.

But don't take our word for how wonderful these stories are! Accept our introductory shipment of 4 Ballad Romance novels – a $22.00 value – ABSOLUTELY FREE – and see for yourself!

*O*nce you've experienced your first 4 Ballad Romances, we're sure you'll want to continue receiving these wonderful historical romance novels each month – without ever having to leave your home – using our convenient and inexpensive home subscription service. Here's what you get for joining:

- *4 BRAND NEW Ballad Romances delivered to your door each month*

- *25% off the cover price of $5.50 with your home subscription.*

- *A FREE monthly newsletter filled with author interviews, book previews, special offers, and more!*

- *No risk or obligation…you're free to cancel whenever you wish… no questions asked.*

Passion-
Adventure-
Excitement-
Romance-
Ballad!

*T*o start your membership, simply complete and return the card provided. You'll receive your Introductory Shipment of 4 FREE Ballad Romances. Then, each month, as long as your account is in good standing, you will receive the 4 newest Ballad Romances. Each shipment will be yours to examine for 10 days. If you decide to keep the books, you'll pay the preferred home subscriber's price of $16.50 – a savings of 25% off the cover price! (plus $1.50 shipping & handling) If you want us to stop sending books, just say the word…it's that simple.

Passion...
Adventure...
Excitement...
Romance...

ll..l..l..ll....dl.l.l..l.l..l.l....ll.l..l.l...l

BALLAD ROMANCES
Zebra Home Subscription Service, Inc.
P.O. Box 5214
Clifton NJ 07015-5214

for his zest for learning is a joy, but I cannot spare the hour I would spend with a paying student."

"The decision is not mine."

"Not yours? But Fraulein, aren't you paying for his lessons?"

"Count Vatutin pays for the lessons. He is Rusak's employer . . . and mine as well." When his bushy eyebrows lowered at her hesitation, she knew he understood what she could not bring herself to say to this man who was not part of the Polite World.

Her brow knitted. Once she had been like this, knowing the clear distinction between right and wrong. Somewhere in the midst of this masquerade that had changed. *No!* It had not. What had changed was caring about what other people thought. Or had that changed either? She cared so much about Herr Professor Waldstein's opinion of her, but it did not bother her that Bartholomew considered her an easy conquest because she was already another man's mistress.

To cover her apprehension at her own thoughts, she smiled and said, "Herr Professor, I shall speak with Count Vatutin. I am sure he will consider an acceleration of the lessons, especially as you have concerns about how much Rusak can learn when they return to Russia."

"Very good, Fraulein." He nodded his farewell.

Hurrying outside, Michelle was struck by the bite of the icy wind. Winter seemed earlier and harsher in Vienna than in Zurich, but it might be nothing more than the fact that she seldom had left the school buildings on the coldest days.

Rusak leapt down from the box to open the door for her. "I could have opened it on my own," she said as she stepped into the interior which was no warmer than the street. "There was no need for you to push aside your blankets."

I thank you, Michelle. He added more that she could not understand.

"Herr Professor Waldstein warned me that you are learning faster than me," she said with a laugh. "Slower."

Glad we come here. Glad we friends. You give me wings to sing again.

Tears threatened to fall. "I am glad, too. You have worked so hard."

Alexei? He learns also?

"Not yet. He is too busy, he says."

Sadness etched Rusak's face as he nodded in resignation. When he closed the door, she swore under her breath. Rusak was doing so well, but it would be for naught if, when he and Alexei returned to Russia, no one comprehended what he signed.

A sliver of pain sliced through her. Alexei would be returning to Russia. He had mentioned several times recently that he was curious about his next assignment. Although she had known this was only a temporary arrangement, as the days, then the weeks, passed, she had persuaded herself that it would continue. The thought of Alexei leaving forever cramped her middle as if she were sick.

"You are want-witted!" she said aloud. "He has told you more than once you are important to him only because you are *Maman*'s daughter." She hid her face in her gloved hands. Nothing, it seemed, that she could offer Alexei was enough to make him change his ways—not even love.

Alexei put down his wineglass and stared at the man on the other side of the table. "You were my last hope, Robert."

"A hopeless hope." The balding man chuckled as he reached for another piece of cheese. "LaTulippe has disappeared. Mayhap we can hope he was banished along with Napoleon to Elba."

Leaning back in his chair, Alexei looked past the man he would not even loosely call a friend. Robert had found himself elegant quarters in Vienna and a lovely woman to share them—the very life in reality that Alexei was living as a sham.

Did Michelle note how he avoided her? Since he had revealed his shame to her last week in front of the fireplace, he had tried to be in the apartment only when she was out or asleep. Mayhap he should move out. Sleeping was impossible when he thought of her only an unlocked door away.

"Did you hear what I said?" asked Robert.

Alexei rested his elbow on the chair's overstuffed arm. "No."

Robert laughed. "Honesty is refreshing from you, *mon ami.*"

"Then I shall honestly tell you that I do not like how LaTulippe has slipped away again."

"What could you do?" Robert shrugged and smiled. "*C'est la vie.*"

"*C'est la guerre.*"

"Ah, but the war is over."

Pushing himself to his feet, Alexei asked, "Do you really think so? As long as LaTulippe and his allies are not at the end of a hangman's noose, the war continues."

"Let him go. What trouble can he cause now that Napoleon is imprisoned far from here?"

Alexei started to reply, then halted himself. He had seen this attempt at self-delusion too many times already in Vienna. Those who should be watching over their shoulders for a backlash from Napoleon's allies wanted to pretend that the emperor was as docile as a house cat. But even that cat could extend its claws when backed into a corner.

Picking up his glass, he finished his wine. He set it down and said, "It has been an interesting call, Robert. I shall see you again before I leave Vienna."

"You are leaving? So soon?" Robert stood, frowning.

"If what I seek is not here, there is no reason for me to be here."

"And it would be uncomfortable to watch your mistress further cuckold you with that German prince."

Alexei laughed. "Do not fret about my mistress and me, *mon ami.*"

"You are a generous man to share her with that princeling."

"Michelle and I understand each other." He bade his host a good day and walked out before Robert could know how completely he was lying.

Bending his head into the wind and snow, Alexei strode toward the address where he had promised to call this afternoon. Mayhap, if luck was once more on his side, the call would last late into the evening, and he would not have to return to the apartment to watch Michelle leave on Prince Charming's arm.

If he did, he might do something stupid that would ruin all his work here. He could not risk that . . . not even for the taste of her soft lips.

You are a simpleton, he had told her during their heated quarrel in front of the fireplace, but he might have been wrong. He could not imagine anyone who was a greater fool than he was now.

As Bartholomew walked into the apartment to escort her to the gathering in honor of Prince Metternich, Michelle saw a flash of disappointment when he noted that Alexei was not there. He was clearly eager to confront Alexei. Had he listened to anything she had said? It was just as well that she would not be seeing Bartholomew again after tonight.

"I am ready," she said with little subtlety.

"Don't you have to leave a message for your protector?"

Her lips tightened. "Alexei trusts me to take care of myself."

Only when he had opened the door to the street did Bartholomew answer, "I cannot believe he trusts *me.*"

"He does not." She went down the steps that were covered with a dusting of snow except where his footprints announced his arrival.

"Then Vatutin is more of a buffoon than I guessed." He motioned toward the carriage.

"Do not underestimate Alexei."

His lips tightened again, but he said, "We shall be late, Michelle, if we linger."

Michelle thought of saying she had changed her mind about going with him, but she knew he would only argue that she had promised. And she had. She sighed as, sitting stiffly in the carriage, she rocked when it started.

"Michelle?" When she glanced at him, he said in an autocratic tone, "Michelle, answer me."

"You have not said anything yet."

He ran his finger along her cheek. "Last time we were together, you allowed me to kiss you. Now you act as if we are strangers."

"I know." She could not tell him the truth. That would hurt him more. Or would he laugh that she was falling in love with a man who was shutting her out of his life?

Bartholomew's arm tightened around her. When she averted her face, he asked, "Do you find me so distasteful?"

"No," she whispered.

"I had planned to ask you a very important question later tonight, but I shall not delay."

"Bartholomew, I would rather speak only of the musicale."

"Vatutin is a rare man to allow his mistress to spend her evenings with another man and never suggest that there has been impropriety between us."

She frowned. She had not expected him to speak about Alexei. Not sure where this conversation was leading, she said, "He has said nothing because he knows the truth."

"Leave him, Michelle," he urged with sudden ardor. "Leave him and come with me. I can make you happy." His hands moved up from her waist. She clamped her elbows to her sides, trapping his hands away from her breasts. "Do you like being used by that Russian bastard?"

"Bartholomew, insulting Alexei is unnecessary."

He bent to place his lips at the crook of her neck. When she stiffened in his arms, he said, "Michelle, don't hide what you feel to protect Vatutin. I harbor him no ill will for discovering you first. If he had not brought you to Vienna, I never would have met you."

She had worked so hard to keep this from happening. She must not hurt Bartholomew, but she also must not speak the truth. "I think you should take me home. I am no longer the proper companion for you to bring to this reception."

He scowled and pounded his fist against the side of the carriage. It stopped. "It would be better if you and I talk without anyone overhearing. Shall we walk?"

"I doubt if you can say anything to change how I feel. I would rather return home."

He pressed her hands to his chest. "We are not far from your apartment. We can walk in that direction, and the carriage will follow. If you wish, it shall take you home after I say what I must." He kissed her fingers fervently. "Or you may decide you don't wish to return to Vatutin."

"Bartholomew, I—"

"Will you listen to me, my dear? You owe me at least that much."

Michelle wanted to retort that she owed him nothing, but she must avoid angering him more. As he helped her from the carriage, she saw four shadows appearing around the end of it. His guards! Fiercely she said, "I don't want them trailing after us."

"Why not?" Honest astonishment widened his eyes. "They are here to assure that no harm comes to me and my friends."

"If you truly want to talk to me alone, Bartholomew, order them to stay with the carriage."

Whether he knew she was serious or he was so eager to

speak to her that he was willing to comply, she did not ask as he snapped an order. His bodyguards slipped back into the dark to leave them alone on the nearly deserted *Platz*.

When Bartholomew offered his arm, Michelle put her fingers on it. She looked around so she did not have to see the recrimination on his face. There were enough within her, for, if she had been honest from the beginning, he might not have thought that she desired him as much as he did her.

He led her across the *Platz*. The street beyond it was as silent as the plaza. Only the hooves of the horses behind them broke the silence.

"I cannot believe that you wish to stay with Vatutin," Bartholomew said. "I have seen how you change when he comes near. Something about him terrifies you."

She almost laughed, for Bartholomew was correct. Something about Alexei *did* frighten her—the strong passions he evoked within her. "I am not afraid of Alexei," she murmured.

"You cannot love him as I love you."

"You love me?"

He stopped on the snowy street and turned her to face him. Snow speckled his top hat and his dark coat, but his eyes burned with longing. "I leave before week's end for Coxe-Saxony-Colburg. Come with me, Michelle. I shall introduce you to my family. They will love you as I love you. Come with me tonight. You need not return to Vatutin. I can give you all you need."

She shook her head. Her vow to maintain this masquerade prevented her from being honest. Now she was not being honest with herself. It was not that promise that kept her from speaking the truth. She could not tell him—or herself—that she wished Alexei were the one speaking to her of love.

Softly she said, "You are kind, but I do not wish to spend my life going from one man to another."

He took her hands between his and raised them to his

lips. His fervor burned into her skin. "Then come with me to Coxe-Saxony-Colburg. I shall never leave your side."

"Even when you marry, Bartholomew? Your wife would be unwilling to share you with me."

He laughed. "Now I understand your dismay. I am not asking you to be my mistress. I am asking you to be my wife, my princess, my partner in ruling the lands I shall inherit. You are wiser than any ministers my father has, and you are beautiful. Why wouldn't I want you to be mine?"

In disbelief, she stared at him. He wanted to marry her? "You have overwhelmed me with your offer," she said when she found her voice. "I wish I could give you the answer you want, but I cannot."

"Are you refusing me? You prefer to whore for a Russian than to be my princess?"

"Bartholomew!"

"Forgive me, my love. Those were the words of a shattered heart. I love you so much. If you will be mine, everything I have ever dreamed of would be mine. Michelle, be mine."

Her eyes closed to dam the tears clinging to her eyelashes. Gripping her cloak, she turned to walk along the street, needing to reach the apartment and shut out the world.

Bartholomew's hand halted her. She looked over her shoulder to see his handsome face so close to hers. If she had not known Alexei, she might have been willing to marry Bartholomew in hopes of falling in love with him. Now it was impossible.

When she said that last thought aloud, he slowly released her hand. "May I call on you again, Michelle?"

"I don't think that would be wise." She held up her hand to halt his protest. "We shall see each other at assemblies, but I think we should avoid any evenings alone. Good night, Bartholomew."

"Don't you mean good-bye?"

She glanced at his coach, where the door was being held open by one of his guards, then turned to walk along the street. Although she heard the rattle of the iron-clad wheels behind her, she did not acknowledge the carriage. She climbed the steps and closed the door behind her. Through the heavy wood, she could hear the clip-clop as the carriage continued past. She took a deep breath to swallow the tears clogging her throat.

It should not have ended like this. Cinderella had sent herself back to the ashes with no hope of rescue by her charming prince. Hearing a door squeak in the shadows at the back of the hall, she scurried up the stairs to the apartment.

Michelle fumbled in her reticule for her key. Her fingers trembled as she unlocked the door. Praying Alexei was not yet home, she pushed it open. Her hopes vanished when she discovered that the front room was brightly lit. As quietly as possible, she shut the door.

"Michelle, I did not expect you home so early." Alexei sat with his feet propped, as usual, on the table. "Good, you can help me with some work tonight."

"It will have to wait until tomorrow."

"Can it?" He scowled at her. "Are you sure of that?"

"Not now, Alexei," she whispered. Dropping to the settee, she clasped her hands. The flames on the hearth could not heat the iciness within her. What had been such an innocent flirtation had blossomed too quickly into something she could not control. Just as Alexei had warned.

When the settee shifted, Alexei sat beside her and asked, "Are you going to tell me about it or just sit in silence?"

"I don't know," she answered softly.

When his arm surrounded her, giving her the haven she needed so desperately, she rested her cheek against his chest and looked up at him. He was not smiling. She was so glad. She could not face his teasing now.

"Tell me, *Liebchen*. Did Prince Charming do something to hurt you tonight?"

"Hurt me?" Her laugh sounded brittle in her ears. "He asked me to leave you and go with him to Coxe-Saxony-Colburg."

His fingertip caught a tear she had not realized had escaped. Balancing it for a moment, he let it fall, forgotten. "He has asked you to leave me before. If you are distressed because you have changed your mind, do not be. Go with him. When you reach his castle, you can tell him the truth, for by that time it will have no impact on my work."

"I am not going."

"Mayhap, if you are so unsettled, you should reconsider. 'Tis a settled life that you would enjoy."

"Be quiet!"

When she stood, Alexei watched her intently. Every motion she made was as slow as if she waded through a field of ice. He waited for her to speak.

"Alexei, have you ever had a dream come true offered to you?"

"A dream?" He went to where she was standing by the hearth. He sat on the arm of a chair.

She smiled sadly. "I had a dream offered to me tonight."

"Love?" He was shocked by the swell of an unfamiliar emotion through him. He knew what it was, but he never had expected to experience it himself. Jealousy. *Verflucht!* He did not want to be jealous of Michelle and Prince Charming.

"Yes."

"That is wonderful," he said tightly as another pulse of jealousy sliced through him. Although he told lies so often, this was the hardest one. Michelle falling in love with her Prince Charming was something he had not anticipated. But why not? She had offered Alexei her soft kisses, but he had pushed her away . . . into another man's arms.

Michelle faced him and put her hand on his cheek. His hand covered hers, holding it against him, for if he let it go, he feared she would go, too. Forever.

"Don't lie to me, Alexei. You do not think it is wonderful. You think it is a disaster."

"A disaster? You should be rejoicing, *Liebchen*, if he asked you to be his mistress."

"His wife."

"His wife?" He stood and arched his brows to hide his amazement . . . and another savage stab of jealousy.

"I told him I could not marry him," she said.

"Why not?"

She smiled. "I don't love him."

"That is no reason to turn down the chance to become a princess, Michelle!"

"What do you know about it?" Michelle cried with sudden heat. Anguish crashed through her. "What do you know of love? Or of life? Or of anything but your job, which requires you to prostitute your life to it?"

When he grasped her shoulders, his lips were a bleached line beneath his mustache. She was seared by the emerald fire blazing in his eyes.

"Are you so blind?" he asked. "I know of life and I know of love. Far more than a woman who has spent her whole life in a convent."

"Alexei—"

"No, *Liebchen*, I have listened to you. Now you will listen to me." A cold smile twisted his lips. "Don't judge what you do not understand. You should find Prince Charming and beg him to let you reconsider his suit."

"I don't want to marry him! I do not love him!"

He stroked her shoulders. "How do you know, Michelle? Have you ever been in love?"

"I don't have to be ill to know what being sick is."

With a chuckle, he sat again. "That might be the best analogy I have ever heard. You are so innocent. If I let you go with him to his court, I would be sending a lamb into a pride of lions."

"I am glad you can see sense, for whatever reason." She

went to the arch. "I don't belong in a castle somewhere amid the German states."

"You are right. You belong here in Vienna with me."

Her heart halted in midbeat as she slowly faced him. Wanting to silence the exultation bursting through her, she could not. "You want me to stay here?"

"Of course." He stretched. Putting his hand over his mouth, he yawned broadly. "You have become a good member of our team, Michelle. You have not faltered in your role as my mistress, although it must have given you much distress while you were with Prince Charming."

"And that is why you want me to stay?"

"Of course," Alexei repeated.

He watched Michelle race along the short corridor. The slamming of her bedroom door warned him that his plan was going just as it should.

Yes, exactly as it should. A plan guaranteed to anger her and make him miserable.

He leaned on the wall and stared at her door. How simple it would be to open that door and answer the passion in her innocent eyes with his own! Just to touch her drove every other thought from his head, except the most important one. She was the one woman in the world he must never possess. No matter how much he wanted her, she could never be his.

Chapter Thirteen

The door of the carriage was opened with a flourish by a footman. Alexei stepped down and held out his hand to Michelle. "Fraulein D'Orage, your admirers await your arrival."

"Admirers?" Her laugh was uneven.

As he helped her down to the brick walkway, he smiled. "You don't believe you have admirers, *Liebchen?* Surely you have heard the rumors that would make any man eager to catch your eye."

"Rumors? About Bar—"

"No, the rumor that you are a lost aristocrat traveling incognito in Vienna while you try to regain what your family has lost."

"What are you babbling about?"

"You have not heard the rumor that you are a Swiss aristocrat traveling in the guise of my mistress?"

In horror, she said with a gasp, "They know about our charade?"

"Not exactly. They think I am your bodyguard."

"You?" She laughed. "A wolf guarding the lambs would be more trustworthy."

The irony returned to his smile. "That shows you how stupid rumors can be, doesn't it?"

If he noticed how her hand on his arm trembled, he said nothing. For that, she was grateful. As storm clouds scudded overhead, obscuring the stars, she gazed at the house, which appeared to be lighted by thousands of stars. The gathering at the home of an English diplomat was the first time she had been among the delegates since she had turned down Bartholomew's proposal three days ago.

Rusak smiled and signed at her: *Lovely Michelle, my pleasure to drive tonight.*

She pulled her hand from beneath Alexei's to answer. With a grimace, she corrected a sign that was not the one she wanted. Rusak reached past Alexei to angle her fingers for the word she wanted. She nodded as he held up his hand in the proper sign.

Understood, she told him.

"Are you two finished?" Alexei asked.

Rusak fired him a glower that needed no translation.

"This was a private conversation," she said.

"Very private, for no one else can understand."

"You could if you came to Herr Professor Waldstein's classes. Rusak is your friend. I would think you would want to learn."

Alexei glanced at Rusak, who turned to climb back into the box. A flash of regret crossed Alexei's face. "Rusak understands I am too busy now." Taking her hand, he placed it on his arm again. "After all, Fraulein D'Orage, you can teach me when we are traveling home."

"Home?" Blanching, she gasped. "Do you want me to go to Russia with you?"

"No, you *would* be a lamb among the wolves there." He drew her up the steps to the door. "Come along, *Liebchen.*" He chuckled.

"What is so amusing now?"

"You are staring at the house like a child at a piece of candy. I hope you are not disappointed."

She pushed back the hood of her cloak. "I realize that this ball is a way for diplomats to continue plotting."

"You have such a high opinion of us," he teased as he led her up the steps to the door.

"Exactly what you have earned."

"Ouch! That one struck deep, *Liebchen*. Can you withdraw that spear from me so I can deal with the ones waiting inside?"

Despite herself, she could not keep from laughing. When Alexei attempted to charm her, she could not resist. Especially when he looked so handsome in his dark blue coat that opened to reveal the white silk of his waistcoat, which was embroidered with vines to match the roses on her gown. Black breeches accented his white stockings. As her gaze rose to his brilliant green eyes, she wondered if she had ever seen a man who was so handsome and so irritating . . . and so tempting.

They were a perfect match tonight, for she was dressed in her most elegant gown as well. Rosebuds embroidered at the edges of the sleeves and at the end of the ribbons beneath the high bodice matched the pink ruffle at the hem. The gown was exquisite, and she had been shocked when Alexei brought it to her along with a pair of slippers dyed the same pink and the feathered fan that was hooked with a gold cord to her wrist. The gift told her that he considered this gathering a very important one.

Michelle wondered what scheme he had in mind for tonight. She smiled as Alexei took her black evening cape and handed it to a servant along with his cloak and hat. Whatever it was, he would not tell her.

She put her hand on his arm, hoping to appear aloof and sophisticated. That hope evaporated when they walked from the plain foyer into a crowded ballroom. She could not keep from admiring the crystalline glow of the chandeliers that reflected in the gilt mirrors edging the walls. The whirling dancers mesmerized her. Listening to the lyrical waltz, she could only stare. She did not belong here.

You could have. She could have been one of them if she had married Bartholomew. A prince had found his heart's desire in the midst of the greatest assembly of allied leaders the world had ever known. It was a fairy tale, but one without a happy ending. She was not a princess, but Fraulein D'Orage of St. Bernard's School for Girls. Nothing had changed for her.

Alexei put his arm around her waist and swept her toward the dancers. That he did not ask her if she wanted to dance did not surprise her. Alexei Vatutin never acted as others did.

She fought not to trip over her feet as he steered her through the crowd. Watching the others, she faced him and placed her right hand in his while her left held up her skirts. She swallowed her gasp as his arm slipped around her waist and drew her to him. Seeing his smile, she knew she was not the only one savoring this sweet embrace.

Without warning, he began to twirl her to the music. When she stumbled, he asked, "Don't you know how to waltz?"

"No, Frau Herbart considers the waltz vulgar and refuses to allow the dance master to teach it at St. Bernard's. Alexei, find someone else to dance with."

"But I do not want anyone else but you, *Liebchen.*"

Something in her center rippled with yearning as she saw the glow in his charismatic eyes. With his arm about her waist and her hand on his broad palm, which was as unyielding as the floor beneath her feet, she pushed aside all pretense. *This* was what she wanted, the happy ending to her fairy tale, a happily-ever-after with Alexei. It could happen only in a fairy tale, but she delighted in imagining it as his gaze moved along her and his fingers stroked her back. She wanted him to pull her closer and caress her with the passions she had discovered in his kiss.

When the music ended, applause broke the spell spun by her craving for him. As the orchestra began another waltz, she walked toward the edge of the dance area.

Alexei's hand on her arm halted her. He grinned and put his arm around her waist again. "Michelle, you still need to learn to waltz. It is simple. One-two-three, one-two-three, one-two-three." As he spoke, he began to turn her slowly to the rhythm.

She kept her eyes on his face. As she relaxed into the music, he smiled.

"This is fun," she said.

His laugh was a low rumble that reached inside her to stir her longings into a frenzy. Her breath became shallow and rapid as he whispered, "It is supposed to be fun, *Liebchen.* Can you envision a better way for a man to spend an evening than to whirl to this music with the most beautiful woman in the room in his arms?"

At his compliment, she missed a step, and his foot came down on her toe. When she yelped, the dancers around them scowled.

"Forgive me, Michelle."

"My fault." When he put his arm around her again, she was shocked that he steered her off the dance floor. "I am not badly injured!"

He nodded, but sorrow stole the lightness from his voice. "I know, but you must excuse me. The person I must speak to just arrived."

"Alexei—" Although she had known that he was coming here to gain more information, she did not want to miss any chance to be in his arms.

"It shall not take all evening." He framed her face with his hands. "I promise you that, *Liebchen.* There will be more dances for us tonight."

"I hope so."

"I promise you." Raising her fingers to his lips, he added in the same intense tone, "You will dance with me later, won't you, *Liebchen*?"

"Yes," she whispered. "As often as you wish."

He smiled as he stroked her cheek before striding away with an air of arrogance that drew eyes from every side.

As she touched the spot on her face that was warm from his touch, she smiled. Mayhap this night could be as perfect as she had dreamed. All she had to do was figure out a way to persuade Alexei to forget his work.

There might be one way, and she intended to find out tonight.

"My dance, my dear."

Michelle turned to see Bartholomew, but a Bartholomew unlike any she had seen. He exhibited a grandeur that diminished her fancy gown. A scarlet sash, topped with gold medals, slashed across his chest. He was every inch a prince from the tip of his tousled hair to his shining boots.

When she started to drop into a curtsy, his hand halted her. He did not release her elbow as he drew her toward the dance floor. Bringing her smoothly into his arms, he turned her to the tempo of the waltz. He did not seem to notice that her feet were stumbling over his. The dance that had seemed so perfect in Alexei's arms was a trial with Bartholomew.

"What a pleasure to see you, my dear," he murmured.

"I thought you were going home," she said in a whisper, knowing many of the guests would be eagerly watching.

"I decided to stay." His gaze edged along her with obvious yearning. "*Gott in Himmel,* you are more beautiful tonight than I have ever seen you. I saw you dancing with Vatutin, and I wanted to cut out his heart so I could have you to myself."

"Don't say things like that, I beg you, Your Highness."

He said in a snarl, "I thought to you I was Bartholomew."

"That was before."

Stopping in the center of the floor, he stated, "Nothing has changed, Michelle. I still love you. I still want you as my wife."

She looked, horrified, at the others who had stopped to eavesdrop. "I wish I could tell you yes," she said as she stepped away.

He refused to release her. "But you cannot."

"Nothing has changed. I still cannot marry you."

He pulled her back into his arms and spun her about the floor with more enthusiasm than the tempo suggested. His medals cut into her, but he refused to allow her to move back even a half step. He whispered in her ear, "I pine for you, my love. I shall not go back to Coxe-Saxony-Colburg without you."

"But I do not want to go to Coxe-Saxony-Colburg. My life, for now, is here."

"For now?"

"For as long as it must be."

He scowled. "What hold does that Russian bastard have on you? Tell me, and I will help you get free."

"I do not need assistance. I am staying because I promised to stay with Alexei while he was in Vienna."

"And then?"

With a sharp tug, she escaped his embrace. She ignored the onlookers who stared at her, aghast. "That, Your Highness, is none of your concern. Good evening."

His infuriated gaze followed her as she walked away. Even when another man dared to ask her to dance, she knew Bartholomew watched. Had she made an enemy of him? She had no choice. A promise was a promise.

She wished Alexei would return from wherever he had gone. In his arms, as they spun to the music, she would find the haven she yearned for. She hoped that she would find a haven and far more.

* * *

Alexei took out his pipe, then tapped it against an ornate ash container. Putting it in his mouth, he puffed on the remnants of smoke and looked at the dancers. Michelle apparently had taken to the waltz as if it had been invented for her.

He noted that she was garnering the attention of many of the delegates. He should be pleased, for that had been his plan when he told her she would be joining him here. Instead he was inflicted with that uneasy emotion he wanted to ignore. *Jealousy!* He swore under his breath. More than one of his supposed friends had been eager to tell him that his mistress had been dancing with Prince Charming.

Although he wanted to deny it, that fact had brought him back to the ballroom. He did not see Prince Charming, but he suspected the prince would remain close to Michelle. If Alexei had told her that Bartholomew would want her even more now that she had turned down his proposal, she would have accused him again of interfering.

He spotted a movement just past where Michelle danced with a member of the French delegation. *Prince Charming!* Swearing again, because even that silly name roused this accursed jealousy, he saw that the prince intended to ask her to dance again.

Alexei stuffed his pipe under his coat. He strode through the crowd, not stopping when someone spoke to him. He reached Michelle and her French partner just before the prince did.

"Can you spare a dance for an old friend?" Alexei asked.

Michelle lost her smile as she met Alexei's intense eyes. "Do you mind, sir?" she asked her partner.

"Of course not, Mademoiselle D'Orage," he said with obvious regret. Nodding toward Alexei, he added, "Your partner, Count Vatutin."

When Alexei did not move, she remembered to translate the words into German. He thanked her partner before holding out his hand to her. Lifting the hem of her gown, she stepped easily into his arms and let him twirl her into the dance. The music enclosed them in the sweet rhythms.

"Will I insult you if I tell you how you have improved?" he asked.

"I had an excellent teacher."

"And much practice."

"You sound jealous!" She lowered her gaze to his waist-coat. "I am sorry. I should not have said that."

"Why? It is the truth."

"Alexei!"

His arm tightened on her, drawing her closer to his lithe body. When he whispered against her hair, she shivered. His breath heated her to her soul even as it wafted the loosened tendrils along her cheek.

"Why are you surprised, *Liebchen?* Just because you have refused to believe how enticing you are does not mean that I have failed to notice."

Her eyes widened. "Alexei, you should not say things like that when they think we are lovers."

He smiled sadly. "No one is listening to be shocked that I am speaking of unsated desire to my supposed mistress. This is not part of the deception. This is the truth. I have been fascinated with you since we met. You are an incredibly lovely woman, Michelle D'Orage."

The flush along her cheeks was so warm that she feared she would burn him where his skin touched hers. She had waited so long for him to say something to her that was not couched in insults. When he had, she wanted to believe the desire in his eyes was genuine.

He stopped abruptly and said in a growl, "Move aside, Your Highness."

In dismay, Michelle looked past Alexei to see Bartholo-mew blocking their path. Other dancers were pausing in curiosity. As a circle formed around them, Michelle remained silent. To speak might escalate the fury.

"I wish to dance with Fraulein D'Orage," stated Bartholomew, every inch the imperious prince.

"She is dancing with me," Alexei replied with quiet dignity.

He ignored Alexei. Looking at Michelle, he asked, "Will you dance with me?"

"I promised this dance to Alexei." She moved closer to Alexei. "Mayhap later, Bartholomew."

"My dear, I cannot believe you would prefer to let this Russian beast paw you rather than dance with me."

When she heard the comment translated into several languages she knew and others she did not, she could not restrain her frustration. "Your Highness, you degrade both yourself and your father's title with such comments. Good evening, Your Highness." Holding out her hand, she said as regally as any member of royalty in the room, "Alexei, shall we?"

"Of course, *Liebchen*." He bowed his head toward Bartholomew before twirling her away. When he had put several steps between them and Bartholomew, he chuckled deep in his throat. "That may not have been wise, but you certainly put that incompetent princeling in his place."

"I do not like being ordered about."

Again he laughed. "You do not need to tell me that."

"I guess I don't." When his arm around her tightened, her breath caught at exactly the spot where her chest touched his. She gazed up and lost herself in the emerald seas of his eyes.

An elbow bumped her, bringing her back to reality. She nodded to the hasty apology, but her brow rutted with disquiet when she saw who had struck her. Although she was not sure of his name, she knew the man was a member of the delegation from Coxe-Saxony-Colburg.

"It is crowded in here," Alexei said, his voice stiff with anger. "I would like to find a quieter place." His fingers moved in a slow, meandering path along her arm. "Do you want to come with me, *Liebchen?*"

Alexei clearly recognized the rude man and wanted to avoid a confrontation that would add to her embarrassment. "I think that would be an excellent idea."

She clasped his arm as they walked off the dance floor, paying no attention to the curious stares that had bothered her when she was with Bartholomew. In other times, in other places, she might have cared what was being said about her. Nothing was going to be allowed to intrude on her happiness of being with Alexei.

He led her into a short hallway. No decorations covered the painted walls. At the end was a door. When Alexei opened it, he bowed with a deep flourish. "My lady, would you wish to enter paradise?"

Michelle could not even gasp as she walked into a miniature Garden of Eden. Plants of every type sprouted in abandon, reaching for the glass ceiling two stories above them. It was wild, free, and urged her to pull off her slippers and dance among the trees and flowers.

"This is incredible!" she said softly.

"The English enjoy their greenery, either in their gardens or like here, in this conservatory." He closed the door behind them. The gentle strains of the orchestra seeped past to soar to the ceiling and then rain back on them in a soft shower. "There is a path amid the plantings. Would you care to explore?"

She smiled. "Yes." When she held out her hand to him, he slipped his fingers through hers.

Sleet coated the windows, but cold could not invade the green world where they might have been the only two humans alive. As she walked by his side, she exulted in how perfectly her fingers entwined with his. The soft hush of water ran throughout the conservatory's garden. At a small bridge arching over a tiny stream, she paused to look at the water tumbling over smooth pebbles. His hands rested on her shoulders, and it seemed perfect to lean her head back against his chest.

He took her hand again as they continued along the path of crushed stone. Gazing up at the trickles of rain and sleet that created changing patterns along the windows, she whispered, "It is so beautiful in here."

"I thought you would like it."

"How did you know it was here?"

He drew her behind a thick bush that was bright with purple flowers. "What better place for a spy to lurk than in the jungle?"

"Don't talk about that. You ruin this beauty with talk of that dirty business. I do not want to think of anything but the aroma of the flowers and the warmth of your hand in mine."

"You French have so much poetry within you."

"We French? I left France after my father died during the Terror. *Maman* decided we would be safer in Zurich. I have lived there since I was less than a year old." She laughed softly. "I have never considered myself French."

"But you are."

She paused and faced him when she realized his reply had been in French. "Alexei, I thought you spoke little French."

"Very little." He sat on a low wall surrounded by flowers.

Knowing how much she risked, she stroked his shoulders. She wanted to touch him, to revel in his fettered strength beneath her fingers. Her hand at his nape tilted his head closer to hers. "But French is the best language for lovers, isn't it?"

She gave him no chance to answer as her lips found his. All the powerful sensations she had experienced in his arms were diminished by the fierce surges that weakened her knees. Alexei's mouth incited a savage rapture that overpowered her, growing stronger and more demanding. She leaned against him, needing his strength as much as his caress. Her fingers sifted through his blond hair as she explored his lips.

He drew her down to her knees as he slid off the wall to kneel beside her. When he pressed his mouth against her neck, her delight burst forth in a heartfelt gasp. Her fingers clenched on his coat, then loosened to stroke the firm planes of his back. Deafened by her own pulse, she shivered as each swift breath brushed her body against his.

With a soft moan, she pressed him back into the soft grass amid the flowers. He tugged her over him, then, with a laugh, pushed her onto her back. She moaned softly when he lifted his mouth from hers.

"Is this my Michelle?" he whispered as he reached to pluck the pins from her hair. "Is this my Michelle who snarls like a wet cat when I speak to her?"

Because he spoke in German, she answered in the same language. She smiled as she ran a finger along his aristocratic nose. "I have not changed. I am still not your Michelle." She paused, then whispered, "But I want to be."

"Do not jest with me, *Liebchen.*"

"I am not."

"Do you realize what I think you mean?"

She took his hand and pressed it to her breast. "Yes, and it is what I mean. I want you, and I want you to want me. You said you would be my teacher, Alexei. Teach me."

His groan came from deep in his gut as he captured her lips. She answered his kiss with her own need. When the tip of his tongue moistened her lips, they warmed. His tongue sought within her mouth for the slick, succulent treats awaiting him. Taunting and pleasuring, his mouth moved along her face, each kiss a new thrill. He tasted the soft whorls of her ear as his breath swirled through her, inflaming the longing into a fierce wildfire. She wanted his mouth to touch all of her.

She quivered when his hand slipped up beneath her gown to stroke her legs. She entwined them with his as his mouth coursed along the curved neckline of her gown.

When his tongue delved between her breasts, caressing each, she reached for the cravat at his collar.

She tossed it aside as he drew her up so he could loosen the buttons along her back. In this hidden bower, she wanted to make her dreams come true, and she undid his waistcoat and his shirt beneath it. Her fingers slid up his chest, and he pulled her tightly to him. His kiss revealed that his need was as overmastering as hers.

As he drew aside the bits of silk she wore, his mouth sought along her body. Each flick of his tongue against her burned lightning hot into her skin. She laughed softly when he traced a moist path along her shoulder and down her arm. As his lips teased the downy skin along the inside of her elbow, unexpected sensations shimmered along her.

She whispered his name with near desperation as she guided his mouth back to hers before he stripped her of all sanity. Lowering her gown to the ground, he slipped one finger beneath the shoulder of her chemise and drew it aside. Her breasts spilled out, and he pinned her against the ground, introducing her skin to his. The frenzy within her would not be stilled. His leg settled across hers when he had pulled away her clothes. When his fingertips trickled up her legs, she entwined them with his, moaning with unfettered longing.

When she eased his breeches away, she admired the masculine lines of his body. Each angle urged her fingertips to explore it, and she refused to be denied. His body was hard from his rough life, but his touch was gentle. His breath burned against her mouth as she surrendered to her desire.

She gasped when he pulled away. Her half-voiced protest became a sigh when he bent to sample the skin along her legs. On a sinuous path, his tongue seared its fire along her. Her fingers twisted through his thick hair, which was brushing her skin, but she could think of nothing other than his mouth on her. Each dazzling kiss stoked the flames within her. She wanted to beg him to stop because she could not stand a moment more of this excruciating ecstasy. She wanted to plead with him never to stop, but words had dissolved into the overpowering craving.

When he leaned over her, she looked up into his glazed eyes. She must share this joy with him. As he pressed against her with each rapid breath, his hands on her hips guided him into her. She clutched his shoulders as his unsated groan aroused the succulent madness. Watching his face, she fought to control her rapture enough so she could enjoy the pleasure fleeing across his features.

His hand swept up through her hair to bring her hungry mouth against his. Unbridled delight captured her as she was enmeshed in the passion melding them together. She was his as he was hers, as they both were part of the need. Each motion, each breath, each pulse stripped everything from her head. When she was sure she could endure no more of the untamed ecstasy, she was swirled into a wild storm, sweeping her away from everything but the man she loved. He shuddered against the force of the tempest, taking her with him as they vanished into its might, lost in rapture.

Michelle twitched when something tickled her nose. She batted it away. It returned. She pushed it aside. It came back. Opening her eyes, she gave Alexei a wry smile as she plucked a leaf from his fingers.

"You are the most irritating man in the world," she said as she tossed the leaf away.

Drawing her head down against his shoulder, he whispered, "And you are the most desirable woman in the world. You cannot guess how much I have yearned to be with you like this, *Liebchen*."

"Then why haven't you?" Her fingers explored the harsh planes of his face. Each angle was as severely sculpted as if the artist had only roughed them in and had never smoothed the lines.

"How can I explain?" he whispered. "How can I explain to you what I do not know myself?"

"Because of *Maman*?"

He smiled. "Mayhap in a way, *Liebchen*. Mayhap I simply felt guilty for bringing you into this life Sophie clearly did not want you to have."

"It is too late for that regret, Alexei."

He laughed at her strict tone. "Now you sound like Fraulein D'Orage, mistress of languages at St. Bernard's School for Girls." His voice became somber as he reached for her clothes and handed her her chemise. "I honestly can tell you that I do not regret stopping in Zurich to find you." His hand stroked the bare curve of her shoulder, the coarse texture of his skin scoring her with yearning to be touched over and over until her mind dissolved again into passion.

"Must we leave?" she whispered as he pulled on his breeches.

"You are a temptress, *Liebchen,* and you know the very way to drive me mad with desire."

"I am learning." With a sigh, she drew her chemise over her and smoothed it along her legs. "I want more lessons from my teacher."

With a growl, he tugged her into his arms and against his naked chest. "As soon as we are home, *Liebchen*, I promise you that our lessons will continue."

"*Our* lessons?"

"I want *you* to teach *me* what gives you pleasure."

"You do." She kissed him lightly, then pulled her dress over her head. He hooked it in place before pulling on his shirt and waistcoat.

She watched from the corner of her eye as he tied his cravat with ease. That he did everything he attempted so well was one of the things she loved about him.

Love! The word popped unbidden into her brain. She

had been trying to hide the truth from herself that she had fallen in love, not with the handsome young prince who offered her a wondrous life, but with a cantankerous, life-scarred man who promised her nothing but the joy of the moment.

And that joy was so splendid. She would not trade it for Bartholomew's castle and title. Glancing again at Alexei, she silenced her sigh. He was hers for now, but she knew he would allow nothing, not even her love, to keep him from doing his work. Yet, if he had, he would not be the man she loved.

As Michelle drew on her stockings and shoes, Alexei caught her hand in his. He touched the ring she wore on her middle finger. "How often I saw this ring on Sophie's hand!"

"And I never saw her wear it. Mayhap it was part of her change from being *Maman* to being a spy." She drew it off and held it up to watch the light play off the lightning bolt. Tilting it, she said, "How odd!"

"What is odd?"

"Look at the initials inside."

"Initials?"

"MML and SR." She frowned. "Sophie Rameau was *Maman*'s name before she wed, but who is MML?"

"Mayhap she was married before?"

Michelle shook her head. "No, that could not be. She told me often enough about how she and my father met at a gathering along the Loire." Her forehead threaded. " 'Tis odd that she told me that story over and over, but told me nothing else about him save about his death."

"There must be an explanation."

"Yes, but what?"

He smiled. "It may be one that we will never know, for all her secrets are buried with her. Odd, I often forget she was married, although I knew she had a daughter."

Drawing her to her feet, he locked his hands behind her. "I never guessed her daughter would be such a delight."

She laughed as he pulled her to him. She answered his fierce desire with her own. His hands stroked her enticingly, and she slipped her fingers beneath his coat to rediscover his coiled strength beneath his silk waistcoat.

"Release her, Vatutin, or you will die!"

Chapter Fourteen

At the imperial order, Alexei sighed. *Prince Charming!* When Michelle became rigid in his arms, he turned her so she could see the fury on Prince Charming's face.

"Bartholomew, what are you doing here?" she asked.

"A question I need not ask you." He reached toward her loose hair.

Alexei stepped between them, blocking Prince Charming's hand. "Your Highness, I do not understand your continued intrusion into Fraulein D'Orage's private matters," he said smoothly. "She has told you that she has no wish to become your wife. Therefore you have no reason to trail after her like a slobbering pup."

"Alexei," Michelle began, but Bartholomew's vicious curse silenced her.

"Vatutin, you have done me grave dishonor. I demand satisfaction."

Alexei shook his head. "I do not duel, Your Highness."

"Afraid?"

He laughed, wondering if Prince Charming would be so eager for a fight if he knew that, in a box somewhere,

Alexei had a fancy medal he had won as a sharpshooter and an even fancier one for his fencing. "I have seen enough dying during the war. Your honor has not been damaged. Michelle was never yours."

"If you are dead, she might come to me, a man who can offer her more than an ignoble position as a bed warmer. She deserves better than that."

"But she does not want you."

When Bartholomew took a deep breath, Michelle asked, "Will you both stop talking about me as if I were not here?" She glanced at Alexei. A smile curved beneath his mustache. She wanted to let his mustache caress her. First . . . "Bartholomew, even if I had agreed to be your wife, your father would never accept me. I am not German. I am not royal born."

He gripped her hands, but did not draw her closer when Alexei shifted from one foot to the other and closed his hands into fists. "My love, if my father will not accept you at first, he shall learn when you are the mother of his grandson."

"No." She tried to tug her hands out of his, but he tightened his grip. When she saw the challenge in his eyes, she realized he wanted her to protest. Why did Bartholomew want to incite Alexei into protecting her? When she saw shadows move beyond him, she understood. He had brought his personal guards.

"Yes, Michelle," he said, his eyes twinkling maliciously, "I have asked you too many times. This time you will say yes."

When he dragged her closer, she wanted to call for Alexei to halt him. She did not, for the sparks in Bartholomew's eyes warned of danger.

Alexei's hand on her arm gently but firmly drew her away from Bartholomew. "Your Highness, will you ask her to consider your suit each time you meet?"

"She shall be mine."

"No!" she cried. "I don't wish to marry you, Bartholomew."

He said in a sneer, "You wish to stay with Vatutin? Where will you go when he tires of you?"

"St. Bernard's School for Girls."

Bartholomew's eyes widened at her quick answer. On her arm, Alexei's fingers tightened. Had she said the wrong thing when she spoke of where she had been living? Too late now to take back the words as Bartholomew's lips tightened with rage. He raised his hand, but his motion was blocked by Alexei.

"I suggest you retire, Your Highness," Alexei said, "before you do something a gentleman would regret. Michelle has given you her answer."

"Vatutin, stay out of this!" At his low growl, his guards burst out of the green dusk. The silent quartet formed an arc behind him, their expressions warning that they awaited his order to attack.

Michelle shuddered, but whispered, "If you cared for me at all, Bartholomew, you would know that I hate this abhorrent behavior."

"Then come with me."

"Is that what you truly want, Bartholomew? Do you want to coerce me into coming with you because I wish to protect Alexei from your men?" When he opened his mouth to answer, she asked more intensely, "Is that what you really want?"

His blue eyes hardened. Whirling on his heel, he snapped an order to his men. They followed him back along the twisting path among the conservatory's flowers. The sound of their angry footsteps echoed eerily.

When she heard a chuckle behind her, Michelle turned to see Alexei sitting on a bench. He held out his arms. Without hesitation, she slid into his embrace.

He brushed her loosened curls back from her forehead and kissed her lightly. "Do you wish to go back to the ballroom, *Liebchen*, or go home?"

"Home."

"Where we may resume this."

"Resume?" She laughed. "How romantic you are, Alexei! Is this how you Russians woo your women?"

"I don't know about anyone else," he murmured, "but this is how I wish to woo you." He branded his answer into her lips.

She softened against him like heated honey, wanting this night to last forever.

Michelle yawned as Alexei walked her toward the carriage. Behind them, the sounds of the orchestra continued over the clatter of sleet on the bricks. She leaned on him, glad to be beneath his cloak.

"Too late for you, Cinderella?" he teased.

"She was home before midnight. It must be past that."

"Far past. Time passes quickly when we are enjoying ourselves, *Liebchen.*"

"I am exhausted. All I want is to go home and go to bed."

"Is that an invitation?"

She smiled. "I hope you think so."

In the distance, through the clatter of sleet, church bells rang. The sound surprised her until she realized it was almost time for matins on the first morning of Advent. The year was nearly over, but she was sure her life was just beginning.

"Be careful," Alexei whispered, steering her cautiously over the icy ground.

"There are advantages to flat slippers that boots do not have." Her feet slipped. "However, even low heels are treacherous tonight."

"This morning. When was the last time you were up all night?"

She pondered the question as Rusak opened the carriage door. Smiling she signed, *Long night.*

Night good?
Best night.

Alexei chuckled as he handed Michelle into the carriage. "Your fingers make magic in so many ways, *Liebchen.*"

When he sat beside her, she gave him that smile that rippled to the center of his gut and exploded along him. He was sure his heart would thud no harder if he had run from Paris to Vienna.

"I believe," she said, "I stayed up all night once when I was about twelve. *Maman* had come to St. Bernard's to pick me up. I had not seen her in almost a year, and we had so much to talk about. We talked all night."

"Knowing Sophie and knowing you, I can believe that."

"Alexei, don't act as if you never get a chance to speak. Whenever you—"

His lips over hers silenced her. Her sweet gasp of astonishment cascaded down his throat, fanning his longing for her. As he wrapped his arms around her slender form, he thought of holding her more intimately in his bed. Her pliant curves re-formed along him, and he knew no woman had ever driven him so mad with fury and yearning.

When she pushed against his arms gently, he released her, but kept her within the curve of his embrace. "Tired of my kisses already, *Liebchen?*"

"It is sleeting hard out there. Rusak should not have to stay out in it any longer than he must while we . . ."

He chuckled. Even in the dim light, he could see the blush tinting her cheeks. She was a paradox, an enchantress in his arms, but still an innocent. He wanted to savor that innocence and her sweet magic again. Leaning forward, he called, "Rusak, let's get home, man!"

Rusak grinned and closed the door. The carriage swayed as he nimbly climbed up to the box.

At a shout from outside the carriage, Alexei peered out the window. "Damrosch! What are you doing out in the storm?"

With a voice slurred by alcohol and a drunken smile on his face, a man rested his arm heavily on the door and lamented, "They asked me to leave, Vatutin. Can you believe that? They think I cannot drink their champagne without getting foxed. Will you go in and—"

"Whoa there, friend." Alexei pushed the door open and managed to keep the rotund man from falling with the same motion. "If our hosts think that it is time for you to go home, allow us to give you a ride."

"Don't want to ride." Damrosch flung out his arms and bowed, nearly knocking himself off his feet again. "Want to dance. Will you dance with me, Fraulein?"

Michelle put her fingers over her lips to silence her laughter. "Mayhap some other time. Why don't you let us take you home, Herr Damrosch?"

"Dance with me some other time, Fraulein?"

"The very next ball we attend, Herr Damrosch, I will save you the second dance."

He heaved himself into the carriage with Alexei's help. Somehow he bowed toward her, a nearly impossible feat in the cramped space. "The second one it shall be, Fraulein. I assume you are saving the first for my dear friend Alexei."

Behind him, Alexei made a motion. She understood immediately and rose to sit on the opposite seat. "Please sit down, Herr Damrosch," she said.

"Always should let a lady ride facing forward," he grumbled.

"Except when you might get sick riding that way, Claus, my friend." Alexei shoved Herr Damrosch's shoulders. The carriage springs creaked as he dropped onto the seat.

"I am not drunk," he retorted in a fuzzy voice.

"Please ride like this," Michelle said before Alexei could speak. She did not want to be further delayed. She wanted to return home and to Alexei's arms. "Herr Damrosch, I do not mind riding backward."

"You don't?"

"Of course not," she lied.

"In that case," he mumbled as he closed his eyes and sagged against the cushions.

Alexei climbed into the carriage and slapped the side to tell Rusak to start. With a grin, he put his arm around her shoulders and whispered in her ear, "Why are you always so considerate of everyone's feelings but mine?"

"You don't like how I treat you?"

"I like the way you are treating me tonight. Before tonight, you never missed any opportunity to smite me with harsh words."

"And do you think that is going to change?"

He chuckled. "Hardly."

Herr Damrosch roused enough to begin singing a bawdy drinking song. Michelle thought that Alexei would halt him, but, when he rumbled with laughter, she knew the song would drag to its ribald conclusion.

Alexei joined in for the lusty third verse, and she giggled. This was a facet of him that she had never seen. As she clapped her hands in tempo with the jumbled words, she watched his face. He was enjoying himself as he seldom did.

"Such a bright smile, *Liebchen,*" he murmured beneath Herr Damrosch's enthusiastic repetition of the final verse.

Kissing him, she delighted in the soft brush of his mustache against her lips. Her hands slipped beneath his damp coat to stroke his silk waistcoat and the strong muscles beneath it. His mouth teased hers with sparks that lilted across her lips.

He nestled her between him and the side of the carriage. With the shadow of his cloak drifting toward her, she was nearly hidden from Herr Damrosch, who was still singing boisterously. Alexei's fingertip brought her lips to his as his other hand loosened the ties holding her cape closed. She could not restrain her soft cry when his mouth sought a luscious path along her throat. His tongue stroked her as eagerly as did his fingers along her back. Unable to control her craving, she pressed to him.

He murmured against her ear, "You taste as perfect as you look, *Liebchen*. Tonight we shall—"

The carriage rocked to a sudden halt. It bounced as Rusak jumped to the ground.

He signed, *Road something.*

"What?" Alexei asked, looking at Michelle.

"There is something in the road."

"What is wrong?" mumbled Herr Damrosch from his wine haze.

"Just a delay," Alexei replied.

Michelle glanced at him uneasily. Although his words were soothing, she sensed his disquiet. He started to add more, then looked out the opposite side of the carriage. He cursed.

"Alexei, what—"

A sharp detonation sliced the night. Michelle froze. What was that? It sounded like guns firing. What was happening? Something whizzed past her, striking the door. More explosions.

Alexei shouted, "Rusak, get us out of here!" He reached past her for the door latch.

"Alexei, what is wrong?" Something struck her left arm just above her gloves. She screamed as pain scalded her, unlike any agony she had ever known.

"Down!" shouted Alexei. More explosions devoured his words.

He shoved her against the wall, and she shrieked as she struck her left arm. That pain was forgotten when another hot needle struck her left leg. Alexei's arms around her held her to the wall of the carriage.

When he groaned with anguish, she cried, "Help us!"

No one answered. All she could hear were the continuing explosions from beyond the carriage.

A screech came from the opposite side of the carriage. Herr Damrosch's coat was riddled with dark, glistening holes. He moaned once and toppled to the floor.

"Alexei! Alexei!" she shouted. His weight on her arm was excruciating, but she could not move him.

Wetness along her left hand drew her strangely unfocused gaze. Darkness etched a path along her gloves. Numbly she realized it was blood. *Her* blood. The same sensation inched along her leg, and she slowly realized she had been shot. The carriage was careening through the narrow streets. Rusak must be fleeing from whoever was shooting at them.

Shooting! It could not be happening. Her brain was deadened with pain and horror. She wanted to hear Alexei's voice as he told her that this was simply another jest.

If only she did not hurt so badly . . .

Michelle moaned as her wounded arm was pressed into the wall when they swerved around a corner. Herr Damrosch rolled over her slipper, leaving it awash with blood. Pain swelled along her leg, but she could not shift it. Freeing her right hand, she touched Alexei's face.

"No!" She moaned.

Blood covered him. Was he still alive? He could not be dead. Not just when they had discovered the beginnings of love.

Her voice scraped her throat as she cried, "Help me! I think he is dying. Help us! Someone, help us!"

Tears burned her face, but she ignored them. The anguish in her leg was increasing as Herr Damrosch's weight bent her foot to a strange angle. She feared her ankle would snap.

The carriage rolled to a stop. Light flashed by the window seconds after someone leapt from the driver's seat. Wanting to call to Rusak, she discovered her voice had disappeared in the void of agony. Herr Damrosch must be dead. He had not moved, not even to breathe.

Just like Alexei. As tightly as he pressed her to the wall, she could not tell if he was alive or not.

"No," she whispered, "do not be dead."

If only she did not hurt so badly . . .

The light vanished. Wondering why they were being abandoned in their greatest need, she struggled to remain conscious. If she surrendered to the tentacles of pain, she might never reopen her eyes. She had to survive. She must survive because . . . No answer entered her head.

The door opened. When she saw several lanterns, she realized that Rusak had gone for assistance.

In a whisper, she begged, "Rusak, help Alexei. Please."

Hearing shouts, Michelle fought unconsciousness as something heavy slid past her feet. A scream echoed in her ears, but she could not tell if it came from her or someone else.

The pressure holding her to the wall lessened. She wanted to whisper Alexei's name, but no sound emerged save for a moan. Someone touched her face, and she focused on a mouth moving in front of her. No words entered the haze separating her from everything but pain.

"Alexei?" she whispered with the last of her strength.

A bright light and hands moving along her hardly pierced her stupor until fingers touched her left arm. She screamed with the renewed agony that journeyed with her into oblivion.

Michelle woke to pain. It cleared her mind of the webs of senselessness. She opened her eyes, but nothing told her where she was or what had happened.

"Alexei? Alexei?" Even to her ears, her voice sounded like a frog croaking.

Where was Alexei? He had been with her only a moment ago. Hadn't he?

If only she did not hurt so badly . . .

"Hush," came a woman's soft voice. "Rest, child."

Forcing her eyes open again, Michelle saw the ceiling of her bedroom in the apartment. Slowly she focused on Frau Schlissel.

"Count Vatutin is alive," Frau Schlissel said quietly. "He shall be in to see you soon."

She closed her eyes, and a smile wafted along her lips. If Alexei was coming to see her, he must not be badly hurt. Joy thudded through her heart.

An arm beneath her shoulders tilted her up enough so she could swallow the warm liquid placed against her mouth. Whether it was tea or coffee or heated brandy, her senses were too deadened to tell. All she could feel was the never-ending pain on her left side.

Slowly that faded as she drifted into a world where there was no beginning and no ending and no now. She simply was.

For that moment, it was enough.

Some time after she first woke, Michelle opened her eyes again. A second or a century could have passed. With the drapes drawn over the window, she could not tell if it was midday or midnight. The caress of rain against the panes comforted her. The sleet must have turned to rain as the day warmed.

She groaned as she tried to stretch. An ache along her back warned that she had been lying in the same position for too long.

"Lie quietly, Fraulein D'Orage."

Michelle saw a strange man bending over her. She screamed. Or at least she tried to scream. All that emerged was a moan.

"Alexei!" she whispered. "Alexei, help me please!"

"What is she saying?" grumbled the man. "Is it French?"

Frau Schlissel answered, "She is distraught and asking for Count Vatutin." Coming into Michelle's view, she whispered, "Hush, child. No one will hurt you again. Here. Drink this. It will help the pain."

When a cup was placed at Michelle's lips, she realized how parched her throat was. She gulped the honeyed tea, and her eyelids drooped. The pillows came up to surround her as she sank into the nothingness again.

The pattern continued over and over. Michelle woke, tried to battle her pain, drank some sweetened tea, and fell asleep again. Finally she realized there must be a sleeping potion in the tea.

When she woke one sunny day, the room was bright. Inching her face toward the right, she saw that the drapes had been pulled aside to let in the sunshine. Ice frosted the panes.

It was cold again. She wondered when it had stopped raining. Then she told herself not to be foolish. Surely more than a day had passed since . . . Her mind veered away from the past.

In the distance, church bells chimed. Sunday, she decided. Only on Sunday would she hear so many bells ringing. It sounded as if every church in Vienna had joined the symphony.

Underneath that exultant clanging came a hushed squeak. The door opening. She had fearfully waited for that sound after the apartment was ransacked. Now . . . was Alexei coming to see her?

When a man entered, she knew that she had seen him before, although she could not recall where. His black frock coat and dark breeches resembled a raven's feathers. White eyebrows matched the few wisps of hair he had remaining.

A tired smile deepened the lines in his face. "Good afternoon, Fraulein D'Orage."

"Who are you?"

"Herr Doktor Telemann." He adjusted the glasses perched on the very tip of his long nose. "It is good to see you awake, Fraulein. How do you feel?"

"Horrible," she answered with a weak smile. All her

muscles, even those in her face, were so stiff, she was surprised she could move them.

He grinned, transforming his angular face. "Unfortunately that is what your recovery requires. I did not want to keep you sedated any longer."

"How long?"

As he placed a dark satchel on the chair and opened it, he murmured, "You were on your way back from a ball last Friday night, correct?"

"A week ago Friday," answered Frau Schlissel from a bench near the foot of the bed. Until now, Michelle had not realized she was there.

He glanced at the housekeeper and away quickly. "Almost a fortnight then. Today is the Feast of the Immaculate Conception." Harrumphing deep in his throat, he continued, "Now let's look at that arm of yours."

Her gaze followed his fingers as he touched the bandages swathing her left arm from the middle of her palm to past her elbow. Two wooden splints lay on either side of it.

The doctor said, "I shall be gentle, but I must examine it."

He lifted her arm slightly, and everything telescoped into blackness as pain surged over her. "No!" she cried, but heard only a moan. She did not want to be lost in oblivion again.

A cool cloth against her cheek offered comfort. She blinked and saw Frau Schlissel leaning over her, concern on her face. "There, child. I know it hurts, but Herr Doktor will be as quick as possible."

"What is wrong with me?"

"Your leg is healing well, for it was little more than a scratch. A ball struck the bones in your forearm, fracturing them."

"Ball?" She gasped.

Memories exploded around Michelle as the gunshots had through the carriage. Clenching her right hand, she fought to silence the echo of her own screams. Again and again and again, the balls had struck the carriage.

"Fraulein D'Orage!"

At the doctor's tight voice, she looked up to see that his face was as drawn as Frau Schlissel's. "I will . . ." She took a steadying breath. "I shall be fine."

"Of course you will be." He smiled. "What you must do now is rest. You need to remain in bed and have quiet for at least another three or four days."

"Can Alexei come and see me?"

His bushy eyebrows jutted. "Fraulein, has no one told you—"

Frau Schlissel interrupted, "Herr Doktor, may I speak to you for a moment?"

Michelle wanted to protest, but she had too little strength. She watched as the doctor and Frau Schlissel stood by the door and spoke too quietly for her to hear. Fear flashed through her, as overpowering as the pain. Until now, lost in her drugged dreams, she had not questioned Frau Schlissel's assertion that Alexei was fine.

"Tell me," she begged in a cracking voice. "Is he alive?"

The doctor came back and took his satchel off the chair. Sitting, he took Michelle's hand. "Count Vatutin is alive, but barely. He was struck many times. Fortunately none of his vital organs was pierced. Frau Schlissel lied to you on my orders. We did not want your recovery jeopardized by your worries for your—" He cleared his throat. "For your employer."

"But will he live?"

"We should know soon."

"Soon? You don't know yet?" Her eyes widened in horror.

"You were both very lucky," he said grimly as he stood. "The assassins appear to have been Herr Damrosch's enemies. You must have been struck by the balls that went awry. Herr Damrosch did not survive."

"And Rusak?"

"He is fine," Frau Schlissel said. Her smile was gentle. "Truthfully, he is fine."

Michelle stared as the doctor accepted his hat from Frau Schlissel. Nodding a farewell, he told her he would be back to check on her tomorrow. Numbly watching him leave, she tried to erase the memories of the attack. She could hear her own screams and, even more clearly, Alexei's moans as he risked his life to shield her.

"Stop!" she cried. "I do not want to remember!"

"Hush, child," soothed Frau Schlissel as she put another cloth on Michelle's aching forehead. "Count Vatutin must have quiet."

"Be honest. Will he live?"

"Herr Doktor is hopeful."

"He must live!"

"No," said the housekeeper with a gentle shake of her head. "Nothing is guaranteed. All we can do is wait and pray."

"I am not good at waiting," she whispered.

Smoothing tangled hair away from Michelle's forehead, Frau Schlissel murmured, "And at praying?"

"I have been doing that since the guns fired." Tears welled in her eyes.

"Then do more, child, for both Count Vatutin and yourself. 'Tis Christmastide. Mayhap you both will be well enough to get out of bed in time for Christmas Day."

"Is that possible?" she asked, clinging to any hope.

Frau Schlissel smiled with compassion as gentle as her fingers, which were tucking a blanket around Michelle. "Anything may be possible. For now, you must rest."

"Frau Schlissel?" She grasped the woman's arm. "Is Rusak really unharmed?"

"Yes, and for that we must be grateful. He has overseen Count Vatutin's care, leaving me free to sit with you." She patted the bed. "Sleep now."

She grumbled, "That is all I have done since . . ." Tears filled her eyes again. So many times she had questioned

Alexei's reasons for being kind to her, accusing him of having an ulterior motive.

"Don't cry, child. It will not help now."

Shocked, Michelle touched her cheek. Tears coursed along it. Sobs gushed out in a torrent.

When Frau Schlissel placed a cup to Michelle's lips, she drank the sweetened tea gratefully. She wanted to be enfolded in the velvet forgetfulness of sleep, where she could dream that she was in Alexei's arms again.

Chapter Fifteen

"Fraulein D'Orage!"

Michelle ignored Frau Schlissel's reprimand. She had meant the curse sincerely and would say it more loudly if she bumped her left leg again while sliding to the edge of the bed. Her eyes narrowed as she gauged the distance to the door. She wanted to get up so she could convince the doctor to let her visit Alexei.

Each day Herr Doktor Telemann brought her a report on Alexei's condition, but trite phrases like "No change for the worse" and "He is doing as expected" did little to ease her anxiety. She wanted to see with her own eyes how he was healing.

A distant knocking intruded. Frau Schlissel said, "Stay where you are, Fraulein. I will see who is at the door."

Michelle nodded but, as soon as the housekeeper left, inched her toes toward the floor. She winced as the bandages around her leg caught on her nightgown. Reaching across the sling supporting her left arm, she loosened her nightgown. Off balance, she clutched the covers as she tipped toward the floor.

She trembled as she righted herself. She was incredibly weak. As she glanced at the pillows against the headboard, the temptation to rest in their welcoming nest again was intoxicating. She fought it. She must escape from this bed.

A soft moan escaped her pursed lips as her right foot stretched for the floor. No matter what she did, she strained her left side, which burned as if it were afire. Half-on and half-off the bed, she panted with the exertion of the simple movement. Gingerly she lowered her left foot to the scratchy rug.

Pain blasted through her. She sagged, brushing her left arm against the covers. The agony escalated until she was sure it would rip her mind away, but she refused to let her wounds halt her. Inching along the bed, she leaned on the mattress with every step.

The room she once had crossed in several paces now seemed as gigantic as the ballroom where she had danced with Alexei. When she reached the end of the bed, she clung to the upright.

"Don't be stupid!" she snapped. "You will never be able to do it until you try."

Her anger at her feebleness spurred her feet forward. Slowly her fingers released the footboard. Swaying, she fought for her balance.

Counting one small step after another, Michelle knew each was a victory. She smiled when she touched the back of the chair. She wanted to shout out her joy, but must not disturb Alexei's recovery.

"What are you doing?"

She smiled as she faced an astounded Frau Schlissel. "I am walking, or at least that is what I am trying to do."

"Did Herr Doktor give you permission to get out of bed?"

" 'Tis time."

"He shall be upset. Come. I shall help you back to bed before he arrives."

"Yes," Michelle replied as her legs trembled with exertion. She knew she must be cautious, or she might jeopardize her healing so far. She let Frau Schlissel help her onto the bed. Leaning her head back into the pillows, she closed her eyes and sank into their comfort. "Who was at the door?"

"No one important, Fraulein. Do not fret about it."

"Frau Schlissel, who was there?"

The housekeeper refused to meet Michelle's eyes and plucked at the brightly embroidered apron she always wore over her dark skirt. "It was a caller for you. His Royal Highness Prince Bartholomew."

"Bartholomew is calling here?"

With unease etched on her face, Frau Schlissel nodded. "Almost every day."

"Why haven't you told me?"

"Would knowing that have helped or hindered your recovery? His visits made you uncomfortable before. I answer his questions and send him away as politely as I can, using the doctor's order that neither you nor Count Vatutin may have visitors."

"And Bartholomew accepts that?"

"If I may be so bold, Fraulein D'Orage, I would guess that he cares very much for you and does not want to risk endangering you."

A hearty laugh resounded along the hall.

Frau Schlissel rushed out the bedroom door. Her gentle face was twisted with anger when she returned. "Prince Bartholomew insists that he will sit in the parlor until you agree to see him."

"Tell him not to be so stupid." Michelle winced as she sat straighter. "It is ridiculous—"

"Not to receive me," Bartholomew said from the doorway.

She gripped the covers and lifted them over her nightgown as he strode into the room. No one could deny that Prince Bartholomew, heir to the German state of Coxe-Saxony-Colburg, had a regal mien. Handing his ivory-tipped walking stick to Frau Schlissel, he removed his leather gloves and tossed them in the housekeeper's direction. In the sunlight, his ebony hair glowed with blue lights.

"Bartholomew," Michelle said quietly, "I do not feel hearty enough to see you yet."

"My dear, did you think anyone could keep me away? You look wondrous." He bent to kiss her.

Averting her face, she began, "Bartholomew, I—"

"Don't say anything, my dear. Let me just look at you. How horrible it would have been if you had died imagining I was angry with you!"

She closed her eyes. "Bartholomew, please go."

He sat on the edge of her bed, ignoring the gasp of outrage from Frau Schlissel. A diffident wave of his hand dismissed the housekeeper, but she remained by the door.

"Don't order my friends about!" Michelle stated, her exasperation strengthening her.

"Friend?" He glanced at Frau Schlissel and smiled coldly. "You have very odd notions, my dear, if you call servants your friends."

"At least Frau Schlissel concerns herself with my recovery. She does not refuse to listen to a polite request to leave so I may rest."

Taking her right hand, he murmured, "Just let me look at you, my dear. I want you to get better so you can come with me to Coxe-Saxony-Colburg."

"My opinion on that has not changed," she said tautly. She almost added that her arm and leg were injured, not her head, but she did not want to insult him more.

He bent to kiss her cheek. His smile dimmed as she pulled away. "The doctor is pleased with your progress?"

"The doctor is very optimistic about my recovery and about Alexei's. Thank you for your visit, Bartholomew."

He stood and bowed over her right hand. "I shall come to see you tomorrow."

"No, you shall not!"

Instantly Frau Schlissel seconded her command. "Your

Highness, it is imperative that Fraulein D'Orage remain undisturbed during her recovery. If you wish updates on her condition, I shall be glad to send them to you, but, please, Your Highness, do not call until you receive word that she has recovered.''

"I do not take orders from servants,'' he said with a snarl as he snatched his cane and gloves from her.

"You will if you care for her.''

With a growl, he stamped out of the room. Frau Schlissel paused to look back at Michelle. With a smile, the housekeeper winked.

Michelle relaxed into the pillows. At last, they had convinced Bartholomew to stay away.

Or she hoped they had.

Michelle waved aside Frau Schlissel's assistance as she paused in the middle of the room. If she showed any weakness, the housekeeper would insist she return to bed. Only Michelle's assertion that she was going to visit Alexei today and Frau Schlissel could help or not as she wished had convinced the housekeeper to allow her to try to reach the connecting door.

Wincing, she put more weight on her left foot. Pain climbed her leg, but she hid it. With her right hand sliding along the wall, she walked with slow, uneven steps toward the door to Alexei's room. Knocking on the door almost knocked her off her feet.

When it opened, Rusak put out his arms to steady her. *How Michelle? You understand me?*

She started to nod, but the motion sent anguish through her head. "I cannot answer you as Herr Professor Waldstein would wish, Rusak, but I can understand what you are saying.''

Concentrating on his fingers, she tried not to let the motion unfocus her eyes. She smiled. He was relieved to be able to communicate with someone again. For the first time, she realized how cut off Rusak had been.

"Are you all right?" she asked.

Hidden by carriage. Shooting at inside. Sorry slow.

"You saved our lives with your quick actions. I—" When she swayed, a hand settled under her right elbow.

Frau Schlissel said, "You should go back to bed. You are not yet healed enough."

"No!" She had come too far to return to her bed without assuring herself that Alexei was indeed alive. Although Rusak was trying to tell her something, her eyes blurred.

Michelle staggered into the room. Rusak's hand on her arm steered her toward the large bed. Her rubbery legs struggled to carry her across the room. Had it grown larger?

"Why are you risking yourself to come here?" Alexei's voice was cold.

"Alexei!" She put her right hand on the bed to steady herself.

Her stomach cramped when she saw he wore many more bandages than she did. One was wrapped around his head and covered his right eye. Another nearly met it along his right cheek. Beneath his dressing gown, the bulge of more bandages widened around his upper arm.

She whispered, "How are you feeling?"

"Better than you, I would wager. I have never seen a face so colorless in my life. How could you be so stupid and come here when you are not yet healed?" Raising his voice, he called, "Rusak, where is your head today? Just because Michelle is being feebleminded, must you be? Get her a chair before she falls."

Michelle stared. Alexei had been terse with her before. He had taunted her for her innocence. He had chided her for her mistakes, but never in a voice as frigid as this one. Even though she could see so little of his face, she could not mistake the fury there.

When a chair appeared behind her, she sat gratefully. She glanced over her shoulder to see the door closing.

Thankful for Rusak's understanding of their need to be alone for a few minutes, she smiled and looked at Alexei again. Mayhap he was just as frustrated as she was with being infirm.

"Why are you here?" he asked in the same demanding tone.

"I wanted to be certain you are alive."

"Barely."

"I am sorry."

He pushed himself forward and gripped her right arm—with his left hand, because his right one was lost within bandages. "Sorry? Why? Because Herr Doktor Telemann doubts I shall ever regain use of my right hand or sight in my right eye?"

"Oh, Alexei—"

"Save your sympathy for yourself, Michelle. I have neither need nor desire for it." He squinted at her, and she wondered if his head ached as hers did. The ache had grown more ferocious since she had come in here. "I understand you were hit twice."

"And my bonnet once." Her attempt at humor fell flat when he scowled.

He became wavy, but not from her dizziness. Tears burned along her cheeks. She reached out to him, but he drew his bandaged arm away. Why was he opening a chasm between them that had never existed?

"Alexei," she whispered through her sobs, "when I thought you were dying, I thought I would, too. I would do anything to—"

"You cannot change what happened. Neither can I. We cannot change anything that happened that night."

Michelle recoiled as his words struck her as savagely as the ball had sliced through her. "Would you change what happened in the conservatory?"

Instead of answering, he picked up a bell set on the table by his bed. He rang it, and the door opened. "Rusak, will you help Michelle back to her room?"

She slowly came to her feet. When she winced as she

put too much weight on her left leg, Alexei's gaze shifted away from her. She raised her chin and forced the rest of her tears back down her throat.

"Thank you," she whispered to Rusak as he assisted her to the connecting door.

She could not keep from looking back at the bed as Rusak opened the door. Alexei was staring at the canopy over his bed. If he sensed her gaze on him, he did not acknowledge it.

As clearly as if he had shouted it, she comprehended the truth. Nothing, but his death, would halt Alexei from doing what he must. All those around him must accept that.

Or leave.

Alexei frowned at the sound of laughter beyond his room. He tossed the letter he had been reading on his desk and slowly stood. Crossing the room, he opened the door to the hallway. Then, knowing that the bandages over one ear had misled him, he realized the laughter came from Michelle's room.

Not just her musical laugh, but a man's laugh. A savage pulse thundered through him. He ignored it. The laugh was not Prince Charming's, but Rusak's.

He fisted his hand on the wall as he opened the door a crack to peer through it. Frau Schlissel set a tray on the table by Michelle's bed and poured a cup of coffee. Handing it to Michelle, she smiled.

How easy it would be to get sucked into that joy again! Raising his other hand, he stared at the bandages that concealed his fingers in a white mitt. Hadn't he learned the cost of letting his attention wander from his work? Exulting in his pleasure with Michelle and the anticipation for more had betrayed him into thinking more about her than about his enemies.

Your enemies never rest. Sophie's voice resonated in his

ears like his own conscience. She had told him that more than once, but the last time had been only hours before she left on the assignment that would be her last.

"Frohliche Weihnacten!" came a voice from the other room. Frau Schlissel's voice.

"Christmas?" he muttered, then swore. *Verflucht!* He had not guessed the year was so near its end. Too many days had been wasted while he was imprisoned in his bed like a mewling baby.

"Frohliche Weihnacten!" At the happiness in Michelle's voice, he knew it was not only his days that had been wasted, but his nights.

He swore again. How much more did she need to suffer before he acknowledged the truth? His hope to keep her safe by bringing her with him had been futile. Instead of protecting her, he had made her a target of his enemies . . . of *their* enemies. That those enemies had been hers as a birthright changed nothing. He should not have brought her to Vienna with him. Instead he should have found a place where she could be hidden for as long as necessary.

When Rusak appeared in his narrow view, Alexei was amazed to see his assistant bend and kiss Michelle on the cheek as he made some of those bizarre signs with his fingers. She must have understood because she laughed and bade him a happy Christmas, too, as if nothing were amiss.

With a sigh, Alexei pushed away from the door. He could not imagine where in Europe the daughter of Sophie D'Orage might be safe now. Going to his desk, he pulled out a drawer. He lifted a small package wrapped in brown paper. It was time for this.

Alexei was not surprised when the laughter faltered as he walked into Michelle's room. He nodded to the house-keeper's halfhearted greeting. Rusak folded his arms over his chest, his smile gone.

Verflucht! He had thought Rusak, of all of the others in the apartment, would understand why Alexei was acting as he did. Rusak knew the perils of this life and the cost exacted from anyone who got in the way.

Looking away from his friend, Alexei glanced at where Michelle sat up against a mound of lacy pillows in her bed. A mistake, he knew instantly, because he could not pull his gaze from her soft lips and eyes that revealed too much— fearful anticipation and stubborn love . . . and the yearning that kept him from sleeping. With her hair drawn back into a single ebony braid and the lace surrounding her, she possessed innocence and sensuality that drove him mad with desire.

Frau Schlissel said, "There is enough for two on the tray. Rusak and I are going to Christmas services, so, Fraulein, why don't you ask Count Vatutin to dine with you? Coming, Rusak?"

When the door closed behind them, Alexei waited for Michelle to speak. She remained silent, so he asked, "Can we ignore such an edict?"

"No." She motioned toward the chair by her bed. "Why don't you sit here?"

He almost laughed with irony. She was treating him with the coldness he had offered her on her single call to see how he fared. As he sat, she peered under the cloth over the dishes.

Her eyes widened, and he saw a hint of the happiness that had been on her face before he came into the room. "Oh, my! Strudel!" Picking up a pastry covered with strawberry jam, she tried to rip it apart.

"Let me help," he said.

"Help? You?"

He ignored her sarcasm as he set the small package on the floor and took the other end of the pastry out of her hand. She gave a sharp tug, and it broke in two.

"Between us," he said quietly, "we have one complete set of hands. This should make for an interesting meal."

"Interesting is not the word I would have chosen."

Alexei did not answer as she spooned eggs onto a dish

for him. Although she appeared outwardly accepting of her infirmity, he knew she hated being unable to do what she once had done easily. Just as he did. He silenced his grim thoughts. It was Christmas Day.

He picked up the small package and placed it on the tray. "Open it."

"A Christmas gift?"

"Not exactly."

Michelle frowned, then set the dish down. Taking the package, she set it on her lap. Glancing at Alexei, she saw his intense expression that even his bandages could not conceal. This was important to him. And her? She almost asked him that, but that would make her as bitter as he was.

Opening the paper where it had been folded together around whatever was inside, she smoothed the paper aside and opened a small box. "Oh, my!" she said softly as she lifted a miniature portrait out. Not a single portrait, but one of a man and a woman. The woman was *Maman*. She had never seen the man before. "Is this my father?"

"Your mother told me that it was of her and Michel, painted shortly after they wed."

She did not trust herself to speak as she stared at the handsome man whose zest for life burned in his eyes. His arm was around her mother's shoulders. On his lapel, he wore the tricolor favored by those who supported the Revolution in France. The Revolution where he had been executed on the guillotine.

"After Sophie died," he said quietly, "I went to where she had been staying. I wanted to collect any materials that she might have left behind." Tapping the top of the frame, he sighed. "I found this. At the time, I did not think of how I was depriving you of it. Now you have it, as you should have years ago."

"Thank you. It is nice of you to—"

"This has nothing to do with being nice," he fired back. She gasped as he surged to his feet. "Alexei—"

"I want you to look at those two happy people," he continued as if she had not spoken, "and see what their ideals cost them. Your father dead because the ones he supported turned on him like rabid dogs. Your mother dead because she was determined to continue the work he had started to bring peace to France." He bent and pressed his mouth to hers.

She should push him away, but she could not. Stroking his uninjured shoulder, she let his kiss sweep her away from pain into precious pleasure. His tongue probed deep into her mouth, demanding more. She wanted his arms around her as she lost herself in his caresses as she had that one magical night.

"No," she murmured when he drew back too soon.

"Exactly."

She gazed at him, baffled. "What do you mean?"

"I mean you are right. I should not be kissing you when I need to be focusing on my work."

Putting the portrait on the bed, she stood. She held on to the tester, not sure if she could move any farther when she quivered with rage. "So that is how you will report the whole of this to your superiors? That you were betwattled by passion and it will never happen again?"

"I will tell them the truth."

"That you were so anxious to take my virginity that you were willing to risk even your mission and that you are sorry for your mistake and it will never happen again. Alexei Vatutin would not be so foolish to ever feel anything but hatred for the rest of his life." She picked up the portrait. "You may have thought you were giving me this to prove your point, but you have failed. My mother and father dared to love each other *in spite* of the dangers they faced. They never blamed those dangers because they were afraid of opening themselves to love."

"Michelle—"

"Are you going to deny it?"

"No." He walked to the connecting door. "I cannot

deny the truth, nor can I deny that I will do anything to keep you safe."

"Even break my heart?"

"Haven't I proven already that I am more than willing to do that?" He closed the door behind him.

Michelle sank to the chair where he had been sitting. She stared at the portrait in her hand, but it was too late to ask all the questions she had. Even if she could speak to her parents, she doubted if they would have an answer to help her now.

Chapter Sixteen

Although Alexei left the apartment no more than she did, Michelle was not surprised when he asked her to help with some correspondence. Occasionally he had visitors. Some she knew. Others were strangers, but all seemed eager to discuss the unwieldy progress of the Congress. She watched as Alexei listened. She remembered how he had told her that he never forgot what he heard, and she knew he was gathering information from his guests.

"You want me to help with your secret work?" she asked, remembering how he had chastised her for coming into his room when he was working.

He smoothed her hair back toward the utilitarian braids she wore. "Who else can I trust as I do you?"

"Rusak."

"Obviously, but Rusak never learned to write."

"Never?"

He smiled tightly. "Now you sound like a schoolteacher again. I need *your* help. Will you help me?"

"Haven't I always?"

"Not always willingly."

She smiled and brushed his face, which was thick with golden whiskers that had swallowed his once neat mustache. As he had told her once, his beard was a splotched array of colors, none alike. The curve of his jaw was shadowed by darker brown, but beneath his mustache, the hair was as blond as atop his head.

His bandaged hand covered hers, holding her but not imprisoning her. When his other arm encircled her waist, her eyes closed in surrender. Sparks tickled her skin as he tasted her cheek. The rough texture of his bandage scraped her face, but she thought only of his heated lips and the softness of his beard against her skin.

She raised her arm to encircle his shoulders, but pain burned her. When she moaned, Alexei asked, "Did I hurt you?"

"No." Her wry smile eased the lines across his forehead. "I hurt myself. I bumped my arm on you."

"I am sorry."

"I am not." She teased the small hairs at the nape of his neck. "Only that you have stopped kissing me."

"That can be remedied very quickly." He pressed his lips against hers, then led her along the hallway.

Michelle wished he were inviting her into his room to exult in passion, but, when she saw his mouth tighten, she knew he was thinking again of work.

"Close the door," Alexei ordered over his shoulder as he gestured toward a chair by his desk. "Sit down."

She did as he requested. The abrupt return of his autocratic tone irritated her. Again the jovial, gentle lover had disappeared.

"You will find writing materials there," he said.

"Where?" She stared at the cluttered desk. Before the attack on them, no papers had been left on it. She doubted if these had any importance, or he would have hidden them.

When he swept the papers aside, he opened an ink bottle and set it beside a stack of clean paper. "I will tell you what I want written. You must write it exactly as I tell you. You are a good speller, I assume.''

"I believe so.''

"Don't worry. I shall check it when you are finished.''

Her hand clenched on the clean paper. "Stop being condescending to me, Alexei! *You* need me to help you.''

"You don't need me?'' He slanted toward her. Yesterday the doctor had removed the heaviest bandages, so only a small one covered his right eye and temple. He could have been a rapacious pirate. "Who pays for the roof over your head and Herr Doktor Telemann for his many visits? You smell beef cooking in the kitchen. Could you afford to buy that?''

"Mayhap! If you paid me!''

He laughed without humor. "So you want an accounting of your wages?''

"No!'' she cried, irritated. She did not want to argue with him. She wanted to help him, for, when he completed his work in Vienna, they could leave and give his enemies no second chance to kill them. "Tell me what you want me to write.''

He grumbled something and dropped into a chair he pulled beside hers. "Put today's date at the top of the page.'' He smiled. "You write with a nice hand.''

"Years of penmanship lessons. You didn't think *Maman* chose St. Bernard's without thought, did you? She often said my lessons would prepare me for life.'' She looked at the page in front of her. "I doubt if she meant a life like this.''

"Doubtlessly you are right.'' He sighed. "All right. Write this. 'Up six, across one. Morning effect.' End of sentence. New sentence.'' He paused, composing his next words. " 'Eager rigid week.' ''

"Excuse me?''

"Just write what I tell you.''

"Alexei, this is absurd. It makes no sense whatsoever.''

"Exactly.'' He placed his foot on the stool in front of

him and winced. "Damn leg. How do you make recovering look so easy?"

"I listen to the doctor."

He ignored her sarcasm. "Write, 'Blue afternoon sings thirty-five. Christmas—' "

"A code!" She stared at the crazy pattern of words. "It is a code!"

"Of course. Now will you please write?"

Michelle bent to her task. When she finished the first page, he told her to start another. As an hour passed, her fingers grew cramped, but she did not complain. It was exhilarating to be doing something other than sitting and waiting for the day to pass. That he spoke slowly enough for her to maintain her pace was a pleasant shock.

Finally, as twilight was inching across the floor, Alexei said, "That is the last of those, *Liebchen.*"

Her hand trembled as she handed him the page. *Liebchen?* He had not called her that since the attack on the carriage. When he lowered his eyes, his jaw working, she knew he had not meant to say that. Why? Because it showed that his feelings for her had not changed?

Alexei read the letter. With a taut smile, he folded it and put it aside. "One more, if you do not mind."

Although she wanted to speak about the word that hung between them, she said, "Go ahead."

"Address it to Monsieur René LaTulippe, Paris, France."

"Paris?"

"Write it in French."

"If that is what you want." Michelle now was completely baffled. Why would he want her to write in a language he could not read?

He smiled. " 'Monsieur LaTulippe, I regret to inform you of the demise of Alexei Vatutin.' "

"What?"

"Just write. 'He was shot by assassins aiming at Herr Claus Damrosch, a diplomat from Prussia. Accept my condolences.' Sign it 'Sincerely' and your name."

"My name?" Michelle frowned.

"It cannot be from me. Dead men do not write to let others know of their tragic deaths."

"But my name? Shouldn't I just make up a name?"

He shook his head and gave her a weary smile. "LaTulippe knows that you are traveling with me. It is most logical coming from you."

"Is he one of your superiors?"

"Do not ask too many questions." He took the letter from her and set it aside so the ink would dry. "I am just trying to forestall any potential problems."

Putting the top on the bottle of ink, she said, "He is sure to discover that I—or rather, that you are lying."

"News travels very, very slowly through the Alps. This should keep him satisfied until we are ready to leave Vienna."

"And then?"

He smiled as he stroked her hair. "Then I shall begin my next assignment, Michelle."

"And me?"

"You shall have an assignment, too."

"With you?"

"It is possible. We have had a rough start." He tilted her face up toward his. "Having you near reminds me that not everyone is accursedly wicked."

"I don't know, Alexei. Sometimes the serenity of St. Bernard's seems to be the most perfect thing I can imagine."

"And the most boring."

"Admittedly, but I must make this decision with care."

He patted her shoulder as he stood. "You cannot escape what you have become by going back to what you were. Many in Vienna remember your mother and want to know if you are related to her. They are determined to discover the truth."

"I should have traveled under an assumed name."

"That would have made no difference. Questions of how

a Russian delegate has an incredibly lovely Swiss woman as his mistress have been eagerly repeated throughout Vienna. Someone with connections in Zurich is sure to discover you left St. Bernard's to join me." He shrugged, wincing as he moved his shoulder. "Your choices are limited. You can work for us, doing what you are told to do—"

"Or . . . ?"

"Or open yourself up for attacks like this." He tapped her bandaged arm lightly. "Choose with care. The wrong choice may be your last."

"Alexei?"

"Hmm?" At Michelle's question, Alexei continued to peruse the newspaper that Rusak brought each afternoon from the shop on the corner. As soon as Rusak delivered it, Alexei sat in the parlor and read every word. He must be looking for information on whatever had brought him to Vienna.

Reaching across the arm of his chair, Michelle drew the pages aside. This was the first time they had been alone in the two weeks since Christmas. The housekeeper, the doctor, or Rusak always kept them company. Frau Schlissel was at the butcher's, Rusak was attending his lesson with Herr Professor Waldstein, and Herr Doktor Telemann was not due back for a week.

"Alexei?" she repeated. When he glanced at her, she asked, "Who fired on our carriage?"

His brow reached toward the smaller bandage across his forehead. "Do you always jump into a conversation with such a question?"

"I would like an answer to that question." *And to why you believe keeping me safe is more important than my heart.*

"As I would." He tapped the page in front of him. "The Prussians are still demanding an investigation to uncover why Damrosch was murdered."

"You know the reason," she whispered, putting her hand on his arm. "He was in our carriage. Whoever fired on us had no idea that Herr Damrosch was in our carriage and sitting where we usually sat. Alexei, they were hoping to kill us. To kill you!"

He rubbed the scar on his cheek, but turned a page as if he were more interested in the latest gossip than in finding out who had tried to murder them. "Such outbursts are not good for your recovery."

She tugged on the pages again. When they ripped, he glared at her, but she refused to be intimidated. "Be honest with me!"

"All right." He put the paper on his lap. "I will be honest with you. I do not want you to get involved in things you need not know about."

"I am involved already." She pointed to her splinted arm.

He shook his head. "No, you are not truly involved. You just got in the way."

"Alexei, you cannot protect me by leaving me ignorant. It is not—"

"Fair? Very little is in life."

"Alexei!"

He sighed. "All right, Michelle. They were shooting at us—or at me, if you prefer. You are right. They could not have known that Damrosch was with us."

"Then who are they? Will they try again?"

"I don't know."

"You do not . . . How many enemies do you have?"

"All I need is one who wants me dead."

Closing her eyes, Michelle sagged into her chair. When she had been at St. Bernard's School for Girls and had longed for adventure, she had not considered it would take such a horrible turn as this.

Alexei's hand covered hers. She looked at him, startled, as her heart pounded. Did he know that she wanted his touch even more than she wanted answers to her questions? Could he guess that she had instigated this conversation in hopes of rebuilding what had been destroyed at the moment those guns had fired?

"Michelle, you know me. Don't you think I would have done something about those bastards by now if I had known who they were?" he asked.

"Yes," she whispered. Transfixed by his strong emotions, she stared, unable to say more.

"Then trust me to do as I must."

"And me?"

His brow ruffled. "What of you?"

"Trust me to do what I must." Pulling her hand from beneath his, she curved it along his face as her mouth slanted across his.

His hand caught her face, drawing her back. Then, with a moan, he leaned forward so his lips touched hers tentatively, as if he feared hurting her. She sighed with eagerness. At the sound, his gentleness disappeared as he pressed her back into the settee. Her need for him burst forth, refusing to be fettered again. He decorated her face with scintillating kisses as he sat beside her. When his hand moved up her breast, heated liquid flowed deep within her, leaving a river of rapture in its wake.

Slowly he opened the neckline of her wrapper. He was careful not to touch her sling as he bent to place his lips against the curves above her lacy chemise. Her fingers twisted through his hair as his tongue slid along her.

This was what she wanted. This was what she was willing to risk anything to have again.

He gazed down into her eyes as he loosened the sash at her waist. His hand paused at the sound of boots on the landing.

Michelle watched Alexei's face harden. "No," she whispered, "it is not wrong to hold me like this."

His hand stroked her cheek. "I know. Wait here."

He stood and walked to the door, pausing to pull a poker from the hearth. He raised it at an assertive knock.

"No!" cried Michelle. "Alexei, it is Bartholomew!"

Alexei muttered his favorite curse as he put the poker aside and reached for the knob.

Bartholomew frowned as Alexei opened the door; then a superior smile twisted his lips. "Good afternoon, Vatutin."

"Your Highness."

"Is Fraulein D'Orage at home?"

Alexei gave a terse laugh. "Where do you expect her to go when she has a broken arm and can walk about only by leaning on the furniture?"

"Will you tell her I am here?"

"Let me see if she is at home for you, Your Highness." Rudely he turned his back on Bartholomew. "Michelle, are you at home for Prince Charming?"

Hearing a grumble beyond the door, Michelle swallowed her laughter. *Poor Bartholomew!* He had added to his worthlessness, in Alexei's opinion, by arriving now. It was tempting to blame Bartholomew for his poor timing, but she must not. "Please have Bartholomew come in. I will push the kettle over the fire."

"You shall do nothing!" Alexei said in the same tight voice. "If you do not promise to sit and forget a hostess's duties, I will not allow Prince Charming in."

"Alexei," she cautioned.

"Promise."

"Yes, I promise."

"Very good." He stepped aside, letting the door open wider.

Bartholomew brushed past Alexei and dropped to his knees by her chair. "My dear, how wondrous to see you well enough to be here." He suddenly frowned. "I can see you and your *employer* were not expecting callers."

Michelle followed Bartholomew's gaze to where her dressing gown gaped. She kept her smile in place as she tightened the sash. "While wearing this sling, I am most comfortable in my wrapper." Uneasily, when he glowered at Alexei, she went on, "I thought you had gone home, and had not heard that you had returned to Vienna."

"With clearer instructions from your father, no doubt." Alexei crossed the room and sat beside her. He showed no sign of any weakness while Bartholomew was in the room.

Bartholomew got up and clasped his hands behind his back. "This is a social call, Vatutin. If you wish to discuss the Congress, I suggest you remember that such things might bore Michelle."

"Michelle bored with politics?" He laughed, but his expression remained cold. "Michelle is as astute as many of the delegates. Mayhap because she has suffered the anguish created by war."

Before Bartholomew could snarl a retort, Michelle said, "Gentlemen, please recall that I can speak for myself. Sit, Bartholomew, and tell us how the news of the Congress has been received in Coxe-Saxony-Colburg."

When Bartholomew sat and began a list of his misadventures of trying to cross the mountains, Alexei listened closely and noticed that Michelle was as well. If this was her attempt to show him that she could be a good partner in his work as well as a delight in his bed, there had been no need. He wanted her in his life and in his arms. But to risk her again . . . He sighed. There had to be an answer. That was something else Sophie had taught him. There always was a way out of any problem. If he found it, he could have his work and Michelle, too.

Asking questions each time Prince Charming faltered, Alexei realized Michelle was watching him. He smiled at her, and her eyes glowed with longing. He struggled to heed Prince Charming, although the chance of learning something valuable from this addle-wit was slight. He would much rather throw Prince Charming out and pull Michelle into his arms.

She asked a question, and the princeling babbled in his attempt to please her. Alexei smiled. She possessed a rare intelligence that outshone even Sophie's . . . and his own. Her touch had beguiled every thought from his head, especially his determination to keep her safe. There *had* to be a solution to this dilemma that would protect her from his enemies and still have her sparkling like the brightest star in a winter sky as she lit his nights with ecstasy.

The droning sound of Prince Charming's voice disappeared as Alexei met Michelle's gaze. In her eyes glowed the desire ravaging him. When he started to move his hand to cover hers, he cursed silently at the bandages encasing his fingers. Soon the bandages would be gone. Then his craving would show pretty, luscious Michelle exactly how much he wanted her. First he had to make sure she was safe. There *must* be some way to do that.

You have to give up everything you love in order to do what you must.

For the first time, Sophie's voice echoing in his head annoyed him. He cursed silently. She had taught him well, but that admonition was one he did not want to accept. He would find a way to have both his work and Michelle. How, he was not sure, but he would. Then he would remind Michelle of the pleasure neither of them could forget.

It would be worth the wait.

Chapter Seventeen

Michelle watched as Herr Doktor Telemann lifted off the bandages that had been on her arm for nearly two months. When she saw the dried blood on the bottom ones, she shuddered. She did not close her eyes as he cut away the layers of filthy linen. The sight before her was not as horrible as her memories of that terrifying night. Her eyes widened as she saw the scar where the ball had struck her.

Fresh air wafted along her skin as the doctor ordered, "Extend your fingers, Fraulein."

She tried, surprised at how cramped they were.

"Do they hurt?" he asked.

"Just stiff."

"And your arm. Bend your elbow. Up first."

She grimaced as her bones creaked from disuse, but her elbow obeyed better than her fingers had. Her smile of pride vanished when he gently touched her forearm.

At her moan, he asked, "Still tender?"

"Yes," she whispered, biting her lip.

"This will take but a moment."

Frau Schlissel came to hold Michelle's hand as the doctor completed his examination. When Michelle's fingers tightened, she feared she was hurting the older woman, but Frau Schlissel said nothing.

"This looks excellent, Fraulein," the doctor said. "A light bandage should be sufficient."

"And the sling?"

"You should wear it for a while longer. If you go out, you must wear it. However, when you are sitting quietly, you should take it off for a few minutes and stretch your arm." He wagged a finger at her. "Only for a few minutes. To do too much too swiftly can harm it. Be sensible, Fraulein, and you should regain full use of your arm. You realize how lucky you are, don't you?"

"Yes," she said as Frau Schlissel retied the sling behind her neck. "Herr Doktor Telemann, what about Alexei?"

He closed his bag. "As soon as I examine him, I will know."

Michelle accepted the scold as her due. Sliding off the bed, she wiggled her fingers and said, "Forgive me, Herr Doktor. I have trouble being patient."

"Mayhap, Fraulein D'Orage, but you have been an excellent patient. Mayhap that is why you are recovering better than I had hoped."

"Did you consider it might be because you are an excellent doctor?"

He chuckled. "I can understand how you have charmed Vienna. If you are as flattering to everyone you have met as you are to this old doctor, you must have them all begging at your feet."

Heat climbed her cheeks. In the past two months while living here quietly, she had given her tongue free rein. She must be careful to watch what she said when she and Alexei were again among the delegates to the Congress, for those diplomats would twist every word she said.

"Do you want help putting away those clothes?" Frau Schlissel asked when the doctor had gone into the other room.

Michelle picked up the small pile. "Thank you, but no. I am glad to have something to do."

"Then I shall return to the kitchen and begin supper."

"A victory supper?"

The housekeeper's eyes twinkled merrily. "That sounds just fine, Fraulein."

Going to the cupboard at the side of her room, Michelle opened the door. She put the clothes on a shelf and started to close the door. With a frown, she bent and looked at where the fabric on the inside of the door had come loose.

An arm snaked around her waist and drew her back against Alexei's hard body. She sighed with undeniable desire as his tongue tickled her earlobe. His finger traced her sling across her throat and along the front of her wrapper. When his hand slipped beneath it to curve around her breast, a craving resonated deep within her.

"Can this come off?" he whispered as he touched the sling. His breath sent quivers along her.

"At night," she struggled to say past her ragged breath. "When we are alone and it is quiet, I am supposed to exercise my hand."

"Perfect, *Liebchen*. I can give you the perfect exercise for your hand. Touch me." He laughed softly as he pulled her to her feet and whirled her to face him.

"Alexei!"

He touched the black patch that covered his eye. "So do I look like a rogue?"

For a long minute, she did not answer. Against his golden hair, the ebony blotch was even more conspicuous. Her fingers trembled as she reached up to the thread holding it in place. "Does your eye hurt?"

"No, but the results of being shot and having the wound become infected are best concealed." He grinned. "Actually, I think the patch is quite dashing."

"It should cause some problems if you wish to go from being Alexei Vatutin to someone else."

Putting his arm around her shoulders, he squeezed

gently. "With all the men wounded from the war, no one will notice another." He looked past her. "Is something wrong with your armoire?"

"The fabric was loose, and I was trying to fix it."

"Let me help."

"A roguish pirate would not offer to do that."

"No, he would offer to do this." He kissed her swiftly, and she smiled as he knelt to poke at the fabric. Her fingers twisted through his hair. "Ah, here is the problem. The fabric came away from its brad. There. Fixed."

"Thank you."

Getting to his feet, he swept his arm around her, pulling her up to his chest again. "So, *Liebchen,* do you want to go dancing tonight?"

"Dancing? Tonight?" She stepped out of his arms so he could not discover how she trembled at the thought. Attending a ball threatened to throw her back into the miasma of horrifying memories.

He cupped her chin. "You cannot cower here forever. Neither can I. There is a party at a French diplomat's house tonight. Come with me, *Liebchen.*"

"Of course. You will need me to translate."

"Not only that," he murmured as he leaned her cheek against his shoulder. "I need you in my arms as we whirl to the music."

She had no chance to answer as he captured her lips as easily as he had captured her heart. She was willing to go anywhere with him, even if it meant going again through the hell they had suffered. She suspected that vow would be tested.

Soon.

Frau Schlissel did not seem surprised when Michelle told her they were going out and she needed help getting dressed. Although the housekeeper prattled, Michelle sensed her disquiet.

Wearing a white gown with a pale pink overdress instead of her wrapper was a pleasure. Frau Schlissel loosened Michelle's braids and arranged her recalcitrant curls about her head, pinning flowers in them.

Michelle's hands shook as she entered the parlor and saw that Alexei was dressed as formally as she was. She had forgotten how incredibly handsome he was in an ebony coat and spotless white breeches. She touched the silver sheen of his waistcoat, so glad that his spirit had not been wounded as his body had. Ready to go among his enemies again, he would not hide behind drab clothes.

"You need a bit of lace for that," he said, draping her sling with a sheer shawl that matched her gown.

"So I can be a well-dressed invalid? Look at you with your black coat and eye patch to match."

"I thought I looked rather dashing." He ran her finger along the scar left by the bullet that had creased his right cheek, then kissed her palm. "I have long aspired to play the roué."

She did not laugh. "I think you look as wonderful as the first time I saw you."

"Do you?" he asked, shocked. He regained his composure as he said, "You were very cold to me that night."

"Looking back, I cannot imagine why I agreed to go with a pompous, self-satisfied Russian autocrat, but I am glad I did."

"Despite everything?"

"Despite everything."

He ran his finger again along the sling. "Even this?"

"Yes."

When his finger glided across her lips, his voice became husky. "Even this, *Liebchen?*"

Her answer was muted by the pressure of his mouth over hers. Why did he ask? Couldn't he tell how much she longed to be in his arms? He was the one who had pushed her away in the wake of the attack on them. Her longing for him had never wavered. Nothing, not even the past that bound them so unexpectedly together, should come between them.

Rusak clearing his throat slowly separated them, but Alexei did not release her from his hungry gaze as he draped her heavy cloak around her shoulders. When Alexei offered his left arm, Michelle put her fingers on it. They remained silent as they walked out of the apartment to face the world together. She did not want to think how easily this joy could be destroyed.

As Michelle walked into the well-lit house, she tried to hide her unease. She did not want to be on display here tonight as if she were part of a gypsy circus. That she and Alexei had survived the assassination should not make them the center of attention, but the bored diplomats would be eager for any diversion.

Alexei smiled as he led her into the ornate room, which was crowded to overflowing. Instantly they were surrounded. Questions were shot from every direction. She tried to answer, but another was fired at her before she could reply. Shocked by the lack of grief over Herr Damrosch's death, she wished she had not let Alexei convince her to make this their first outing. If they had emerged slowly, mayhap to a restaurant or for a ride about the city, she could have dealt with the curiosity more easily.

The words of one overplump dowager caught her attention. "Excuse me?" Michelle asked, sure she had misunderstood the woman.

"Fraulein D'Orage, I do trust your baby was not lost. You appear as slender as ever. It would be such a great tragedy if—"

"I don't know what you are talking about." She was about to add more when she saw Alexei's lopsided smile. Obviously he had heard this rumor.

"Michelle is alive," Alexei said with his most charming grin, "and that is what we must be grateful for." He slipped his arm around her waist. "I trust there will be other opportunities."

The dowager fluttered her fan and hurried away, clearly disconcerted by Alexei's outrageous comments. His quick answers to the others came as he steered Michelle toward a bench by a window. A servant appeared as soon as she sat. Alexei took two glasses and handed her one. Gratefully she took a deep drink of the champagne.

"Are you all right?" he asked, sitting beside her. "You look very pale."

"All for the better, if I am supposed to be quickening." She arched her brows. "And exactly when were you planning to tell me about this?"

He smiled. "I heard the rumor for the first time the night you seduced me in the conservatory." His finger traced her ear as his gaze softened. "Needless to say, I forgot it along with everything else when I was in your arms."

"Anything else you have forgotten to tell me? Some other deep secret that I should know?"

"Yes. I love you."

She blinked, wondering if she had misheard him. "What?"

"You heard me, *Liebchen*. I love you." He brushed her lips with his.

"Really?"

He laughed. "Have I been dishonest with you in the past?"

"Yes."

"And didn't you always know when I was lying?"

She nodded. She *had* known so often when he was spinning her a tale, because she had seen the sincerity in his eyes when he spoke the truth. The truth of his admiration for her mother. The truth of his concern for his work. And now the truth of his love for her.

His broad fingers stroked her shoulder. "So am I being less than honest when I say, 'I love you, Michelle D'Orage'?"

Searching his face, she was not sure whether she hoped to see his ironic smile or to discover that he was being truthful. Her errant heart did not dare to believe that he loved her. Yet, as she thought of the nights spent in their cozy parlor, she realized she had never been happier. But to have Alexei love her complicated their lives.

"I wish I were back in Zurich," she whispered.

Fury edged his voice. "What? Do you want to run back to your convent and hide from the world and my love for you?"

"You don't understand!"

"I don't? I tell you that I love you and you want to flee. What are you running away from?"

Putting her glass on a nearby table, she caressed his cheek. "I am afraid of losing you, Alexei. Really losing you next time. I want to go home, but I want to take you with me. I love you too much to lose you forever."

The hard lines vanished from his face as his mouth lowered toward hers. Everything in the room vanished beneath the flood of desire that swept her away from anything but him. Too quickly he drew away.

"Don't stop," she whispered. "Please don't tell me there is someone important to whom you have to talk."

"There is no one more important than you, my love." Standing, he brought her to her feet. "Let's go home. Not to Zurich, but to *our* home."

Michelle nodded as she put her hand on his arm and walked with him out of the room. She accepted a footman's help with her cloak as Alexei shrugged his on. When she saw the carriage waiting in the brilliant splash of moonlight, she knew there was nothing she wanted as much as this night with Alexei.

No, that was not true. She wanted all her nights with him.

Sitting in the carriage, Michelle leaned her head against his chest and listened to his steady heartbeat. She sat up with a cry as the coach halted abruptly. Alexei's hand on her shoulder kept her from leaping up from the seat. The carriage began to move again, and they rounded a corner. Embarrassment filled her as she realized it had stopped to let another carriage pass.

"It is all right, *Liebchen,*" Alexei whispered as he brought her back into his arms. "Do not shake so. I swear you shall fall apart if you continue."

"I thought— I was afraid that—"

"Hush, *Liebchen.* I know what you thought. Why do you think I have not kissed you since we got into the carriage? I did not want to remind you of that night."

"Hold me, Alexei. Hold me and never let go."

"Gladly." Alexei smiled as he rested his cheek on Michelle's head. Petals from the flowers in her hair drifted along her shoulders as she snuggled closer to him. As she slowly calmed, he wondered how long the bestiality of the ambush would haunt her. It had been a rude introduction into the world he had come to call his own.

Stroking her back, he wished he could promise her that she would become inured to violence. That would be a lie, for he had not in the years he had been skulking across Europe on one assignment or another. Mayhap he was a jinx. Rusak, Sophie, now his beloved Michelle, all hurt because they had become involved with his life. That was nonsense. Those were the risks taken by anyone who dared to work for peace.

When Rusak brought the carriage to a stop in front of their door, Alexei opened the door. Michelle smiled gamely as he took her trembling fingers and assisted her to the walkway. Telling Rusak good night, he led her to the door.

The parlor was empty. As he hung their cloaks on the pegs, Michelle asked, "Do you want me to put the kettle on for some hot chocolate?"

"No, because, *Liebchen,* you already have me steaming." He drew her toward the arch.

When she gave him a smile as rakish as his own, he was

sure every muscle was taut with desire. His gaze swept along her. She was so beautiful in her silky gown, but he wanted her out of it so her even more silken skin was against him.

He paused in front of his door, and she started to step past him. "No." His right hand clumsily caught hers as he put his left on the doorknob.

"I was going to get—"

"You need nothing but me tonight, *Liebchen*. Tonight and every night."

"Every night?"

"For as long as we can."

When her eyes dimmed for a moment, he wanted to take back those words. But he would not lie to her tonight. He could not offer her marriage and the conventional life she might have dreamed of. All he could offer her now was making her charade as his mistress a reality. The woman she had been in Zurich would have slapped his face and walked away.

"Yes," she whispered. "Tonight and for as long as we can."

"Are you sure?" Again he wanted to silence the words, because he did not want to risk losing what they could share. Michelle had changed, but he had as well. She urged him to think of something other than his work, which had eased his grief for so many years. He had not expected that his guilt that he had not been there to save Sophie would be eased by the love he had found in her daughter's arms.

When he drew her into his room, he closed the door behind her and slipped the bolt into place. Nothing must intrude. "Wait here," he murmured.

Michelle nodded and went to stand by the hearth. Although she heard the connecting door between their rooms open, she did not turn. She suspected Alexei was locking her door as well. In front of her the flames burned no hotter than the fire within her.

Michelle heard Alexei's footsteps nearing her. She

closed her eyes and surrendered to the luscious madness as his lips caressed the nape of her neck. His fingers fumbled with the knot holding her sling, and she was tempted to assist him, but she guessed he wanted to undress her himself.

When she turned to face him, he was frowning. She asked, "Is something wrong?"

"With you? Of course not!" He sighed. "I had fantasized about sweeping you into my arms and tossing you onto this bed, where I would shred your sanity with my touch."

Hearing the pain in his voice, she asked, "I love you, Alexei! Not the man you imagined yourself to be. You have not changed, for I fell in love with you before we were shot. I do not want a rake who will ravage me. I want you. I want you exactly as you are."

"Exactly as I am now?"

Letting her fingers curl through the golden silk of his hair, she whispered, "Exactly as you are now, except I want to feel your skin next to me."

"I like a woman who knows what she wants." He chuckled. "No, I *love* a woman who knows what she wants."

With a laugh, she pushed against his shoulders. When he fell back on the mattress, she leaned over him. "I want you, *mein rogue.*"

He swept his fingers up through her hair, scattering the flower petals around them. Brushing her loosened curls back from her eyes, he grinned and pressed her back into the pillows. His lips found hers with the ease of the luscious nights she had dreamed of being again in his arms. Taunting and pleasuring, his mouth moved along her face, each kiss a new thrill. He tasted the soft whorls of her ear as his breath swirled through her, inflaming the longing into a firestorm.

He undressed her quickly, his right hand not hampering him. He delighted in her naked breasts against him and slid his hands along her back, drawing her tight to his hips.

Another soft gasp escaped from her lips as he found the most responsive spot on her throat. Her fingers clenched on the back of his shirt when his tongue stole along her skin, lighting every inch of it with desire. Caught between his hard body and the cloying caress of the bed, she surrendered to her craving. She reached for the buttons on his shirt. All she wanted was his body on hers, to explore him intimately, to surround him with herself.

Sparks glowed along her skin wherever his lips touched her. When he tasted the warm valley between her breasts, she ran her tongue along his ear. His quick breaths were puffs of fire on her.

His clothes dropped to the floor with hers as he drew her beneath him. His rapid breaths mingled with hers before his lips spiraled along her, leaving her writhing and driving her to the very edge of sanity.

She giggled as he sampled the curve of her instep. "That tickles."

"Serves you right," he whispered. "Let me see where else you are ticklish."

Her laughter dissolved into a moan as his mouth moved along her leg. Gasping his name, she became the escalating pulse of her body as it moved with the tempo of his probing tongue. He cupped her hips, pulling her even closer to him.

Desperately she gripped his shoulders and urged him to share the ecstasy. His mouth covered hers as he found welcome deep within her. The ripples of rapture became a wave and crashed over her, sweeping away every thought but one. Whether she should or not, she loved this man.

"My love, where are you?" The breathless caress of Alexei's voice cooled Michelle's face and drew her back from the sweet fire.

Opening her eyes, she looked up at his face. Her finger wobbled like her rapid pulse as she touched the angle of his high cheekbones underlined so perfectly by his scar. "I don't know, but wherever it was, it was wonderful."

He chuckled. "I agree, *Liebchen*. Wherever it was, it must be paradise." Kissing the curve of her throat where her uneven heartbeat pounded, he smiled at her sharp intake of breath, then pressed his mouth over hers.

Lifting her arms around his shoulders, she delighted in the passion that had controlled them so completely. She smiled when he raised his lips from hers.

"Will you stay with me tonight?" he asked as he drew the covers over her. He laughed when she shivered against the cool sheets. "I will be glad to keep you warm all night."

"All night tonight and every night for as long as we can."

"For as long as we can."

It was a vow she meant, although she knew the time they had together might be short. But, in the afterglow of ecstasy, she wanted to let herself be lulled into forgetting for this one night the rage waiting to destroy them.

Chapter Eighteen

The moon reflected off the wet roofs of the city. Melting clumps of dirty snow edged the street. In the carriage, Michelle ran her fingers along the wall. She gasped when her hand was caught and drawn away from the leather edging the window.

"It is over, *Liebchen.*"

She closed her eyes and put her forehead against Alexei's shoulder. Without her sling, she could move much more easily. As his arm swept around her, she said, "When we ride in this carriage, I cannot look away from the holes left by the balls shot at us. That reminds me that the ones who fired on us are still free."

"It has been a long time since the night we were attacked. Mayhap they wished only to give us a warning."

She raised her head and frowned. "You don't believe that."

"Of course not, but I was hoping you could. At least for tonight. I enjoyed dancing with you." He tweaked her nose and laughed. "You are not going to be able to use that injured leg much longer as an excuse for stepping on my feet."

"Who stepped on whose feet?" she retorted.

Laughing, he settled back and crossed his legs. "It will soon be of the least importance."

"Are we leaving Vienna?"

If he was surprised at her insight, he did not let any hint of astonishment color his voice. "Soon, *Liebchen.* I would guess by the end of the month, we will be on our way."

"Where?"

"Does it matter?"

"Don't you trust me enough to tell me?"

He took her hands and pressed the palms to his lips. "I trust you, but I am not exactly sure where I will be sent next."

"Not to Russia, I hope."

He chuckled. "You have an obvious aversion to the czar's empire, *Liebchen.*"

"I do not want to go where I cannot speak the language."

"What about England?" he challenged.

Her eyes widened. With the alliance between the Allies eroding as each day of the congress passed, it would not surprise her that the Russians would send agents into King George's realm. She thought about the English she had met in Vienna. They were self-satisfied and eager for power. She almost laughed at the thought, for that description fit every diplomat in the city.

"It might be interesting," she said.

"Who knows where we might go? Mayhap America."

"Never!"

"Such vehemence! You would like that wild world, *Liebchen.*" He sighed. "Unfortunately, we probably will be sent to another capital here in Europe."

"Unfortunately?"

"I would like to visit America. I met an American once. He was outspoken and quite cocky that his nation whipped King George's troops."

She laughed. "That was over three decades ago. Are they still talking about it?"

"Glory comes seldom for a backward nation. They are conspicuously absent from the Congress. That is the fate of an insignificant nation clinging to the Atlantic seaboard."

"They are much larger since they purchased that land from France."

"Napoleon was an ass to sell so much valuable territory to finance his imperial aspirations." Suddenly he laughed. "Why are we discussing politics when I could be sampling the wondrous flavor of your lips, my love?"

"Why, indeed?"

As his kisses sparkled across her skin, she pressed closer. His fingers moved along her, inciting the fervor that increased every time he touched her, and she delighted in the passion that soon would overwhelm them.

The carriage rolled to a stop in front of the house. Alexei did not wait for Rusak to jump down to open the door. He swept Michelle out onto the brick walkway and, grasping her hand, hurried with her up the steps. Their laughter trilled through the shadows.

As she climbed the steps to the landing, Michelle hummed the melody of the final waltz they had enjoyed this evening. It had been a wonderful evening with the symphony first, then a gathering where they could be part of the music as they danced.

Alexei laughed, but she paid him no attention. The music had been thrilling, and she wanted to savor it as long as she could.

Pausing by the apartment door, she waited for Alexei. He stopped two steps below her so their faces were level. When she put her arm around him, he grinned with the happiness she knew was on her face.

"So you liked the evening's entertainment?" he asked.

"So far." When his arm tightened around her waist, she kissed him and smiled. "What do you say we go in and have a cup of Frau Schlissel's hot cocoa before bed?"

"Frau Schlissel is asleep by now."

Her finger traced the hard line of his jaw as she whispered, "Then I guess we shall have to go directly to bed, won't we?"

"Now you are getting the idea." He climbed the last steps and opened the door to the luscious aroma of hot chocolate.

Rusak met them with a smile. *Frau Schlissel. Chocolate waiting. Good.*

Alexei draped his cloak over a peg. Taking Michelle's scarlet-lined cape from her shoulders, he hung it next to his. She spun about, humming the melody that would not be banished from her head.

"Pay her no mind, Rusak," Alexei said.

"Next time you must come with us." Michelle laughed. "You must hear this Beethoven. He is a genius." She pulled off her gloves, her left hand still slow. "His music reaches into you and stirs every drop of blood in your veins."

When Rusak's fingers moved with the speed she could not copy, Alexei ordered, "Slower, man! Slower! Our eyes will cross at this speed."

Rusak's grating laugh drowned out Michelle's chuckle. She put her arm around Alexei and chided, "If you would attend Herr Professor Waldstein's lessons, you would have learned to understand him."

"Do you understand him when he talks so fast?"

"No." She smiled.

"I thought not." He looked back at Rusak. "Slow down, so Michelle can do the job she was hired to do and translate for me."

As Michelle interpreted Rusak's signs, she smiled. These two men were so similar: passionate, dedicated, devoted to their allies. She understood how, in the midst of Napoleon's horrible campaign in Russia, when Alexei had come close to losing Rusak to their enemies, they had become friends.

She stroked Alexei's arm as he answered Rusak's questions about their plans for the morrow. From the moment she had seen Alexei standing in Frau Herbart's house, she had been drawn to him. So many times she had questioned that attraction, but she could not deny it.

When she yawned, Alexei laughed. "Why don't you get ready for bed, *Liebchen?* I have a few more things I want to discuss with Rusak. Come back out, and we will have some hot chocolate before we retire."

"I will need some help to unhook my gown," she murmured, running her hand up his face.

With a chuckle, he said, "I guess I should volunteer." He walked with her toward their bedchamber. His fingers caressing her waist suggested the feverish touch he would unleash later.

"Unless you want Rusak to do it for me?"

The intensity in his voice sent a shiver along her back. "No, *Liebchen,*" he whispered as he drew her into his arms. His voice was warm against her skin, and she sighed with eager delight. "Rusak is a good friend, but I do not want any other man touching you. You are my *Liebchen.*"

She brought his mouth to hers. At the brush of his lips, she pressed to him.

He groaned with throaty longing. "Drink the damn chocolate quickly, *Liebchen.* If it would not hurt Rusak's feelings, I—"

"Chocolate first," she whispered, awed by the desire in his eyes. "Then we shall have the rest of the night for making our dreams come true."

"You have made mine come true already." He loosened the back of her gown, kissing her nape. When her breath caught, he murmured, "Hurry, my love. I shall have your cup waiting."

"With cream?"

He kissed her bare back. She trembled with ecstasy, and he chuckled. "With whatever it takes."

Michelle smiled as he walked out of the room. He could not hoax her. He must have something important to share with Rusak. Otherwise Alexei would not have left. Her smile broadened. She loved this man who loved his work.

Slipping her dress down her arms, she stepped out of it and tossed it over a chair. Warming weather had brought mud. A dark stain ringed the hem, and she hoped Frau Schlissel could clean it.

As she pulled on her wrapper, Michelle loosened her hair. She shook her head, and the ebony strands floated around her as she walked back to the parlor.

All the lamps but one had been extinguished. The crackle of the fire matched its dancing light climbing to the ceiling on the opposite wall. Sitting next to Alexei on the settee, she accepted the warm mug from Rusak.

"Thank you."

You welcome. Good party tonight?

"Very nice." Then she glanced at Alexei. "We are talking about the gathering tonight."

"I guessed that. Some of the . . . what do you call them?"

"Signs."

"Some of the signs are obvious." He took a sip from his cup. "Mayhap I shall be able to master a few."

"Both of us are going to have to study hard to keep up with Herr Professor Waldstein's star pupil." When she saw Rusak blush, she almost laughed. Then she realized he was not embarrassed by her compliment, but proud of his progress. She must return with him to class if she wanted to understand all he said.

"Do you think you can be ready to leave by Thursday?" Alexei asked as he put his hand over hers. "It is short notice, I realize. I have asked Frau Schlissel to stay on during our *vacation.*"

"Thursday should be no problem."

"Good. Rusak, have the carriage checked over. I do not want to lose a wheel in one of the mountain passes. I—"

The door crashed open. A flood tide of men cascaded into the room. Rusak jumped to his feet and knocked one man back into the others.

Alexei shouted, "Run, Michelle!"

She leapt up from the settee.

He grabbed her right hand and pushed her toward the arch. "Go! Get help!" he ordered.

She whirled. Help? What was happening? She turned to run, but a jungle of hands and arms and strange faces tried to entangle her. She screamed as an arm encircled her waist. Another order was shouted, but not by Alexei. A hand clamped over her mouth, and her head was jerked back painfully against a man's chest. She clawed at the fingers, then stamped on her captor's feet. He laughed, not letting her escape. When she tried to pull away, his hand shifted to cover her nose.

She fought to breathe as dull thuds were followed by something falling to the floor. Blackness surrounded her. The man's hand moved again, and she could breathe. As she gasped, another hand grasped her chin and tilted it back farther. Her gaze met a pair of dark eyes set beneath thick brows in a narrow face. Their evil glint sent fear roiling through her.

In thickly accented German, he ordered, "Don't faint. We are not done with you yet."

He gave her no chance to answer as he turned away to call something to his men. She paid no attention to his words as she saw Alexei facedown on the floor. She tried to break free, screaming, "No! Don't hurt him!"

When her captor growled in her ear, she froze.

"You are French!" she cried. "What are you doing here?"

"Idiot!" snapped the man who was clearly the leader. "She understands French!" His scowl lessened as he stepped over Alexei's prone body and toward her again. When his gaze moved along her, she struggled against the hands holding her. She wanted to put something between her and this man's icy eyes. "Of course, it is not important what she knows. What is your name?"

"Collette," she said, hoping he could not guess she was lying.

"Collette? What happened to Michelle D'Orage?"

"She is gone."

"Where?"

She tried to shrug, but could not move. "The count did not tell me. We do not speak of such things."

"So you replaced the infamous Michelle D'Orage as this traitor's mistress?"

"Traitor?"

"No questions from you, Collette."

Trying to peer past him, she wanted to find out if Alexei and Rusak were still alive. He caught her face between his fingers. When she saw blood on his hands, she gasped.

With a broad smile, he mused, "How much might you truly know, Collette? Enough to make it worth my time to drag you across Europe? Or are you simply the latest pretty plaything he has collected?"

"Who are you?" she whispered.

His smile was frigid. "No questions." He shrugged, but his eyes examined her minutely. "You really have no idea who I am?"

"Do you think I would have asked if I had known?"

"You look as if you regret asking that." He patted her cheek. "Don't. Such a witless question convinces me that he kept you around for something other than conversation." He eyed her up and down. "I can see why. If I were not so anxious to be on my way . . ." He chuckled when her face grew cold. Turning his back on her, he called over his shoulder, "She is worthless. Take care of her."

Michelle opened her mouth to scream. The sound came out in a moan of pain as something struck her head. Agony swelled to encompass her as she crumpled into a pile on the floor.

* * *

Michelle roused to something itchy against her cheek. Just the thought of moving seemed impossible. The teasing sensation continued, irritating her awake. As she put her hand against her cheek, she discovered she was lying on the carpet. Pain blared through her head.

What had happened?

She groped for anything solid and tried to stand. She collapsed to her knees. Hanging her head, she tried to breathe. She dropped back to the floor as she fought the pain rippling across her skull. Weak tears dampened the carpet beneath her cheek.

Pushing herself up to her knees again, Michelle leaned her head against a nearby table. She wiped the tears aside, as everything in the dark room remained wavy.

Seeing someone on the floor not far from her, she knew she must check. As fiercely as she had been struck, she feared what the men might have done to Alexei.

The men! Memory erupted through her head. The Frenchmen who had stormed into their apartment!

Taking one step forward on her knees, she folded again. She refused to be halted. She crept toward the shadow, whispering, "Alexei? Alexei, wake up! Please!"

She moaned. If they had killed him ... Pain rushed through her.

"Alexei?" she whispered again. "Alexei, please wake up. Don't be dead."

Her fingers stretched out in the flickering light of the flames on the hearth. Fear slashed her. Murmuring a prayer, she touched the shadow, then groped about the floor. It was just her dark cloak that had been tossed onto the floor. She slapped her hand against it and swore in French and German.

She rolled to sit and gasped, "Rusak!"

His face was battered and already swelling. He offered a hand to help her to her feet. Leaning on him, she lurched across the floor to a chair.

"Where is Alexei?"

Rusak handed her a damp cloth, pointing to her head. Instead of putting it on her aching skull, she dabbed at his swollen face.

When he winced, she whispered, "I am sorry. Rusak, do you know where Alexei is?"

Before he could answer, she heard a shriek from the arch. Frau Schlissel stood there with a candlestick in her hand. In the bright light, the housekeeper's face was as pale as the wax dripping down the candle.

"Come in," urged Michelle. "Rusak, is there more cocoa? I think Frau Schlissel could use some to soothe her."

He regarded her in awe. Her voice sounded calm, but it was a ploy to convince them—and herself—that she was not panicking.

"Please, Rusak," she added when he did not move.

Nodding, he poured a cup and held it out to the housekeeper. Frau Schlissel dropped into a chair and stared as Rusak lit the lamps. Each one showed more of the destruction in the room. The chair where the housekeeper sat was the only one not broken.

Sipping her chocolate, Frau Schlissel whispered, "Where is Count Vatutin?"

"I don't know." Michelle looked at Rusak, who stood by the hearth. "Is there any chance he is here still?"

Look for Alexei. Not find him. Find only you.

Michelle closed her eyes in horror. She had not realized how much she had hoped that Alexei was in another part of the apartment. He must have been taken away by the men.

Rusak's broad fingers pushed a hot cup into her hands and closed her shaking fingers around it. She saw more bruises darkening on the side of his face.

"Who?" she whispered. "Who are they? Where will they take Alexei?"

His hands fairly flew with his anxiety to share what he knew. She watched, trying to understand. Rusak scowled when she could not understand what he was trying to say.

"Gone? Yes, I know that. But where?" When he shook his head, she asked, "Did you recognize these men? Yes?" She tried to guess what the next sign meant. "Enemy?"

At his nod, she shivered. "Where do you think they will go now that they have Alexei?"

His fingers formed a sign and repeated it emphatically.

"France?" she asked in disbelief. "Why France?" When he looked at her, clearly frustrated, she asked, "Where in France?"

As he tried to answer, she realized she was not going to be able to understand what he had to say. She needed someone to interpret for her.

"What time is it?" she asked.

Frau Schlissel whispered, "About two in the morning."

"Rusak," Michelle said.

Go teacher?

"Yes. Frau Schlissel?"

The housekeeper did not move. She stared at the shattered furniture and the cloak on the floor.

"Frau Schlissel?"

The housekeeper remained silent and motionless.

Michelle sighed. She had no time to comfort Frau Schlissel. "Rusak? Come with me."

He followed her into her room. Reaching into her armoire, she pulled out a dress. When she loosened her wrapper, he turned his back. She pulled on her dress.

"Help me, Rusak, please." She struggled not to give in to tears. Such a short time ago, Alexei had teased her about not allowing any other man to touch her. Now he was gone.

He quickly hooked her gown. They hurried out into the main room, where Frau Schlissel was on her feet and trying to right some of the furniture.

When Michelle pulled on her cloak, the housekeeper cried, "Where are you going?"

"To the one man who can talk to both Rusak and me." Michelle pulled the hood of her cloak over her head.

"It is the middle of the night."

"I cannot wait until morning to speak with Herr Professor Waldstein."

"But Fraulein D'Orage, what if the men come back?"

"They will not be back. They got what they wanted. Lock the door, if it makes you feel better, Frau Schlissel."

Rusak put his hand on Michelle's arm and pointed to the door. Biting her bottom lip, she shivered. The bolt had been broken off, leaving the wood shattered behind it.

She took a deep breath. "Frau Schlissel, you might be safest in your room with the door bolted."

"Be careful." The housekeeper wrung her hands.

"You can be sure of that." When Rusak took her arm, she stepped over the fragments of wood littering the carpet and went down the stairs that were shrouded in shadows.

Stay here, he signed when they reached the door to the street. *I get carriage.*

"All right," she whispered. When the door closed behind him, she huddled to one side where she could see out the etched window.

Nothing moved on the street. In the distance, she could hear bells tolling the hour. Tears were a hot pressure in her eyes, but she tried to ignore them. It seemed impossible that only a short time before, she had been walking up these stairs with Alexei and they had planned a night of love.

Who? And why? And what would happen now? If Bartholomew had been the one kidnapped, she would guess that his abductors wanted ransom. That could not be why they had taken Alexei. If his captors wanted a ransom, they would not be taking him farther from Russia.

Somehow his enemies had discovered where Alexei was.

They must want the information he had. That he would die before revealing any secrets only added to her fear. The cruel man who had taunted her would delight in torturing Alexei. She moaned and pressed her face against the wall.

Rusak tapped her shoulder.

"All set?"

He waved aside her words and signed his own.

"What do you mean the carriage is gone?"

Gone. Carriage. Horses. Gone.

"They took it, didn't they?" She laughed without mirth. "They wanted to be sure we did not follow too closely. All right, Rusak. Let's go."

To teacher?

"We need his help more than ever." She put her hand on his arm. "They hit you hard. Can you walk there?"

Go now.

Agreeing with his vehemence, Michelle walked with him onto the deserted walkway. It was not far to Herr Professor Waldstein's house. She hoped the information he could help her understand would offer the clue needed to save Alexei.

If not . . . she did not know what they would do.

Michelle had passed from pain into a debilitating fatigue by the time they reached Herr Professor Waldstein's house. Lifting her heavy feet, she climbed the steps. She knocked and glanced worriedly at Rusak. His assertion that he was fine had been a lie. He leaned against the wall and panted.

Impatiently she knocked again. No answer.

"Herr Professor Waldstein?" she called as she banged on the door. "Herr Professor Waldstein, are you here?"

The door was opened a slit by the housekeeper.

"We must see Herr Professor Waldstein immediately," Michelle said.

"Fraulein, come back tomorrow."

"We must see the professor. Now!" She pushed the door open.

The housekeeper scowled, but said, "I will see if Herr Professor Waldstein wishes to speak with you."

"No need," came a voice from the dimness at the top of the stairs. Herr Professor Waldstein followed his voice's bass rumble down the steps as he tied his robe in place. Making no effort to hide his surprise, he asked, "Fraulein, why are you here at his hour?"

"Forgive us for waking you, Herr Professor Waldstein. It is an emergency."

He touched the unbuttoned cuff of her dress. "I can see that, Fraulein, but why are you coming to me?"

"I cannot understand all that Rusak is trying to tell me. I must understand. It is vital."

Herr Professor Waldstein signed at Rusak too quickly for her to comprehend. When Rusak nodded, the professor said, "Come to my classroom." Over his shoulder, he added, "Bring coffee, Matilde. Lots of it, for this may take a while."

As soon as they were seated at the table as if it were an ordinary lesson, Herr Professor Waldstein said, "You shall ask your questions, Fraulein D'Orage. Feodor, you will sign the answers to me. I want all your concentration on me. Is that understood?"

"Yes," whispered Michelle as Rusak nodded. Dampening her lips, she clasped her hands on the table. "Who?"

Herr Professor Waldstein watched Rusak's fingers. "The man's name is René . . . René La—"

"René LaTulippe!" cried Michelle.

"Calm yourself, Fraulein D'Orage," ordered the professor.

She nodded. That one answer told her so much. She recalled the letter she had written to a Monsieur René LaTulippe. Alexei had called him a problem he did not want to deal with. It seemed that the problem had found them. Fear lashed her, but she warned herself to listen to what Herr Professor Waldstein was saying.

"The man's name is René LaTulippe," Herr Professor Waldstein continued. "He works for Napoleon." His forehead rutted as he made some signs back to Rusak. "He is Count Vatutin's most deadly enemy."

"Tell me where they are going."

Although he clearly was curious about what was happening, Herr Professor Waldstein translated, "Either to Geneva or Paris. Most likely Paris, for that is where the Bonapartists are congregating in the hopes of resurrecting Napoleon's empire and putting Napoleon back onto King Louis's throne. Because Count Vatutin—" He hesitated, then added quickly, "He betrayed them and helped bring about Napoleon's downfall."

"Betrayed them?" That must be why LaTulippe had called Alexei a traitor.

"Count Vatutin," answered the professor, his eyes wide, "ingratiated himself with Napoleon's closest advisers and passed along information to the Allies."

"How could a Russian infiltrate Napoleon's inner circle?"

Rusak did not wait for Herr Professor Waldstein to interpret his answer. He grabbed her face and turned it toward him. *Not Russian. French.*

"Alexei is French?" She gasped. "Being Russian is a disguise?"

Reluctantly Rusak nodded. It was obvious he would have preferred not to divulge that information.

"What is his real name?"

He shook his head.

She understood. He would tell her what was necessary to save Alexei, but no more. Alexei had guarded the secret so well that she had never suspected his name was not his own. So many more questions careened through her head. If Alexei was French, he had hired her for the very reason he had told her so many times. He had come to St. Bernard's to safeguard her from her mother's enemies who were seeking her. Was Monsieur LaTulippe that enemy?

"Rusak—" She faltered, wanting to ask if Rusak was his real name. Then she realized it did not matter now. "Do you think it is possible for us to find Alexei in Paris?"

Possible.

"Then we must go there."

Rusak's smile became malevolent, and she knew he shared her determination to free Alexei from his captors.

Rising, she said, "Thank you, Herr Professor Waldstein. I doubt if we shall see you again soon."

Herr Professor Waldstein stood as she did. "Fraulein D'Orage, you cannot be serious about chasing Count Vatutin's enemies across the Alps."

"Rusak has experience in these matters. If we do not go, Count Vatutin may die." Her breath caught on the last word. "Shall we go, Rusak?"

As they left, the teacher said nothing. She suspected he believed that he would never see them alive again. Although she was afraid that he was right, she could not let LaTulippe win. The prize would be Alexei's life.

Frau Schlissel had regained her composure by the time they returned. She met them at the door. "Come and eat your breakfast."

Michelle was about to refuse, but Rusak signed, *Eat. Need food. Long trip.*

As she gulped the coffee that she had craved during the long, cold walk home, Michelle listed what they would need for their trip. The few gold coins she had brought with her from St. Bernard's would pay for most of their travel. She wished she had taken more from the box.

"Frau Schlissel," she asked, pouring another cup, "will you stay?"

"Count Vatutin has paid my wages through the end of

the year." She lowered her fork to her plate. "I shall stay, if you wish, Fraulein, past that time."

"The lease on the apartment lasts only until the end of September. If we have not returned by then, you must find another position. I shall write a recommendation for you before we leave today."

"Today?" choked the housekeeper. "You have not slept!"

"There will be plenty of time to sleep on the coach. When does it leave, Rusak?"

Three hours.

Tossing her napkin on the table, Michelle rose. "I cannot eat. I am going to pack what I am taking with me."

Rusak caught her hand. *Bring little.*

An exhausted smile loosened the ridges of anxiety from her face. "I shall bring no more than I can carry in my small satchel. Excuse me."

Going into the room where she once had slept alone, Michelle opened the wardrobe door. She lifted the board at the bottom and reached in for the bag containing the gold coins. A frown furrowed her forehead as a piece of paper crackled. Drawing it out, she saw that a folded page was attached to her bag. She opened it and read,

Michelle, Liebchen,

If you want to succeed as a spy, you must devise a more original hiding place than under a loose board. I considered taking your little cache to teach you a lesson, but I thought you might truly need it, so I am leaving this note and what I owe you for your first two months of working as my interpreter.

If you are reading this because you are leaving me, reconsider. Many things are not as innocent eyes see. If you are reading this because something dreadful has happened, do not forget what I have taught you, Liebchen. It is too bad because we would have made a hell of a team.

I will close with the words I may never have been bold

*enough or foolish enough to speak. I love you, Michelle, as
I have since the moment you swooned in my arms. What
man could resist such a compliment?*

Michelle sank to the floor. There was no date on the
letter, but it must have been written before the ambush
that had crippled Alexei's right hand. Even then, he had
loved her.

When a hand touched her shoulder, she saw Rusak
standing behind her. "From Alexei," she whispered, looking back down at the letter.

Move, Michelle. Please. He pointed at her armoire.

Curious, she stood. Folding the note, she put it in her
bodice, wanting it close to her heart.

He knelt by the wardrobe and opened the door. Taking
the lower edge of the fabric that lined it, he pulled it away
from the brad that held it in place.

She gasped as it opened to let a score of pages and a
small book cascade to the floor. "Alexei's?" she whispered.
No wonder Alexei had not been concerned when the apartment was searched. Once he had seen that her room was
untouched, he had known that his hidden materials were
safe. "Are these Alexei's?"

He nodded. Scooping up the papers, he shuffled them
together. She picked up the small book, which was bound
with brown leather. He halted her from opening it, shaking
his head.

"If I read it," Michelle said, "there may be a clue to
where he is."

Only Alexei reads. Secret words.

"Code?"

He nodded. *Michelle knows nothing. Safe. Orders. Alexei.*

"Let me keep this." She placed the book in her satchel.
"LaTulippe thinks I am Alexei's mistress Collette and useless."

Who? When she explained her lie, Rusak chuckled, but
signed, *Michelle no have book. Alexei angry.*

"I will risk that." A sob scraped her throat. "Alexei can scold me when we find him."

Frau Schlissel was waiting when they came back to the parlor. "Contact the Russians," she urged. "Or someone in Talleyrand's entourage, if you think they are taking Count Vatutin to France. You cannot go after him by yourself."

Pulling on her cloak, Michelle said, "Rusak has suspicions about where Alexei will be. We shall find him quickly." She did not add the words that resonated through her brain: *if he is still alive.*

"These may be the same men who arranged the ambush."

"Yes."

The housekeeper's timeworn hands took Michelle's. "They are criminals. How can you fight them?"

"Because we must." She relented when she saw Frau Schlissel's tears. In a gentler tone, she whispered, "How can I wait here?" She tied her cloak under her chin. "I shall send you an address if we decide to stay in Paris."

"I thought you were coming back!"

"If we find Alexei before the end of the Congress." She did not add that both might take far longer than anyone had planned. "Oh! Your letter of recommendation. I—"

"Do not fret about it. Do what you can to rescue Count Vatutin."

Michelle hugged the housekeeper. "If you are willing to remain, stay here, Frau Schlissel. If Alexei can elude his captors, he will come back here. He must know where we are."

She nodded. "I shall stay, Fraulein D'Orage. Send me word as soon as you decide what you will do, or if . . ." She lowered her eyes, but not before Michelle saw the truth. Frau Schlissel did not believe they would find Alexei alive.

Picking up her satchel and reticule, Michelle asked, "Ready, Rusak?" When he nodded, she motioned for him to open the door to begin a journey she could not have imagined yesterday. She had no idea what they would find at its conclusion, but she knew it would not end until they discovered where Alexei was.

Even if it took the rest of their lives.

Chapter Nineteen

The spring sunshine struck the cobbles, but nothing could warm Michelle as she hurried along the Paris boulevard. Beside her, Rusak was scowling. He was furious that she would not heed him.

How could she when doing so meant turning her back on the search for Alexei? It had taken them weeks even to reach Paris. Warm weather had softened the mud and mired the coach every few miles. When her money for their fares had run out, they had walked the rest of the way.

The city was in an uproar, for Napoleon had reclaimed it. That Napoleon had escaped from his island prison and won the loyalty of the king's men at the same time as Alexei was abducted warned Michelle that the two events were connected in some way. She could not convince Rusak to explain how. Although she had become more proficient at signing during their long journey, this one topic he refused to discuss.

But he must soon. They had been here for nearly the whole month of May, and now they were broke. There was another alternative to coming to Monsieur Mauriac's jewelry store today to sell *Maman*'s ring, but she did not want to think about it.

Yet how could she push from her mind Rusak's excitement when he had burst into the single room they had rented over a pastry shop where the scent of cakes taunted them when another hungry day was over?

She had been reheating the thin broth that would be their supper. "What is it?" she had asked, seeing him sign, *Good news.* "Did you find Alexei?"

Rusak's smile wavered.

Putting her hand on his, Michelle sighed. "I am sorry, Rusak. What is your good news?" She could not imagine any tidings that would be good, except that Alexei had been found alive.

Rusak get job. Money for Michelle and Rusak. Money for food and house with two rooms.

"How?"

Go to school for deaf children. Teacher learn signs there. In Paris. Job for Rusak. Teaching. Money for Rusak and Michelle.

"But Rusak, if you teach at the school, when will you have time to help me look for Alexei?"

His lips tightened.

"Are you giving up?"

No. He added nothing else.

"Do you think Alexei is still alive?" When he shrugged and turned away, she took his hand and shook it. "Answer me! Do you think he is still alive?"

Want Alexei alive. Do not know.

"So you are ready to give up?" She dropped onto the edge of the pallet where she slept while Rusak curled up on a patched blanket under the table.

Men die.

"No!" Her anger collapsed into sobs as she hid her face in her hands. How long could she continue on this quest alone? She would never stop looking for Alexei.

When an arm encircled her shoulders awkwardly, she

clung to Rusak. He drew her face up so she could see his fingers.

What else we do?

"I can sell *Maman's* ring to get some money." She touched the ring.

No!

"It is just a ring, Rusak. Is an heirloom more important than Alexei's life?" Running her finger along the lightning bolt, she whispered, "It is the only thing I have left to sell, and I know *Maman* would have wanted me to help Alexei." She raised her eyes to meet his. "Rusak, with what I should be able to sell this for, we can buy some allies to help us find Alexei."

One week. Told school come in one week.

"And we shall look for Alexei until then?"

Sell ring. Try find Alexei one week. Michelle and Rusak find Alexei or stop looking.

Although she wanted to argue, she knew he was being sensible. They had found no clue to Alexei's location in the past week. Her heart shattered as she whispered, "If we have not found Alexei in one week, you will take the job at the school." A sob bubbled up from deep within her. "And I shall look for a teaching position also."

Rusak had gently wiped her tears away, and the motion had undone her. She had sobbed against him, knowing that, in doing as he wanted, she was betraying the man she loved. That Alexei would have expected her to do as Rusak requested had not lessened her pain.

Now she and Rusak had arrived on the street where Monsieur Mauriac's shop was. She stared at the door. MAURIAC'S JEWELRY STORE was written across the sign over it.

Michelle's fingers trembled as she reached for the door-knob. The clamor of the streets was muted when the heavy door closed behind them. Her nearly ruined slippers sank into the crimson carpet. She looked about in confusion.

No jewelry was on display. A trio of overstuffed chairs

waited around a table to one side of the small room. A lamp glowed near them, and she wondered how anyone could see gems well enough in that light. On the other side of the room was a single table, higher than the first, and a stool.

"Monsieur Mauriac?" she called.

Michelle whirled as she heard a rustle. A curtain covering a door was shoved aside. It was clear they had interrupted the man during his midday meal, for he held a crust of bread. Her stomach growled, and she heard a low laugh from Rusak. She almost retorted that he would not find starving amusing, then realized that they would not starve. His job at the school would buy them food. All they would lose if she could not sell this ring was their last chance to find Alexei.

"Yes?" the man grumbled. Popping the last bite of bread into his mouth, he rubbed his fingers across a napkin and stuck it into his breeches.

"Are you Monsieur Mauriac?"

"Yes."

Uncomfortable under his scrutiny, she said with feigned serenity, "I would like to sell you something."

"I do not buy from anyone who has not been introduced to me by another customer, mademoiselle. Do you have a reference?"

She took a steadying breath. If she appeared desperate, he might become suspicious. "It is a piece purchased here."

"Really?"

Realizing she had piqued his interest, she said, "Actually it is half of a set of wedding rings. Made for Monsieur and Madame D'Orage."

"D'Orage? That name is not familiar to me, mademoiselle."

"It would have been more than a quarter of a century ago, Monsieur Mauriac."

He waved aside her words. "Even if they had been my

father's patrons, I would know. I recall no name like D'Orage."

"The rings were purchased here." She twisted the strings of her reticule nervously. Recalling how Alexei had teased her for tangling her fingers in them, she let the bag drop against her skirt. She glanced at Rusak, but he could not help her.

"Do you have proof of that?" Monsieur Mauriac asked.

"No, but would you look at the ring?"

He sighed, "Mademoiselle, I—"

"Sir, we are starving."

When he looked from her to Rusak, he said, "Let me see the ring." Gesturing toward the tall table, he ordered, "Over here."

Drawing off her right glove, she started to place it on the table. When she saw his distaste, she stuffed the tattered glove into her reticule. Regret ached through her as she pulled off *Maman*'s ring and put it on the table.

He picked it up and gasped. "Where did you get this?"

"It was my mother's."

Suddenly he was smiling. "I may have good news for you, Mademoiselle . . . ?"

"D'Orage."

"Ah, yes, so you said. Will you and your companion please be seated? I believe I have a buyer for you. I shall send a lad to contact them."

"I can leave the ring with you, if you wish." She did not want to lose a moment of the time she had to look for Alexei.

"No, please wait. It should take no longer than an hour for them to arrive."

"But—" Michelle bit back the rest of her words when Rusak tugged on her arm.

No sell. We go now.

She wanted to agree. This was too peculiar. But if there was a chance the money she could get for the ring would help her save Alexei, she must play this game. She went to sit in one of the trio of chairs by the other table. For a moment she thought Rusak would storm out. Then he sat beside her.

An hour had never seemed so long . . . or so short. Michelle was tossed between expectation and despair as the hands on the clock by the door slowly moved, then seemed to leap forward like a runaway horse. Beside her, Rusak was lost in his thoughts, and she guessed he was thinking about his new job at the school. It was a wonderful opportunity for him, but . . .

The door opened again, and two people entered. The dark-haired woman was dressed in the height of fashion. Beside her, a tall man also had jet black hair, but when he passed the window, the sparkle of a gold earring glistened in his left ear.

Monsieur Mauriac rushed forward to greet them. Turning, he said, as Michelle and Rusak came to their feet, "Mademoiselle D'Orage, may I introduce Lady Sommerton and the *Duc* de Tonnere du Grêlon, who are interested in your ring?"

A *duc*? Wearing a gold earring? And the lady's name was decidedly English. What was going on here? She knew it did not matter. All that mattered was selling *Maman*'s ring. With the aplomb she had honed in Vienna, she held out her hand.

The *duc* took it in his gloved hand and bowed over it, then glanced at Lady Sommerton. His mistress? But why would a French *duc* have an Englishwoman for a mistress? She almost laughed. Alexei had been pretending to be a Russian with a Swiss mistress. The wisest thing would be to sell them the ring and leave.

Quietly Michelle said, "I would like to introduce my friend Feodor Rusak." She tried to smile.

Rusak nodded in their direction. She did not explain that he could not speak. She wanted to conclude this deal and continue her search for Alexei.

The *duc* said smoothly, "Mademoiselle D'Orage, we are pleased you agreed to meet us."

"Monsieur Mauriac led me to believe that this meeting was necessary to complete our business."

"May I examine the ring you are offering to sell?"

"Certainly." Despite her attempts to remain calm, her fingers quivered as she drew off the ring. She did not want to sell her last connection with *Maman*.

He ran his finger along the raised lightning bolt. When he offered it to Lady Sommerton, Michelle was shocked to see tears in her eyes.

"Mademoiselle D'Orage," Lady Sommerton asked, her voice cracking, "is it possible that your mother's name was Sophie?"

"Yes, but how—"

"Dominic, it could be her!"

He put a calming hand on her arm. "Don't jump to conclusions too hastily, Brienne." His piercing ebony eyes reminded Michelle so much of Alexei's green ones as he asked, "Would you be willing to answer a few questions?"

"About what?" She was losing valuable time here. She wanted to say that, but heated words might destroy the chance to get the money she needed.

"Your mother's name was Sophie. Sophie what?"

"Sophie D'Orage."

He rubbed his chin. "D'Orage. That is French for 'storm.' It could suggest Tonnere du Grêlon."

"Thunderstone?" repeated Michelle in confusion, noting for the first time his odd title. "Like the one on *Maman*'s ring?"

Lady Sommerton smiled. "And your father's name?"

"Michel. I was named for him."

"Not Marc-Michel?" Lady Sommerton asked.

"No. I told you; now can we speak of the ring?"

"Your father is where?" asked the *duc*.

"He is dead."

"When?"

"Your Grace, I do not believe that this conversation is necessary in order for you to purchase my ring. If this is how business is conducted here in Paris, I shall wait until I return to Zurich to sell it." She was bluffing, but she hoped they would not realize that.

"Zurich?" asked Lady Sommerton as she sat. "Is that where you have been? You have been so close all the time?"

Icily, Michelle said, "If you will give me back my ring, I think we shall leave. This has gone on long enough."

"Please be patient, Mademoiselle D'Orage," Monsieur Mauriac urged.

Michelle shook her head and held out her hand. She refused to be taunted because she needed money.

The *duc* said, "Forgive us, Madeomiselle D'Orage, but we have a reason for asking these questions."

"Then mayhap if you were to explain, I, too, might understand."

"Monsieur Mauriac asked you to meet us," the *duc* said, "because we offered him, as we have every jeweler in Paris, a handsome reward if he found this ring. But we asked to meet the owner face-to-face."

She looked from the *duc* to Lady Sommerton. She wanted to trust them, but she had learned smiles sometimes hid the truth. "You still have not explained your interest in *Maman*'s ring."

In a voice raw with emotion, Lady Sommerton said, "Mademoiselle D'Orage . . . Michelle, I think you are my younger sister."

"Sister?" She shook her head. "You have made a mistake. I am not the one you are looking for. I do not have a sister. It was only *Maman* and me."

"Because your father was beheaded during the Terror?"

Rusak clutched Michelle's arm, but she did not need his warning to be careful.

"Many died then," she answered coolly. "I am sorry you lost your parents and sister, Lady Sommerton." Holding out her hand again, she said, "My ring, please, Your Grace."

When he did not return it to her, she hesitated. The *duc* stood a head taller than Rusak. As Rusak shifted his stance and clenched his fists, she motioned for him to do nothing. If he tried to get her ring back, someone might be hurt.

"Mademoiselle D'Orage," the *duc* asked, "will you let us explain?"

Grudgingly, she nodded.

"As Brienne said, we believe you are our sister."

"*Our* sister?" She sat and stared at him.

He drew off his left glove. Her eyes grew wide as she saw the ring on his hand. It matched *Maman*'s. Taking it off, he handed it to her. "Our father's ring. Our father, Marc-Michel Levesque."

"Marc-Michel Levesque?" She tilted his ring and saw the engraving inside. It was just as in *Maman*'s ring. "MML and SR. Marc-Michel Levesque and Sophie Rameau?"

"We had hoped," Lady Sommerton said with a tentative smile, "that when *Maman* fled Paris after our father was executed, that she took her wedding ring along with our baby sister." She took Michelle's hands. "Our father's name was Marc-Michel Levesque. Michelle, you are our sister. Whether you believe it or not, I do."

"I do not know what to believe."

"I know exactly how you feel. Like you, I was raised far from home."

"Home?"

Monsieur Mauriac grinned and interjected, "Mademoiselle, your brother and his wife have returned to France to claim your family's estate, Château Tonnere du Grêlon. You, Mademoiselle D'Orage—or, I should say, Mademoiselle Levesque—are a *duc's* daughter."

Michelle fought to breathe. She looked at Rusak, but his face was as ashen as hers must be. *Maman* had been a *duchesse*? How had *Maman* kept this secret for so many years? Had Alexei known? He had been so closemouthed about other things. He might have known and never told her.

"Are you all right?" Lady Sommerton asked.

"Yes," she whispered. "I believe I am."

The *duc* chuckled as he handed her *Maman*'s ring. "I suspected you would be. Such tidings are not enough to defeat a Levesque. Will you and Monsieur Rusak join us at the family's house here in Paris? We can speak further there."

As she opened her mouth to answer, Rusak gripped her face, turning it toward him. He signed furiously. *Say no, Michelle. Think first.*

"Why?"

Not sure. Mayhap lies.

"I am not sure either, but—" She switched to sign language. *Duc help find Alexei. Must try.* She saw the others watching with curiosity. "Rusak was injured in the war, and this is how he speaks."

"Fascinating," said Lady Sommerton. "You talk with your hands, Monsieur Rusak? Did you know there is a school that teaches that manual language here in Paris?"

"He has been offered a position as an instructor there."

"Perfect! Our house is convenient to it." She smiled at her brother—not just hers, but Michelle's. "I cannot believe we have finally found her. Who would have guessed that Armistead LaPorte was honest when he told me that my sister was in a place that would be difficult to reach in the winter? Zurich fits that description perfectly, and now here she is."

"Armistead LaPorte?" Michelle asked.

Lady Sommerton smiled. "A long story about an old enemy, Michelle."

"Shall we go?" asked the *duc*. "You can tell her that story in the carriage, Brienne."

Again Michelle hesitated.

"Is there a problem, Michelle?" the *duc* asked as he opened the door.

She should have guessed any man who reminded her of Alexei would not miss something as obvious as her distress. "Your Grace, I—"

"Please call me Dominic." He gave her a roguish smile. "You are unsure of our familial ties, but I am not. You look exactly like the paintings of Sophie Rameau that are still hanging at the château."

"That is how we knew instantly it was you," said Lady Sommerton—no, Brienne.

A sister and a brother? Michelle wished her mind would stop whirling. When she stepped out of the shop and saw Brienne run up to a man and a woman standing by a carriage, she took a steadying breath. The man and woman were obviously waiting for them.

With a sparkling laugh, Brienne said, "Michelle, come and meet my husband, Evan." She put her hand on the arm of the man, whose hair was a tawny brown, and smiled up at him. Then, looking at the woman who had the most amazing red hair Michelle had ever seen, she added, "And this is Dominic's wife, Abigail."

Michelle's smile grew uncomfortable as she greeted this sudden family. So many questions teased her to be asked, especially because she realized Evan was English, and Abigail was an American. Michelle blinked back tears as she thought of how Alexei wanted to travel to America.

"We should go," Brienne said, her smile widening even more. "By this time, Lucile will be awake from her nap."

"Lucile?" asked Michelle.

"Our daughter," Evan replied, putting his arm around Brienne. "And she already has the Levesque contrariness and determination."

Michelle shook her head in amazement. "I cannot believe all the relatives I now have." She glanced at Rusak, and saw her uneven emotions reflected in his frown. She was so happy to have found this family, but her joy was diminished by her fears for Alexei.

Mayhap can help.

She nodded. Mayhap her family could help her find Alexei. A *duc* must have allies who might be able to unearth even a hint of Alexei. She shuddered, wishing she had not thought of the word *unearth*. He could not be dead.

Michelle waited for the other women to climb into the carriage. She smiled as Dominic handed her in. His hand was as rough as Alexei's, surprising her, because she had not guessed a *duc* would lead a rough life or wear an earring like a pirate.

Rusak stepped into the carriage after Michelle and sat facing Brienne and Abigail. Michelle sat next to him as he continued to sign his concerns and his hopes to her. He still did not trust these people. As Dominic sat beside Brienne and joked about the crowded carriage, her breath caught. It was as if she looked at the picture of her father, for they both had the same determined expression in their dark eyes.

As the carriage jerked into motion, Michelle gasped. Too late she realized how she was sitting. She clenched the edge of the red velvet seat.

Evan smiled. "I realize it is not comfortable, but we need go only as far as Îsle Saint-Louis."

Michelle could not answer as she shivered. Since the ambush on them in Vienna, she had been careful not to ride backward. Her stomach roiled.

"Evan," cried Brienne with abrupt concern, "something is wrong. Michelle's face is as gray as the cobbles. Stop the carriage."

"No! Don't stop the carriage! Don't!" Michelle hid her face against Rusak's shoulder as memories pummeled her with the pain of that horrible night.

"Michelle?" Abigail put her hand on Michelle's arm. "The signs Monsieur Rusak is making . . . Were you shot in a carriage?"

Taking deep breaths, Michelle tried to banish her panic. "Yes," she whispered. "In Vienna." She started to explain, but Evan stood awkwardly and motioned for her to take his seat.

"Michelle, you will be much more comfortable here," he said.

She dropped gratefully into his seat, glad that he had not suggested that they stop the carriage to change places. "Thank you," she whispered.

"Let us speak of something else," Brienne said softly. "Tell us about *Maman*, please."

As Michelle glanced at the entreaty on Brienne's face, she pushed aside her terror. Her sister longed for any connection with their mother. Touching *Maman's* ring, she whispered, "*Maman* was always kind and laughing and making everything more exciting. I wish I could have spent more time with her."

"I thought she died only a few years ago," Dominic said.

"Yes, but I did not see her as often as I wished when I was growing up because *Maman* . . . worked. She was a . . . a . . . a spy."

"A spy?" Evan laughed, shocking her. "That seems to be a profession the Levesques excel at. For whom did she spy?"

"Whomever Alexei works for."

"Alexei? Who is he?"

Michelle looked again at Rusak. How could she describe Alexei? What words would give life to his quicksilver personality? How could she explain to her family that she knew nothing about him other than how he made her heart dance with joy?

Alexei loves Michelle. Michelle loves Alexei.

She smiled and squeezed his hand. Rusak was right. This was one truth that could not be denied. Looking at her family, she said, "He is the man I love."

"But he abandoned you in Vienna?" Dominic's brows lowered. "A man does not abandon the woman he loves."

His wife smiled up at him. "That is true."

Michelle wondered how much of the truth she should

reveal. Then she remembered what Alexei had told her soon after she had left St. Bernard's. Her family had become a part of his work by their kind act of welcoming her. Alexei's enemies, who had become hers, would believe she had told her family the truth.

Taking a deep breath, she began the tale from the beginning. She had to trust these people who had opened their home and their hearts to her. What the result of her honesty would be, she could not guess, but she hoped it would not be another disaster.

Chapter Twenty

Michelle was reaching for a cake on the plate held out to her when she heard a footman announce she had a caller. Looking across the grand room with ceilings that must be fifteen feet above the floor, she wondered who would be calling for her here.

Brienne asked, "Who do you know in Paris?"

"No one." Michelle stiffened on the gold settee that matched the elegance around them. "And no one knows I am here."

"Monsieur Mauriac is a skilled jeweler, but he has an unfortunate habit of gossiping."

"But to whom?"

The footman said, "Mademoiselle, he said he has a message for her from a Monsieur LaTulippe."

"LaTulippe?" Leaping to her feet, Michelle cried, "Show him in! Now!"

"Michelle—"

"No!" She faced Brienne as the footman went to do as ordered. "Don't try to protect me. He . . . he may know where Alexei is."

"Because he abducted Alexei?"

"Yes."

Slowly Brienne nodded, then turned as a man entered the room. He was unshaven, and, from the odors rising from him, Michelle guessed he had not bathed since he last shaved.

Michelle stepped between the man and her sister. "You asked to speak to me?"

"*You* are Michelle Levesque?" He laughed. "Not Collette?"

"Yes." She hid her flinch. He must have been among the men who had attacked them in the apartment in Vienna. "I understand you have a message from LaTulippe."

"You are to hear it alone," he said in a growl.

Brienne cried, "No! I am not leaving—"

Michelle shook her head as she looked into her sister's dark eyes that were so like her own.

Brienne sighed and nodded. Holding her skirts close so they did not brush against the man's filthy clothes, she left. Michelle suspected she would not go far.

"We are alone," Michelle said. "What is the message from LaTulippe?"

He smiled as his gaze swept along her, leaving a slimy sensation in its wake. The tip of his tongue scraped along his bottom lip, and he stepped toward her. Fighting her desire to flee, she did not move. He muttered something, then scooped up a cake and took a generous bite.

Around his mouthful, he mumbled, "You look very good now, Michelle."

"Thank you." She folded her arms in front of the light green gown that Abigail had lent her. Ruffles had been hastily added to the hem to make the dress long enough for her.

"Of course, fear makes you very pale, doesn't it?"

"Give me the message and leave."

"You may order your lover around, but not me. I will tell *you* what to do." He chuckled as he dropped into the chair where Brienne had been sitting. Motioning toward the settee, he commanded, "Sit."

She did not hesitate. If she argued with him, he would withhold the message. She lowered herself to the very edge of the settee.

Picking up a cup, he held it out to her. "I am sure the *duc* has some excellent brandy in the house."

"I am sure," she said, but did not take the cup.

With a shrug, he set it back on the saucer. "It was worth a try. LaTulippe is anxious to meet with you."

"I guessed that," she answered serenely. When she saw his astonishment, she smiled.

"You have something he wants."

"Do I?"

He scowled as he crossed one leg over the other. Flicking mud from his boots to the rug, he said with a growl, "Aren't you curious about your lover?"

"Yes."

"Good." He rubbed dried dirt from his hands and reached for another cake. "If you want to see him alive, be ready for a ride tomorrow at one."

She nodded. "I will be waiting by the front gate."

"Alone."

"LaTulippe would not want to risk meeting anyone more dangerous than a woman, I realize."

Grumbling a curse at her insult to his employer, he snapped, "And bring your lover's journal with you. It is a small brown volume. Do you know of it?"

Michelle blinked, trying to maintain her composure. She kept her gaze from the mantel, where she had placed the book last night after showing it to her brother. She had hoped Dominic might have some suggestion of whom it should be taken to. With the upheaval since Napoleon's arrival in Paris, no one knew who was trustworthy.

"Tomorrow at one." She rose and was surprised when he did the same.

"If you have anyone else with you, LaTulippe will pass by on his way to watch your lover's death."

She could not hide her flinch this time. Smiling, he set his battered hat on his head and bade her a good day.

Closing her eyes, she pressed her hands over her heart. Alexei was alive!

Michelle ran to the fireplace and took the small book off the mantel. She would hold on to it until the time she was to meet LaTulippe. Her smile faltered. Alexei had not wanted LaTulippe to have this.

No, she would not choose his work over his life. Her mother had died because of the work they did. Alexei must not become a martyr as well. She was going to try to save his life, even if she ended up destroying all he had worked for.

Michelle looked out through the trees edging the window of her room and watched the traffic on the Seine. Before the day's end, she would see Alexei again. Although Rusak was worried that LaTulippe was lying to her, she believed that Alexei's enemy would have delighted in sharing the news of Alexei's death. LaTulippe wanted the book she held in her hands enough to trade Alexei for it.

She opened the book and yawned. A few of the cryptic phrases she recognized as ones she had written in the letters for Alexei. It was gibberish. She hoped she had not made a mistake about this.

Closing it, she stared at her colorless face in the glass and forced a grin. "Are you ready to be a heroine?" The face reflecting back had no answer.

Her family and Rusak were waiting when Michelle descended the stairs.

Brienne handed her daughter to Evan and rushed forward to embrace her. "Why do you have to put yourself in such danger when we have just found you?"

"I must do what I can to save Alexei."

"Take someone with you," Abigail urged.

"No one. The message said I was to come alone."

"They may kill you." Dominic caught her by the shoulders. The fury on his face had not dimmed since their discussion yesterday when she had revealed her plans. Her ears still rang with his bellow that he wished they were on his ship where he could order her to heed common sense. His scowl eased as he said, *"Ma petite soeur,* you do not know if Alexei is alive. They could be lying to you to get what they want."

Although she wanted to smile as he called her *little sister,* she squared her shoulders. "He must be alive." She looked from his frown to the distress on her sister's face to Rusak's silent acceptance. He understood what her family could not. "I must try. I cannot let Alexei die to save my own life."

"I understand," Evan said, squeezing her hand. "This Alexei is so much a part of your life that you are incomplete without him." He put his arm around Brienne. "The Levesques hold on to what is theirs. She is no different from you or Dominic."

"Be careful, Michelle," Brienne whispered.

Michelle hugged each of them. When she turned to Rusak, he signed, *Rusak walk Michelle to gate.*

"LaTulippe said I must be there alone."

He made a sign she did not recognize, and she guessed by his tight face that it was a curse. *No see Rusak.*

She nodded, glad to have a concealed ally. With a strained smile for her family, she hurried out to the ornate gate. The door closed behind her, and she shivered. Mayhap she was mad not to heed their advice, but she could not let Alexei die now.

Michelle be safe.

"I will try." She watched as he hid out of sight from the street.

Exactly as the church bells tolled the hour, a carriage slowed to a stop in front of the wrought-iron gate. The

carriage was as elegant as the one she had traveled in with
Alexei to Vienna. When she saw the garish wheels, she
realized it was the same one. She forced her dismay deep
within her. LaTulippe wanted to disconcert her. She must
not let him.

The door opened, and a deep voice commanded, "Come
in if you are alone and have what I requested, Mademoiselle
Levesque."

Michelle stepped forward. A footman assisted her into the
familiar carriage, giving her no time for second thoughts.
As a hand grasped hers and tugged her down to sit, the
carriage sped along the busy street.

An arm around her shoulders kept her from striking
the side of the carriage as it rounded a corner at a dangerous speed. She stared at the hated face she had seen only
once before. She pulled away.

LaTulippe chuckled. "I was being gentlemanly. I understand you hurt your left arm during the winter, and I did
not want you to reinjure it."

"Do you do all your dirty work in carriages, Monsieur
LaTulippe?" she shot back.

He gaped at her, shocked at her daring words. Then he
smiled coldly. "I can understand why your lover has been
lamenting about you since we left you behind in Vienna,
Mademoiselle Levesque."

"You made an error by believing me in Vienna." She
gave him a condescending smile.

"Not if I get what I want."

"How did you know where to find me?"

He laughed. "I have many ears that listen for me
throughout Paris. One happened to hear how Mademoiselle Michelle D'Orage had a heartwarming reunion with
her family, the Levesques. A few questions, and I knew
where you were." His gaze swept over her. "Intelligent
women disgust me. I want one who knows only enough to
serve my needs. Too bad, for you are a sweet morsel. If
you ever tire of—"

"Never!"

He smiled coldly and crossed his arms over his chest. "Mayhap you are not so intelligent after all, if you prefer him over me."

"I hope you *will* be insulted that I would prefer Satan over you." Her laugh was as callous as his. "Unless, of course, you are one and the same. No, Satan would not make so many careless mistakes."

He spat, "Did you bring it?"

"Until I see Alexei is alive, I will not answer your question."

"I doubt if you can halt me if I decide to search you."

She hoped her cloak hid her shiver as his gaze raked her again. It took all her strength to answer in the same tranquil tone. "You are probably right, but would that give you as much satisfaction as forcing him to watch as I give you the information in exchange for his life?"

He pyramided his fingers in front of his face. "Very questionable, Mademoiselle Levesque." Suddenly he laughed. "He told me you were a novice and to leave you out of my attempts to gain the information I need. As usual, he was lying. Would you be interested in employment by the same people who hired your mother?"

"I thought—" She halted herself. The malicious twinkle in his eyes warned he was trying to trick her.

"A woman with your obvious talents could be as skilled at dealing with gentlemen as your mother was." His fingers stroked her cheek. "In the satiation of desire, a man tells a lovely lady things he might not at other times."

She slapped away his fingers. *"Maman* did not prostitute herself."

"While you were being educated in that stuffy school, she was roaming Europe on the arms of some of the Continent's lustiest men. Do you think she charmed them with only her bright wit?"

"You are lying!" When her hand rose, his fingers caught

her wrist and pressed her against the wall. Her breath came sharp and fast in fear as he leaned toward her.

Before he could fulfill the threat visible in his narrowed eyes, the carriage stopped. He glanced out the window and snarled a curse. Releasing her, he stepped from the carriage. Holding up his hand, he assisted her out. She tried to pull her fingers away, but he held them tightly. With a growled order, he led her around a stone house.

Her nose wrinkled as they stepped into a reeking alley. "Where are we going?"

"You will see when we get there." He laughed, the sound ricocheting through the narrow alley. When he paused before a door set several paces below street level, he motioned for her to precede him.

Uneasily she did. Every sense waited for betrayal, but she heard nothing but his footsteps behind her. She opened the door and went down a flight of dimly lit stairs. Trying to breathe shallowly so the hideous odor did not sink into her lungs, she took each step cautiously. She was not surprised to see water pooling on the floor. A chill clung to the stones.

LaTulippe pushed past her, grasping her arm. When he stopped before a wooden door with a metal grate at eye level, he called, "Vernier, you have a guest."

"Vernier?" She gasped. When LaTulippe glanced at her, she masked her shock. This must be Alexei's true name.

With a key pulled from beneath his coat, LaTulippe unlocked the prison cell. A shadowed form stood, and she heard the clank of iron. She cursed, and LaTulippe chuckled.

Stepping into the room ahead of her, he lit a candle on the wall. "Aren't you going to pay a call on Alexandre Vernier, onetime spy?"

She ran to be enfolded in Alexei's arms. She heard him gasp her name, but she wanted only to touch him. His lips found hers through the tears engraving a path along her face. As his arms closed around her, she forgot that Alexei was chained to the wall by one ankle and that his hair and beard were long. Nothing mattered but the caress of his loving mouth on hers.

"Isn't this sweet? Another reunion for you, mademoiselle."

LaTulippe's sarcastic words separated them.

Alexei glanced from her to his captor. "Michelle, *Liebchen,* you should never have come here." He edged between her and LaTulippe.

With a victorious laugh, LaTulippe toyed with the key in one hand and held a gun in the other. "You might as well speak French, Vernier. Your charade as the Russian is over. Even Mademoiselle Levesque is no longer betwattled."

"Levesque?"

LaTulippe laughed again. "It seems you were not the only one traveling under an assumed name. Alexandre Vernier, allow me the supreme pleasure of introducing you to Michelle Levesque, sister to the *duc* of Tonnere du Grêlon."

When Alexei regarded her with astonishment, she wanted to explain. Her voice dried up in horror as LaTulippe pulled back on the pistol's hammer. She had not stopped to think how easy it would be for LaTulippe to kill both of them. The first shot from his gun would be for her, for he would want Alexei to suffer as long as possible.

LaTulippe smiled. "I have fulfilled my share of this agreement, Mademoiselle Levesque. Give me what I want."

"She will give you nothing!" In one smooth motion, Alexei shoved her aside and slammed his fist into LaTulippe's face. Before he could swing again, men appeared as if from some hidden spring, drowning him in a cascade of blows.

She shrieked and tried to pull one of the men away from him. A strong arm pushed her backward. She fell on a filthy pallet, striking her head against the stone wall. Fuzz filled her mind.

Someone jerked her to her feet. When she swayed, her slipper hit something more pliant than the stones. She saw Alexei facedown on the floor. Time collapsed into itself. Again she was in Vienna, and the horror was only beginning.

With a moan, she dropped to her knees and put her hands on his shoulders. "Alexei. Alexei, look at me."

"He is alive," said LaTulippe with a snarl. "Get up." He wiped blood from his nose. "Give it to me, Mademoiselle Levesque."

Clutching her reticule close to her chest, she watched as Alexei—no, she must think of him now as Alexandre— shook his head and sat. "If I give you this," she asked, "will you let both of us go alive?"

"Alive?" He snickered and tossed the key on the floor in front of her. "Give me what I want, and you and Vernier are of no further use or interest to me."

She pulled the brown book from her bag. Holding it out, she heard Alexandre's curse as LaTulippe snatched it from her.

"Move a muscle, Vernier, and your mistress is dead." LaTulippe riffled through the book and smiled. "Thank you, Mademoiselle Levesque. What you have done will be remembered throughout history." He motioned to his men, and they followed as he sauntered out, leaving the door open behind him.

Michelle dropped to her knees next to Alexandre. She started to put her arms around him, but his scowl halted her. He put his hand up to his head.

"Your right hand!" She gasped. "You can use it."

"I have had nothing else to do since I was caged here but to practice using it." He struggled to his feet. Grasping her shoulders, he brought her upright. "Michelle, how could you be so stupid as to come here?"

She shoved his hands away. "I would not let you die."

"Instead now hundreds of allied men may die to fulfill Napoleon's dream of regaining his empire." He reached for the key on the floor and unlatched the rusty manacle around his leg. "LaTulippe is correct, *Liebchen*. You may be remembered throughout all history for giving Napoleon the information he needs to beat the allies."

"That is what is in that book?"

"I was in Vienna to obtain military intelligence from the allied leaders. It was to be used to halt Napoleon if he tried to annex Europe again. LaTulippe let me live after I convinced him I could not get him what he wanted. I did not understand then, but I do now. He knew he could lure you into giving the information to him with me as the bait. *Verflucht*, Michelle! How could you be so stupid?"

"I would risk the whole world for you."

"Even though I lied to you right from the beginning?" He took her hands and pressed them to his chest as he stood. "LaTulippe was being honest. My name is Alexandre Vernier, not Alexei Vatutin."

"It does not matter who you are. I love you. Let's go home."

"Home?"

"My family's house here in Paris." His brow wrinkled in confusion, and she smiled. "It is lovely outside. While we walk, I shall try to explain everything that has happened since we left Vienna."

"Outside? I have been in here so long, that seems like a dream."

"Let's go," she urged gently. "Once you get cleaned up, we can decide how to halt LaTulippe."

"You make it sound so simple, my love."

"Isn't it? Do you think he is any match for us when we work together?"

She thought he would smile, but his eyes narrowed as he said, "Yes, *Liebchen*, I think he is our match. I only hope he is not more than our match."

* * *

Alexandre sat in an overstuffed chair of Michelle's bed-room and puffed contentedly on his pipe. This had been an amazing day. He chuckled as he thought of his reunion with Rusak, who had been glad to see him and eager to rout LaTulippe from his hole.

It should not have amazed him that Sophie had hidden her past as the *duchesse* of Château Tonnere du Grêlon. He wondered if even her superiors had known the truth.

That Michelle had a whole family waiting for her in Paris had been the greatest surprise of all. He had been uncertain of a welcome when he learned Michelle's brother had served as a privateer for Napoleon in the blockade of England, but Alexandre Vernier had been greeted as a hero, although he had made a mess of the whole situation.

Several times Michelle had tried to speak to him of the book she had handed over to LaTulippe, but he had cut her off each time. He did not want anyone else, not even her family, to know of what was in it. There might be a way to undo this muddle, but he was not sure how. He needed some time to think of a solution. Yet all he could think of was Michelle and how he wanted her. When a door opened, Alexandre smiled as his dream was given life.

Michelle's bare skin above the open collar of her wrap-per glistened with droplets from her bath. "I wish *Maman* had lived long enough to see this day when we are all here together." She put her hairbrush on the dressing table. Sitting on his lap, she waved away the smoke from his pipe.

He set the pipe aside. "I forgot how it vexes you, *Liebchen.*" When she smiled, he said, "I can get no more accustomed to calling you *ma chérie* than you once could imagine calling me anything but Alexei."

"Rusak is Russian, but if you are French, how . . . ?"

His lips hardened, creasing his freshly shaven cheeks. "The work I do creates strange friendships that are not bound by political alliances. He was a contact I had made several years before the Russian campaign. When I returned there, I met with him. Unfortunately our rendezvous was witnessed by my enemies. You see the result."

She leaned her head against his shoulder. When his arms tightened around her, she whispered, "You must not blame yourself for what happened. Rusak does not."

"How do you know?"

"He told me." She raised her head and smiled. Pleasure and the need for her curled through him, making him taut. Her breath brushed his cheek as he wished her fingertips would when she said, "We talked often of you. It helped me believe you were still alive. I even laughed about all our conversations that had ended in angry words."

He stroked her damp hair. "I feared that I would be mad and fall in love with you if I was honest with you about anything."

"You do a very good Russian accent in both German and French."

"I thought so."

She batted at his hand teasing her cheek. "You need not sound so smug." Running her finger along the collarless neckline of his shirt, she asked, "How do we find LaTulippe?"

He did not want to talk about his enemy. He wanted to make love with this beguiling woman. "We start first thing in the morning. With the funds your brother so generously has offered, we should be able to buy more information about LaTulippe's comings and goings than he can remember himself."

Suddenly Michelle slipped off his lap. Frowning, Alexandre stood. She whispered, "Alexandre, he said *Maman* was . . ."

He tilted her face up. "*Liebchen,* what did that cur say?"

"He said *Maman* once worked for his organization."

"That is true, but she grew disillusioned with Napoleon, as many of us did when it became clear he was not France's salvation but the road to her ruin. Then she approached my superiors to help them destroy Napoleon's empire."

"Is it true that she used her skills to gain information?"

"She certainly was skilled, for she could urge reticent men to tell her things that they soon regretted that they had."

When Michelle walked away from him again and ran her fingers along the covers of the bed, he frowned. She was hiding something from him. He cursed under his breath. How had LaTulippe poisoned her mind?

"LaTulippe offered me a job," she said so softly that he could hear her only by drawing her back against him. "The same one he said *Maman* had."

"And you wisely refused. *Liebchen*, you are not upset because LaTulippe tried to twist you into his web. What is wrong?"

Whirling, she cried, "He said *Maman* prostituted herself to get information."

He slanted her head against his shoulder as she flung her arms around him. "How could you believe him? Your mother was a skilled spy. She flirted with men, but, if she had a lover other than your father, it was because he offered his heart, not because he had information she needed." He leaned his head against her soft hair. "As I have offered you mine."

"If he had killed you, there would never be happiness for me again." Her fingers stroked his jaw. "I love you, Alexandre."

"And I love you."

"Alexandre, I know you are angry that I gave the book to LaTulippe, but—"

"No more about him now, *Liebchen*."

"But Alexandre, I wanted to explain—"

He captured her lips. For a moment she tried to pull away; then she answered his kiss with her own longing. Whatever she had to tell him could wait. Nothing mattered now but that she was in his arms. With a laugh, he gathered her up and dropped her onto the bed. Leaning over her, he whispered, "And that is not the only fantasy I want to make come true with you tonight."

Her lips were soft beneath his as he held her to the pillows with his kiss, soft and willing and eager for the passion that had been denied them too long. It would not be denied them any longer.

Chapter Twenty-one

Walking to where brilliant blossoms overflowed a planter on the edge of the terrace, Michelle wished Alexandre would come back to the house. She had tried since they had returned here yesterday to talk to him about the book she had given to LaTulippe. He had not given her a chance to explain.

She smiled as she ran her fingers along a ceramic planter. Last night any opportunity to talk had ended with feverish kisses and an ecstasy that still sent shivers down to her toes, which curled with delight at the memory.

Dominic walked toward her, smiling. He had suggested at breakfast several "friends" who might help Alexandre find LaTulippe. She had been shocked to discover that her brother and her brother-in-law had once made a living smuggling art across the channel. Alexandre had smiled and thanked Dominic for the offer, but had left to seek an ally of his own.

"How are you doing, Michelle?" Dominic asked, sitting on the low wall.

"I shall do better when Alexandre gets back."

He sandwiched her hands between his. "Why don't you and Alexandre come with Abigail and me at the end of the week to Château Tonnere du Grêlon? It is relatively inaccessible, and you will have time to decide what you must do."

"I do not think we have any time."

With a grim expression, he nodded. "I guessed that, but I fear what will happen if you stay here. LaTulippe knows you are here."

"He knows about the château as well." She pulled her hands away and looked at the river. "We are not safe anywhere until he is arrested."

"Let Alexandre take of that," urged Brienne as she came to join the conversation. "He knows what he is doing."

Michelle gasped. "Would you let your husband go into such danger alone? Wouldn't you help him?"

"She has you there, Brienne," Dominic answered with a smile. As a maid walked toward them, he added, "Here comes lunch. Shall we wait for Alexandre?"

"No," Michelle said, "for I have no idea when he will be back. He may have to chase Napoleon's army north through the Low Countries to find LaTulippe." She looked at the table where the luncheon was being set out. "Where are Abigail and Evan?"

"Evan took Lucile for a walk in the park," Brienne said. "The *Teatro* Caparelli is playing there, and they are friends."

"A traveling theater troupe?"

"Evan has friends everywhere." Brienne sat at the table and poured lemonade for each of them. "Where is Abigail, Dominic?"

"She was not feeling well this morning." He sat and picked up a glass, his eyes twinkling.

"Again?" Brienne laughed. "Is she pregnant?"

"It is possible."

Michelle laughed as Brienne slapped his arm and said, "I have no doubts it is *possible.*"

"We shall know soon." He took a sip. "Or so she tells me."

Taking the glass Brienne held out to her, Michelle leaned back in her chair. She never had guessed how much she wanted a family. She had relished the days she and *Maman* had together.

She looked over her shoulder as she heard footsteps in the house. "Who . . . ?"

Half a dozen men swept through the door to surround them. Dominic started to stand, but sat again at the click of a hammer being drawn back on a pistol.

When another man pushed forward, Michelle said with a gasp, "LaTulippe!"

He held her gaze as he walked along the table to approach her. She fought to hide her fear.

"What a charming familial scene!" He bowed toward Dominic. "Forgive the intrusion, Your Grace." The venom returned to his voice as he looked at Michelle. "Where is Vernier?"

"He is out," Michelle said coolly.

"Is that so? Where?"

"I don't know. He left before I rose this morning."

He leaned on the table and held his gun directly in her face. Ignoring Brienne's horrified gasp and Dominic's curse, he smiled. "Does this help you remember?"

"It would if I had forgotten, but I truly do not know where Alexandre went."

"You have seen that he is not here," said Dominic smoothly, in spite of the rage lining his face. "Why don't you leave? Or is it the way of Napoleon's lapdogs to threaten innocent women?"

"Threaten innocent women?" LaTulippe put his hand over his heart. "You wound me. I would not suggest harm to your *innocent* sister."

"My brother has been a genial host," Michelle said. "If you expect to stay here until Alexandre returns . . ."

He shook his head in fake sorrow. "What a shame he

corrupted you! You are as magnificent as your mother in her heyday. However, you shall have to do as I say now, Mademoiselle Levesque, or you will force me to do something painful.''

"I will not help you betray Alexandre. Nothing you can do—''

He pointed his gun at Brienne. With a cry, Michelle jumped to her feet and reached for his arm. He caught her hand and twirled her into his grip.

"Such fire,'' he mused in the same irreverent voice. "To think of it wasted on Vernier brings me great sorrow.'' Again he bowed. "I bid you *adieu*. Or, I should say, we bid you *adieu*. If you make an effort to follow us, it will be your sweet sister who will die.''

Dominic stood slowly. "I assume you have a message for Alexandre.''

LaTulippe laughed and tightened his grip on Michelle's wrist. When she gasped with the pain that raced along her arm, he said, "Of course, for he is sure to stop here first to kiss his mistress good-bye. Tell Vernier to go to Madame Nicollet. He will know what I mean.'' He chuckled. "You may also tell him that I look forward to seeing him die. When I am done with him and your lovely sister, I will return her to you . . . mayhap.''

"Please leave Michelle here,'' begged Brienne. "You do not need—''

"But I do. Simply to even the stakes.'' He shoved Michelle into the arms of one of his men. As the man bound her hands, LaTulippe added, "Tell Vernier I want the key to the code. Before midnight tomorrow at the location he will be told by Madame Nicollet. Otherwise I can promise you that none of you will ever see Mademoiselle Levesque alive again.''

Michelle wanted to say something to ease her sister's terror and her brother's fury, but she whispered, "Tell Alexandre not to do anything ill-advised. Tell him I love him.''

LaTulippe laughed. "And I hope he loves you in return, because then he will not hesitate to do as ordered." He tweaked her cheek.

She spat in his face. She heard her sister's scream in the moment before LaTulippe's fist struck her, sending her into a blackness as thick as his soul.

"Wake up!"

Michelle started to roll over, but moaned as her bound arms ached. When a lantern flashed close to her face, she wanted to recoil, but it was impossible. The rest of her body hurt as deeply as her arms.

She cowered as she saw a raised hand. In the past two days, she had suffered LaTulippe's beatings. He used any excuse, although he had not hit her again as hard as he had when he abducted her from the house on Île Saint-Louis. He wanted to be sure she missed none of the torment he had in store for her.

"Where is he?" LaTulippe's shout rang through her head. Only exhaustion had granted her a few moments of sleep, almost her first since the night before she went to Mauriac's jewelry shop.

She forced her eyes to focus on his furious face. It was a sight she had become familiar with since she had been bound and thrown in the corner of what she guessed was a barn. She had become more accustomed to the odor of animal droppings and the damp than to LaTulippe's tantrums.

"If you mean Alexandre," she replied, "how do you expect me to know?" She cringed as he struck her hard enough to start her ears ringing again.

"Harlot! To think I wasted my time with you."

"I did not ask you to kidnap me!" When he lifted his hand, she glared at him, agony fueling her bravado. "You cannot blame me for your mistakes."

"My mistake *and* yours. We both believed your lover

would come here before the deadline passed this morning." Standing, he looked at the men leaning against the opposite wall. "We shall go to where the army is encamped," he announced. "The book is already there. I will have to explain to Marshal Ney that it may take a bit longer to have the code broken."

Michelle swallowed her gasp. If LaTulippe had access to one of Napoleon's most trusted men, the information could be in the emperor's hands as soon as it was decoded.

Jerking on her arm, he dragged her up to a sitting position. "Do you want to go for a ride?"

"I would be delighted to go back to Paris."

"Paris is not your destination." He laughed as he motioned to his men. All but one left the barn. "You can bring him now. Mademoiselle Levesque is ready to leave us."

Michelle bit her lip as the man ran out. Who was LaTulippe sending for?

"What? No questions?" he taunted as he pushed her to sit on the filthy pallet again. "That is unlike you, Michelle."

"I see no reason to give you pleasure by asking what you plan to do with me." She wondered how long she could maintain this haughty dignity. Fear was nibbling away at it like a rat eating a cracker. "You would not tell me if I asked."

He squatted in front of her. His loosened waistcoat flared over the knees of his breeches. Twisting his fingers through her tangled hair, he murmured, "It is really a shame to send you away. You are a pretty little thing, although you have the disgusting habit of talking too much." His eyes slitted into an icy glare. "It might not be such a loss at that. Vernier did not consider you worth saving."

She tried not to react to his cruel words, but it was impossible. She was sure Alexandre would have come if he could. That left only one alternative. He was unable to save her. When LaTulippe laughed, she knew her fear had flashed across her face.

"I will be right back. I want to speak with your new friend before he comes in." He patted her head. "Believe it or not, there is someone willing to take Vernier's mistress and save me the problem of disposing of your corpse. Relax. I doubt if he will grant you much time for sleep tonight."

"Go to hell, you whoremonger!"

"If I get there before you, I will be sure to pay you a call when you arrive." His horrible laugh rang through the barn. The door crashed closed behind him, and a bar dropped into place.

Michelle sagged against the wall behind her. The stones cut into her back, but the pain in her heart was sharper. When hot tears trickled along her face, she drew up her knees and leaned her cheek on her filthy dress. She moaned as the motion strained her arms.

"Alexandre," she whispered, "be safe."

She shuddered. When she was sent away with LaTulippe's ally, she might never know what happened to Alexandre. She could not imagine a worse torment.

Voices beyond the door cut through Michelle's misery. Sunlight burst around the opening door, blinding her. Dampening her chapped lips, she vowed to let neither LaTulippe nor his crony learn how terrified and heartsick she was.

Her resolution vanished as the sunshine glowed off a familiar face. "Bartholomew!" Hope made her sit straighter. How had he heard of her predicament and sought out LaTulippe to save her?

He flashed her a smile, but spoke to LaTulippe. "As you said, she is unharmed. Name your price."

"Nothing has changed." He leaned with false nonchalance against the wall. "Exactly what we discussed before. I am understandably in a hurry, Your Highness. Pay me, and you can take your tattered princess back to Coxe-Saxony-Colburg with you.''

Bartholomew held out a leather bag with obvious distaste. "There is what I agreed to pay you for Michelle. Count it, so we can be done with this. I wish to be on my way before dark. If Napoleon is to move his men at dawn—''

"Be silent," said LaTulippe in a growl as he stuffed the bag beneath his coat. He reached down and jerked her to her feet. A shove sent her reeling into Bartholomew's arms. "Untie her if you wish, Your Highness, but you may find she will be more cooperative if you let her stay as she is for a few more hours.''

"Yes," he answered slowly. "I understand very well.''

When Bartholomew pulled on Michelle's arm, she hurried out with him. She blinked in the bright sunshine. In horror she stared at the fields before them. In what must be the French army camp, thousands of men were waiting for the signal from Napoleon. Then they would attack the allied forces for one final grasp at glory.

"By the morrow, my dear, you will be very happy I have taken you away from here," Bartholomew said.

"Can we get to Paris tonight? My brother—''

He laughed. "Paris? Why would I want to take you to Paris?" Pulling her tightly to him, he ran his fingers up to her breast.

She tried to pull away. His mouth clamped over hers. *Du lieber Gott!* She had not believed that Bartholomew was truly LaTulippe's ally. Raising her foot, she stamped on his foot. He screeched, his grip loosening.

She ran as fast as her weak legs could go down the hillside. She saw Bartholomew's carriage on the road below and tried to stop. As her feet slipped out from beneath her, she screamed. Dirt sprayed over her as she fell. She drew her feet under her to stand.

"Think twice, Michelle," came a cold voice.

Michelle capsized against the torn earth as the barrel of

Bartholomew's pistol pricked her ear. To think she could run away had been absurd, but she had to try.

He grabbed her bound arms and pulled her to her feet. When she shrieked in pain, something cold brushed her hands. Abruptly they were free. Bartholomew checked first one arm, then the other. She gasped as he touched her left shoulder.

"It is not broken," he stated tightly. "Get in the carriage."

"No!" Her voice was faint with pain. If her shoulder was not broken, it ached as if it were.

A footman came at Bartholomew's command and picked her up. He pushed her onto the carriage seat. Bartholomew sat beside her, grabbing her arm before she could flee. She moaned as another sliver of pain sliced across her shoulder.

He glared at her as the carriage lurched into motion. His once kind blue eyes were filled with fury. He took her hand and stroked the ring her mother had worn. "You will obey me. I did not pay so highly for you so you could flee back to Vatutin's arms."

She stiffened as Bartholomew used Alexandre's alias. Didn't Bartholomew know the truth? If he was LaTulippe's ally, he should know. Mayhap he did not realize why LaTulippe had abducted her. She had to know, for that might help her devise a way to escape. "What did you give LaTulippe for me?"

"Just a few gold coins and the promise to bring Coxe-Saxony-Colburg into the new alliance."

"New alliance?" She frowned. "You know what has happened to Napoleon's so-called allies in the past. He swallowed them whole. There will be no more Coxe-Saxony-Colburg."

"That is not your worry, my dear. You need think only of the pleasure you can give me."

Michelle tried to evade his hands. In the carriage, there was no place to escape as he lowered the leather shades.

She moaned in horror when he caught her shoulders and pinned her to the seat.

"Bartholomew, you are hurting me," she cried as he touched her wrenched arm.

"Why should I wait?" He laughed coldly as he ran his fingers along the rips in the shoulder of her gown. He tore them more to leave her sleeve hanging on her arm. "It is not as if I would marry you after you have embarrassed me so publicly with your lover."

"Then why—" She screamed when he tore a hole in the sleeve on her other shoulder.

He pushed her hands away as he bent to press his mouth against the skin above her modest gown. When she moaned with horror, he slipped his finger into the tatters and ripped her other sleeve away. "Think how the gossip will stop when the delegates learn that you have crawled back to me on the eve of the announcement of my betrothal to another woman." He gripped her face painfully. "You shamed me, Michelle. For that, you are going to pay."

"Bartholomew—"

"I think you should call me 'Your Highness.' "

"If you do not want me to call you Bartholomew, I shall call you Prince Char—" She cringed as he raised his hand.

"Do not become tiresome." He gave her the smile that she once had thought was kind. "Mayhap, if you beg, I will spare you such a life, Michelle. Beg me as I begged you to be my wife."

"And you will give me the same answer."

"You are right." He laughed and forced her mouth beneath his. She tried to keep his hands away, but his strength was too much for her.

The carriage stopped, nearly rocking them to the floor. Michelle clutched the seat. At the sound of gunfire, she screamed and waited for the pain that she recalled all too well.

A man shouted her name.

"Alexandre!" she cried when he called her name again.

"Shut up!" said Bartholomew with a snarl. Pulling a handkerchief from an inner pocket, he stuffed it into her mouth. He drew his gun and pressed it against the cloth. "Make a sound, and it will be your last one."

She tried not to moan with despair as he dropped a cloak on her. Through it, the weight of his gun centered in the middle of her stomach. If she moved, he would fire it.

Straining, she sought to hear what she could not see. The coach rocked as the driver and footman alighted, but the door remained closed. Beyond it, she could hear the hoofbeats from more than one horse. She hoped Alexandre had brought many allies with him.

Bartholomew growled a curse just before she heard Alexandre say coolly, "What a pleasant surprise, Your Highness! As you are heading south, I should offer you a welcome to France, but I admit little pleasure at having you in my homeland. Now, before you continue on your way, I think you have in your possession something that belongs with me."

"I have nothing of yours, Vatutin. Why don't you go after LaTulippe? He is northbound toward where the armies are amassing in—"

She could hear Alexandre's grim smile in his taut voice. "I know exactly where they are, but that you are familiar with his location suggests many different things, Your Highness. Such as bargains your father would not sanction. That, however, is none of my business. What is my business is that I also know you are holding Mademoiselle Levesque against her will. If you would be so good as to return her to me, I shall let you continue on your way."

The gun poked painfully into her ribs, and she fought not to gasp in pain.

Bartholomew laughed tersely. "You are chasing shadows, Vatutin."

"Actually, the name is Vernier. Alexandre Vernier."

"I do not give a damn what your name is. Get out of

here. I have dinner waiting for me at an inn in Namur. Why don't you let me get to it?"

Alexandre's voice lost its easy negligence. "Dinner for two? I have given you enough opportunities, Prince Charming." He ignored Bartholomew's curse as he went on, "If you do not want to listen to me, mayhap you will listen to my Pauly."

Recognizing the name as a type of pistol, Michelle slipped her fingers under the cloak and pulled the material out of her mouth. Carefully she waited for Bartholomew to answer Alexandre. At that second, the prince's attention would be centered on his foe.

"Vatu— What the—"

Michelle kicked at him at the same time she shoved the heavy cloak upward to knock his arm away. She scrambled past him for the door. An arm jerked her back.

"Let me go!" she screeched in frustration. The tip of a pistol in her cheek silenced her.

Bartholomew's voice was as agitated as his heartbeat beneath her ear as he said, "Leave us, Vernier, if you do not want to see her with a ball in her skull."

Alexandre smiled. "How are you faring, *Liebchen?* Forgive me for being so slow to come for you, but I shall explain later."

"You will do nothing but . . ." Bartholomew tensed.

Alexandre opened the door with a grand bow. "Prince Charming, if you do not want me to order Rusak to fire his shotgun in the back of your head, I suggest you release Mademoiselle Levesque posthaste."

For a trio of heartbeats, no one moved. Michelle saw Bartholomew fingering the trigger of his gun. Abruptly he drew it away and shoved her forward. Alexandre caught her before she could strike the ground. He steadied her on her feet and set her beside the road. Although he offered her a smile, he turned back to the carriage.

"Have a pleasant journey home, Prince Charming. If

you will excuse us, we have a bit of unfinished business to deal with north of here.''

"You need not waste your time looking for me, Vernier. We can finish that business right here.''

Michelle whirled as she heard LaTulippe's mocking voice. The pistol in his hand was pointed at her.

LaTulippe continued in the same falsely genial tone, "I expected you would turn up as soon as I sent your mistress off with this young fool who thinks more of his tarnished honor than his father's wrath.''

"Shoot him!'' urged Bartholomew. He choked back his next words as the jab of the shotgun barrel reminded him that Rusak stood behind him out of sight from the road.

"Why don't we let this princeling go?'' suggested LaTulippe as he dismounted from his horse. Two other men appeared from the trees to flank him. "Then we men can discuss this matter, Vernier.''

Alexandre did not move away from the carriage. Any sudden step toward Michelle would guarantee LaTulippe's pulling the trigger. Keeping his pistol hidden behind his coat, he rested his foot on the step of the carriage. The door remained at his back to block an attack from behind, although his own safety was not his highest priority as he waited for LaTulippe to make a mistake.

"Why don't you make this easy on all of us?'' LaTulippe asked. "Give me the code, and we will find you a place in the new government.''

"A place for a man who betrayed his ideals to save his life?'' Alexandre snorted in derision. "Such a man would have as little worth to Boney as to any leader.''

" 'Tis not your life you are bargaining for, but hers.'' He emphasized his words by waving the pistol at Michelle. "Give me the clue to the code.''

Alexandre chuckled. "Do you think I am carrying it with me? What good is it when I do not have my book that Michelle gave to you? Once, I might have been able to recall what was said to me in Vienna, but you beat it quite literally out of my head." Michelle moaned, but he did not look at her. "Neither of us has anything worthwhile. We both have lost."

"Have we?" LaTulippe's finger caressed the hammer of his gun. "Or could it be that you have both and are here only to save your mistress?"

"I am here to save Michelle, but I do not have the damn information any longer. You have it!"

LaTulippe laughed as he looked at Michelle. "Why didn't you tell your lover about how a candle burned in your room all night before you brought me his book? Haven't you shown him the pages you copied?"

"You are mad, LaTulippe!" Alexandre said with a snarl.

"Am I? Am I, Michelle?"

"No," she whispered. Her gaze reached out to Alexandre as he knew she wanted her hands to. "Alexandre, I tried to tell you. At first there were too many others around; then we . . ."

Alexandre cursed under his breath, then louder. *Verflucht!* She *had* tried to tell him, but he had not heeded her, although he should have guessed she would do anything she could to help him with his work. If he had, he would not have needed to chase after LaTulippe and leave her unprotected.

LaTulippe said, "It seems we are back where we started. You have the coded information *and* the key to it. I have your mistress. Is she worth the trade?"

"Yes."

"Alexandre!" she cried. "You said I should not have given him the book to save you. You said—"

"I was wrong." When he heard LaTulippe's laugh, he did not react. Instead he held Michelle's wide-eyed gaze as he added, "It seems there were some more lessons I had yet to learn."

"May I suggest you make your next lesson getting your copy of the information and the code and bringing it to me without delay?" LaTulippe chuckled again. "Tell him where it is, Michelle."

"No! You will send your men to my family's house again."

"Tell him, or . . ." He drew back the hammer.

"No!" Michelle moaned, but her voice was swallowed by Bartholomew's shout.

Guns fired along the road. A splotch of red exploded across the front of the man standing next to LaTulippe. She huddled on the ground. A hand grasped hers, and she tried to pull away. She shrieked for Alexandre as she looked up at LaTulippe's vicious smile.

When he raised the pistol to aim it at her, she grabbed a handful of dirt and flung it in his face. He shrieked a curse as he clawed at his eyes, but was drowned out by the ear-shattering crash of a pistol firing. She watched LaTulippe fall into a widening puddle of blood.

"Liebchen?"

She flung her arms around Alexandre's neck and clung to him as she sobbed out all her fright. "Thank you for saving me," she whispered.

"I didn't."

"You didn't?" When a finger tapped her shoulder, she moved away reluctantly, then said in a gasp, "Rusak! Thank—"

Come, Michelle. Hurry.

"Yes, we should leave," Alexandre said.

She glanced at him and smiled. He must have been learning more signs in the past days.

No. Michelle, come, carriage. Hurry.

Looking at Alexandre, she saw he was as confused by the emphatic signs as she was. Carefully not looking at the dead men at the back of the carriage, she went with Rusak to the open door. She covered her mouth with her hand as she stared at Bartholomew's blood-soaked coat.

In a barely audible whisper, he murmured, "I could not let him kill you."

Michelle tore her gaze from him to look at Alexandre's shocked face. Her eyes must be as wide with amazement. Putting her hand on Bartholomew's arm, she said, "LaTulippe is dead, and I am alive. Let us get you to—"

He asserted in his most imperious tone, "No . . . doctors. I . . . I . . . dead man. Tell me . . . tell . . . me . . . Do you . . . did you . . . ever love me?"

"Of course," she lied as she took his already cold hand between hers. "How could I know you and not love you, Bartholomew? You made me believe I could be a princess. You—"

Alexandre's hand on her shoulder silenced her. He drew her away from the carriage door. Reaching past her, he closed Bartholomew's sightless eyes. Then he pulled her into his arms. When he bent to kiss her, she answered his passion for only a second.

Tugging away, she cried, "Why did you wait so long to come for me?"

He pulled off his coat and wrapped it around her ruined dress. "We have been here since about three hours after LaTulippe put you in that barn. The two of us could not storm his stronghold and be sure we would keep him from killing you. We knew he would bring you out eventually. He did." With a sigh of regret, he shook his head. "Unfortunately we did not consider that your prince would be caught in the cross fire."

As tears bubbled up in her eyes, he turned her toward where his horse waited. "What about the carriage?" she whispered.

"When we get to the allied camp, we can send someone back for it."

"The allied camp?"

"This game is not yet done," he said as the excitement returned to his voice. "We have to get the pages you copied and deliver them with the code to my contact at Charleroi, *Liebchen.* Shall we go and see what we can do to free France from Napoleon's dreams of conquest once and for all?"

She smiled as he lifted her onto the horse. His enthusiasm was contagious. When he mounted behind her and sent the horse along the road with Rusak riding close behind, she did not look at the carnage behind them. She must think only of the future bought with those lives.

A future she wanted to spend loving Alexandre.

Epilogue

. . . and that is why I brought you to Zurich, dear daughter. Here we could be safe from the French government. I had intended to take you back to France, so we could find your brother and sister. All my attempts to seek Dominic and Brienne's whereabouts have failed, blocked by that pint-sized dictator. Mayhap someday he will be gone and our family will be together.

In the meantime, I have worked to further the goals of his enemies. Not against France, but against Napoleon. It has been simpler to leave you at St. Bernard's, because I could not take you with me during my trips out of Switzerland. It would have been too risky for you as well as inconvenient in my guise as an unfettered woman.

That is in the past. What concerns me, my dear child, is your future. Although I have concluded each day with a prayer that my beloved Marc-Michel will watch over all of you, I know the time is coming when I can help you no more than I can your brother and sister.

Dear Michelle, you must be aware of your past. If you decide to return to Château Tonnere du Grêlon, you may need assistance. I suggest you find my most recent partner. He will help you deal with any problems you encounter in France. His name is Alexandre Vernier, but he might be using another name. I would describe him to you, but he changes his appearance like a chameleon changes color. You will know him by his green eyes and irreverent humor. Just contact the people at the address below, and they will help you find him wherever he might be.

God bless you, my child. If someday you should chance upon your sister and brother, tell them how much I have dreamed of holding them again. I pray your life is filled with the peace and the family that I was denied. All my love.

Michelle glanced up from the crumpled page to see tears running along Brienne's face. Dominic's mouth worked with strong emotions when he put his arm around Abigail, who wept as her month-old son nursed in her arms.

In a choked voice, Michelle whispered, "It is signed, 'Your mother, Sophie Rameau Levesque.' "

Silence filled the room, which was small by the standards of the grand Château Tonnere du Grêlon. Larger than the refectory at St. Bernard's, it did not feel crowded with the many people sitting on the faded brocade settees. The room might once have been grand, but the wallpaper was now peeling and the floors were dull. In a corner between a floor-to-ceiling window and the hearth, which was decorated with garlands for Christmas, Lucile played with an old woman Brienne called *Grand-mère*. Madame LeClerc had raised Brienne during the years they lived in London, hiding from Marc-Michel Levesque's enemies. Beside her sat a woman a generation younger, Madame St. Clair who had been Dominic's foster mother. They were now a part of the Levesque family.

Sensing Alexandre's gaze on her, she looked at him. "Are you all right?" he asked softly.

"I think I shall be." She smoothed the note on her lap. "If only I had had this months ago . . ."

She could not fault Frau Herbart, who had lamented losing this letter before Michelle left St. Bernard's. In the months since, Michelle had forgotten about it. Never had she suspected that the headmistress would find it weeks later and send it on to Vienna. Slowed by the weather and the events that had exploded across Europe before Napoleon was sent into what she prayed was permanent exile, it had reached Vienna after she and Rusak left. Frau Schlissel had brought it with her when she came to Paris, but she and the letter had found their way to Château Tonnere du Grêlon only this morning. This had been the first time all day that everyone had been together so Michelle could share the letter.

Alexandre took Michelle's hand and led her out of the room. Climbing the wide stairs, he said nothing as they went to their room. She did not look at the bed on its raised dais or the frayed cloth of gold curtains as she flung her arms around him.

"How much simpler our first meeting would have been if I had only known!" she whispered.

He stroked her back. "You cannot be certain of that. You had no reason to suspect that Alexei Vatutin and Alexandre Vernier were the same man."

"It is Christmas Eve again." She breathed in his intriguing male scent. "Who would have believed a year ago that you and I would be here at a French château with my family?"

"Who would have believed that we would be anywhere together? Last year at this time, we were recovering from that mad attack on us. I wish I knew who had ordered that. It might have been LaTulippe. It might have been someone else." When she shivered, he said quickly, "Forgive me, *Liebchen*, for reminding you of that."

"I wonder what 1816 will bring. I hope it is peace."

"I think that is everyone's wish, and you, *Liebchen,* made it possible by not listening to me."

She smiled as she locked her fingers behind his nape. "I do believe you usually remember everything you hear."

"Except when you tell me you love me."

"You forget that?"

"Only so I can exult in hearing you say it again." He kissed her with slow, lingering hunger. "But I am glad you heeded me about looking for a better hiding place for important items."

She laughed. "Do you think LaTulippe's men would have found the copied pages in a torn stocking beneath a pile of discarded clothes in the wardrobe at Brienne's house?"

"You have learned your lessons well."

"All of them." She drew his mouth down to hers. When her tongue brushed his lips, he moaned with the need that swept over her.

He drew back, shocking her. Quietly, he said, *"Liebchen,* I got my new orders yesterday."

"I know."

"How—" A flash of astonishment was replaced by a grin. "You have learned too much from me."

"Are you telling me that you are leaving?"

"After the new year begins. It will be strange to go without Rusak, but he enjoys working at that school for the deaf." Smiling, he stroked her shoulders. "Who would have guessed he would be the one teaching school now?"

"He was so proud to show the Americans and Dr. Gallaudet that he could learn the French signs without previously speaking French. It seemed perfect that he would replace Monsieur Clerc as an instructor when Monsieur Clerc went with Dr. Gallaudet to the United States."

Alexandre's smile faded as he murmured, "You are babbling. You always do that when you want to avoid talking about what is really bothering you."

"Your leaving bothers me." She closed her eyes and whispered, "No, that is wrong. Your leaving breaks my heart."

"I can tear myself from that part of my life no more than I can halt breathing. We have been lucky to have had the summer together, but I must leave as soon as the holidays are over."

"Oh." She drew away. That her sister and brother had found a lifetime of love had been no guarantee that she would, too. If only she could stop dreaming of the future she wanted for her and Alexandre.

He turned her back into his arms. Gazing at his face, which displayed the scars of his last assignment, she wondered how she would be able to kiss him farewell, knowing he could die before he came back to her.

"I already talked to Dominic. As your brother, he is your closest male relative. He has agreed to—"

"You talked to him about this already? And what did you two agree to? For me to sail with him about the world on his ship or simply to stay here to watch my niece and nephew grow older while I pray for a home and a family of my own?"

"Michelle, I—"

"No! Don't say it! I love you, Alexandre Vernier. I loved you when you were Alexei Vatutin, and I love you now. Changing your name does not change my love for you!"

He silenced her with his lips over hers. She leaned into the kiss, wanting to savor it with every inch of herself. Nothing had changed, especially her heart.

Slowly he raised his head. "If you would be silent for just a moment, you might understand."

"I understand." The sorrow stripped the sweetest edges from the passion. "You are leaving, but let's not argue about it tonight. Just kiss me, Alexandre. Kiss me, and don't say a word about the future."

"Even about our wedding?"

"Wedding?"

Laughing, he asked, "And why else would I speak to your brother about this before I talked to you? I wanted his permission to ask you to be my wife. Will you marry me? I know this question is long overdue, but, to be honest, I never thought about marriage until I thought about leaving you. I want you in my life. Will you marry me, Michelle Levesque?"

"Yes."

He crushed her to him as he tasted the love he had not planned to find when he went to safeguard the daughter of a late partner. Somewhere, in the realms of memory, he could hear the sound of Sophie's laughter. He wondered if this was what Sophie had plotted all along. Giving no time to the teasing thought, he concentrated on the tantalizing woman in his arms.

It was only hours later, when she rested in Alexandre's arms amid the incredible peace of sated love, that Michelle asked where they were going for their honeymoon.

He laughed. "Are you sure you want to know? It will be, of course, the site of our next assignment."

"Where?"

Pressing her back into the pillows, he whispered in her ear, "Russia."

Her eyes widened as she stared up at him. "You are joking!"

"I wish I were, *Liebchen*. Not my choice of assignment either. If you thought Vienna was cold . . ." He gave an exaggerated shiver. "Of course, I shall have you to keep me warm."

"Always." She ran her finger along his nose. "How do you say 'I love you' in Russian?"

"I will be damned if I know." He grinned. "I do not speak Russian."

She laughed, and he joined in until the sounds of their amusement became a soft murmur of joy as he brought her back into his arms. It was where she would stay, no matter where their quest for adventure took them.

Author's Note

I hope you have enjoyed my series *Shadow of the Bastille*. Writing about the Levesque family was so much fun, because I got to create three happily ever after endings.

My next Kensington release will be *Highland Folly*, a Regency available in June 2001. When a stubborn Scottish lady meets an engineer trying to build a bridge over a river that has long separated enemies, neither suspect that a matchmaking llama might help them create a bridge of their own . . . between their hearts.

I like hearing from my readers. You can contact me by e-mail at: jaferg@erols.com or by postal mail: Jo Ann Ferguson, P.O. Box 575, Rehoboth, MA 02769

Please include a self-addressed stamped envelope.

Happy reading!

Also look for these books by Jo Ann Ferguson

A Christmas Bride
A Brother's Honor
(Book #2 of Shadow of the Bastille)
Lady Captain
A Daughter's Destiny
(Book #1 of Shadow of the Bastille)
Sweet Temptations
The Captain's Pearl
Anything for You
An Unexpected Husband
Her Only Hero
Mistletoe Kittens
An Offer of Marriage
Lord Radcliffe's Season
No Price Too High
The Jewel Palace
O'Neal's Daughter
The Convenient Arrangement
Just Her Type
Destiny's Kiss
Raven Quest
A Model Marriage
Rhyme and Reason
Spellbound Hearts
The Counterfeit Count
A Winter Kiss
A Phantom Affair
Miss Charity's Kiss
Valentine Love
The Wolfe Wager
An Undomesticated Wife
A Mother's Joy
The Smithfield Bargain
The Fortune Hunter

And writing as Rebecca North
A June Betrothal

COMING IN JANUARY 2001 FROM
ZEBRA BALLAD ROMANCES

__SUMMER'S END: THE CLAN MACLEAN #1
by Lynne Hayworth   0-8217-6882-4 $5.50US/$7.50CAN
Some called Clemency Cameron a witch, with her mysterious potions and
healing ways. Jamie Maclean had certainly fallen under her spell. Pledged
to avenge his kin, he must find a way to lay his past to rest ... or risk
losing the woman who has claimed his heart.

__RUNAWAY RANCH: TITLED TEXANS #3
by Cynthia Sterling   0-8217-6764-X $5.50US/$7.50CAN
Cam Worthington comes to Texas as a new member of the clergy. Suddenly
upon his arrival he finds himself facing a farmer with a shotgun, a nervous
young woman named Caroline Allen, and a preacher ready to perform a
hasty marriage ceremony—with Cam as the groom. Soon he discovers
that the strongest faith of all comes in a love that no one can destroy.

__THE OUTLAW TAKES A WIFE: THE BURNETT BRIDES #2
by Sylvia McDaniel   0-8217-6766-6 $5.50US/$7.50CAN
Grieving the death of his best friend, Tanner Burnett walked away from
the Battle of Atlanta. Now a deserter, he lives the life of an outlaw—until
the day he rescues Elizabeth Anderson from stagecoach bandits. Tanner
is unprepared for the emotions Beth inspires in him. But thanks to a
scheme, Beth is bound for his hometown of Forth Worth, Texas ... and
promised in marriage to his brother, Tucker!

__A MATTER OF PRIDE: THE DESTINY COIN #2
by Gabriella Anderson   0-8217-6765-8 $5.50US/$7.50CAN
In England, Boston-born Eden Grant is determined to make the most of
her freedom before she weds. She becomes the toast of society, but the
only gentleman who interests her is Trevor St. John, Earl of Ryeburn—
when scandal threatens Eden, Trevor hastily marries *her*. Now, what began
as a marriage of convenience has become the melding of two hearts ...

Put a Little Romance in Your Life With
Constance O'Day-Flannery

__**Bewitched** $5.99US/$7.50CAN
   0-8217-6126-9

__**The Gift** $5.99US/$7.50CAN
   0-8217-5916-7

__**Once in a Lifetime** $5.99US/$7.50CAN
   0-8217-5918-3

__**Second Chances** $5.99US/$7.50CAN
   0-8217-5917-5

—**This Time Forever** $5.99US/$7.50CAN
   0-8217-5964-7

__**Time-Kept Promises** $5.99US/$7.50CAN
   0-8217-5963-9

__**Time-Kissed Destiny** $5.99US/$7.50CAN
   0-8217-5962-0

__**Timeless Passion** $5.99US/$7.50CAN
   0-8217-5959-0

Call toll free **1-888-345-BOOK** to order by phone, use this coupon
to order by mail, or order online at **www.kensingtonbooks.com**.
Name _____
Address _____
City_____ State _____ Zip _____
Please send me the books I have checked above.
I am enclosing $_____
Plus postage and handling* $_____
Sales tax (in New York and Tennessee only) $_____
Total amount enclosed $_____
*Add $2.50 for the first book and $.50 for each additional book.
Send check or money order (no cash or CODs) to:
**Kensington Publishing Corp., Dept C.O., 850 Third Avenue, 16th Floor,
New York, NY 10022**
Prices and numbers subject to change without notice.
All orders subject to availability.
Visit our website at **www.kensingtonbooks.com**.

BOOK YOUR PLACE ON OUR WEBSITE AND MAKE THE READING CONNECTION!

We've created a customized website just for our very special readers, where you can get the inside scoop on everything that's going on with Zebra, Pinnacle and Kensington books.

When you come online, you'll have the exciting opportunity to:

- View covers of upcoming books
- Read sample chapters
- Learn about our future publishing schedule (listed by publication month *and author*)
- Find out when your favorite authors will be visiting a city near you
- Search for and order backlist books from our online catalog
- Check out author bios and background information
- Send e-mail to your favorite authors
- Meet the Kensington staff online
- Join us in weekly chats with authors, readers and other guests
- Get writing guidelines
- AND MUCH MORE!

**Visit our website at
http://www.zebrabooks.com**